THE BLACK
GARDENIA

ELLIOT PAUL

Blackstone Studios, Inc.

THE BLACK GARDENIA

Elliot Paul

COACHWHIP PUBLICATIONS

Greenville, Ohio

The Black Gardenia, by Elliot Paul
© 2015 Coachwhip Publications

The Black Gardenia published 1952.
Elliot Paul (1891-1958)
No claims made on public domain material.

Front cover: Background © Flypaper Textures;
    Movie camera © AnthonyCZ

CoachwhipBooks.com

ISBN 1-61646-313-9
ISBN-13 978-1-61646-313-7

CONTENTS

1

Quicker Than the Private Eye

HOMER EVANS AND FINKE MAGUIRE were seated on stools at the bar of the Brown Derby in Beverly Hills, California, watching the dinner customers arrive and take their places. From where they sat they could see through a small service window the main entrance from Rodeo Drive and Wilshire Boulevard and the principal part of the dining room. From time to time, waitresses would appear in the absurd brown costumes, with stiff hoop skirts which ballooned out and exposed the back of their legs above the top of their long nylon hose whenever they had to lean forward. It is possible that one of the founders of that world-famous restaurant had imagined that skirts like those would suggest out-size bowlers, chapeaux melons, or derbies. Actually, the fantastic uniforms served to reveal the charms of the enticing young women who waited on an even more fantastic assortment of customers. In a region where bodies, forms and faces assailed the eye from all directions, the alluring legs of the Derby waitresses caught the eyes of yokels and connoisseurs, lone wolves and trained seals, amateurs and professionals, alike, from an effective angle which, since the days of the French cancan of the 1890's, has been somewhat neglected. Emile, the gifted Mexican bartender who had started his long experience with the film colony several decades before as a small bashful bellboy in the old Paramount Hotel, was at his post, mixing drinks.

The patrons, on that fragrant June evening in 1949, included, as usual, the cream of the motion-picture celebrities,—stars, producers, directors and agents; character actors and actresses who divided their time between Broadway and the West Coast; always a number of prosperous sightseers, tourists and hero worshippers; a quota of hopeful unknowns who wished to attract the attention of talent scouts; and a few racketeers who found good pickings wherever folks with money congregated.

As soon as Evans' glass was empty, Emile refilled it from a bottle of pre-war French Calvados, aged in the wood. Finke, who had been sipping absent-mindedly, drained his glass, too, and pushed it toward Emile, nodding somewhat uneasily. The moment Finke had dreaded, without being willing to acknowledge it, was drawing near, and the only thing Finke disliked more than feeling one of the softer emotions was showing that he was feeling it.

Since the days when together, in Paris, they had tracked down the murderer of Lieutenant Bob Kitchel and Nurse Agnes Welsh, U.S.A., they had not been in touch constantly, but they were on the same continent and each could contact the other promptly, and ask for what help was needed. Of course, Finke understood that he had been the one on the asking end, most consistently, although Evans, whom Finke described, none too graciously, as "the cerebral type," had kept the relationship on an even footing by calling on Finke for aid whenever prompt action was *de rigeur*. When Finke had decided, with Homer's full approval, that during the post-war epoch there would not be enough Americans in trouble abroad to keep a young and somewhat impractical private eye busy, Evans had decided to make the crossing at the same time, in order to attend a performance of the Berlioz "resurrection music" that Monteux was preparing in San Francisco.

Seeing Homer Evans and Finke Maguire, side by side, leaning on a bar, almost anyone would have said that two men more unlikely to have compatible interests could scarcely have been found the world over. The casual observer would have been wrong. Evans, with his well-trimmed Van Dyke, amazing erudition and extreme refinement, was almost as familiar with the past, from the hazy dawn of recorded history up to and including our own bloody problematical century, as with the daily events which passed before his eyes. Finke Maguire, on the other hand, a couple of inches shy of

Homer's six feet one, but stockier, was an Irish-American from Boston's South-End slums whose formal education consisted of a few years in grammar school, when the truant officers could catch him, and a few more in night school, of his own volition. Finke had been on his own since he was a small boy, and had improvised his course from day to day. As an operator with G-6 in France, during World War II, he had picked up the language of the street, and knew more French than was contained in the dictionary of the Académie Française. Homer spoke sixteen languages, living and dead, correctly or in the vernacular.

They had landed, about two months before this story begins (and, incidentally, although neither of them mentioned the fact, almost sixty days before the concert in San Francisco which Evans was so eager to hear), from the old *De Grasse*, at Pier 57, New York, and Finke had decided, aware that it was really Homer's suggestion, that the West Coast, to be exact, the Hollywood region, would be the best field for a private detective, unknown and with experience abroad. They had made the trip across the continent together, by train as far as Detroit, where Finke had bought a Chevrolet coupe.

While Finke had been in the most active branch, behind the lines and at the front, of the secret service during World War II, Homer had been assigned to a Government organization the existence of which was known to very few indeed, and had spent much time in Hollywood, screening aliens, refugees and foreigners, as much for the protection of the worthy ones as for the exposure of underground enemies and Fifth Columnists. His secretary and principal assistant had been Kay Cougar, a lanky and intelligent woman in her late thirties who had spent her life in show business, but never as an actresses. Kay, restless and discontented after the exciting war years under Homer's brilliant direction, was the ideal choice of colleague for Finke, and although they kidded each other unmercifully verbally, in a brief six weeks had become friends.

It was natural that Kay (after consultation with Homer) should select a location on the Strip and a small swanky suite of offices

for Finke, as far in effect from the drug-store book conception of a
detective's small, bare, scrubby, ill-furnished single room as could
be imagined. At the extravagant layout, the ritzy situation and the
ultra-modern *décor*, Finke had grumbled, then beefed, then roared.

"Keep your shirt on six months, and you'll like it," Kay had said,
and he had signed the lease and paid the bills with the stubborn
Irish determination in the back of his mind to prove his "long-
haired" counselors wrong. For Kay, like Evans, was a walking
encyclopedia of everything Finke said was too deep and useless
for a roughneck like him or the palookas who might be dumb
enough to retain him.

That balmy evening in June, Homer was starting back to Paris,
via San Francisco. Finke, who had always thought of himself as
self-sufficient, would be on his own. So what, he asked himself,
was he anxious about?

"What's this dirge you've got to hear in Frisco?" asked Finke,
somewhat forced and gruffly, with a glance at the Derby clock.

Evans smiled at Emile, who also smiled understandingly.

"He's referring," said Homer, "to one of the greatest of musical
compositions, in the class with Beethoven's Ninth. I mean the
Berlioz 'Judgment Day.' Monteux is conducting a performance two
days from now, with full male and female choruses, augmented
symphony orchestra, a band, and additional groups of trumpets to
sound from behind the audience the sudden hair-raising blast of
Gabriel's horn. The Day of Doom, which was heralded from the
beginning, has come. Graves open, the dead arise and assemble
with the living, for the Final Judgment. No fixing of witnesses now.
No use for fancy-priced lawyers. For the first and only time since
Creation, nobody will get away with anything before the bar of
Justice. The evocation of that event-to-end-all-events, by a great
neglected master of music, interpreted by a sensitive conductor,
sung by vocalists and played by instrumentalists who have assembled
from everywhere traveling is possible, that is, this side of the Iron
Curtain! That is what my friend, Maguire, dismisses as a dirge. The
Mass was composed by Berlioz on order of the French Government in

the 1860's. The Government refused to pay. The clergy scorned it. There was a makeshift performance at Berlioz' funeral, at which the members of the French Academy, called 'The Immortals', were present. Incidentally they had refused to admit Berlioz as a member, year after year, while he was alive. I missed that first audition because it took place before I was born, and for no other reason. That music has been performed only twice since that sad occasion in 1869— once at the Invalides in Paris, again in Notre Dame, in 1928. Needless to say, I was in the audience both times. Monteux' rendition will be the first in North America. I just couldn't miss it."

Emile's dark expressive eyes, always sympathetic, were glistening. His thick black hair was parted in the middle but never plastered down with grease, and his heavy eyebrows lifted to emphasize his meanings.

"I should like, myself, to hear such music, and dream of ten-thousand-dollar graves in Forest Lawn flapping open, and souls and half-souls in dry bones and live pot bellies, or slim forms artificially reduced, mingling and preparing for what is coming to them. It sounds like a natural for Cecil de Mille."

"I'll still take Kid Ory and his band, at the Jade," grunted Finke.

"Well, all right, then," said a voice behind them.

Kay Cougar had come in, according to appointment. She was to drive Evans to the airport in time for the eight-o'clock plane, ostensibly because she had "an errand to do" in Burbank. Actually, she knew how Finke felt about farewells, particularly the one at hand, and had sacrificed her free evening to spare him an awkward moment before the take-off. Kay thought of everything.

The two men greeted her. Emile smiled and bowed. She nodded toward Evans' glass and said, "The same." As soon as Kay had downed her drink, and they all had had another, Evans shook hands with Emile, then Finke, and followed Kay out the door, seemingly as casually as if he were going no farther than the hotel across the street.

Doggedly, Finke sat at the bar, staring through the little service window.

"Well," Emile said, philosophically. "It's always a pleasure to serve Mr. Evans. He was most helpful to several of my country-men during the war."

"That's a hobby of his, being helpful," said Finke. "He was help-ful to me, all right, in that murder case we mentioned, over there. He made me look like Simple Willie Stevens. He thinks I should settle here, at least until Europe gets itself straightened out. . . . Say, a couple of hundred years."

"There's no lack of Europeans hereabouts," Emile observed, in a tone that could be construed in divers ways. "Are you getting acquainted?"

"A guy can get by. But so far all the work's been steered my way by Evans, and it's all routine. Nothing happens much, and why should it? For four bits you can see a swell crime on the screen, and after some of those hams play detectives—Philo Vance, Sam Spade, Nick Charles, Sherlock Holmes—who's going to hire a licensed private eye who hasn't got a script cooked up by four or five smart writers to find his answers in?"

"Be patient," Emile said. "I've spent most of my life here. Things happen when you least expect it."

"That's what Evans told me, and he's never supposed to be wrong," said Finke.

One of the waitresses, a pretty Tennessee girl named Diana, dainty, well-formed, and with a musical Southern intonation, placed her tray on the shelf behind Emile.

"One small beer, one iron-worker's cocktail and one Pernod old-fashioned," she said, dead-panning except for the roguish light in her eyes, which seemed to imply, "Now you've heard everything "

Emile, startled, faced about, almost dropping the bottle in his hand. And it took something quite extraordinary to startle Emile.

"*Mi madre!* What a combination!" he said, softly, and gave a curious but discreet glance out into the dining room over Diana's shapely shoulder. She, aware that Finke was also intrigued not only with her, but the amazing order for refreshments, leaned grace-fully to one side, so he also could give the once-over to the trio who had voiced it. He saw, sitting in one of the best booths on the

Wilshire Boulevard side, three men who would have looked less out of place in a Dashiell Hammett dive.

"All mugs," he exclaimed under his breath, and glanced at Emile for confirmation. The bartender nodded.

The impressive one of the three was a man of mild manner, in advanced middle age, a swarthy European type who dressed as his tailor thought a conservative American businessman should appear. He sat quietly and pensively, as if detached not only from his table companions, but the animated restaurant, the assortment of celebrities and nonentities, and current events. Nevertheless he conveyed, somehow, more menace than his companions. He was unquestionably the boss, the No. 1. At his left, in the middle, was a handsome, rakish type of thirty-eight or forty. He was sturdily built, cock-sure of himself and loudly dressed to a degree that, even in Hollywood, was hard to grasp at first sight and harder to believe on closer examination. The third, who surely was due for the iron-worker's cocktail, was young, hard-boiled, as blasé as only one can be who has never had to think for himself or even has been discouraged from so doing, and seemed ready to take any orders and carry them out without question. The first question in Finke's mind was why Gregory, the snooty Greek manager or maître-dee, had escorted the trio, personally, to one of the most desirable locations reserved for big shots, and was hovering nearby in his most obsequious manner

"Italians?' asked Finke, of Emile, who was mixing the drinks.

"Neapolitans," said Emile, and added, "from Chicago."

"Brothers?" continued Finke.

Emile nodded confirmation.

"Ricardo, Antonio and Pietro Manello. Ric, Tony and Pete. Ric's the oldest. He's got the brains. Tony's the middle one, with the taste for bright colors—the wrong ones. The young one's called Pete."

Diana shrugged and sighed. She had to wait on them.

"What are they doing out here?" Finke asked. An Easterner, and certainly no film fan, he still thought of Southern California as somehow detached from the United States proper.

It was Emile's turn to shrug. "They moved in, about six months ago."

"Moved in?"

"On E.P.U. You know. One of the major studios. Ric must have something on the executives there. Anyway, the Manellos have the run of the place, to some extent at least, and do about as they please. Nobody understands exactly why—no one who dares to talk about it frankly."

Having nothing to do to kill the evening, and not relishing the idea of being by himself, Finke paid the bar check and wandered to the inner door to the main dining room. A table in a booth across the aisle from that of the Manellos was unoccupied. It was also one of those Diana served. Finke headed that way, and Gregory, the watchful manager, tried to steer him elsewhere. Ignoring the Greek, Finke tossed aside the card marked "Reserved" and sat down on the leather-upholstered circular seat. Just as he was doing so, however, he saw two women approaching—one old and the other not old—and realized that the table had been held for them. They looked like mother and daughter and it was the mother, small and friendly, with humorous eyes and silver hair, who touched Finke's heart, so that he rose and was about to give them back their places. The older woman smiled and said, with a quaint Russian accent, "What's the hurry? There's room."

She made a gesture indicating that the booth would seat her daughter, Finke and herself, with room to spare. It seemed to Finke that Tony Manello, across the aisle, was somehow displeased by the seating pattern that was arranging itself and was trying to catch Gregory's eye. In fact, Finke was quite sure, when he reviewed it afterward, that the flashily dressed type who looked like a gangster in Technicolor in an otherwise black-and-white sequence had made a sign intended for Gregory and attempting to convey his desire that the new arrivals be seated farther away although tables were at a premium.

As usual, when exigent clients had conflicting notions that might embarrass him, Gregory was carefully looking the other way, except from the corner of one eye. He turned questioningly to the daughter, who evidently was a steady customer of some standing.

"Are you satisfied, Miss Mesker?" the manager asked.

"It's O.K., Gregory," the daughter said. She was a cool, determined young woman whose efficient, self-possessed manner was softened by her large blue-gray eyes, like her mother's, but, in repose, suggestive of the tragic. She looked Finke over without hostility, introduced her mother, and then herself, as Ruth Mesker. Without fuss they got settled, with the mother in the middle, Finke at the right, and Ruth at the left of the semicircle. Finke saw Ruth's face cloud slightly as she bowed to the trio in the booth across the aisle. Ric, the oldest Manello, responded with habitual Latin courtesy; Tony with too deliberate and prolonged a stare; and Pete with boyish indifference, until he caught a side-glance from Brother Ric. Then the kid relaxed and bowed properly. It was all the same to him.

The problem of what Mrs. Mesker should eat absorbed Ruth's immediate attention. She ordered the white meat of chicken, with a certain sauce, not too highly seasoned, and other items with as much care as if her mother, who looked unusually healthy for her age, was an invalid. But having taken so much pains to select a harmless meal for her mother, Ruth's resourcefulness seemed temporarily exhausted. Finke saw that she was tired, if not worried, or both.

"Want me to order?" he asked, smiling a sort of experimental challenge, and Mrs. Mesker beamed so approvingly that Ruth acquiesced. The enigmatic blue-eyed husky young man beside her looked like anything but a gourmet.

Aware that Diana was intrigued, somehow, by the set-up, that Gregory was still lingering nearby, and that he was being overheard, in part, by the Manellos, Finke could not resist assuming his most nonchalant manner and going the limit. He had not lunched and dined, off and on, with Homer Evans in the course of several months to no purpose. His assurance was ironic, if not comical, to himself, but not to anyone else among those present. He chose a *pâté Belge* as an appetizer, a brook trout in Alsatian style, with white Montrachet; an unbreaded cutlet, with Beaune; fresh fruit, Swiss cheese and coffee, with Armagnac brandy as a liqueur. Finke, who loved the old lady already, winked and patted her hand. He was, at last, at ease.

"That's right! Make her eat," Mrs. Mesker said, happily. "She thinks of me, too much." That was O.K. with Finke. He liked the feeling that two such nice persons were always thinking of each other. He had experienced nearly everything within the scope of his unscholarly limitations, but never what is loosely known as "family life."

Again, but very dimly because of his unexpected pleasure in the company of the Meskers, he was aware that the Manello brothers were not happy, and that the friendly women, old and relatively young, in the booth with him, were somehow the cause. He noticed that Tony nudged Pete, who detained the elusive Gregory by clutching his sleeve. Pete, by pulling on the said sleeve as if it were a bell rope, also caused the Greek maître-dee to lean over so that Tony, half-rising, could whisper in his ear. Gregory's face showed mild consternation because all the booths and good tables were occupied. He broke loose from Pete's grip and registered frustration. But Tony pointed out to him, without too much attempt at concealment, a booth twice removed from the one the Manellos were in and less desirable because it was too near the entrance to the bar. At the moment, Finke did not remark especially the tall, correct young man with a huge blonde woman and a quiet small one. The latter was dressed in a somewhat unusual way that had a suggestion of the Oriental in it, although her face was American, of the cultured or artistic sort. She wore a dyed scarf, the pattern of which featured plants with folded yellow-green leaves, veined darkly, on long stems, flowers somewhat like inverted tulips facing downward. The flowers were a most arresting hue, suggestive of pale garnet, with a touch of saffron or henna, and a texture as smooth as the petals of rose. Finke had a chance to enjoy, in detail, the color of the leaves and flowers because, after having been prodded by Tony Manello, Gregory had gone to the young man's table, conveyed a message that might have been an order or request. Suppressing an expression of natural annoyance, the young man, most certainly with some connection with "the industry," in some "artistic" capacity, rose, as did the two women with him. Neither the big blonde, of decidedly Teutonic cast, nor the small one with the batik scarf, offered any objection as they shifted tables.

Ruth Mesker apparently did not know the Amazon with the wheat-colored hair and stature of a Rhine maiden. But she nodded and smiled at the American woman with the unusual dyed scarf, and less familiarly to the correct, well-dressed young man who had been so complacent at being moved in mid-meal at the Manellos' behest.

By that time, Finke realized without question that Ruth Mesker was troubled about something, but he thought it better, especially in the presence of her mother she protected so carefully, not to ask questions. As far as he was concerned, the farther away those mugs were, the better he liked it. It had been so long since any strangers, presentable or ominous, had interested themselves in Finke or what he was doing that he felt a glow of satisfaction just to be sitting with someone whose presence bothered gents who, if they were not out-and-out public enemies, had surely missed their calling.

Before coming to the "Coast," Finke had given little thought to motion pictures, analytically. To him, E.P.U., Inc., (for E Pluribus Unum Pictures, Incorporated), meant nothing but the screen bison, the switching of whose tail on the studio trademark preceded so many elaborate films. Like most intelligent people, wherever their education had come from, he disliked nine-tenths of the movies heartily. In spite of that, he bought his ticket now and then and sat through quite a few, and did not complain if there were a few good gags or passably funny situations. It had only been brought to his attention recently that the stars did not think up their own lines and business. The cinematic functions of financiers, producers, directors and agents had escaped his attention. So had the contributions of cameramen, cutters, designers and a host of technicians and artisans. Because Ruth Mesker received more than her share of salutes and greetings at the Derby, Finke assumed that she must be of "the industry." It was equally clear that she was not an actress, and for that he was thankful, without having known many of them well.

Suddenly the attention of everyone was focused on the entrance. A young brunette had come in through the revolving doors, a girl so striking in appearance that she was immediately the center of all eyes in a company where beauty and shapeliness was the rule rather than the exception.

"The Black Gardenia," Finke heard the waitress murmur, having sensed that he had no idea who the vision of health and loveliness might be.

"She's Mexican," supplemented Ruth. "I think she holds some records as a swimmer."

"I haven't seen her on the screen," said Finke. He saw, with relief, that the muscles of the Gardenia, so-called, were not unpleasantly overdeveloped. No sculptured nymph could look less athletic. She had thrown back her cape and her bare arms and shoulders were like those of a Psyche or Diana, except that instead of being dead white, her smooth skin had a subtle mezzotint of cream or tan. Her gown, cut low in front and without any back worth mentioning, was of faint Nile green.

When Finke recovered from the stimulating shock of seeing such a woman without warning, he noticed that she was followed, possessively, by a large good-looking elderly man, unmistakably an American, and most certainly not an actor. The impressive, if not ponderous escort wore evening clothes and rated veritable kowtows and salaams from Gregory, who never failed to show reverence to a bank account.

"An oil man from Texas—Mills Harmon," Ruth whispered to Finke.

"Texas, my eye," replied Finke.

"The oil's from Texas. Mr. Harmon was born in New York, where he's listed in the *Blue Book*," Ruth admitted. She added, "They're engaged."

To Finke's further astonishment, as the stunning Mexican beauty and her multimillionaire came up the aisle, Ric Manello rose to his feet, and his brothers did likewise, Tony with alacrity that was much too pointed, and Pete, as ever, blasé.

Ric Manello accomplished the introductions of Harmon to Tony, Pete and himself, with something remaining from his native Neapolitan grace. Tony had no regard for old-fashioned manners or social rank. He nodded to Harmon and eyed the Gardenia with frankly lustful admiration.

"Sit in here beside me, sweetheart," Tony said, in a tone loud enough to carry all the way to Finke, because of the hush that had descended on that section of the dining room.

The Gardenia took no offense. She smiled, politely, either unaware of or ignoring any impropriety, squeezed herself in and was about to seat herself between Ric and Tony. Finke could scarcely believe his ears and eyes, but no one else seemed to find the situation bizarre. Mills Harmon, however, asserted himself. He was of the type who not only had to be at the head table, but preside. He motioned Ric to get up and step into the aisle. Then the oil man took his place at the Gardenia's right, so all the tableware and drinks had to be redistributed.

"I don't get it," Finke said.

Ruth dropped her eyes. "Hells bells," she said, in an undertone.

"Eat, my children!" prompted Mrs. Mesker, who took things as they came, a practice she had formed when she first landed in America at the age of thirteen.

Finke thought he had never seen a dinner party go as badly as the one involving the Manellos, the ravishing Mexican *señorita* and the oil magnate from one of the first ten of America's Sixty Families. The way it started off was awkward enough. Once they all got seated, the Manellos ordered meat balls and spaghetti, and it was the night off of the cook who turned out specialities that neither the French *chef* nor the Chinese *ga-chuew* could handle (including macaroni in various forms, enchiladas, tamales, chile con carne, Pennsylvania scrapple, ham or bacon and eggs, and what is called up North, "Southern fried chicken"). Mills Harmon had to have a peeled parboiled tomato, stuffed with chopped chicken, white celery and mayonnaise. The Black Gardenia had an appetite to match her physique, if physique is not too crude a word to apply to a body so shapely, a face so expressive and lovely, and a spontaneous charm that seemed to be naive. For a starter she had cold boiled lobster with French dressing which she mixed herself, displaying to advantage in the process her slender hands, bare arms and smooth shoulders. Afterward she ate a slice of rare roast beef and some fresh fruit which, had it been sentient, would have been thrilled to have been bitten by such teeth.

Little was said until the coffee came along. Nevertheless the jealousy and resentment of Mills Harmon was painful to witness. He suffered not only for himself, but for all elderly lovers of young exciting women, whenever his fiancée was bombarded with crude attentions by Tony Manello.

Dining with the trio from Chicago certainly was not Harmon's idea. It must have been the Gardenia who had planned the meeting for some purpose of her own then hidden from Finke. Little by little, something was cautiously being revealed, or proposed to the fuming multimillionaire by the Gardenia herself, with Ric Manello to second the motion. There was something the Gardenia wanted, and to which Harmon was indignantly, then violently opposed. Finke sensed that Ruth, who also was watching covertly, had an idea or inkling of what the argument was about. Again Finke thought it better to ask no questions for the sake of Mrs. Mesker's peace of mind. Mrs. Mesker, it seemed, lived and had lived for decades, in a small harbor of her own, shielded from the storms outside. Remarks Ruth had made indicated that she and her mother had been in Hollywood quite a number of years, but Finke was sure that Mrs. Mesker knew less than he did about its intrigues or hazards.

About ten-thirty, just after the two women and conventional young man who had changed booths with the Manellos had departed, and their places had been filled by a group from Iowa who had waited for a table an hour, some kind of crisis was reached between Harmon, on the one hand, and his betrothed, on the other. The jealous and harassed millionaire was at the end of his patience. He rose abruptly, grabbed the check from Ric and signed it. Anyone could see that he was insisting that his fiancée accompany him, and that they quit the Manellos and the Derby at once. The Mexican beauty looked annoyed and disappointed, if not angry, but she held her temper in check as Harmon seemed to be losing his. After shaking hands and saying "*Au revoir*" punctiliously to the three brothers, in turn, and somehow conveying that their project, whatever it was, was not to be abandoned, she followed her ruffled fiancé to the door and into the commodious limousine at the curb, which shimmered blackly in the incandescence of street lamps and the soft June starlight.

The Manellos, outwardly unruffled, walked along the aisle in order of seniority and paused at the cigar counter to fill their pockets with slim inexpensive panatelas, for which Tony paid in cash, indulging in small talk with the salesgirl and telephonist the while. It was there that Finke and the Meskers passed them on the way to the Derby parking lot across the street, where Finke had left his Chevrolet. Finke had the distinct impression that the Manellos, especially Tony, were interested in his identity. It seemed to him that Tony made an inquiry of Gregory, who was unable to answer the question, and passed the buck to Emile, whose head chanced to be protruding through the service window behind the bar. So, perhaps within hearing of the Manellos, although indifferent as to whether they overheard or not, Finke told Ruth that after he had taken them home he would come back to the Derby for a nightcap, having in mind that he would find out from Emile if Tony had asked any questions and, if so, what about. Ruth, smiling ruefully and shrugging her shoulders, intimated that Finke might be returning to get better acquainted with Diana.

"I don't blame you. She's cute," Ruth said, but so that her mother would not hear.

When Finke got out of the roadster at the Meskers' apartment house, less than a mile from the Derby, Mrs. Mesker stretched impulsively up to her tiptoes and kissed him on the cheek. What she said was on her usual theme.

"Ruth is too much with me. She should go out and enjoy herself."

"Don't mind Mama," Ruth said. "She always tries to palm me off on some man. Any man." In spite of herself, Ruth showed her anxiety and weariness. "God!" she exclaimed. "What's more of a washout than a tired woman!"

Finke looked into her eyes, and both were jolted by their unforeseen reaction. "You scare me," he said.

"I do?" she asked, it seemed to him, almost plaintively.

"Those eyes. A guy could fall in there and get lost," he said, and added, grimly, "Just the same, I spent a damn pleasant evening."

Mrs. Mesker had discreetly disappeared into the house, and Ruth followed. Finke got back into his Chevvy and drove back to the Derby parking lot. He did not know exactly what happened after that. He found his old spot, in the dimmest corner, turned off the ignition, removed the key and stepped out beside an adjacent car about which he had noticed, casually, that it had been backed into place, so that it was headed right to drive out. Sailors often parked like that, as if cars were skiffs or launches. Without warning Finke felt a tap on his head, and conscious memory lapsed for a time.

When he regained his faculties, he was told by the parking attendant and a couple of taxi drivers from the stand nearby that they had found him, half in and half out of the baggage compartment of his own roadster, in such a position that they concluded the lid had accidentally dropped on him, striking the top of his head. Finke knew better than that, but he let it pass. Whoever had conked him had had plenty of practice. Of that he was sure. Quite exhilarated, he thanked the men who had revived him and strode over to the Derby, but the lights were being turned out and Emile had gone home. And the Derby never closed before two A.M.

2

An Object Lesson

AFTER FIVE OR SIX HOURS OF SOUND SLEEP, in the course of which he had dreamed of roaming aimlessly, but with no oppressive sense of being lost, through swamps and forests in which the foliage ranged in color from the faint translucent greens of the Gardenia's sheer gown and the exotic plants portrayed in the other woman's Oriental scarf to the subdued shades of rust and saffron he remembered from the flowers, Finke woke up, stretched, touched the bump on top of his head and got out of bed with perverse satisfaction. He was on his own. Homer Evans was gone. He still felt funny about that. But in Hollywood he was no longer an outsider. He had been crowned, in spades, and by a master with a sack of shot. He must have been out at least two hours. And why? He had a hunch that reasons would reveal themselves, in time. He was not in a hurry, and felt no pain and no strain.

He breakfasted heartily at Armstrong-Shroeder's, and then drove to the small park on Beverly Drive where he sat on a bench, shaded with magnolias, read the morning papers leisurely, and watched some large patched goldfish nosing around the pool that was centered and splashed by a miniature fountain. The sun was warm, the sky clear and the air of late spring most tempered with summer fragrance.

At first, when he had been inclined to jump out of bed, scan the headlines as he swallowed his food, and go early to the office, Kay had put her foot down. She knew show business and the town. He would lose face, she told him, with prospective clients of

23

importance, if he made himself available before ten-thirty or eleven in the morning. It simply wasn't done. Finke had beefed, as usual, but had found that Kay was right, and had taken her advice. Furthermore, he had begun to enjoy those morning hours, between rising at seven and checking in for business just before the cocktail hour preceding lunch. The climate of Paris is one of the most trying in the world, and that of Southern California ideal, all magazine, vaudeville, burlesque and television jokes to the contrary. Finke liked the verdant little park in Beverly Hills. No one else seemed to use it. It was as if he had a luxurious estate, without any of the accompanying headaches. In cases of emergency, of which there had hitherto been none, Kay knew where she could find him.

So that morning at ten, a good half-hour before he would have dared show up, he was surprised to see Kay's absurd little Austin, which because of her extra long legs seemed to bring her knees up under her chin, turning into the drive. She got out, like a long female Houdini extricating herself from a packing case, and waved as she came toward him.

"Good morning, boss," she said.

"That's no reason for leaving the phone unguarded," was his comment.

"I've got a message for you," she said, ignoring his crack.

He could not help grinning, because his hand had gone up instinctively to touch the sore spot on the back of his head. He'd already had what might be termed "a message," but he let that pass.

"At this hour? Couldn't it wait?" he asked.

"It's from a woman," she said. "She left a number, and no name."

Kay handed Finke a slip of paper. The phone number meant nothing to him. So he nodded, thanked Kay and pretended to watch the goldfish again.

"Come off it," Kay said. "This dame is in trouble. I could tell by her voice. You'd better make it snappy."

He rose, stretched and walked over to his Chevrolet.

"Don't crowd too close behind me with that Kiddy Kar. Folks might think we're together," he said.

Whenever he approached the office Kay had selected, Finke had to shake off misgivings. The white plaster edifice, labeled "Griffith Building, 1930," named for the neglected genius who created *The Birth of a Nation*, was on what was known as "The Strip." The rooms of Finke's "suite" were numbered 201 and 202, with "Enter Here" lettered in gilt on the door of 201, which had a clouded glass panel, and "Enter 201" on the solid oak door of Room 202, which was kept perpetually locked. The reception room, in which Kay's desk and the master telephone were located, had on its walls some reproductions of modern paintings which always caused Finke to do a double take. There was a batch of beat-up sunflowers; a dame with three kissers in a crooked chair; a night jungle number with an outsize moon and a tiger that would have brought back Frank Buck; an African tropical forest with trees strictly from Oz, one chocolate native and a cream-of-wheat waterfall.

Kay had explained that the paintings would help them classify the clients. Those who liked the specimens of modern art would have plenty on the ball, but would have to be watched, if they led off by reciting E. E. Cummings or listening for worms.

"And what about those who get sore when they look at them?" Finke had asked, as if he might be one of those.

"They're smart, but set in their ways," Kay had replied. "The ones who are indifferent are uncomplicated types, slow on the trigger. We'll have to do all their thinking for them. Wait six months, and you'll see what I mean."

So when Finke had found in 202, his private office, a picture of a bunch of crumb bums in a third-class railway carriage; another of some lopsided fruit on a slanting table top; and a third with what passed for a newspaper, a couple of European oysters and a swollen ukulele, he had swallowed hard and let them stay.

That morning, in spite of the Austin's cramped dimensions, Kay was so close behind Finke that by the time he got to his inner office and sat down, his phone rang.

"Your party, Mr. Maguire," Kay's voice announced.

"Mesker speaking. Ruth Mesker. Remember?" a voice said that was unmistakably Ruth's.

"Well all right, then," said Finke, bewildered.

"Could I come right over? I can't talk freely by phone."

"The sooner the better," replied Finke. Ruth's tone was so strained and tremulous that Finke was caught way off his base. How was it possible that she could have got so panicky in just the few hours since he had bade her good night at her door? A horrid thought flashed across his mind.

"Your mother? Is she all right?" asked Finke, almost matching the anxiety of Ruth's voice.

"Yes. Oh, yes. It's not Mother . . . It was nice of you to think of her," said Ruth, and hung up, to be on her way.

It was Kay's theory that all clients should be kept waiting at least five minutes in the reception room, before being shown in to Finke, so that it would never appear that he had no other business on hand. Finke forgot all about that when he heard the sound of Ruth's voice by means of the listening device. He barged out to the reception room to greet her.

"Short time no see," he said.

He had not had occasion, the evening before, to mention Kay's name or her connection with his office, but he was pleased to note that Ruth and Kay seemed to know each other, and favorably.

"You'll excuse us?" Ruth asked Kay, indicating nervously that what she had to say was for Finke's ears alone. Kay smiled reassuringly and reached over with a long thin arm to click off the listening switch.

The moment Ruth and Finke were alone in his room, she lost her self-control and her eyes filled with tears. As soon as she got her voice back she looked at him apologetically.

"Fine start," she said.

"I didn't think you'd come for a social chat," said Finke. "But spare me the waterworks. What's wrong?"

"It's all so damned unfair," she said, achieving a sort of control.

"Look," said Finke evenly. "Nobody's going to shove you around. Not unless he's tougher than me. Suppose you tell me what's got you in such a dither. And for God's sake, dish it out straight, the first time. I always say that, and nobody ever does it. The smartest detective I know told me, 'We have to solve our clients first, then the case is usually easy.'" He reached out and lifted up her chin. "After all, there isn't anybody dead!"

Shuddering piteously, Ruth looked up at him with those fathomless eyes. "There is," she said quite desperately.

Finke came up out of his chair. "Are you serious?"

She nodded.

"There's a body? A corpse?"

"Yes," she said, and again swallowed hard.

"Where?"

She tried to compose herself. "In a crumby little graveyard out Santa Monica way," she answered.

"Already buried?"

"Yesterday morning," said Ruth. "I went to the funeral."

Finke sighed, a little disgustedly.

"Does that make sense? I see you last night with your mother at the Derby. You polish off a five-course meal. I leave you without trying to kiss you good night—because I like your old lady better than you. Now in the morning, when the sun's shining and all these bloody mocking birds are singing full blast, you come running to me, more dead than alive, and tell me what you knew all the time—that some guy died."

She took it without smiling and continued, more earnestly, "But I didn't know he was murdered. Not till late last night, after you had left," she explained.

"You found out who killed this bird?"

"Nobody's come out into the open," answered Ruth.

Finke grunted. "Murderers are almost always self-effacing types."

He was not as skeptical, however, as he sounded. A vague pattern was forming itself in his mind. That tap on the head he had got the night before. That was real and earnest. It had meant, perhaps, "Lay off." And in that case it had been done by someone who had seen him with Ruth, in what could have looked like a huddle.

For an instant he was on the point of telling Ruth that he, too, had got a message last night after they had parted. He thought better of his impulse and encouraged her to go on.

"Relax," he said. "Begin at the beginning . . . If there's time."

"There's time . . . I think," she said.

He could see that she was making a heroic effort to keep calm and put the case to him as accurately as she could.

"I'll have to give you a lot of background, to make you understand," she began.

"I'm listening," he said.

As briefly as she could, Ruth told him how she had got started in "the industry." Her first job she had landed in New York, in the Eastern office of a major studio. She had been a "reader," and had picked a few smash hits, right off the bat, so that the famous producer, Sol Goldstein, had got excited about her "story sense." She had come out to Hollywood as Sol's secretary, and stuck it out five years although he was one of the most unpredictable, vain and exigent men in a field where self-centered screwballs are a dime a dozen. The last two years with Sam she had drawn down $500 a week, but eventually had to take her choice between the five C's weekly and a nervous breakdown. A firm of agents, real master burglars called Champsberg and Blut, had taken her on, offering salary (which they had to pay) and commission (on which they cheated). In their employ, she had bucked competition that would have disillusioned Ali Baba. When she could no longer put up with Champsberg and Blut, she had hired an office for herself and built up, from scratch, a small agency.

Without prompting, Finke understood that all her hard work had been done, not for herself, but to give her mother security and comfort. There could have been no time for love or recreation.

An agent, Ruth explained, to stay in the running, must have under contract two or three stars who are in demand at the studios, will follow the agent's advice and stick with the agency through thick and thin. Of those, Ruth had two: Shirley Hall, a superb dancer who was only passable as an actress; and Bob Reynolds, a good singer to whom acting was as natural as breathing.

"I've seen them both. Not bad," said Finke.

"I got Shirley into the big money at E.P.U., with an airtight contract that prevents the studio from fouling her up," Ruth said.

"She plays opposite Reynolds, it seems to me. I don't go to musicals, but once in a while I get caught because they're on the bill with some comedy I like."

"Shirley couldn't get by without Reynolds. She's crazy about him, for one thing, and suffers when he's out of her sight. And he's in love with her, in his way, and generous enough to try to give her the credit for their hits."

"What's bad about that?" asked Finke.

"Nothing much," said Ruth. "Only he's built up the idea, in Shirley's mind, that she's a great actress, when, as a matter of fact, in every film they've done together, Bob's held up the hard end. I could get other dancers for him, but no one but Bob would do for Shirley."

It hardly seemed likely to Finke that these details of the Shirley Hall–Bob Reynolds relationship had some bearing on the murder case at hand, and he was anxious to get on with it.

"From the way you talk, it's neither Shirley Hall nor Bob Reynolds who's dead, and buried in Santa Monica."

Ruth shuddered again, and bowed her head. "Let me tell the story, as best I can," she begged.

"I'm waiting," answered Finke.

She took a deep breath and continued, "Bob Reynolds phoned me last night, after you'd brought Mother and me home. He said he had to see me. I was tired as hell, as you know, but I told him to come ahead."

"Wasn't he at the funeral you spoke about?"

"Yes," Ruth said. "Be patient just a little while longer."

"Take your time," grunted Finke.

"I'll try to tell you what Bob said, just as he said it," continued Ruth.

"Your mother was asleep, I trust."

Ruth nodded. "She doesn't know a thing about all this," she said, and choked up again.

"Nix on the tears. Go on," Finke said, gruffly.

She braced herself again. "Just now, E.P.U. is planning a big feature, with Laslo Sitchev producing and directing, and an Hawaiian setting, in which Shirley will star, but with almost no dancing."

"Where do you dig up pictures like that? Where dancers don't dance?" asked Finke.

"The script's almost finished. My third best client, Jack Oehler, a very good writer, is writing it. *Sin on an Island*—that's the title up to now."

"Does Reynolds sing?"

"He'll be most of the show, as usual," Ruth said.

"What's wrong then?" interrupted Finke. "Who got killed, when, where, how and why?"

"Here's what's wrong," Ruth said bitterly. "The Manellos, Ric, Tony and Pete—the thugs you saw at the Derby last night—chiseled into E.P.U. six months ago. They're pals of Willie Bioff, who went to prison a while back on about a dozen counts of blackmail, extortion and conspiracy to defraud. The fact is that the Manello boys have, somehow, got the E.P.U. executives and all the rest of the outfit scared stiff."

"Just how do the Manellos put *you* on the spot?"

"They're trying to steal Bob Reynolds," Ruth said. "Ric, the oldest—he's the brains of the family—got hold of a few cheesy properties. By that I mean screen rights to stories, books or plays. It was all third-rate stuff, but E.P.U. began buying it like mad, and at fancy prices, too."

"You mean the studio had to buy, or else?"

"That's the size of it. But that's not the worst of it, from an agent's point of view. E.P.U.'s got enough money to buy properties, right and left, good or bad. The hell of it is, out here, when it looks as if some new clique has got the inside track, a number of actors, actresses and all kinds of talent want to climb on the bandwagon. In the case of the Manellos, some pretty fair names have already switched agents, and signed up with them."

"That still isn't murder," Finke said.

"Not long ago, a few weeks, Ric Manello called on Bob Reynolds at the Omar Gardens, where Bob lives. Ric didn't try to get tough. He simply outlined the advantages the Manello Agency offered in promoting careers at E.P.U. Naturally, he let Bob understand that whoever strung along with the Manellos would better himself."

"This mug didn't approach Shirley? How come? Did he figure Shirley'd trail along with Bob, wherever he went?"

"I can't say, for sure. I don't think so. He ignored Shirley, knowing she and Bob were in love up to their ears, and that they had starred together in six big features, all hits."

"And Bob? What did he say to the proposition?"

"Bob told Manello that he was satisfied with me as an agent, and didn't want to make a change."

"That didn't end it, I take it."

"Ric let the matter ride for a month or so. Then he cornered Bob again, was more insistent, and Bob, who doesn't like being pressured, told him to take a flying jump at the moon."

"And Ric?"

"He was smooth as glass. 'Don't blow your top, Bob,' he said. 'This is just a business proposition. Nothing personal, you know.'"

"So?"

"Since the war, Bob has had a stand-in, a nice guy named Barney Rice. Barney was an ex-service man with lung trouble. He was built much like Bob, and even resembled him in the face. We find those doubles everywhere. Barney was broke and had no other way of making a living when Bob took him on. They became pretty close friends. Barney not only did the usual work at the studio, taking Bob's place while scenes and sound apparatus were being set, but he lived in the bungalow with Bob at the Omar Gardens, drove his car, answered his telephone and kept him company whenever Shirley had a fit of jealousy and made Bob's life a hell—if she could find him. As a matter of fact, Shirley, in a pinch, would cry on Barney's shoulder, herself. Barney was the type who was always sympathetic with the troubles of others. He had no axe to grind, himself."

Ruth, at that point, could not hold back a half-sob.

Finke was on his feet again, hands clenched. "You don't mean to say it was Barney Rice they picked on?"

Ruth nodded, sick with misery, and Finke started pacing the floor. "How does it tie in?" Finke asked, at last.

"Here's all I got from Bob, all Bob knows. About six weeks ago, Barney complained of internal pains. Bob knew that Barney would take a lot without complaining, so he called in a doctor no stand-in could afford on his own. The doctor rushed Barney to the Balm of Gilead Hospital, and got a bunch of consultants who would have cost a top executive six figures."

"What was the matter?" interrupted Finke.

"Nobody could decide. Barney's case became a watchword in medical circles. He was tested for all poisons, germs, organic diseases and injuries. Nothing fitted. He lost what little was left of his tolerance for nourishment. The pain, at first spasmodic, stayed with him day and night. He wasted away and died."

"No post-mortem?" demanded Finke. His voice sounded angry now.

Ruth made a gesture with both hands uplifted. "The works," she said. "No one had seen a case anything like it before. Not one of the doctors could make a stab at the cause."

"Then how in hell do you know it was murder?"

"Here's what happened yesterday," Ruth said, trying her utmost to be brief and explicit. "You saw the lovely Mexican *señorita*, Eulalia Noguera, with her rich oil man at the Derby."

"Having dinner with the Manellos," added Finke.

Ruth nodded. "Yesterday afternoon, although Bob was pretty badly upset by Barney's funeral in the morning, he made a screen test with her. Bob's a sweet guy about helping beginners get a break. Shirley, of course, raised holy hell, but Bob had given his word and wouldn't retract it."

"Don't blame him," grunted Finke. "I couldn't say no to that tomato, myself."

"They were both of them pretty well stripped, in tropical movie style. And after the test was over, to duck a row with Shirley, Bob got himself lost in some bar off the regular beat."

"I don't blame him for that, either," Finke said.

He got home about midnight and somebody called him to the phone, not the private one in his bungalow, but the pay phone in the hotel garage."

"What was the call?"

"Bob heard a voice he didn't recognize. It sounded to him like a man who'd gone to Oxford, or maybe Harvard or Princeton. Afterward he had the feeling that it might have been recorded, because when he tried to get a word in, edgewise, the voice went right on."

"Well! What did it say?"

"It said, 'You're having an object lesson. What happens to someone close to you can happen to you. Think well about the matter. Don't be obstinate. What happens to someone close to you can happen to you. You're having an object lesson. Think well . . .'"

Ruth looked appealingly at Finke.

"That's all I can tell you," she said.

3
The Omar Khayyam Gardens

THE YEAR ROUND, but especially in the springtime, the Omar Gardens, resting on the gentle slope above Sunset Boulevard, backed by woods and hills forming an intimate horizon, presents a vista that cannot be adequately reproduced by million-dollar movie sets in Technicolor. The landscaping in the patio, between the sheltered bungalows and in the bottom of the garden, with flowering shrubs, bushes in bloom, trees in bud and with new green leaves along the drives and pathways, combines natural beauty with the gardener's art and features tastefully the vegetation of the temperate and subtropical zones.

Entering those premises for the first time, Finke, in company with Ruth Mesker, experienced a vague uneasiness, as if he regretted that he had not brought more money with him.

He parked the Chevvy near the entrance and administration lodge, and they walked one hundred yards or more, in shadow and sunshine, to the bungalow which had been occupied by Bob Reynolds and the late Barney Rice. Since Barney's death it had housed only Bob, who depended on the hotel service for the bare details of his bachelor's existence.

Before starting out from Finke's office to talk with Bob, Ruth had phoned him, without mentioning that she was bringing a detective with her. He had been up most of the night and, after Ruth's phone call, had fallen asleep again, so that when she appeared, at eleven o'clock, he was still dozing, in pyjamas, robe and slippers.

To give Bob time to dress and pull himself together, Ruth had taken Finke on a short walk through the grounds.

As Finke strolled and tried to adjust himself to such visual splendor, he had the strange sensation of having been transported back into the dream he remembered from the night before. They had passed the bungalow Ruth told him was occupied by the Gardenia, the corner bedroom windows of which were shaded by a hedge of jasmine bushes which sheltered a colony of nocturnal moths. Nearby was a bed smelling of fertilizer and freshly turned loam which had recently been raked and spaded. The modern cottage, with white walls in plain Spanish style, was secluded by a mariner's pine and some lotar palms. Farther along the pathway, leading away from Concord Drive to the east, was a thicket of stout bamboo, stalks standing straight upright to a height of more than sixty feet and, in spite of the dryness of the season, in flower.

When they came to some feathery clumps of much shorter ornamental bamboo, called Calcutta grass or Indian cane, the illusion to walking in the dream began to manifest itself. And just beyond where some greenhouses stood, with fantastic flower beds all around, some screened and hazy, others exposed and enlivened by insects and bees, the colors—faint greens of pitcher plant petals lined with metachrome and the rose texture of the garnet and wine-brown flowers—prevailed. They had been implanted in Finke's mind, he knew, by that batik scarf the mousy little woman with the tall nance and enormous German blonde had worn at the Derby, combined with the diaphanous lime and chervil of Eulalia Noguera's low-cut gown, and her flawless brunette skin so effectively exposed.

At first Finke thought that no one but he and Ruth among the hotel guests and morning visitors seemed to be taking time off to enjoy the amazing horticultural display, which meant nothing to him except that he liked it and also felt a recurrence of the doubts he had had as a boy in South Boston about anything that might be called sissified. Then he saw a wrinkled, wizened old woman who might have been one hundred years old, it seemed to him. The crone was kneeling on the edge of a bed of pitcher plants that were distinctly different from the big ones with the tall inverted flowers. The ones the hag was examining intently, and with a furtive guilty air, had little pitchers not more than twice the size of thimbles that hung right-side up, suspended by a twisted tendril, and having a lid that was open.

Instinctively Finke had halted, detaining Ruth also with a slight pressure on her arm, so that they could watch the strange old creature amid the still stranger plants. Finke's hair stood on end, the nerves in the back of his neck tingled and Ruth clutched his hand in terror as both of them, and the old woman who reminded Finke of Old Goody Two-Shoes, heard a loud roar, a single shouted word: "*Raus!*"

It came from somewhere behind them, quite far behind them. Finke thought, as soon as he could collect his wits, that someone had bellowed at the old dame, or Ruth and him, as intruders, from one of the front bungalows, way up near the patio. Finke's German was of the Army brand, picked up in conquered territory, and was not fluent like his French, but he knew that "*Raus*" was a very strong way of saying "Beat it!" or "Get out."

By the time he had got that far in his mental processes, the weird old woman was completely gone from sight. She had vanished.

That rap on the sconce he had acquired the night before, Finke concluded, had had a more lasting effect than he had counted on. The surroundings, the witch, the startling shout, and the mood his dream and Ruth's disclosures had engendered seemed unreal. Nevertheless, he was functioning, somehow. His sharp ears caught something, he wheeled about, saw at the corner of the Gardenia's bungalow a fluttering of disturbed moths around the jasmine bushes and thought he heard the click of a door latch.

Ruth, still holding his hand tightly and trembling, breathed deeply.

"That was Latacassi," she managed to say, at last.

"Lata who?" demanded Finke. It made him gruff to be startled.

"The old woman. She was originally from Java or Borneo or somewhere out there. Since the first South Seas picture was featured, she's worked part-time as an extra, and done housekeeping on the side, to make a living for herself and her cute little granddaughter named Tani. The little girl—now she's twelve and not so small—gets a few days' work as extra, too, sometimes. As a matter of fact, Latacassi did a little housecleaning for Bob and Barney, once in a while, while Barney was alive. Bob hasn't called her in since Barney went to the hospital, because Latacassi burst out crying, now and then, and it got on his nerves."

"Too bad about his nerves!" muttered Finke.

"Don't worry about old Latacassi. She's in demand. Plenty of the folks who live here hire her by the hour or the day. She's neat—that she learned the hard way—and she's honest. Has no sense of property at all."

"You have to have a hell of a sense of property to be honest. That one sure moves quick, for an honest dame of any age," said Finke.

With a sigh, as if she dreaded the interview, Ruth turned and took Finke back to Reynolds' bungalow. This time they found Bob in an easy chair by the window, staring toward the boulevard without seeing anything in particular. He did not notice at first that someone had entered with Ruth.

"What was that old fat-head yelling about? How does he get that way?"

"Someone was shouting at Latacassi. She wasn't doing any harm in the garden. Just looking at the flowers," said Ruth. "And who was it who sounded off like that? I jumped out of my shoes."

"That grouchy old squarehead who works for Harmon, I guess. He thinks he owns the whole place."

Ruth braced herself, urged Finke forward, and Reynolds looked puzzled.

"Bob Reynolds—Finke Maguire," Ruth said, uneasily.

Because he was so nervous, Reynolds acknowledged the introduction more coolly than he intended. Finke tried not to react with resentment, but he stiffened in spite of himself.

"Mr. Maguire's a detective," Ruth volunteered, lamely. She realized that what Bob had told her was in the strictest confidence and that, even though she was a trusted agent, she should, perhaps, have asked his express permission before bringing another party into the situation.

Reynolds flushed with astonishment. Ruth continued, quickly, "Bob! Something had to be done, and pronto. The Los Angeles police are the dumbest in the world, and corrupt in the bargain. The Beverly Hills police act as goons for the residents who're filthy with dough. I don't have to tell you about Pinky Johnstone, and the E.P.U. force."

"The devil," exclaimed Finke, disgustedly. "How many kinds of cops do we have to deal with?"

"Those I've already mentioned, plus the County gang, the F.B.I., the U.S. Treasury agents, and the State Cossacks," Ruth said.

"Good God! As many as that?" Finke said.

Reynolds, trying to reconcile himself to Ruth's high-handed procedure, could not help glancing at Finke appraisingly.

"You called in a private eye?" he asked Ruth, incredulously.

Finke, near the boiling point, kept relatively calm.

"Get this straight," he said to Reynolds. "I represent Miss Mesker and her interests, which, I understand, include you."

"Up to a certain point," Reynolds said.

"You can string along, if you like, or make other arrangements," Finke continued.

"I've always managed to take care of myself," Bob said, shortly.

For Ruth's sake, seeing how she was distressed, Finke tried being diplomatic. "If I've got this set-up straight, the odds are too heavy against you for you to play it solo. Why don't we all have a talk?"

Bob looked again at Ruth, more uneasily. "You told him . . . everything?" he asked.

Finke answered for her. "About Barney Rice, if that's what you mean, and the trick phone call you got late last night. Also that Ric Manello's trying to get you away from Miss Mesker, and put Shirley Hall out of business, maybe. Is there more?"

"Shirley's sore as hell," Reynolds said, revealing all too clearly what was uppermost in his mind. "She comes all unstuck when she sees me with another woman—on the set or off." He turned to Ruth, with a plaintive expression on his handsome face. "Have you talked with her?"

"No," Ruth said. "And I hope you haven't said too much to her, either."

Bob looked at Ruth reproachfully. "Now, you know I couldn't do that. Can you imagine what Shirley might do, if I suggested that the Manellos don't care about her work, and are hot after me? She might commit murder, herself. And that damn-fool doctor of hers doesn't help. I don't think he knows his pratt from his elbow."

"Both of those are outside his specialty," Ruth said, touching her forehead with a forefinger.

"Psychiatry. Bah," Reynolds said.

"Who is this bug doctor?" asked Finke.

"Another German refugee! Hershel Harms. Cripes, what a name!" Reynolds said.

"And for what is he treating Miss Hall?"

"For jealousy. Can you tie that one? Path-o-logical, he calls it. If she lies on the couch in his office and tells about her dreams— catch a woman being frank about that—and whether she roasted ants or stole pickles as an infant—if she does that, at twenty-five smackers an hour, mind you, two or three times a week for two or three years, then, according to this monkey, she can take a *rational* view of love and sex affairs, and the conduct of normal but sensitive men. God! He knows as much about women as I do about those plants in the garden that eat hamburg and wasps! *Rational*, my eye!"

"You know enough about women to expect that when you play a scene with practically no clothes on with a *señorita* as sharp as the Gardenia Shirley would raise the roof."

Reynolds, for the first time, looked sympathetically and appealing at Finke.

"You know how it is, Maguire," he said. "A fellow doesn't run into half as much grief on account of tramps as the faithful respectable kind."

"You can say that again," Finke agreed.

"Shirley's suffering, all right. But I think that will take care of itself. What I want to know, from you, Bob, is whether this Mexican tamale can act."

"To tell the truth," Reynolds said, in a manner that was quite credible, "I was so upset by the way Shirley was behaving that I can't be sure how the test I made with Miss Noguera will look on the screen. We'll have to wait until this afternoon for that. Of course, I gave it all I had. An actor instinctively does that. The rushes will be shown at 4:30, in Projection Room A."

"Projection Room A," repeated Ruth. "They don't use that one, with the velvet plush on the chairs, and a secret box for big shots who don't want to be seen and asked questions, unless the test is important."

"There's a lot of hush-hush at the studio, and no one except a few who've been invited are supposed to get in," said Bob.

"And *who's* been invited?" demanded Ruth.

"I don't know. I couldn't say," replied Reynolds. "Only, for the love of Jesus, if somehow you could keep Shirley away . . ."

"Shirley'd like nothing better if the Mexican girl is lousy."

"I got to see it, first, for myself," insisted Bob.

"And what about Mills Harmon?"

Reynolds face showed distress. "Miss Noguera tells me he's frantic. Until last night, at dinner, he didn't know about the test. He's as jealous as Shirley. He roars and dances like a bear."

"You mean, that girl didn't tell him until after the test was made?"

Bob looked uncomfortable. "You get the picture. A rich old duffer like him, who's always had his own way, and a young attractive woman. Eulalia had to tell him she was at the hairdresser's or somewhere while she was at the studio."

Ruth raised her eyebrows sarcastically, but philosophically.

"So it's *Eulalia*, now. Does she call you Bob?"

The expression on Reynolds' face was indicative enough that she did.

"She called me last night, late, after I'd talked with you. She'd had such a row with Harmon that she had to talk with somebody in a position to understand."

"Here, in your bungalow?" asked Ruth.

Again Reynolds looked reproachful and hurt. "As God is my witness. Nothing like that," he said.

"You went to hers, perhaps. That's more Continental."

"We sat in the patio until dawn," Bob answered, "She's not a girl who'd go back on her word. She likes the old guy, and respects him. She's marrying him for himself, as well as oodles of dough. She tried to make him listen to reason. She told him, and promised on her honor, that if he'd go to E.P.U. this afternoon, see for himself, and talk with the experts, that if the professionals say that she stinks, she'll chuck the whole idea, settle down and be a dutiful wife."

"Did she get away with that?" asked Finke.

"Not so you'd notice it,' said Bob. "Harmon gave her an ultimatum. He forbade her to set foot in E.P.U. or any other studio again."

"So the whole thing's off?" continued Finke, in a tone that implied it was most unlikely.

"You can't talk that way to a spirited girl like Eulalia," said Bob, more uneasy than ever.

"She told him to go to blazes?"

Reynolds nodded. "She said that they aren't married, yet, and even if they were, she'd live her life as she pleased, as long as she did only what was right."

Ruth interrupted determinedly. "Who arranged that screen test?" she asked, forcing Bob to look her square in the eyes. "Was it Sitchev or the Manellos?"

"I honestly don't know," Bob said. "But there's something I ought to tell you about. Harmon and the Manellos didn't hit it off at all. He'll have no dealings with them, ever again. So Eulalia, trying to pacify the old boy, told Harmon it was my agent—she didn't actually mention you by name . . ."

"Exactly how did she pin it on me?" Ruth demanded, eyes blazing.

"Well," said Bob. "She said my agent noticed her, first, and thought she had what it takes to be a star. And that you fixed it up with Sitchev about the test, and asked Jack Oehler to write the scene."

"That's not all. Come out with it," Ruth insisted, relentlessly.

Reynolds sighed and squirmed, but he came through.

"She had to tell Harmon something, to explain your interest and mine. So she mentioned that Shirley wasn't feeling very well, and was under a doctor's care . . . that she might have to take a little rest."

"Now that's just fine! I think I'd better have a talk with Harmon, myself."

"You're not sore?" Bob asked, with such naif anxiety that Ruth glanced at Finke, and he at her, and they could not help bursting out laughing, in spite of the gravity of the situation.

"And what did Harmon have to say to all that?" Ruth asked, stern again.

"He bellowed something fierce," admitted Bob. "He swore he'd put us out of business. But you know, yourself, he wouldn't go as far as that."

Ruth expressed no opinion about that. "Has Miss Noguera, or Eulalia, as you call her more familiarly, fallen for you, by any chance?"

Reynolds fidgeted and shifted his feet. "The girl's grateful, if you know what I mean. And I suppose, being so much with an older person, she enjoys the company of somebody her own age, within six or eight years."

"You've been seeing her, then?"

"So help me God. Not until last night, when we sat and talked, just like I said. Ruth, you know I love Shirley, and owe everything to you. Just tell me what you want, and I'll do it," Reynolds said.

"First of all, keep everything under your hat. Don't say a word about Barney's death—the mystery about the cause—not to the police or anybody at the studio, or anywhere. Nor about the threatening phone call."

Finke interrupted with a question.

"Who brought you the message that someone wanted you on the phone?"

"Enrico, the night garage man," said Bob.

"Another Mexican?"

"I guess so. Sure," Bob answered.

"Any idea why the call should have come to the pay phone out there?"

"Not the foggiest," Reynolds assured him.

"Anybody ever call you that way before?"

"Not a soul," said Reynolds.

"What's the number of your phone here at the bungalow?"

Reynolds read it off and Finke jotted it down. Bob phoned the office, to get the garage pay-phone number.

"Don't a lot of calls come through the hotel office?" Finke asked.

"They have a list—not many, about fifty people in all—whose calls are to be received for me, if I'm not here, and the numbers taken so I can call back from the house, if I am at home."

"I've a copy of the list," Ruth said to Finke.

"You're sure of the way the call was worded?" asked Finke.

Bob repeated it, word for word, exactly as he had transmitted it to Ruth the night before, and she to Finke that morning. Bob memorized his lines, or anything else, very readily by ear, although printed matter of any kind meant little to him, unless it mentioned his work in a flattering way.

"Now I want you to take on Finke as your new stand-in, so he can get a pass and have access to the E.P.U. lot," Ruth said.

"I'll co-operate," Bob said.

4
A World in Storage

THE E. P. U. LOT IN CHEVIOT HILLS, eight or nine square miles devoted to the actual making of pictures, is a wonder of the hodge-podge modem world, with relics of ancient epochs thrown in. There is a spacious jungle for films in which apemen live in trees; period sets for stories in which men write with feathers; a block of skyscrapers complete with sidewalks of old New York; a white-pillared mansion with embowered veranda for lost-cause dramas in which men sip mint juleps; and an even rarer assortment of unrelated and unique settings enclosed in cavernous "stages." These are ranged in Gargantuan rows and consecutively numbered. There are barber and beauty shops in which stars are trimmed, waved or plucked each day, when they appear in roles shot in six weeks or less and covering dramatic periods of months, years and sometimes generations. A zoo houses trained bears, elephants, crocodiles, monkeys, black kittens which may be streaked with whitewash to serve as skunks, a trained python that can do everything but talk, yapping house dogs, bleary-eyed St. Bernards, owls, parrots, macaws, magpies and crows. The music department has a library of tunes in public domain, the classics, "standard" music, Strauss waltzes, Stravinsky, Debussy, jazz, bop, bebop and rebop, and the product of Tin Pan Alley. There is a warehouse of books, uncatalogued, to fill shelves on the sets, at random; a huge pond with docks and wharves; wind, rain and ocean-wave machines; sea-going vessels, launches, tugs, pirogues and dories; spaceships, rockets, exteriors of moon landscapes and Martian scenes; fields of cotton for the Deep South; Arctic wastes for the Frozen North; iron maidens, torture racks, execution blocks and axes; gallows, gas chambers, guillotines and switchboards for the hot squat, the chairs for which are seldom shown because of superstitious censors.

In contrast with the variety and color of the main lot, the two-story administration building is an architectural banality with a flat roof. Because, for many reasons, high-salaried film executives are more fearful about their persons and possessions than most adults in peace time, and not without cause, the yard surrounding their offices has rectangular green lawns and beds of flowers not more than knee high, so spaced that no cover for snipers exists.

Above this fantastic miscellany—material, imaginative, bestial, historical and even human—lurks the California sky, false blue and, for the most part, cloudless and serene. At any rate, the spring weather was clear and ideal on the afternoon of which I write, when Finke Maguire, anxious to have a look around what to him was a triumph of matter over minds, approached the main entrance after lunch, with his newly stamped pass, which described him as a "stand-in." Not only did the gatekeeper on the boulevard entrance admit Finke, but he called him by name, and told him Mr. Reynolds had not yet arrived.

The feel of the place, not like anything in heaven or on earth, gave Finke the willies. He meandered through the broad passages between the mammoth stages; read the names of renowned directors (of whom he had never heard) on the office doors; and saw a few actors getting haircuts and shaves. The sound of Kid Ory's band drew him toward the music department, where a record of "High Society" was being played, with Barney Bigard on the clarinet.

The door of the music library was ajar and Finke, a sucker for Dixieland jazz, went in. A few clerks nodded or gestured perfunctorily, and then half-rose with their faces wreathed in smiles, but not for him. Behind him, pale and distracted, a slim and beautiful blonde was entering and even before she was greeted as "Miss Hall," he recognized her as Shirley. The fine recording of "High Society" might as well have been "The Good Old Summer Time,"

as far as Shirley Hall was concerned, although, instinctively, as a
dancer, she kept in step with the march. She walked gracefully, as
if in a nightmare.

Finke pretended to be looking at a catalogue of records, and
let her pass, but he watched closely as she entered a room beyond,
through an unmarked door. Allowing her a few seconds' leeway,
he followed. He heard her footsteps clicking on the board floor and
saw her near the end of a narrow dismal corridor. When she was
out of sight, he hurried his own pace so as not to lose her. At the
next corner he caught a glimpse of her as she opened another door
which appeared to be unguarded. He had the feeling that she had
desperate intentions.

The hall she had entered contained long rows of bookshelves
with narrow aisles between. She traversed it, and it chanced that
the doorkeeper of the next department was having a late lunch that
day, and consequently was absent. Shirley went in, unaware she
was being followed, and Finke again hesitated, to give her time to
get ahead, so she would not be likely to discover him. When he
opened the door cautiously, and closed it softly behind him, he
could hear her steps, but no others, or no voices. What he saw
around him took his breath away. He had never dreamed of such
an assortment of weapons, from the most primitive slings and war
clubs, through the ages of arrows and spears, swords, lances and
other weapons of chivalry, the early types of firearms and, lastly,
the most modern.

Finke ducked behind a Civil War cannon just in time to avoid
being detected when she halted nervously and threw back a quick
glance to make sure she was unobserved. Reaching into a glass-
fronted case with shelves, she selected what looked to Finke like a
small automatic, tucked it fearfully into her handbag, and started
back toward the entrance, accelerating her steps. Finke had to stay
in his hiding place until she had passed him on her way out, and
before he could open the door safely to follow, she had taken a
turn through a maze of narrow corridors and he had lost her.

Disgusted with his luck, he hustled back into the weapon warehouse, and walked the full length of it to the case from which

Shirley had taken the object she was now carrying in her bag. His worst premonitions were confirmed. The empty place from which the automatic was missing was easy to find. Finke picked up identical ones on either side. They matched in make, workmanship and calibre. Both were .32 special automatic pistols with handles of mother of pearl. Ladies' guns. While he still had the two ornamental but deadly weapons in his hands, and before he had time to ascertain if they were empty, loaded or filled with blank cartridges, a door opened a few feet from him, startling him so that he almost dropped them, and appeared to be juggling them when the returning attendant confronted him with bulging eyes.

"As you were," said Finke, lamely. "I was looking around."

The attendant acted more unnerved than Finke, as the latter put back the automatics in the case, but he stepped near enough to glance in, and saw that a weapon was missing.

"You took one," the attendant said, with a tremor in his voice.

"Think nothing of it," said Finke. "I'm new around here. They sent me down for a gun, and you were out to lunch."

"Did you have a requisition?" the attendant asked, and seeing from Finke's face that he had none, continued, with what courage he could muster. "You can't take out weapons without a requisition, countersigned by Captain Johnstone."

About to reach for his pass, Finke realized that would be the worst thing he could do. He had to act fast, and think even more so. There seemed only one solution. He let the guy have it, on the point of the jaw. The man slumped, peacefully. Finke caught him and let him down softly so he wouldn't bump his head, then hot-footed it out of the rear door and into the open. He had to get away from that part of the lot without attracting attention. He had to find Reynolds and Ruth, and head off Shirley before she took a shot at herself or somebody else. And he hadn't the remotest idea where he was, or which way to go.

In his haste to get away from the scene of his encounter, he had turned a couple of corners and was standing in what looked like a normal city street, except that the houses had fronts but no backs and the shop signs and posters seemed to be in Polish. What

appeared to be a tandem of open buses, wide enough for two in a
seat, was approaching. A man in his shirtsleeves, stepping out of
nowhere, signaled the bus driver with his hand. The shirtsleeved
man got in, and Finke, following suit, took the other half of the
seat. The driver continued, following a route that seemed to be
prescribed, but which further bewildered Finke until he spotted
the barber shop near the boulevard entrance. The bus stopped at
Stage 1, where a herd of tame reindeer was being corralled. A few
extras dressed as Laplanders got out, and Finke with them. No one
paid him the slightest attention. From where he stood, uncertainly,
he glanced at the barber-shop clock and saw that it was a few minutes past four. Continuing to the main gate, where the man with
the amazing memory had spoken to him so kindly, Finke addressed
him again, "Mr. Reynolds in yet?"

"You'll find him at 4:30, in Projection Room A," the doorkeeper
said. And observing that Finke did not know where that was, he
gave him detailed directions. He had to show his pass to a studio
cop at the cubicle which commanded the concrete walk between
the main lot and the administration building. There the elevator
man told him the projection room he sought was one floor down
and invited him into his car. There was a smooth brief descent.
Beyond the cozy landing was an elaborate reception hall, with a
thick carpet, red leather upholstered easy chairs, pedestal ash trays
and reading tables equipped with magazines. Finke had barely time
enough to look around when he heard voices approaching. Finke
stepped into a secluded alcove, plumped down in a red leather
chair, grabbed a copy of the *Hollywood Reporter*, and held it in
front of his face.

He was astonished to see Ruth escorting the Gardenia and Mills
Harmon through the reception room and into a dim corridor which
led, according to the elevator man's directions, to Projection Room
A. The Gardenia seemed pleased as she clung to Harmon's arm
and he was responding fatuously to her affectionate attentions.

"Now what the hell?" Finke asked himself. The last he had
heard, the multimillionaire was beefing to heaven and swearing to
put Ruth in the poorhouse. Now all was loveydovey between the

affianced couple, and Ruth was obviously in the good graces of both of them.

"This is a screwy set-up," Finke thought. He would have liked to attract Ruth's attention and warn her that Shirley was on the prowl with a stolen automatic, quite possibly intended for use on Bob, or even Señorita Noguera. Before he could think of a pretext, he had to duck behind the *Hollywood Reporter* again. Pinky Johnstone, Ric Manello and a small, spry Central European he quickly recognized from descriptions as Laslo Sitchev hove into sight. From what they said, when they caught sight of Harmon, the Gardenia and Ruth in the corridor ahead, Finke understood that Ruth's presence was an unwelcome surprise, and that they had not counted on Harmon's being there with the Gardenia.

The minutes were passing, and there was no sign of Reynolds. For all Finke knew, Shirley might be lurking inside, in the darkness, with the gun. So Finke, as soon as the way was clear, started down the now empty corridor toward Projection Room A just as the green light above the doorway changed to red.

As Finke opened the projection-room door cautiously his eyes, unaccustomed to the dimness, could not make out all the occupants clearly. Ruth, the Gardenia and Harmon had joined a group seated a few rows from the front, in the center, including Tony Manello. Over on the right-hand side, near the back, sat a round-faced young man Finke assumed was Jack Oehler, with his secretary. Sitchev and his raven-haired receptionist, Natalia Borodin, were in a dim corner farther back. There was no sign of Pinky Johnstone.

Finke took a seat in the last row, left of the projector, so that if either Bob or Shirley came in, he would be sure to spot them.

Suddenly there was dead silence, except for the faint droning of the projection machine. The few shaded house lights up front went out, and the conical glare from behind him sought the screen, wavered, then steadied itself. No one moved or said a word. All eyes were converging on the same blank objective. It confused and annoyed Finke to find himself sharing the general tenseness in the small auditorium, the excitement, curiosity, hope and defense against expecting too much. What was at stake, of such grave moment? It was as if the scattered few who sat in that room were feeling for the multitude of movie fans the world over and wondering what was in store for them—disappointment, banality or a miracle? There were fewer amateurs present than professionals, and each individual was tough, self-centered and also sentimental, in his or her way. The most cynical were likewise the most impressionable. A novice, the lovely Mexican girl, was confident. Ruth, with years of disillusioning experience behind her, seemed equally sure that the test would be a flop. So many tests were. So many were called, and so few were chosen. There was the element, too, of chance. The yearning for the long shot to win, at high odds.

Finke tried to be objective but, to his dismay, he realized that his muscles were aching. The seconds of suspense prolonged themselves, and when the click of flash wiped off the blank with an image, he felt it way down to his toes. He was seeing on the screen a close shot of the Gardenia. She was as bare as any native of a South Sea Island. She had a lei around her neck, scant breast coverings and a sash that blended with her satin-smooth skin. Her eyes were looking straight into the camera, very nervous and afraid.

"Relax, darling," said a voice on the sound-track, off-screen, which was all too recognizable as that of Bob Reynolds. The Gardenia relaxed. It was a kind of magic, a response to an hypnotic suggestion.

"Here goes nothing," Finke said to himself, as it came to his mind that Shirley, with that snub-nosed automatic, could not be far away.

Reynolds' voice again, off-screen, said, encouragingly, "That's better, sweetheart. Smile."

Finke hoped fervently that Harmon was unarmed.

The Gardenia seemed to have shed about ten of her twenty-four years. Her face and movements had become girlish. Her image smiled, as if happy to oblige, and then the smile lingering slowly, died away.

"Profile!" commanded Sitchev's voice. "Right. Now left. Cut! Thank you, Miss Noguera."

Another card was being held up by a man in his shirtsleeves. This one was marked Scene One, Take II. Reynolds' voice was saying, off-screen, "Now don't be nervous, Miss Noguera. You're doing all right. You're *in*."

The second shot was so close that every eyelash, each hair in her eyebrows, all her features were magnified. The Gardenia's expressive face was solemn. She looked frightened, as she was. Her dark eyes were wet. She was not in tears, exactly, but as near to them as was photogenic.

Again Sitchev's voice: "Ready, sound? All right! Camera!"

A third card was displayed. Finke no longer bothered about scenes and numbers. That one was brief—a two-shot of Reynolds and the girl in a bamboo go-down, garlanded with white moon lilies. Bob, wearing nothing but a jock strap, was facing the Gardenia. She was barer than before, and lovelier. Both looked aghast and terrified, in character.

"Mumu," murmured Reynolds. He was giving what he had, all right, and since the role had come from one of the best films ever made, and originally had been acted by a native of Tahiti who never had been spoiled by professional direction, Reynolds was able to imitate the native. That Bob could do, very well, indeed. Finke grasped, without briefing, that the handsome native couple were in love, in a frank and primitive way, and in trouble which might mean life or death. Mumu, as the Gardenia had become, raised one hand to her pulsating throat.

"I shall be strangled."

She panted, as if already being choked. Her breasts rose and fell.

Sitchev's voice cut in, on the sound track.

"Just a minute," he said as he stepped into the shot. "Don't put all the expression into the words. To hell with words. Act. Say 'I shall be strangled'."

The way the little Hungarian, in Hollywood slacks, impersonated a young island girl in danger was astonishing to Finke. He had no impulse to laugh. "These cookies know what they're about," he said to himself.

Mumu was repeating the lines, using Laslo's inflections, without the Hungarian accent. "I shall be strangled . . . I shall be strangled with the tendrils of a buru vine."

"Fine! Magnificent!" exclaimed Sitchev as he stepped out of the shot. The take was cut, abruptly, and the man in shirtsleeves held up another card.

It was then Finke noticed that the door was being opened behind him, cautiously and soundlessly. Ready for anything, he leaned forward slightly, resting his weight on the balls of his feet, and held his elbows close but not tightly to his side. Then he saw that the newcomer was a messenger in uniform. He was holding a slip of paper in his hand.

Afterward Finke could never explain exactly why he acted as he did. He was expecting momentarily either to see Bob Reynolds or Shirley or to hear a pistol shot. He had been watching the door from one eye, like a cat, while the performance had been in progress on the screen. A message was coming for somebody, from someone, and he had to know about it. So he slipped out the door, motioning the messenger back into the corridor.

"What is it?" Finke asked, with an air of authority.

"Mr. Sitchev gave orders that no one was to be interrupted . . ." the messenger said.

"So?" demanded Finke.

"There's a phone call for a Mr. Harmon . . ."

"Oh, that," Finke said, nonchalantly, reaching for the slip of paper. "I'll take care of it."

On the paper was written simply, as a memorandum, the word "Harmon."

Looking relieved, the messenger led him along the plush corridor and showed him into a booth de luxe, with upholstered chair, arm rest, adjustable lights, ash tray, pad, pencils and an extra telephone instrument in case more than one at a time was needed. Finke nodded his thanks and closed the sound-proof door behind him. He sat down, took up the receiver, and this is what he heard, spoken in a voice, quite obviously recorded, of a chap who might have been to Oxford, Harvard or both.

"You're having an object lesson. What happens to someone close to you can happen to you. Think well about the matter. Don't be obstinate. What happens to someone close to you can happen to you. You're having an object lesson. Think well . . ."

As carefully as possible, Finke replaced the receiver, backed silently to the door of the booth, turned the knob deftly, and, opening the door swiftly, stepped out.

As he hustled back to the shelter of the dim projection room, he was filled with satisfaction. Whether he had got a break or blundered into a heap of extra trouble, he could not decide. But he was getting action, at last. Immediately, before he took his seat, he was aware that the small picked audience had reshuffled itself. Laslo Sitchev had absented himself, and in the seat the famous director had occupied sat Ric Manello. Natalia, Sitchev's secretary, was beside him. What gave Finke a jolt was to see Bob Reynolds with the group around the Gardenia. Bob must have come in, and the producer must have ducked out, while Finke had been at the phone.

Whether his nerves were on edge or he was responding to the warning an alert man often has when someone is glaring at his back, Finke threw a hasty glance toward the projectionist's small balcony. He saw, just for an instant, behind the projectionist and his assistant, the pale drawn face of Shirley Hall, with an almost maniacal glitter in her eyes. She vanished, rather than moved, and stare as he might, he could not catch sight of her again. Still, he had seen her. She must have been following Bob. Finke's first impulse was to go up there and investigate, but he figured that no one could shoot from a brightly lighted booth into the dark auditorium and expect to hit a given individual. And if Shirley tried to enter he could nab her.

5

An Armed Anthropoid

THE PLOT OF THE FAMOUS FILM, *Tabu*, as revised by E.P.U., Inc., revolves around the fate of two young Tahitian lovers. The Girl was chosen by the ageing regional high priest as the ceremonial virgin who is tabu to all other males. Any other man who looked upon the sacred maiden was ostracized. If this Girl expressed amorous feelings toward any of her youthful companions, she was garotted and all traces of her body and possessions destroyed.

Mumu (Miss Noguera) and Timomo (Mr. Reynolds) found love stronger than tradition or tabu, escaped the high priest by fleeing to an island under jurisdiction of the French, were safe and ecstatic for a while, then were sacrificed by petty French officialdom to preserve "tranquility" on the Islands and Johnston-code morality.

Reynolds, the Gardenia, and a character actor who was playing Egali-gali, a French colonial police inspector, were on the screen. The *décor* was the interior of a South Sea bamboo love nest. Egaligali had been tipped off that Mumu, the fugitive ex-virgin who was wanted by the native ruler and shocked inhabitants of Tahiti, was in French territory and should be deported. Timomo, Mumu's lover, was refusing to give her up to the law, which would ship her back to where an executioner was waiting to choke off her young life with the tendril of a buru vine.

The tenseness of the atmosphere in the projection room had mounted until it could be cut with a knife, and Finke was continuing to feel it as keenly as anyone, with the possible exceptions of Mills Harmon and Shirley Hall.

Ruth, as she watched, was filled with growing consternation. Nothing moved according to her desires or expectations. She had been misled in every particular. Sitchev, instead of considering the test a trivial matter, a mere favor to catch the good will of a man of wealth and influence, had directed it himself. As cameraman he had chosen Hagup Bogigian, three times winner of the Academy Award, and one of the best in the business. The scene Jack Oehler had lifted from the old French masterpiece was not one to be played casually in an afternoon, then discarded. It had possibilities that anyone who knew anything about pictures could foresee. It was haunting and fairly cried for a build-up and expansion. Reynolds, aware of it or not, had outdone himself. Eulalia Noguera had shed her initial stagefright. As Mumu and Timomo, they were expressing tenderness, defiant courage, wild passion, black despair. No one could remain unmoved by such a performance. It would impress the toughest critics and roll fans in the aisles.

It was clear to Ruth, and even to Finke, that Laslo Sitchev must have become convinced that the Manellos were going to take over the studio, and he was playing into their hands, with a view to his own future, in his bland and unscrupulous way. What stuck out most prominently from the tangle of interests and intrigue was the incontestible fact that the Gardenia, as an actress, was terrific, that the invading trio of Chicago gangsters had been tipped off and were trying to take possession of her, as a tremendous asset. Between Sitchev and the Manellos, it was hard for anyone to guess "which serpent would devour the other" but Ruth was overwhelmed by the likelihood that she would be wiped out between them.

On the screen, the touching scene unfolded itself. When, at one of the most dramatic moments, Timomo took from its case the prize pearl for which he had risked his life and shown phenomenal skill as a diver, to offer it to Egali-gali as a bribe, Mumu threw herself into his arms and begged him, instead of giving up the treasure, to let her die. If there was a dry eye in the projection room it was not one of Finke Maguire's. He saw their young bodies blending. Timomo was conscious only of Mumu's nearness, her ardor. She was dizzy with love.

Timomo dropped the pearl. The corrupt French official re-trieved it, greedily, and exclaimed with wonder. He held it to the light. Mumu's fate was in the balance.

Then pandemonium started breaking loose out in front. Mills Harmon, letting out a tormented roar, sprang up from his seat. He faced about, shaking a fist into the blinding cone of white light from the projector.

"Stop this, I say! Turn the damn thing off!" he shouted.

In the projector's booth, coincidentally, there were blurred signs of a scuffle, and sounds of voices—horrified, entreating and hysterical. A second later, Shirley Hall, chattering, panting and brandishing her open handbag, lipstick, handkerchief, keys and a pearl-handled .32 automatic in her frenzied hands, ran into the auditorium. Buzzers sounded. The house lights went up, catching everyone in the act of rising, turning, gesticulating, questioning and adding to the general confusion.

Shirley's initial impetus got her past Finke before he could waylay her. Her eyes riveted on Bob Reynolds, she made for him. Bob, caught unprepared, took a couple of strides to meet her. Tony Manello, who, unlike Bob, had spotted the gun in Shirley's ner-vous fingers, stuck out one foot to trip Bob and spill him to the floor, out of range. Evidently, in the Manellos' book, Bob was not expendable. Then Tony, on his own account, ducked between two rows of chairs.

Dazed, Shirley halted, stood shaking but otherwise immobi-lized, just long enough for Finke to catch her from behind and dis-possess her of the automatic, which he slipped hastily into a side coat pocket. Mills Harmon, unable to command attention while Shirley held the center of the scene, motioned her aside.

"Young woman! You're overexcited," he said. "Go away!"

Shirley, with concentrated fury, fixed Harmon like a huge bird before a snake. "You old dodo!" she cried. "Can't you see that this golddigger you fished out of a swimming tank is making a fool of you? Methuselah!"

She shot a final frantic glance at Reynolds, spun around and dashed from the room. Bob made a faltering attempt to follow her, overwhelmed with embarrassment. He felt himself detained by a firm strong feminine hand on one of his coat lapels, and realized that he was staring ineffectually into the smoldering eyes of Ruth Mesker.

"You chump!" she began.

Rattled as he was, Bob knew what Ruth meant.

"I couldn't shoot off my mouth about how good I was, till the scene had been shown," he said, lamely.

"You could damn well have let me know how good *she* was!" Ruth countered, indicating the Gardenia. The Mexican beauty was so excited by the furor she was creating that she tried to embrace her foaming fiancé.

"Miss Mesker thinks I'm good. You promised, darling, to abide by the verdict of the experts!"

Mills Harmon held her off gruffly and confronted Ruth.

"You got me into this! You lied to me! You assured me that Eulalia could never be an actress. That she . . . that she would see how hopeless it was, and behave like a dutiful wife. Dutiful! Stripped naked as a jay bird! Mumu! Buru! Goo goo! Bah!"

Quite as furious, but more restrained, Ruth yelled back at him, "That two-faced weasel, Sitchev, swore she stank!"

"Where's this Sitchev?"

"Please find him, someone. We want his verdict!" the Gardenia said.

"I'll strangle him," said Harmon.

"Mr. Reynolds," the Gardenia appealed to Bob, "you're an expert. Was I good? Can I act?"

Harmon interrupted, even more forcefully. "Fine! Ask Mr. Reynolds. He's an actor. He is what you call good. He admits it, himself. So do I. He's engaged to a famous actress, the kind *you* want to be. We've just had a sample of their love life!"

A telephone rang. Natalia was standing by.

"It's for you, Miss Noguera," Natalia said. It was clear that the Russian secretary was hanging around to pick up information and that Sitchev had made himself scarce to escape the consequences of his double-dealing.

Harmon took the instrument instead, and slammed down the receiver, without listening or speaking.

"Not a word! We're leaving this insufferable place for good," Harmon said. "I'll buy every foot of every last copy of that indecent film."

The Gardenia, who was making an heroic attempt to keep her temper, flared dangerously.

"That film is not indecent. It's lovely."

"I'll buy it and burn it myself, every inch . . ."

"You think everything's for sale."

Harmon, who had been sizzling like a fuse, reached the firecracker stage. "Not your figure! . . . Undraped! That's not for sale. For fifty cents admission. No wife of mine . . ."

"We're not married . . . not yet. You keep forgetting that!" the Gardenia said, with spirit.

As Harmon's jaw dropped in horror, Laslo Sitchev, having tried unsuccessfully to phone the Gardenia, entered suavely, smiling and rubbing his hands.

"You should be proud, Mr. Harmon," the producer began. He was practically purring.

"Did you see anything wrong with my figure? Anything indecent?" the Gardenia asked the little Hungarian.

Sitchev shrugged and appealed again to Harmon.

"After all, Mr. Harmon," he said. "We can't make the girls wear red flannels in a South Seas picture." To the Gardenia he added. "I want you should come to my office for a chat."

Ruth stepped forward, defying the Manellos and Sitchev. "Don't let them stampede you, Miss Noguera," she said. "Be careful about signing anything."

"Now, Ruth, darling . . ." protested Sitchev. The Gardenia looked at him sardonically.

"Did you tell everyone that I stink, Mr. Sitchev?" she asked.

"May God strike me dead!" the Hungarian objected. "In my office we can talk things over. Mr. Harmon's a smart businessman . . ."

"I'll never consent. I shall sue you if that film we saw today is shown again. There'll never be another!" Mills Harmon asserted.

"I'll speak for myself. No one else has the right," the Gardenia said.

Ruth warned her again. "If one producer and one agency wants you under contract, you can write your own ticket in every studio in town. Look them all over. Take your choice. You've shown what you can do. Don't let them sew you up and swindle you."

"Eulalia!" barked Harmon. "We're leaving this detestable place right now."

She turned on him, eyes flashing. "Go ahead, if you wish. Mr. Manello arranged for my test. Mr. Reynolds was kind enough to act with me, and Mr. Sitchev directed us. I'll hear at least what Mr. Sitchev has to say."

Leaving Harmon gasping, she took Sitchev's arm and went with him up the aisle and out of the auditorium.

Finke made his getaway from Projection Room A as promptly as he could, after the Gardenia allowed herself to be led away by Laslo Sitchev. He had to avoid Harmon, at all costs. The raging millionaire had not taken particular notice of him, and probably, Finke thought, would not recognize him by sight if they chanced to meet again. And surely, in the end, Finke would have to tell Harmon about that intercepted telephone call. He was not sure about the law regarding telephone messages. Did they, like letters in the mail, belong to the sender, even after delivery? Or did the party to whom they were addressed have an equity in them, so that anyone who took them under false pretenses could be charged with theft, and sued for damages? Would it not be difficult, if not impossible, for anyone to prove or disprove, legally, that he had talked, or not talked, with any given party by means of the telephone? Could the failure to disclose to the police the text of a telephone message be deemed deliberate or malicious withholding of information? Could anyone swear, in court, under oath, that he or she had recognized a "voice" coming over the wire?

Quite willing to let Harmon stew in his own juice for the time being, Finke was much more concerned about having a talk with Ruth.

From behind the same copy of the *Hollywood Reporter* that had shielded him from observation before the performance, he had seen Harmon storm out of the place, alone. Finke had hoped to waylay Bob Reynolds, as much to keep him under control as to find out what Bob had learned, if anything, that he had not known that morning. Finke was all at sea concerning Bob. Was the actor as naif and simple-minded as he seemed? Or did he, on the contrary, find it more convenient to put on an act? Having seen for himself how Bob with the aid of a little body paint could pass himself off as a South Sea Island native, Finke was willing to believe he could act like a none too bright young American with equal facility, and at the same time be stupid, like a fox.

Of one thing Finke was sure. Ruth was on a worse spot than she had feared, in a business way. She could not hope to hold her own if Bob let her down. When finally Ruth came along, Finke attracted her attention and she joined him in his alcove, plumping herself down, wearily, in a red leather chair.

"We've got to find Shirley. Right away," she said, as if nothing else mattered just then.

"What about Bob?"

"He's already started out to find her," said Ruth.

"He didn't go out this way."

Ruth sighed. "You never can tell. He may be hiding—in some bar—again. That's his solution, whenever life gets too complicated."

"He may have something there," said Finke.

Their talk was interrupted by the entrance of a pretty girl, who looked as if she might be of grammar-school age. She was very graceful and, in studio surroundings, completely at ease.

"Tani! Where did you come from?" asked Ruth.

"Where's Mr. Reynolds?" the girl asked, her eyes wide and shining. Finke could not understand why she looked hauntingly familiar, although he had never seen her in his life. As the kid asked her eager question of Ruth, she was sizing up Finke from the corner of her eyes. This is the pay-off, Finke thought to himself. This kid, not a day over twelve, is flirting with me.

"Mr. Reynolds has gone. But I saw your grandmother this morning."

A number of pieces clicked together in the jig-saw puzzle that was forming in Finke's mind. Tani, who was giving him the eye at the age when she should have been learning square root, was a

South Sea islander, or at least, an American-born descendant of one. She had had a small part, as one of a group of girls surrounding Mumu, in the scene from *Tabu*. And, divested of her clothes appropriate for school, she was not as childish as she looked when dressed. The girls of the tropics mature in their earliest teens and wither by the time they are thirty on their native sands, beneath the sheltering palms. How Tani would develop, in Free America, remained to be seen, but she had got a wonderful start. She was self-possessed without being fresh, and precocious without seeming unnatural or unattractive.

"Granny works for Mumu," Tani said. "I'm sorry she left Mr. Reynolds. Wasn't he wonderful in *Tabu* today?"

"Mumu wasn't bad, either," said Ruth.

"I'll say she wasn't," agreed Tani. "She acted just like me."

"Tani hates herself," said Ruth to Finke. "Did you see the rushes just now?" she asked Tani.

Tani nodded. "I never miss seeing Mr. Reynolds, if I can help it," she said.

Finke grinned. "I can see, maybe, why Granny went over to work for Mumu," was his aside, to Ruth.

"I know," Tani sighed. "I'm just at that age. But Mr. Reynolds never made a pass at me, if that's what Shirley's afraid of."

"Shirley? Afraid? What are you getting at?" asked Ruth.

"She's jealous. She made Mr. Reynolds promise to get rid of Granny, on account of me. Can you tie that one?"

"I didn't see you in the projection room," Ruth asked. "Where were you?"

"In the secret booth with Captain Johnstone," Tani said. "Captain Johnstone's never made a pass at me either, which a lot of the girls can't say, who treat me as if I were a baby, and colored, at that." Tani bared her arm and offered it for inspection. "I'm not quite as dark as Mumu. They had to make me up for the test, so she wouldn't look too brown, and I wouldn't be too white."

Ruth was looking hard at Finke, and allowed herself a sarcastic smile for the first time that afternoon. "I don't like the gleam in your eye," she said.

Tani looked up at Finke, mischievously, and sidled a little nearer. "Your friend is nice," she said to Ruth. "Are you having an affair?"

"Never mind that," Ruth said sternly. "Did Captain Johnstone like the show, and, if not, why was he there?"

"I think he was watching your boy friend . . ."

"Mr. Maguire!" Ruth said, firmly.

"I think he was watching Mr. Maguire, but he sure was surprised when Shirley pulled that rod."

"Revolver."

"No. Revolvers spin around. Shirley had an automatic that can shoot twelve times," Tani said. "Gee. If Shirley doesn't pull herself together, she'll have to take a good long vacation."

"Who told you that?" Ruth asked, so sharply that Tani clammed up.

"Oh, that's just some talk that's going around," she said.

The amazing child gave another frank look of approval to Finke and smiled. He got so rattled that he blushed. He had found himself wondering, seeing Mumu and her Tahitian playmates, one of whom had been Tani, that afternoon, how a man would act if he got stranded on such an island, where "the age of consent" meant just what it said.

"Tell me, Miss Mesker. How old does a girl have to get before it's lawful for men to make passes?"

"Never mind. Run along!" Ruth said, more sternly than she meant to.

Tani skipped over to the elevator, where the elevator man said, "My! Tani. You've grown."

"Thank heaven, not like a string bean. I've filled out, in proportion, don't you think?"

The car door rolled into place and the cage presumably ascended.

"That kid has the run of this place. How come?" Finke asked, looking after the elevator with lingering amazement.

"Oh, everybody loves Tani. She was knee high when the Central Casting first used her, and still attends the E.P.U. school. I used to see her report cards, X'd by Latacassi. You know how it is, when a child appears on the screen. A brat steals the scene from the smartest grown-up actors without trying. In the studios, the kids get an even better break. They have two strikes on everybody, from directors to bootblacks."

"That one's got three on me," admitted Finke.

Ruth rose, after extinguishing her cigarette on the silver-plated ash tray.

"What's so important about finding Shirley right now?" Finke asked, to get Ruth back to the subject she had been so intent upon when Tani had come in.

"She's played right into Ric Manello's hand," Ruth said. "With more than a dozen witnesses looking on, including the police chief, Tani, a couple of working projectionists, two secretaries who spread gossip the way Typhoid Mary scattered germs, Ric and Tony Manello, the Gardenia who expects to take her place, and most likely her man in the bargain . . ."

"But why get excited about that? Miss Hall and Bob have their little tiffs, two or three times a week. Who cares?" asked Finke.

"'Twould serve them both right to get shot," Ruth said, exasperated. "I'm thinking about Shirley's contract. There's a clause in it that E.P.U. can terminate it without notice if she creates a public scandal 'that might be injurious to her reputation and reflect discredit on the studio or the industry.' That's one of the gems we have Will Hays to thank for. If one of our stars commits bigamy or is exposed as a link in a dope ring, or gets pinched for drunken driving, and the papers play it up all over the country, the box office suffers, the producer's association has to make a gesture to pacify the church crowd, and the star has to go."

"I never thought of that," admitted Finke.

"Shirley attempted to assault Bob with a dangerous weapon. If the Manellos have such a drag at E.P.U. that Laslo Sitchev's already gone over to their side, and they want to ditch Shirley, without giving Bob any legal pretext for breaking *his* contract, Shirley's exhibition this afternoon is made to order for them."

"She's already spilled the beans," Finke said. "What can we do about it, if we find her?"

"The afternoon papers have gone to press. If Shirley and Bob give out a statement, and stage a touching reconciliation scene, with plenty of photographers present, that will make the scene this afternoon look like a touching lovers' quarrel. The fans will eat it up, with such a happy ending. E.P.U. will get some fine publicity. That means dough."

"Will Bob have to marry the girl? I mean, right away?"

Ruth's face took on that stern look again. "By God, he will if I say so."

Finke nodded. He got the drift all right. The lawyers who drew up those studio contracts stuck in a couple of jokers which left holes in them through which any shyster could drive a big truck.

"My car's on the parking lot," he said. "I'll drive you where you want to go."

As Ruth assented, she was reminded, all of a sudden, that the man on whom she depended so readily had been a stranger less than twenty-four hours ago. There was something in the tone of her voice when she responded, almost meekly, "I'll meet you outside," that gave her a start.

It was the custom at E.P.U. for the executives, producers, writers, agents and distinguished guests to enter and leave the lot by way of the administration building, which had a canopy from marble steps to the curb irreverently called "The Porte Kosher." Finke, a mere stand-in, had to "go out by the same door that in he went," that is to say, the main exit on Washington Boulevard, which was used by most of the rank and file of talent and low-paid employees, to the number of several thousand. Each man, woman or child was put on record as he or she entered, with the minute and the hour of entrance, and on leaving the lot, the entry was completed with a notation of the time of exit. Finke, after having watched Ruth ascend in the elevator to the ground floor, walked two hundred yards through a tunnel to the main lot, and came up into the slanting sunlight within sight of the barber shop, which had become, for Finke, the principal landmark on the studio grounds.

When he glanced toward the exit, another fifty yards away, he saw that a serious bottleneck had developed there. Pinky Johnstone, a few studio cops in uniform, the regular gate attendants

and the guard Finke had slugged after lunch in the firearms warehouse were giving each man who went through the turnstile the
once over. In cases where the weapons guard seemed uncertain,
the studio police were frisking the outward-bound employees without ceremony.

It occurred to Finke that the gun they sought was still in his
right-hand jacket pocket, and that he was the man they were after.
Since he had no trouble in recognizing at a considerable distance
the guard he had socked, there was no good reason for Finke to
assume that the latter would not spot him at sight, at close quarters.
As to the automatic, it was probable that the studio had a record of
the make, calibre and serial number of the pearl-handled gun.

Finke dropped out of line, as casually as he could, and walked
back toward the barber shop again, on the pretense of buying an
evening paper from the Negro bootblack there. The neat little tandem bus, bringing a number of extras to the wardrobe department,
to turn in their costumes at quitting time, came alongside. Finke
had to have a chance to think about his new problem. He got
aboard. He was aware that Ruth was in a hurry to get going, and
was waiting for him on the parking lot, but he had to figure some
way to get to her without being arrested by Pinky.

It was not that Finke had done wrong in disarming Shirley to
prevent bloodshed in Projection Room A. He could not simply ditch
the gun. The telltale gun must be accounted for. Pinky himself,
and Tony Manello, among many others, had witnessed the gun-
play and knew that Finke had put Shirley's weapon in his pocket.
If he produced the gun, at the gate, and the arsenal guard accused
him of assault, battery and larceny, Finke could not take the rap.
That would tie up the gun with Shirley, and connect Shirley with
Finke. The truth of the matter, as so often happens, would sound
too fishy for any authorities to believe or accept.

After passing the huge building in which were housed the music department, the false library containing thousands of unlisted
books, and the grotesque warehouse filled with Iron Maidens,
racks, guillotines, tomahawks, shillelaghs, blunderbusses, muzzle-
loaders, and revolvers, the bus, in which Finke was now the only
remaining passenger, and therefore uncomfortably conspicuous,

brought up at the studio zoo. The driver looked at Finke expectantly, as if there were nowhere else to go in that direction, so Finke
got off.

In cages, the great cats were pacing restlessly, as if the spring
air stirred memories. The smaller monkeys were chattering in
cages, and a few attendants were currying the more docile beasts
like yaks, hartebeestes, zebras and camels, or cleaning the cages
of the bears. In the doorway of a small shack, like a railroad gate-
tender's office, sat a large white-haired easygoing-looking man in
shirtsleeves, glancing, over brass-bowed spectacles, at the headlines of the evening news. Finke, so as not to attract attention, stood
on the far side of a cage in which was a solemn, mangy drill, with a
bright blue behind and disillusioned, beady eyes. In order to look
over the back stretches of the lot, Finke, staying close to the cage,
surveyed the area between the zoo and the twelve-foot back fence.
Had he but known it, some of E.P.U's most colossal outdoor pro-
ductions and expensive flops, involving chariot races, Mormon
migration and Chinese farming had been shot in that uncultivated
field. Between times it was used as pasture land for studio sheep
and cattle, and to exercise the horses.

In the corner of the lot farthest removed from the inhabited
streets of Cheviot Hills stood a dismal conglomeration of exterior
sets, with buildings, as always, having fronts and no backs, or vice
versa. The day shift of gardeners had been transplanting a field of
cotton and some magnolias. Backless cabins were grouped to represent the hovels of plantation Negroes. Nearby was an old Southern mansion, with veranda, white pillars, mint beds, shade trees
and all the traditional fixings. Why it had such a bewildering as-
pect was that half of it was freshly painted and in good repair, while
the other half was in process of being loused up for a sequence in
which the distinguished old Southern family had seen better days.

Absorbed for the moment in his own immediate problems,
Finke was paying scant attention to the drill, and had leaned
against the bars of the cage. Startled by a tug at his right jacket
pocket, Finke's hand strayed down there. He jumped a foot off the

ground, and outward, having grasped, then more quickly released, a monkey's paw.

"Aw nix, monk! Nix! Give it back," he pleaded. The drill had fished in his pocket for peanuts, found the pearl-handled automatic and appropriated it. Frowning and chattering, the blue-bottomed monkey had retreated to a safe distance, where Finke could not reach him, and was examining the automatic, tipping it, tapping it, tilting it, peering into the barrel, flipping the trigger guard, balancing the gun, sniffing it, and holding it to his ear. When Finke stuck his arm into the cage, in a futile effort to grab the weapon, the drill sounded off, with such a scolding and scuffling that the zoo-keeper, eyes still on the newspaper, yelled, "Take it easy, Monty."

Either because of his master's voice, or Finke's quick withdrawal of his hand, the drill stopped chattering and fuming, cocked his impertinent head on one side and again peered into the barrel of the gun. The safety catch was on, but the monkey's exploring fingers had missed it but narrowly, more than once. Finke had to take a chance and get away from there, fast.

There was nowhere to go, without being spotted by the zoo-keeper and his men, except toward the field of cotton and the old Southern mansion with the before-and-after exterior. He had no sooner reached shelter behind the false front than he heard a shot, and the squat four-foot monkey squealing and yawping—also the alarmed voices of the zoo-man. From his hiding place, Finke watched the big drill bounding, rebounding, banging the bars, turning indignant somersaults and making a phenomenal hullabaloo. The monkey must have been more startled than hurt, and it seemed unlikely that any innocent bystander had been shot. As it appeared to Finke, the monkey must have contrived to unlimber the safety catch and pulled the trigger. Then when the explosion had scared him, he had thrown the automatic to the bottom of his cage, and was carrying on so furiously that the zoo-keeper and his helpers could not retrieve the weapon.

The drill proved to be a monkey whose emotions were violent but transitory, and to whom experience meant little or nothing.

While still surrounded by the zoo-men outside his cage, the monk stopped screaming and cavorting, cocked his head, took another look at the gun on the floor, and picked it up again. Without exception, the men scattered and scampered for their lives, the head keeper, being the most experienced, several paces in the lead. Finke saw the flare of another explosion, heard the report, and made up his mind that he must escape, then or never. Inside the shell of the fake plantation housefront, he saw an extension ladder which the workmen had used in attaining the post-bellum effect on the right half of the mansion. Also he found a rubber doormat marked "Welcome." Keeping the house front between him and the zoo, he dragged the ladder and lugged the mat as far as the high fence. Without being observed, he climbed to the top, protected himself from the charged electric wires by means of the doormat, pulled the ladder up after him, and descended, mat in hand, to the other side. He was free from E.P.U. at last, in a vacant section of Cheviot Hills occupied by a couple of jerry-built factories which had served some obscure purpose during war time. As a precaution, he hid the ladder and mat in one of the deserted factories, and as he did so he was startled, but not too violently, by the distant report of another pistol shot.

The nearer he got to the parking lot and his Chevrolet, the less inclined Finke was to redeem it. Ruth, most certainly, could not have waited all that time. And if Pinky Johnstone had reason to suspect Finke in connection with the theft of the automatic, the chief would not be stupid enough to omit keeping Finke's car under surveillance. Furthermore, the records would show that Finke had checked into the lot just after lunch time, and that, officially, he was still there. When the E.P.U. police now caught up with him, he would have to explain promptly how he happened to slug an attendant and steal the gun, turn it over to Shirley, recover it and then put it into the hands of an irresponsible blue-arsed monkey. Since he had disarmed Shirley in the projection room where such a state of excitement had prevailed, he had not had a moment to examine the contents of the clip or the firing chamber. It might have been, and still be, deadly, or merely filled with blanks.

His best course seemed, at first, to taxi straight to his office, and, with Kay's help, recover the loose threads of his contacts. Then, in the taxi, it occurred to him that, if Pinky Johnstone had caused a dragnet to be spread for him, as he most certainly would have, he might have tipped off the County police to watch his office on the Strip. So he ordered the driver to take him to the Tropics.

6

A Clue, at Least

THE TROPICS IS A FEW BLOCKS EAST of the Derby, on Rodeo Drive. It is the rendezvous of those who like to imagine themselves beachcombers, or who actually are. Its refreshments are of a high order: genuine Cuban rum, Chinese food cooked by Japs who had to be clever and competent to avoid exposure, and a small band equipped with Hawaiian and flamenco guitars, a marimba, and a makeshift gamelan. Finke, who knew nothing about it technically, enjoyed the exotic music of the islands. As he sat on the open terrace, listening to it, he liked its effect on the nerves. He phoned Kay to join him, ordered a bottle of Bacardi, so that the soft-footed waiters would not have to interrupt them too often, and tried to get himself into a detached frame of mind.

He had, before meeting Ruth Mesker, been ignorant of the details of the motion-picture industry. Otherwise he would not have followed her suggestion that he try to pass himself off as a stand-in in order to get the run of the E.P.U. lot. There must have been a better way, but it was too late, now, to mend the damage that had been done. He had stuck his neck out, and Pinky Johnstone, the Manellos, and all their pals and social equals would take a crack at it. By appropriating the telephone call belonging to Mills Harmon, he had committed a crime the gravity of which he could not even estimate. The police might regard it as trifling, or take the solemn view. Finke felt like the eagle carrying the monkey. He was flying upside down. That brought his thoughts back to the drill at E.P.U., who still might be terrorizing the lot with the automatic that was balling up the case. Pinky Johnstone, Finke felt sure, must know quite a lot about him by now. It must have occurred to the E.P.U. chief to look for Finke's name in the phone book. And there it was, with his office address and phone number, for anyone to see. And it was not the one he had written on Pinky's application blank. To a cop of Pinky's type, any stranger or intruder was an object of suspicion and rested in the pigeonhole of his mind marked "Unfinished Business." Pinky would not care a hang about justice, but in an area where more than a half-dozen police forces were operating, information of any kind had a trade-in value.

"What kept you?" Finke asked, curtly, when Kay put in an appearance, but he called over the waiter for a bowl of fresh ice, since the cubes in Kay's drink he had poured were melted.

"A Dutchman, who's been trying to talk with you, off and on, since five o'clock, phoned again, and Emile, from the Derby, called to tell you that the same Dutchman, apparently, has been trying to reach you there."

"The devil!" said Finke. "What's his name?"

"He wouldn't leave his name or number. I think he's been in the East Indies. He referred to you as 'Tuan Maguire'."

"That's a hot one. *Tuan Maguire*. He wouldn't be Harmon's man?"

"Has Harmon got a Dutchman?"

"So I hear."

Kay noticed that Finke looked annoyed, or troubled, which for him was about the same thing

"What's bad about that? Mills Harmon's a very rich man. Maybe he wants to retain you to get his girl back for him."

"Who told you Harmon had lost his girl?"

"Ruth told me what she knew, after you'd stood her up on the E.P.U. parking lot. She's looking for Shirley on her own."

"What about Reynolds?" asked Finke.

"In some sawdust foxhole, I suppose. Ruth hoped that you could find him."

"Will Ruth keep in touch?"

Kay nodded, and tapped her flat chest. "They also serve, who sit at a damn phone and wait."

"It's unguarded now, I suppose," Finke said.

"You must have had some prize dumbbells work for you in Parree," said Kay. "I left instructions with the confidential service to have calls relayed here."

"Police and all?"

"My face is red," said Kay. "I should be in two places at once, and you should be invisible."

Finke took another drink, then summarized for Kay the afternoon's developments. Kay assimilated them as fast as he dished them out, but the intercepted phone call took precedence in her mind over all the rest.

"You've got to tell Harmon right away," Kay said, positively.

"What's the hurry?" demanded Finke, defensively. He suspected that Kay was right, but he did not relish the assignment.

"A man who's life is threatened by parties we know are in earnest has a right to know about it," insisted Kay.

"It's Miss Noguera's life that's threatened. She's the one in danger. If anyone's entitled to the information, she is. Who else is 'close to Harmon'? She ought to be guarded night and day."

Kay looked at him quizzically. "That cookie'll take care of herself," she said. "She's got around Laslo Sitchev, Tony Manello, and has her hooks in Bob Reynolds. Now it's you."

"A murderer threatens to bump off Miss Noguera. So what's *your* reaction? All you worry about is whether some rich old stiff will miss her when she's gone."

"Somebody phones E.P.U., asks for Mills Harmon, a messenger writes his name on a slip . . . and the messengers, by the way, make daily reports to Pinky Johnstone . . . so you take Harmon's call, leave him in the dark, and want to go into a huddle with his girl."

"Think it through, you dope!" said Finke. "What does a rich old guy do, who's out of his mind from jealousy on account of a pippin about one-third his age? He grabs the phone, calls Pinky, the L.A. cops, the Beverly Hills force, the County bunch, and the F.B.I. Then where does Ruth stand? Or Bob? Or for that matter, you and I?"

"You may have something there," said Kay. "But aren't communications between a client and a licensed detective privileged? Aren't we exempted by the law?"

"Not where murder is concerned," said Finke.

"The doctors haven't fixed the cause of Barney's death," suggested Kay.

"At first glance, that looks like our only possible out." Finke rose. "I'm going to the Gardens. Tell anyone who wants me that I've flown to San Francisco to hear four or five hundred clunks play a Cecil de Mille arrangement of the 'Dead March' from *Saul*."

"My! We've finished the rum," Kay said, and straightened her hat, which should have been tilted instead.

Nearing the Omar Gardens, Finke had the taxi driver let him out on the wooded stretch of Concord Drive. A short walk brought him to the ornamental wrought-iron gates which were wide open. He continued through the patio to the pathway that led to the Gardenia's bungalow. No one seemed to pay attention to him or any others who entered, departed or strolled around. That was in every way disconcerting to a detective who had reason to believe that one former resident had recently been murdered on the premises and that at least one more was on the list, and surely would be missed.

When he and Ruth had been there that morning, she had pointed out the house occupied by Mills Harmon, and in which his valet, bodyguard and gardener (all in the same person) also slept. It was quiet and dark. Finke would not be able, even if he wanted to, to tell the oil tycoon about the death threat. Farther along, as he approached the Gardenia's cottage, he saw, or thought he saw, a faint light. As he stepped off the trodden path to investigate, he crossed the soft garden bed. His feet sank an inch or two into the fresh loam and he hoped he was not damaging any seeds or sprouts. At the nearest window, partly shaded by Venetian blinds, he tried to peer in.

Without warning, he felt a hard knee in the middle of his back. A couple of big horny hands which smelled of fertilizer seized him from behind and started squeezing his neck. Finke feigned limpness and dropped straight downward with all his weight. When his assailant tried to shift his grip, Finke let him have a backswipe with one elbow and knocked the wind out of him. The man made a noise like a coffee can being punctured with a key, and would have slumped had not Finke, aroused by the suddenness of the attack, clipped him three times before he hit the dirt. A little ashamed of his unnecessary violence, Finke bent over to examine the man. He was "the Dutchman" all right. He had shaggy eyebrows, ash blond in color, long limbs with knobby joints, and hands the size of Rodin's "Thinker's." The soles of his boots, heel to heel and turned outward, would have served as airplane propellers. Flat on his back, his rugged blondness framed by the dark soft dirt, beneath the star-studded sky, enveloped in the blended odors of jasmine and manure, the furtive giant looked like an ogre out of Hans Christian Andersen.

It was then nearly nine o'clock. Finke found the mechanic, Enrico, alone in the garage. The Mexican had been expecting Finke, since Emile had told him Finke was coming. Mexicans in California stick together in a way that is not at all characteristic of Americans in foreign lands.

"I was hoping Señorita Noguera would be at home," Finke said.

"She hasn't been here since mid-afternoon, when she left for E.P.U. with Mr. Harmon," Enrico said. He was obviously a little anxious about the situation.

"I saw her test shown," Finke said. "She was great."

"If one has such a longing to act it's better to be good. But wasn't Mr. Harmon also present? He came back here just after six o'clock, in a rage, dressed for dinner and stormed away again, alone. He was in such a state that he scraped the front fender of his limousine when he drove out through the iron gate. He's usually a careful driver."

"He would be," said Finke.

"He and the *señorita* have had little tranquility since she let him know about her ambitions."

"To be an actress? Is that all?"

"No, Señor. There's also the Dutchman."

"What about the Dutchman?"

"From the first, Señor Van Vleeck has disapproved of the *señorita*. He's stubborn and speaks his mind. Before Señor Harmon and Señorita Noguera met, he found life with Mr. Harmon ideal—from his point of view. The Dutchman's not an ordinary gardener, Señor. He's a botanist. I've seen his picture and his name on articles in foreign magazines. With Mr. Harmon, he had a small steady income and a chance to carry on his work. . . . Señor Van Vleeck is most remarkable about growing things. I've never seen such plants, trees and flowers, not even in the royal park in Mexico City."

"Where did Harmon pick him up?"

"In Batavia, I've heard."

"Long ago?"

"Ten years or more," Enrico said. "Today Señorita Noguera refused to admit Van Vleeck in her house, and declared she would not marry Mr. Harmon as long as he was still in his employ."

"What brought that up?" asked Finke.

"The Dutchman reported to Mr. Harmon that Señorita Noguera had spent last night with Mr. Reynolds."

"Did she?"

Enrico shrugged. "A Mexican girl of her quality, Señor, once she has made a promise, keeps it to the letter."

"The *señorita* has been seeing Mr. Reynolds at the studio each day," Finke remarked.

Enrico shrugged again, in a slightly different way. Enrico's shrugs had been so eloquent and expressive that they had cost him the movie career he had craved when he first came to Hollywood. All the good directors struck out the accompanying lines as redundant whenever Enrico shrugged, so he never got a speaking part.

"You were on duty last night?" asked Finke.

This time Enrico nodded, and said, "Sí, Señor."

"Did you chance to be in the patio, between two o'clock and dawn?"

Enrico sighed. "I wanted to be frank with you, and gallant at the same time," he said, apologetically. "You evidently know that Señor Reynolds and my impulsive countrywoman were together. I would bet anything, nevertheless, that the señorita's behavior, if indiscreet, was not improper."

"Harmon found out about the moonlight rendezvous?" asked Finke.

"The Dutchman saw to that."

"Who else did he tell?"

"Most probably no one. He's a glum old fellow. Talks mostly to himself. The only time he notices the rest of us is when we take an interest in his plants."

"I heard him yell at old Latacassi this morning when she took an interest. She was only looking at the flowers."

"The Dutchman hates Latacassi. She's been hired by Señorita Noguera to do some of the work Van Vleeck used to do."

"Van Vleeck likes housework that much?"

"The *señorita* says he took every pretext to enter her house, unannounced, and that while she was away he read her mail and searched her belongings."

Finke was glad, indeed, that he had not volunteered any information to Harmon about that telephone call. Was it not possible that the threatening Voice had reference to the Dutchman, as being close to Harmon? If the Manellos were turning on the heat, and needed the Gardenia alive, they would not care a hang whether Van Vleek lived or died.

"I try to do my best for the guests here," Enrico said, sighing. "I should not be discussing their affairs even with you, Señor, if it were not for Emile. He assured me that your interests are sympathetic."

"They have to be. I'm a detective," said Finke.

"That would have been my third choice, for a calling," Enrico said wistfully. "First, the screen; second, to grow beautiful plants; and third to be a Latin Carlos Chan. Come to think of it, Señor, we have almost no detectives in Mexico. My countrymen are not afraid to die, but as a rule we do not like to have our faces pushed in and our heads broken, daily, to fight with our fists at close quarters, to shoot so accurately that later we may be sorry, to drink whiskey by the tumbler night and morning, and particularly we find it unpleasant to take ice-cold showers whenever there seems nothing else to do. Instead, we prefer to sleep in the sun."

"Your countrymen may have something there," Finke said, and bade Enrico good night.

Before leaving the Gardens, Finke had to take a look at the Dutchman, to be sure he was all right. He needed that Dutchman badly, for future reference. When he got as far as the bed of freshly turned loam, he saw it was not only empty, but that all traces of the one-sided struggle had been swept or raked smooth. Again he tiptoed across the redolent earth and tried to get a glimpse of the interior of the bungalow between slits of the Venetian blinds. So doing, he found himself looking into a pair of dark glowing eyes that were watching him from inside. They disappeared, and as their possessor made herself scarce in a jiffy, Finke recognized in the shadows the enticing shape of little Tani. He would have liked to talk with her, but at the same moment she left the window, he heard behind him footsteps on the gravel path and, forgetting the colony of moths, he ducked into a jasmine bush and stirred up quite a silent commotion. The night butterflies which had been feeding at their leisure fluttered this way and that, until the dust from their wings made Finke's throat itch. He restrained his cough, however, and the tall well-dressed young man in the dimness of the pathway did not notice the moths. Finke could not get a clear look at his face, which was obscured by the brim of the stylish felt hat. The toilet water the young man was wearing, however, was so strong that Finke smelled it over the fragrance of the jasmine that engulfed him.

Had not the tall young man, with broadly padded shoulders and slim waist, been so intent on something in the direction of the Dutchman's greenhouses and gardens, he might have spotted Finke. Instead he walked, erect but noiselessly, past the small grove of straight bamboo in flower, stalking more cautiously as he got nearer the beds where the pitcher plants were. When he got abreast of the clump of feathery East Indian cane, the young man concealed himself there, and Finke tailed him until he reached a point where he could see not only the furtive young man, but old Latacassi, kneeling silently in the same place she had squatted that morning when the Dutchman scared her off. The moonlight, by that time,

was almost strong enough to read by, and the old crone from
Borneo was admiring or examining, without once touching them,
the thimble-like flowers which seemed to be suspended from the
tips of leaves, and had lids that were open and caught faintly the
glimmer of the moonlight.

Some pollen drifting on the mild breeze must have tickled the
young man's throat, and he was less successful than Finke had been
a moment before in suppressing his desire to cough. He made a
scraping choking noise in his throat and almost before it had made
itself audible, the place where Latacassi had been was vacant and
she had vanished without trace.

After slight hesitation, the tall young man straightened his coat
lapels and squared his padded shoulders, as if he wished to attain a
more dignified position. He stepped from the shelter of the Indian
cane, went over to the same flower bed Latacassi had been studying, and, leaning forward without bending his knees, looked down
at the strange meat-eating plants in a critical, somewhat reverent
manner, as if they had been designed by someone who had asked
his judgment or opinion about them. Then the young man lifted
the screen that protected the flowers of a nearby bed from insects,
and gave them the once-over with the same supercilious air.

"A touch of swish," said Finke to himself, and he did not refer
to the plants.

Finally, the tall young man, whose face had all the time remained in shadow, strolled toward a back gate in the bottom of the
garden. He took a key that must have been hanging on a nail in the
wall nearby, unlocked the gate or door, and was about to leave without bothering to take the key from the look, or to relock the exit.

"Oh, I say," said a man who appeared, but not, it seemed by
appointment. The tall young man who fancied pitcher plants by
moonlight, and used toilet water stronger than wild jasmine in
June, waited for the other, and they went out one by one, leaving
the door slightly ajar.

"So what?" Finke asked himself. Again he felt the urge to find
Tani and, through her, if possible, to gain the good graces of old
Latacassi, as a source of inside information. He took the pathway

which led near the wall between the hotel lot and Concord Drive. If the management wanted to be as careless about the obscure back exit, for the convenience of murderers, as the front entrance and patio, Finke could only groan and bear it.

He was just about to tap on the door of the Gardenia's bungalow and whisper to Tani when he heard footsteps on the sidewalk beyond the wall. The two men, both tall and well dressed, and both wearing gray felt hats with turn-down brims, whom he had just seen go out the back way, were talking. One was saying to the other:

"Self-government may be all right as a sop to the natives, but how will it affect credit arrangements and trade? Will the poor fools give their stuff away, or . . ." The speaker, whichever he was, drifted into some language Finke did not know, and which surely was not European.

An answer began, from the other chap, in the same exotic but musical lingo and switched back to English again. "By the way. May I give you a lift, Tuan?"

"Tuan!" Then suddenly Finke's hair stood on end. He brought himself up short, his heart thumping hard, then skipping a few beats. He measured the distance to the top of the wall and strained to reach it by jumping. Try as he might, Finke could not quite make it.

He dashed for the back gate, shoved the door open and ran outside. Veering between inanimate objects that looked hazardous by moonlight on the vacant back lot, he got as far as Concord Drive. There he skidded to a stop, cursing under his breath. For he saw, in the dim haze beneath a street lamp, the tall, slender, well-dressed young man who had scared Latacassi away from the flower bed. That one stepped into the driver's seat of a car that looked like a Plymouth—a maroon Plymouth. Finke could not be absolutely sure of either the make or the color. It had been parked near the corner of Concord and Crescent. The guest rider, the man who had accepted "the lift" and who resembled at a distance the driver, in a superficial way, got in by the right-hand door, in front. The car started easily; there was little or no traffic to impede it. Without mishap, the maroon Plymouth sedan rolled out of sight in the direction of Sunset Boulevard.

Finke, on foot, had no chance to follow. But he had a clue, the first, and that is the one that starts cracking a case. He had heard, from outside the wall around the Omar Khayyam Gardens, while he was trapped inside, the Voice. He had an ear for voices, and did not think he was likely to be mistaken about that one, either then or any time. He had heard it once before, over the telephone, repeating monotonously:

> *"You're having an object lesson. What happens to someone close to you can happen to you. Think well about the matter. Don't be obstinate. What happens to someone close to you can happen to you."*

7
A Psychoanalyst's Fixation

WHEN FINKE PULLED UP and was about to dismiss his taxi in front of his office building, he noticed that an elegant black limousine was parked near the curb, and called the cabman back. The big car was empty, but a quick examination revealed that the front right fender was badly scraped and dented. That must be Harmon's car.

No other offices but Finke's showed a light in the windows of the Griffith Building. Ergo: Harmon, improbable and embarrassing as it seemed, must be up there, presumably with Kay. And there was more than an even chance that somehow, perhaps through the E.P.U. messenger and Pinky Johnstone, the oil man had been tipped off that Finke had accepted the telephone call for him, and had failed to disclose its text. And Finke had a strong feeling, also, that whatever the E.P.U. chief knew that was useful to the Manellos, and vice versa, was promptly exchanged.

Finke's office, he decided instantly, was no place for him just then. He directed the taxi driver to take him down Beverly Drive, so they dodged in and out of the late dinner and picture-show traffic, the tourists, competing taxis and the flashy cars of figures and figureheads of "the industry." The building in which Ruth maintained her office was dark, and none of the doormen of the Savoy, the Derby, Mike Romanoff's, Dave Chasen's or the Beverly Wilshire was sure whether or not he had seen Ruth or Shirley or Bob Reynolds that evening. Each time Finke leaned out of the taxi window to ask a question, he half expected to feel a heavy hand on his shoulder, and hear the harsh voice of some shamus, in uniform or out.

Finally, Finke had a hunch. Wherever Ruth was, she would not leave her mother without word too long, so he directed his driver, from memory, to the corner of Reeves and Charleville, where the Meskers lived. He asked the driver to circle around, and look for any signs that they were being followed, and then to wait for him halfway down the block.

"As you say, Mac," agreed the chauffeur. He was a veteran in Beverly Hills and assumed that nine-tenths of his passengers would be harmlessly nuts.

It was only when Finke saw the distressed solicitous expression on Mrs. Mesker's face as she opened the door in response to his buzz that he realized that his clothes were somewhat awry, his face was scratched and bruised, and one of his hands was still bloodstained from his tiff with the Dutchman. Enrico, of course, had been too polite and reserved, in his Mexican way, to indicate that he had noticed anything unusual in Finke's appearance. Murmuring sympathetically, Mrs. Mesker led Finke straight to the short stairway leading to the mezzanine floor on which were the bedrooms and the bathroom. In spite of his protestations that he was unhurt and that she was taking too much trouble for him, the silver-haired old lady washed and bandaged his hand, straightened his jacket and dabbed spots from his shirtfront.

"What a pity Ruth's not at home! That's how it goes. She's here too much, then she goes out and you come to call," said Mrs. Mesker. "I want you should sit down, and maybe she'll come back."

"Don't worry about Ruth," Finke said, assuming at once that Ruth's mother had no inkling of what was going on outside those cozy walls. The Meskers' taste in decorations inclined more toward Maxfield Parrish and Wallace Nutting.

"Could I get you some viskey, or Scarch?" Mrs. Mesker asked, hospitably.

"I dropped in, just on the chance that I might find a bite to eat. I've had no dinner yet," Finke said.

The old lady's face showed distress, then brightened. She took up the phone, dialed the Derby and ordered chicken sandwiches, with lettuce and tomatoes, potato salad, beer and Swiss cheese, sent "but quick." She pronounced the last two words "boot keveek," but Gregory of the Derby was multilingual and understood the meaning of almost any sounds.

"Ruth won't let me keep a thing in the 'hooze'," Mrs. Mesker complained. "She says food brings ants and roaches. The truth is, she knows I don't cook good enough. I never learned. When I came to this country at the age of thirteen (Mrs. Mesker spoke as if that were a week or two ago), I married right avay mine English teacher. Another Rooshian. So I never learned to speak the language, or keep hooze, or anything else, believe me."

"You wouldn't have any idea where Ruth might go looking for Miss Hall?" Finke asked. He was perfectly relaxed in the quiet apartment with the wonderful old lady who was so utterly unworldly and still so keenly alive.

"I'd hoped she was with you, like she said, to please me, when she phoned at dinner time," Mrs. Mesker said, smiling happily.

"We'll get together later," said Finke, and added: "I hope."

Mrs. Mesker looked at him, knowingly. "God forbid, Ruth's in trouble. No?" she asked, and laid one tiny hand lightly on Finke's unbruised one.

That caught Finke way off his base, and he forgot to slide. Mrs. Mesker went on, encouraged.

"My Ruth's what you call 'up against it' and calls on you for help. Yes?"

"Well, in a way," admitted Finke

To his further confusion, she clapped her hands with satisfaction. "I felt it," as she touched her heart, "in here."

"Understand. In a professional way," he stated, lamely.

"Personal. Professional. Confessional. Who cares? You'll be with her often, maybe every day?"

Finke loosened up, unable to hold out any longer.

"I've got to find her now. But keveek. See. Now you got me talking like you do."

"As long as she's with you, and you're with her, I'm not afraid," Ruth's mother said, serenely. She should have been an actress. Ouspenskaya could not have expressed herself more effectively.

"My life is Ruth, and she has so little of her own. It's better for something to happen, even something dangerous, if she doesn't personally get hurt, than to go on days or years, and nothing happening at all but work. The money comes in, goes out. I get older. She gets no younger. Mine husband was no English teacher, of which I am the proof after nearly fifty years together. At least, I was in love when I was young."

The door buzzer sounded. The order from the Derby was delivered. Mrs. Mesker, overjoyed to have something to do, laid out everything tastefully on a tray at Finke's elbow.

"Ruth won't let me have a dining room. Just a breakfast nookie. Again to save me work," Mrs. Mesker explained.

"You and I should go out together," Finke said, then dropped that line, the look of disappointment on her face was so touching.

"Young folks should be together, and old wimmen, alone," she said.

While he was eating hungrily, she talked.

"You're not an actor, God be praised. That I could see at once. Ven ve met at the Doiby, I couldn't figure you out, so I looked in the book for your name."

Finke sighed. "A private eye," he said, then, aware that his slang had gone over her head, added: "Detective."

The old lady looked at him calmly. "And, in this free country, where are detectives also is homicide. No?"

That floored Finke again. Before he could recover, she continued: "All right. You can't talk. Private poissonal business. So let me. Last night, late, comes to Ruth the actor (ektor) Bob Reynolds. They talk in whispers, down here."

"You overheard?" asked Finke, alarmed.

"Not the woids." Mrs. Mesker touched her forehead. "I put two and four together. Up here!"

"Bob Reynolds is a cloth-head. He should have met Ruth outside."

"Bob's been before in trouble, plenty times, but not so bad as this time, I think. It used to be wimmen. . . . Ruth is used to that. Last night was different."

"He's on the outs with Shirley," Finke began, but his heart was not in it. He could not deceive Mrs. Mesker, and wanted to less and less.

"Bob thinks Barney Rice was moidered. No?"

"I suppose so," conceded Finke.

"And was he?"

"I can't say for sure, one way or another."

"You'll find out," the old lady said, as confidently as if the case was already in the bag. "But that maybe isn't all, about Barney Rice, I mean. I've seen plenty films, and where there's one death at the start, later on comes more."

"No one wants to murder Ruth. I give you my word," Finke said. "And if someone did, I wouldn't let him."

The telephone rang and both of them reached for the instrument. Finke deferred to Mrs. Mesker and heard her say:

"*Da!* That's me . . . No. Vait a minute. It's my daughter you vant . . . *Niet*, Lieutenant. She's out. I don't know when she comes back . . . I couldn't tell you vair she is . . . Oiky Doke . . . And good luck, Lieutenant, in Korea or wherever they send you . . . Oh, excuse me. The police. Vell. Good luck, anyvay. I'll tell her, Lieutenant Mox Klop."

Finke reached for the phone, but Mrs. Mesker had hung up. She shrugged. "Some vun from the police, yet. My Ruth don't drive, I'm heppy to say, so it can't be a ticket."

"Mox Klop? That's the hell of a name for a loot," Finke said. He was disturbed, and no mistake. If the cops were after Ruth . . .

Mrs. Mesker broke into his train of thought. "Not Mox Klop. I told him I'd tell Ruth that Mox, that's his name, call up."

"Mox."

"You've seen Hippo and Gaucho Mox. Mox. Like the brothers Mox."

"You mean Marks?"

"That's right. Mox."

"Too good a name to waste on a cop, but, I suppose by any other name they'd smell the same. I'd better beat it, in case this Mox takes a notion to drop around here. And if you hear from Ruth, tell her to meet me later, at the Tropics, in the dimmest booth, and not to show up around here till further notice."

"The Topics. All right," agreed Mrs. Mesker, not at all panicky.

"Tropics. On Rodeo Drive."

The old lady shrugged. "Tropics, Topics, what does it matter? She understands almost everything I say, after thoity-one years. So. I've let it out. Her age. Believe me, Mr. Finke. No woman's a woman till she's thoity, at the very least. Take my vurd."

"One thing more," Finke admonished her. "If anybody you don't know calls and asks about Ruth or me, tell them we flew to San Francisco, on a military plane, to hear Chopin himself play his own funeral march."

"But Chopin's dead, in person," she objected.

"Sure. That makes it all the better."

She caught on, nodded and smiled.

Finke hustled out the front door, after kissing Ruth's mother on both cheeks. He spotted his taxi, and just as he climbed in and told his driver to take him back to the Griffith Building, and not to spare the horses, nearby a siren sounded on a police car that rounded the bend of Charleville and passed them.

"*Gesundheit!*" the driver said to Finke.

They got as far as Beverly Drive, headed east, when Finke banged on the window, opened the door before the driver could come to a halt, and motioned him to find a space and park. That was about as easy, on that street, as checking on the address of the Unknown Soldier. But the driver was game. Somehow he had decided that Finke was not daft, but merely wanted. For a fugitive from California justice, lots of good men will go out of their way to lend a hand.

What really had happened was that Finke, as they were riding along, had caught sight of Bob Reynolds. The taxi's spectacular stop on a dime had piled up traffic all the way back to the intersection. That was nothing strange to anyone familiar with the neighborhood. Reynolds was breezing along, looking purposeful, for him, with his head in the air. He prepared himself, sartorially, as if he were about to step into the glare of klieg lights on a set, hitching up his belt like a sailor going into a strange saloon. Then he barged resolutely into the foyer of a swanky but conservative-looking office building. It was only a matter of seconds before Finke entered in his aromatic wake, but Finke paused to glance at the plaque on which was lettered the directory of tenants. The edifice was called the Hippocrates Building. Most of the occupants seemed to be doctors, with a dentist or two and a few laboratories thrown in. By the time Finke looked toward the elevator, there was no sign of Bob. The indicator revealed that the cage was aloft, and as soon as it descended, Finke asked the elevator man if he had seen the actor, Bob Reynolds.

"Sorry, sir," the elevator man said. He had the grave manner of an undertaker's assistant, but there were signs galore that in former days he must have trod the boards.

Hearing a commotion in the corridor, Finke stepped quickly into the elevator with the former Thespian. The door was left open.

"Dear me," said the elevator man, clasping and unclasping his hands.

What Finke saw was Bob Reynolds, resisting and gesticulating, as he was propelled by a huge woman in white along the slick marble floor. Man and boy, all the way from South Boston to the Place de la République, Finke had seen men given what is known as the "bum's rush" but never more expertly than Bob was getting it. The white-uniformed Amazon had one firm hand on Reynolds' fashionable shirt collar, tightening it so that Bob was clutching and gasping for breath. The female bouncer's right hand was gripping the seat of Bob's pants and causing the maximum of discomfort on the beam end.

When they reached the swinging doors a few feet from the exit, the huge nurse gave Bob a brisk heave. He hit the doors with both hands upraised to protect his face that was insured by E.P.U. at a very high figure. Bob described a creditable parabola to the sidewalk, and the doors swung shut of their own accord.

The nurse, whom Finke now recognized as the out-size blonde he had seen at the Derby the night before, with the scarf woman and the tall young man who had given up his table to accommodate the

Manellos, said good evening to the elevator man as she went back along the corridor and into an office in the rear, at the right. She was not even breathing hard and there was an exalted gleam in her eye.

"Good evening, Miss Kahler," murmured Potts.

As soon as Potts seemed to be recovering from his mixed disapproval and awe, Finke said, "I like to see fine workmanship. Big Mary has style. A real technique."

"I assure you, sir. Such a thing does not happen here often. Our tenants and their patients are of the most respectable element. Naturally, sir, the patients suffering from mental or nervous derangements get overexcited, sometimes."

"You mean Bob Reynolds comes here to consult with some psychiatrist?" asked Finke, incredulously. Then he had a flash of comprehension and changed his approach. "Of course not. How stupid of me! He must come to ask about his fiancée, Miss Hall."

The elevator man was discretion personified. "You'll understand, sir, that I am not at liberty . . ."

"I know. You can't talk about the customers. I'll have a chat with Dr. Harms, myself. What did you say that nurse's name was?"

"Kahler. Lukie Kahler," the elevator man said, without cracking a smile.

"Well, thanks for everything," Finke said. He had inferred from Potts's unctuous tone that Shirley was a regular caller at the office of Dr. Hershel Harms, whom Bob had referred to that same morning as a bug doctor who, for a handsome fee and after protracted treatment, made pathologically jealous women "see sex and love in a rational way." Potts, the operator of the elevator dedicated to Hippocrates, had such personal dignity that Finke hesitated before slipping him a five-dollar tip. Luckily, the former actor's self-respect was equal to the occasion. He pocketed the bill, and bowed.

Again they were interrupted by an unexpected event which caused Potts more dismay than Bob Reynolds' violent expulsion. In came Bob again, through the same swinging doors, each arm in the grasp of a uniformed policeman. One of them seemed to know Potts.

"Did you just chuck this party out on his ear?" one of the cops asked Potts.

"Oh, no, sir. I'd be quite unequal to such discourtesy to an artist of Mr. Reynolds' achievements."

The cop turned back to Reynolds. "So you're the famous Bob Reynolds, trying to pass yourself off as Tim Omo."

Bob had spotted Finke, who was standing behind Potts in the elevator. Drunk as Bob was, he gave no sign of recognition, and for that Finke awarded him two gold stars on his report card.

"I insist on seeing my lawyer. Where's the phone?" demanded Bob.

"You can phone at headquarters. It just happens that the Captain called all cars and patrol boxes not too long ago, and mentioned your name," the cop said.

Finke had made a quick decision. If Bob was going to be hauled in, the more reason for Finke, himself, to be out. He must make his talk with Dr. Harms and Fräulein Kahler very snappy, and then *find Ruth.* Bob did not seem to be in such bad shape that he could not be left to his own devices in the Beverly Hills police headquarters until he could be sprung. The moment the two Beverly Hills cops, with Bob Reynolds between them, were out of sight, Finke made a gesture of farewell to the elevator man, and started down the corridor, toward the office of Dr. Hershel Harms. On the door of the suite was the legend "Enter Without Knocking."

The reception rooms were empty when Finke entered. There were really three rooms, so arranged with walls that were sliding panels that as many separate groups or individuals could be accommodated at the same time, without one interfering with the privacy of another. Each section was furnished in old-fashioned style, including everything from horsehair sofas to woven fabrics. No article was easily breakable, and the heavy picture frames had been screwed to the walls. The pictures were mostly of rural or pastoral scenes, with tame fowl or dumb animals. All windows were shaded discreetly, but always from the outside and the glass was unbreakable. The carpets corresponded with the wall paper and chairs. But in one of the rooms all the seats were covered with upholstery whose colors and design reminded him instantly of the batik scarf he had seen at the Derby, and in his dream. The pattern comprised pitcher plants, shrimps, playing cards and steamboats, the elements of which were rearranged according to the artist's fancy. The tints and hues ranged from that translucent yellow green to the brick red, tinged with wine and saffron, and suggested even to Finke, who knew less about art than he did about classical music, the Technicolor which had been applied to the sets of Jack Oehler's rewrite of *Tabu*.

Alone in that weird suite, wandering from room to room, his footsteps muffled by the thick carpets, an idea hit Finke between the eyes. Technicolor. That screen test, photographed on Monday, was shown Tuesday afternoon, that very day, in Technicolor. And Finke had read in the *Hollywood Reporter* he had used for camouflage at E.P.U. that major studios were kept waiting as long as six months for Technicolor, because of the post-war scarcity of materials needed for the next one. Somebody, in connection with the Gardenia's test, had pulled some powerful strings. That must have been Sitchev, who had made Ruth believe, before the test was shown, that "Miss Noguera" stank.

When the door opened from the doctor's inner office, and Lukie Kahler stepped out, in a professional, almost military manner, Finke was standing near her desk and the filing cabinets, whose corners had been inconspicuously padded. "Also!" she said, fixing Finke with a pale blue eye as cold and almost as large and round as that of a porpoise.

"*Gesundheit!*" said Finke.

"You have an appointment?" she gave a quick glance to her desk calendar pad. "No!"

"With Mr. Reynolds. You know. Bob Reynolds, the actor."

"Impossible." She thumbed through a sheaf of cards as if they showed the action of some famous prize fight. "No Mr. Reynolds is a patient here."

"I'm glad to hear it," Finke said. "It's Mr. Reynolds' fiancée, Miss Shirley Hall, who's Dr. Harms's patient. Mr. Reynolds and I were to meet her here and take her to dinner. If you don't mind, I'll wait."

He plunked himself down into a horsehair armchair. "Impossible," Nurse Kahler insisted.

"What's impossible? You have three waiting rooms. I've plenty of time." It cost Finke somewhat of an effort to make that last remark.

"Patients here are never permitted to make rendezvous after consultations," the huge nurse said, sternly, as if she were reciting to a backward recruit the Articles of War.

Finke rose and smiled in his most charming manner.

"All right, baby! I'd like to see the doctor. He's a wow at curing jealousy, I'm told. I've got a complex. See?"

"Dr. Harms sees patients only by appointment," said the Teutonic Woman-Mountain Dean. "I must ask you to go."

"I'm staying till I see the doctor," Finke said.

Lukie Kahler moved fast, but Finke was ready. He had foreseen that she would try for a grip to give him the bum's rush, and that with one hand up and the other down, she would leave herself wide open. So he stepped in close, caught the hand that was reaching for his collar, spun her around and pressed her arm tightly over her shoulder. With the leverage he could exert, from behind, she was unable, as strong as she was, to free herself without dislocating her shoulder. She tried to kick his shins and he bore down enough to stop her, but in so doing, somehow the nearest filing cabinet tipped over. Finke could not hear much of any noise, but the door opened from the inner office and Dr. Harms stood in the doorway.

"Is something wrong?" he asked, softly, as self-possessed as if Lukie and Finke were sipping tea. Finke grinned. The psychiatrist was not over five feet three, and of such slight stature that, compared with Fräulein Kahler, he looked like a civilized pigmy. His brown hair was wavy and cut long, like that of a trombone player; he had heavy eyebrows, a high domelike forehead and delicate hands.

"What made you think something was wrong, Doc?" Finke asked, still holding the statuesque nurse from behind her. "Miss Kahler and I were practicing *jiujitsu*. She's pretty good, but needs more practice."

"*Schweinhund!*" exclaimed Miss Kahler, gutturally, and struggled ineffectually. Finke, watching the doctor closely, was astonished to see that the spectacle somehow thrilled and excited him, almost to the point of fascination.

"Most unusual," he whispered. "In years of practice . . ."

"You need more practice, too. That's what I came for. To have a talk with you. Miss Kahler was opposed to that, at first, but now she's agreeable."

The doctor smiled quite meekly, or so it seemed, as he bowed, clicked his small heels together, and said, "Sir. Come in."

Finke followed him into the office, closed the door behind him, tried it and found it had locked itself securely. The doctor shrugged, went to the door, opened it an inch or two, and pressed the release button so that when he reclosed it, the door could be reopened at will.

"You do not like locks and bars," the doctor remarked. "Many of your countrymen, I find, have that phobia to a high degree."

"I'm looking for Shirley Hall. It's important," Finke said.

The little doctor smiled again, in a deprecatory way. "You understand, of course, that I'm not at liberty . . ."

"I know. You can't discuss your patients."

"I haven't said that Miss Hall is a patient," the doctor said, reproachfully.

"Big Lukie said so."

The doctor's face showed pained astonishment. "Impossible," he said.

"In effect," corrected Finke. "When I asked her if Bob Reynolds was a patient, she said 'No,' and when I asked her about Shirley Hall she gave me the line about not discussing your patients. The inference is plain, *nicht wahr?*"

The doctor was disconcerted, and while he was trying to decide how to proceed, Finke took from his pocket his detective license, stamped and signed by the Los Angeles County Sheriff, and countersigned by the State Attorney General in Sacramento. Seeing that, like all Germans, Dr. Harms was impressed with papers, seals and signatures, Finke took out, as a topper, his E.P.U.

pass granted by Pinky Johnstone and identifying him as Bob Reynolds' stand-in.

"I came here to warn you, Doctor. You are on a hot spot," Finke said.

With a face as straight as a die, Dr. Harms said, plaintively, "But, Tuan . . . Excuse me, Herr Maguire! I'm not a patron of any night club. I flatter myself on my command of colloquial English. By hot spot, is that not what you mean?"

"You're in trouble," Finke said. He had not missed the "Tuan Maguire" but thought it better to let it pass till later.

"Impossible," murmured the little doctor.

"I want to help you," Finke repeated. "My interest is in Bob Reynolds. Bob came here this evening, to see Shirley or discuss the case with you. Your husky Fräulein Kahler threw him out on his ear. The cops were passing by, assumed because Bob had had a drink or two he was creating a disturbance, to the detriment of public tranquility, and took him to the hoosegow. He is at present being questioned, and unavoidably will have to mention what happened to him here."

Finke's speech was so long that the doctor had time to get back his equanimity before he had to reply. He glanced at the unlocked door, flipped off the listening and speaking device on his desk so Nurse Kahler could not hear, seemed to relax, sighed patiently, and said, "From the nature of my specialty, it follows that my patients occasionally lose control and get violent, when the moon is high, toward the first of each month when bills come in, or when domestic conditions are trying. As you see" (the doctor made an eloquent gesture, brushing with his lily-white hands his coat lapels and downward to the seams of his neatly pressed trousers) "I am reasonably fit, as you Americans say, and able-bodied, but not phenomenally strong."

"So the *Fräulein* takes care of the rough stuff? Is that what you're driving at? . . . I can see that she could. But why give Bob Reynolds the works? And especially, if Bob's not a patient. And if Bob is not a patient, and you cannot admit that Shirley Hall is under treatment here, why should Bob crash this office, and tangle with your lady bouncer?"

The doctor sighed. "Mr. Reynolds had been drinking."

"Not much. He'd only got started," Finke said.

"I'm not criticizing him for that," said Dr. Harms. "I envy him. How often I wish fervently that I, too, could cut loose and enjoy a real—how do you express it?—'bender'. And, naturally, most of my best patients are alcoholics."

"You've never treated Bob for the jim-jams?"

"I'll be candid. My acquaintance with Mr. Reynolds is slight. Some time ago he brought me, because someone he knew had recommended me highly, a young man in his employ. His stand-in, to be exact. The case, I found after the briefest questioning and a cursory examination, was not in my line. So I sent the young man— I don't even remember his name but Miss Kahler, no doubt, has a record—to the Balm of Gilead Hospital. That's all there is to it."

"Except that the young man died," Finke said.

The doctor shrugged. "I'm sincerely sorry," he said.

"But," Finke continued as if Dr. Harms had not interrupted, "that doesn't explain why Bob was manhandled by your seven-foot nurse . . ."

"Fräulein Kahler is only six feet, three," corrected the doctor, as meticulous as ever, even in his protestations of innocence.

Dr. Harms paused, as if searching for the exact words, and continued, "Miss Kahler, because of her stature—how can I explain? exerts a peculiar fascination over certain types of men. Especially those who are noticeably small, and who have been embarrassed all through life with such cruel nicknames as 'Peewee', 'Shorty' or 'Runt."

The doctor's expression grew quite rapt and intense.

"When Lukie was in training, at the Eitel Friedrich hospital in Berlin—she was only eighteen then but had attained her full height and breadth—a distinguished sculptor who was no taller than I am, and if anything, more slight, became desperately infatuated with her. He followed her, in secret, for weeks without declaring himself. Then, one day, he accosted her passionately, with such earnestness that . . ."

The doctor shrugged and sighed.

"She fell but wasn't pushed," suggested Finke.

Whether he realized it or not, the doctor was betraying almost infinite sadness that took possession of him then, as it must have years before, in Berlin. Finke, as sensitive as any doctor could be, respected the little man's feelings, and understood. Psychiatrists choose that specialty because they know what mental and nervous suffering means, and many of them land in the same institutions to which they have sent their patients. Psychiatrists who specialize in treating cases of pathological jealousy must have had long and devastating experience with the green-eyed monster, to the point where they cannot do otherwise than sublimate their thwarted desire by immersing themselves in the similar afflictions of others. Finke did not think in terms of five-syllable words, but he grasped also that the tendency toward self-torture would impel such a victim of unrequited love to keep its object near him ten years, twenty years, a lifetime, if he could.

In short, Finke had to put aside his impulse to commiserate with the little bug doctor and get back to brass tacks.

"I still don't see," Finke said, in his gentlest tone, "how Bob Reynolds fits in. Bob is six feet one, if he's an inch."

The doctor sighed again, if anything, more disconsolately than before. "Again I must explain. For other reasons, quite as logical, tall men are seized with strong urges to—possess Fräulein Kahler, the more irresistibly when intoxicated. And most male screen stars are tall, and all of them drink heavily, excepting possibly Lew Ayres. An actor like Mr. Reynolds, for instance, has to play in his stocking feet most of the time, because his opposite is the slender dainty type the public likes best among women. Such a man as a boy has always had to take the back seats in school. Always, when he has tried to dance, he has had to lean over. To clasp a girl in his arms he has been obliged also to lift her. He develops, subconsciously, a longing for statuesque women, whom he can reach without bending his knees, and look fondly in the eye while standing. It is, perhaps, a refinement of the mother fixation."

"You mean that Bob Reynolds has a yen for Big Lukie?" Finke demanded, incredulously.

The doctor shrugged again.

"Well, anyway, Doc, Bob's longing for the *Fräulein* didn't get him anything tonight but the old heave-ho. I witnessed it myself. And I saw the cops take him away. Maybe, if he's got the Galahad complex, along with the rest, he won't speak her name. But that won't let you out. The police, dumb as they are, can find out he was in your office. The press may get wind of it."

"*Barmherziger Gott!*" exclaimed the doctor. "If Miss Hall reads that Mr. Reynolds and Miss Kahler have any kind of relationship whatever, I would not answer for the consequences. She well might attempt to blow up this building or burn it down."

"Miss Hall is your patient, then?" said Finke. "Where is she?"

"She left here just before you came in," the doctor said.

"Have you suggested to her, in the course of your treatment, that it might help her to see her love life in better perspective if she should take a nice long rest?" Finke asked sharply.

His tone and the text of the question made Dr. Harms wince. The little psychiatrist looked appealingly at Finke.

"One has to try everything," he said. "If only to gain time."

Finke thanked him, and left him, if not in peace, in company with the Amazon he had loved and lost and nevertheless retained. Dr. Harms, Finke thought, had been telling the truth when he said that Shirley had just left the premises, but since he had been in a position to know for certain that she had not used the corridor and the front door on Beverly Drive, there must be some other way. Furthermore, if Shirley had been in the doctor's suite of offices while Bob had called and riled Lukie Kahler the rooms must be well sound-proofed as well as equipped with dictographs and inter-communicating devices, and at least one secret exit.

"I thought all that stuff went out with Dr. Fu Manchu," Finke said to himself. He took a chance on leaving by the front door, found his taxi waiting and stopped at the next drug store to tele-phone Kay.

His office did not answer.

He tried Kay's apartment, and got no answer there. He called Mrs. Mesker. She had not heard from Ruth. Lieutenant Mox had called, in person, and Mrs. Mesker had given him the message. He had been sore, but had written it in his notebook—that Ruth had flown to San Francisco to hear the funeral march. And he had said that that was the second time he had heard that baloney tonight.

"Thanks, Mrs. Mesker. Don't worry. And don't tell anybody a thing."

As he hung up, he deduced that the police, one kind or another, had caught up with Kay before she had left the office, and she also had given them the San Francisco story.

So he started for the Forty-Niners Towers, on the strip about a mile from his office, to find Shirley Hall. She lived there, and, if the doctor had not given him a bum steer, he might catch up with her and, possibly, Ruth. On the way, since he had to pass so close to the Derby, he thought he'd take a chance to snatch a quick one and find out what he could from Emile. In fact, he could send in his taxi man to ask Emile, on the Q.T., if the coast was clear.

The taxi man, by now, had decided that his client must be either J. Edgar Hoover or John D. Rockefeller, 2nd. No one else would be likely to have a cab wait on Beverly Drive, where cruising taxis were passing in either direction continuously, day and night. He got the O.K. from Emile, conveyed it to Finke, and while the latter was entering the Derby, the cab driver took a few minutes off, to get a bite in a relatively inexpensive lunchroom (where the food was as good or better) and a couple of snorts of gin. Ordinarily the chauffeur did not drink while on duty, but tonight seemed to be an exception. He was doing so well for himself.

A plainclothes officer, who was in the vicinity, happened to stroll past the cab. One or two minor details about it seemed to set it apart from ordinary public conveyances, so the dick glanced inside. Firstly, it was parked outside the Derby, not twenty yards from a cab stand at which cabs were waiting, and almost always available. Secondly, there was no driver. Thirdly the meter read $23.80. As the officer stared at it, the meter clicked merrily to $23.90.

The dick walked over casually to the lunchroom and peered in the window. A cab driver was holding up his glass for a second slug of gin. That was contrary to regulations. The officer waited for the driver to emerge, then braced him and asked him where his passenger, who had ridden nearly twenty-four dollars' worth, was keeping himself, and who he was.

"Some rich palooka. He's in the Derby. So what?"

"So you're drinking on duty," the dick said, but he shrugged as if to say, to hell with that. He went into the Derby by the bar entrance, and took his place beside Finke. Emile smiled his usual genial smile of recognition.

"Any screwball in here, with a cab outside that's waiting?"

"Not that I know of," Emile said.

The officer was not much interested. But he took from his pocket a small notebook and consulted a list of names, moving his lips as he read.

"What brings you here, at this time of night?" Emile asked, to be sociable. Detectives from the L.A. force usually dropped in either earlier or later. They had no authority, technically, in Beverly Hills, but that did not mean that they did not pick up plenty of information there.

"Know a dame named Mesker? Ruth Mesker?" the officer asked. Finke kept as still as he could, without attracting attention.

"Miss Mesker hasn't been in tonight," Emile said.

"And what about a fink named Maguire?"

Emile shook his head.

"You know him?"

"He's been here once or twice," Emile said.

"No idea where he might be now? The orders are to pick him up."

"He might be in San Francisco," said Emile.

The plainclothes man checked him with a sarcastic grimace. "Don't tell me he's listening to some funeral march."

"He might be," Emile said, brightening. "He and a friend were discussing the other day the Monteux performance of the Berlioz Requiem Mass. It's a big event in the musical world."

"It must be," the plainclothes man snorted, disgustedly. "Half L.A. seems to have gone up there . . . and all on military planes."

The officer sauntered out, without paying for his drink.

"Mind telling me who that bird was?" asked Finke, getting ready to take his own departure.

"Lieutenant Marcus . . ."

"Mox, for short . . ."

"Of the L.A. Homicide Squad."

"Did you say homicide?"

Emile nodded, unhappily, and Finke's frown deepened.

"Weren't you taking quite a chance?" Finke asked.

"He has no real authority here . . . in Beverly Hills. The L.A. boundary's two blocks over this way" (Emile thumbed to his right) "on Olympic Boulevard."

Finke took three ten-dollar bills from his pocket, and handed them over the bar. "A few minutes after I'm gone," he said, "would you mind having Diana pay off my taxi man?"

Up went Emile's arched eyebrows. "Shall he keep the change?"

"Why, yes. Let him keep it," Finke said.

8

The Massive Requiem

THE CATHEDRAL IN SAN FRANCISCO was filled to capacity for the first performance in America of the Berlioz Requiem Mass, with Pierre Monteux conducting and the Very Reverend John J. Mahoney, S.J., D.D., L.L.D., officiating. Twelve rows from the front, on the aisle just left of center, sat Homer Evans, engulfed in the magnificence of sound and symbolism.

Bach had set the Last Judgment to music profoundly. Verdi presented it histrionically, as a kind of glorified *Traviata*. Berlioz, whose Mass music has been the most neglected, dramatized the event to end all events on a scale commensurate with the occasion. The score calls for a full orchestra, a band with extra brass for Gabriel's horn blast, a large mixed chorus and a number of inspired soloists. The tremendous concord of sound to which earth, heaven and hell each contribute is made colorful to the eye by the scarlet and gold trappings of prelates and priests, the pipes of the great organ, the altar and the twisted smoke of incense, rising from the nave and transept to the arched roof and the dome.

Homer did not concentrate as he listened to music. He tried to reverse that process, and clear all extraneous thoughts from his mind. When attending ordinary concerts, he had made it a practice to buy two seats, side by side, and sit in the one on the aisle, so that he would be sure not to have anyone too near him to cause him distraction. In the case of the Berlioz Mass, he could not bring himself to deprive one human being of the privilege of hearing it and missing the musical experience of a lifetime.

The Mass had progressed through the Requiem, the Kyrie, the Dies Irae, Tuba Mirum, to the almost unbearable pathos of the Lacrimosa and the serenity of the Sanctus. The Sanctus, in the Berlioz conception, is a tenor solo. For this Monteux had selected an Irish singer whose voice and temperament were suited to the melody, but just as the climax was approaching, Homer was astonished and outraged to see one of the ushers escorting down the aisle a heavy-footed square-shouldered type who, the world over, in church or out, could only be a plainclothes man. At each row of seats, the officer paused to look over the members of the audience, and once or twice he even had the audacity to flicker the beam of his flashlight across some man's or woman's face. This happened to women who were neither very young nor very old, and men in their thirties, of the active type who looked fit and were clean shaven. That simplified the plainclothes man's preposterously difficult assignment, in a way, because of the two hundred and fifty male performers, and two thousand males in the audience, nearly two-thirds had lilacs, fringes, sideburns, goatees, Van Dykes, Prince Alberts, full whiskers or other face decorations. Homer, who wore a neatly trimmed Van Dyke, was passed up after a hasty glance, but he noticed that the shamus seemed fascinated with the young Irish soloist, not because of his rare voice and musicianship, or the sublimity of the Berlioz Sanctus, but on account of the tenor's husky and capable shoulders, his solid build, and almost aggressive stance which the conventional black of his attire did not counteract. Homer, for whom the spell of the music had been broken momentarily, gave the soloist the once-over, himself, and concluded that, before his voice had been discovered, he must have been a baseball player—one who had to keep in training and whose work did not damage his face.

After the Sanctus was concluded, Homer's mind got farther astray from the music, in preparation for the overwhelming finale, and he could not shake from his thoughts the fleeting similarity to Finke Maguire he had seen, or thought he had noticed, while the San Francisco plainclothes sergeant, who clomped in where angels fear to tread, had been glaring at the young Irishman. Homer wondered how Finke was getting along, and whether the routine under which he had chafed in filmland still obtained.

When the Mass was over, and the dazed audience streamed out of the cathedral, Homer noticed that the plainclothes man and his usher were stationed near the holy water font and were still looking for a man and/or a woman. His curiosity was stirred. He had several hours to pass before plane time to New York, so he sought out the sacristan, feigned indignation and complained that his enjoyment of the sacred music had been shattered by the vulgar intrusion of cops into the cathedral. The sacristan, who had been forced to grant permission to the plainclothes officer to perform his duty, Mass or none, apologized. He not only shared Homer's displeasure, but his wrath exceeded it.

"Those notorious criminals and reprobates from Southern California hold nothing sacred," the sacristan said. "And our police have to kowtow to them. Whoever has to escape from Los Angeles and can't speak enough Spanish to cross the Mexican border passes through our fair city, on the way back east or to Canada."

"Who is it Los Angeles is looking for, at a solemn Requiem Mass?"

The sacristan consulted a scribbled memorandum he took from a pocket of his elaborate dress uniform, and in so doing lost hold of his mace, which Homer courteously recovered and handed back to him.

"Some fugitives mixed up in a murder investigation. One is a private detective. They're all as crooked as a dog's hind leg. The other is an agent, some woman who's supposed to be a material witness. Material strumpet, more likely, who hasn't been inside a church in years, and thinks that's the last place anyone would look for her," the sacristan said.

"But," Homer objected, in a tactful manner, "the seats for this performance, and even standing room, have been sold out at least sixty days. If any man or woman involved in a capital crime were hiding here, the getaway must have been planned at least two months ago. To whom were the applications for tickets addressed?"

The sacristan's face became so woeful and horrified that Evans was moved. "To me, sir. To me! And I was supposed to keep them all, in case of complaints. Please, I beg of you, do not put any ideas in the ears of the police. I shall have to confess that I detest music, especially church music which I have to hear almost constantly. So, during the Mass, when I could sit quietly in my quarters, I tore up those letters, all of which I'd had to answer in longhand, one by one, and flushed them. . . . Our cathedral is modernized, sir, to an extent."

"I'll make a deal with you," said Evans. "Answer just one question, and I'll hold my peace about those applications. Is, or is not, the private detective from Los Angeles, and sought by the police, named Finke Maguire?"

The sacristan's eyes widened and he looked really scared. "Why, yes. That's his name."

"Thank you," said Evans.

The sacristan was by no means reassured. "You! You, sir! Are you a detective, yourself?"

Evans smiled, and set the man at ease with a gesture.

"An amateur, only. You need have no fear of being molested by me. If there is honor among thieves, there is at least as much among catchpoles. Good night."

From his suite in the Mark Hopkins Hotel, Homer phoned Finke's office in Los Angeles. He was informed that all Mr. Maguire's calls were being handled by the special service and would be relayed to the number which Mr. Maguire's secretary had designated.

It did not take Homer three seconds, once he was connected with the Tropics, to recognize the sound of the gamelan and the words of an old Javanese song which warned one and all not to tie a pony to a young mulberry tree. He was informed by a voice he remembered as that of Bob Kertojoyo, assistant maître d'hôtel, that Mr. Maguire was not on the premises. Homer told Bob who he was, and learned that Finke had been there earlier in the evening, that he had been joined by a lady with arms and legs as long and angular as those of a Javanese shadow puppet, that Finke and the young lady had consumed a full bottle of Cuban Bacardi while engaged in earnest conversation, and that Finke had departed in a taxi a few minutes before the angular young woman got her little Austin from the Tropics parking lot and drove into the night, practically at the pavement level.

"Is that all?" Homer inquired, quite sure that Bob was withholding something

"Did you expect more, Mr. Evans?" Kertojoyo asked. Homer, during the war, had been very helpful to many of Kertojoyo's displaced compatriots, but, even to Homer, the Javanese disliked to talk about police. He still retained an ancient native superstition that to mention an evil helped perpetuate it.

"Any calls from the police?"

"Three on the telephone, and one in person. In fact, Mr. Evans, it is possible . . ."

"I know. They may have tapped the wire. Who was the officer who came to call, in person, as you say?"

"He made me promise not to tell."

"Naturally, Bob. But who was it?"

"Lieutenant Marcus."

Homer whistled softly. "Of the L.A. Homicide Squad?"

"Yes, Mr. Evans."

"Thanks. Good night."

Homer hung up, and called Finke's hotel. No trace of him there. He did, however, get the party he wanted at the Western Air Lines, cancel his reservation to New York that night, and in a certain military headquarters arrange with the pilot who had flown him from L.A. to San Francisco to take him back again. It required ten minutes for Homer to pack, five minutes to taxi to the military field, and an hour later, just before midnight, which in Hollywood is the beginning of the evening, he stepped off the B-69. On the stroke of midnight, he entered the Beverly Hills Brown Derby and walked leisurely to Emile's bar. While Homer refreshed himself with Calvados from Normandy, Emile, immeasurably relieved in behalf of his friends who were in difficulties, told Evans, briefly and succinctly, of the high spots of the situation in which Finke was involved: The haphazard meeting with the Meskers, mother and daughter; the dinner party at which the three Manellos and the lovely Mexican, Eulalia Noguera, who wished to be a screen star, had so little success in winning over the wealthy Mills Harmon, her fiancé, to the idea; Finke's being retained, and induced to pose as Reynolds' stand-in, to get the run of the E.P.U. lot; the unusual impact of the *señorita's* screen test, which Laslo Sitchev and the Manellos pretended, in advance of the showing, was a flop; Shirley Hall's frantic outburst of jealousy; Harmon's ultimatum which the Gardenia threw back in his face; the feud between the *señorita* and Harmon's valet, the Dutchman, and the latter's unsuccessful attempts to contact Finke; and the dragnet set for Finke and Ruth Mesker by Lieutenant Marcus, of the L.A. police.

"Kay has made herself scarce, for obvious reasons," said Evans. "Bob Reynolds is the one I should approach, since Finke cannot do so without walking into a trap."

"Reynolds," Emile explained, "had some misunderstanding with a nurse, who works for Dr. Hershel Harms in the Hippocrates Building. Unfortunately he was taken to the Beverly Hills police headquarters where he promptly fell asleep."

"Before they started questioning him?"

"So I've heard," said Emile. "I'm sorry my information is so sketchy. I hear all kinds of rumors and gossip, mostly misleading. But there is soundness in your American proverb that: 'Where there's smoke there's fire'. The difficulty is that the fire may be tended by wild Indians, scouting on the war path, or like Shakespeare's little candle, it may cast its beams 'like a good deed in a naughty world'."

Evans smiled, unworriedly. "Some of my best friends are Indians. And my ancestors not only dipped their own candles, but made bullets by dropping molten lead into the family rainbarrel."

Emile sighed. "Ah, climates! Your New England is the cradle of revolution because rains lend themselves to the household manufacture of bullets at a nominal cost. California is a land of conquests which have to be financed from outside, since the sky is always clear."

It was a matter of a few minutes for Evans' taxi to weave its way through the capricious traffic of Beverly Drive, which got whackier as the evening wore on. As becomes the richest little city (per capita) in the known Western world, the city hall of Beverly Hills is a rather beautiful building of yellow brick trimmed with granite, imposing in height, yet moderate, its masses well distributed. One wing is devoted to the police headquarters, the municipal court and the jail, from the barred windows of which the occupants may see a rather luxurious vista, indicative of affluence and the advantages of private enterprise. On that June night, the mocking birds were singing with abandon in the surrounding trees, drunk with the scent of jacaranda, the faint purple blossoms of which decked all the branches and carpeted the pavement below. Not in Tyre or Sidon, Ur or Nineveh, or in any of the Cities of the Plain, could nature have incited men to wilder or more pleasurable extravagances.

The thoughts of Homer Evans strayed along such lines as he entered the office where a police sergeant ordinarily was left to carry on through the night while his superiors cavorted or slept. Instead, behind the desk was a very disgusted captain.

"Why, Captain Strongfort. I'm glad—and astonished—to see you. What brings you here on such a night? Can something unusual be afoot?"

The Captain eyed Homer, not with hostility as much as caution. He had had experience before with that "bird from G-6, with the spinach."

"What is it, this time?" the Captain asked.

"I've come to save you from yourself," Homer said. "In short, I want Bob Reynolds released without delay."

As he voiced that request, he fingered idly the leaves of the record book that was spread on the desk.

"No soap," replied the Captain, tersely. "Any further questions?"

"This isn't exactly a request," Homer said, without losing an iota of his equanimity. "And, as I've already observed, it's as much, or more, in your interest than mine."

"I'm the best judge of that," the Captain said.

"You haven't thought it through," suggested Evans. "You are informed by Lieutenant Marcus, of the L.A. Homicide Squad, that he wants you to find and hold a reputable agent, Miss Ruth Mesker; a licensed private detective, Mr. Finke Maguire; and the singing actor, Robert Reynolds, who has, behind him, aside from inalienable rights guaranteed by our Constitution and all that sort of thing, the backing of E.P.U., Inc.; the Motion Picture Association headed by Eric Johnston, custodian in chief of public morals; the chain of banks which dispenses credit all the way from Rome to Shanghai, California, and doubtless, Timbuctoo; not to mention a film audience of 150,000,000 souls, 100,000,000 of whom are relatively free Americans."

"If I had your line, and a hundred million cases of snake oil, I'd be in big business. Why don't you get wise to yourself and put those famous brains of yours to some practical use?" said Captain Strongfort. Nevertheless, he looked slightly uncomfortable. He had had Bob Reynolds in for drunken and disorderly conduct—although it had been much more drunken than disorderly—once or twice before, but Reynolds, off screen, a man of few words, had been content to thank the officers for a good night's rest, and let it go at that. Now here was Homer Evans, criminologist and wartime G-man, who was the champion of all who had the gift of gab.

"Has Lieutenant Marcus stuck his neck out? No," Evans said. "Has he apprehended Miss Mesker, Mr. Maguire, or anyone else involved in this case, which may be murder or leapfrog, for all you know, or he, either, for that matter? Again, no! What is the charge against Mr. Reynolds?"

Homer reversed and extended the large flat book, wide open.

"How can you charge a guy who goes to sleep with his elbows propped on your desk?"

"You have something there. Let's wake him up. In that event, what is your charge?"

"He made such a disturbance down at the doctors' building, and was in such condition, that a nurse—a lady nurse, mind you—bounced him out. He fell flat on his face on the sidewalk. Is that a wholesome example for a public idol to set 100,000,000 dopes?"

"Mr. Reynolds wouldn't strike a lady, or even a woman," Homer said. "The fact remains, Lieutenant Marcus hasn't the proper grounds to take action himself, so he leaves you holding the bag. Now I can call Dr. Hershel Harms, who is a qualified expert, you'll admit, on all kinds of alcoholism and artistic temperament. I can wake up Attorney Sol Flato to raise bail, up to any amount you could name. I can wake Judge Weiner from his couch of ease and get him to sign a writ of *habeas corpus*. If I were pressed far enough, I could attach your home, automobile and personal property, in a suit of false arrest. That would be boorish and unfriendly. Let me make this suggestion. Lieutenant Marcus is ambitious. He has little regard for the Beverly Hills police, the County officials, the State police, or the district attorney's office. Supposing I promise that if there is a murder case in which either Miss Mesker, Mr. Maguire or Mr. Reynolds is implicated or can furnish clues to the solution, you, Captain, and not the L.A. Homicide boys, will get the tip-off, and receive the credit."

"Blackmail," grunted the Captain.

"But, as it should be, without witnesses," Evans said, with a comradely glance at the two cops, who pretended not to notice. He held out his hand. "You have my word, Captain Strongfort," he said.

The Captain, irresolute for a split second, climbed down. As he groped for words, Evans smiled and said, "Your line, Captain, in case it has slipped your mind is 'Some day you'll stub your toe.' And no doubt I shall. Caesar had his Brutus. Sherlock his Moriarty. But my Nemesis shall not be Lieutenant Marcus."

"It's your lower jaw that moves," the Captain said, disgustedly, as he signaled to an officer to take Homer to the cell in which Reynolds was blissfully sleeping. The other cop, at Homer's request, started in a police car for Dave Chasen's to get for Homer a bottle of Calvados, aged in the wood.

"Ask the barkeeper to uncork it, please," was Homer's admonition as he started down the corridor to the section that served as a detention house.

If the richest little city (per capita) can boast of mocking birds by night and warblers by day, the purple mist of jacaranda in season and at least four drinking emporiums where Calvados aged more than twenty years in the wood is available, it cannot be said that the Beverly Hills jail falls below standard. The cop, on whom Homer had two strikes plus for the way he had got around Captain Strongfort, without attempted bribery, bluster or nocturnal writs of replevin, simply opened the door and returned to the wardroom.

"Not bad. Not bad at all," Evans murmured as he looked around. First he ascertained that Reynolds, whom he had never met, had received no bodily injury beyond a few bumps and bruises. That, spiritually, Bob was unsullied, was made plain by the smile that hovered on his lips, indicative of pleasant dreams. Homer felt a glow of satisfaction. The singing actor, who perforce he would see a lot of while the case was in progress, seemed to throw off the effects of alcohol as artistically as he sang South Sea ballads or caused women's hearts to flutter. The "cell," if that is not too harsh a word for the sleeping quarters Beverly Hills provides its wealthy well-known drinkers and philanderers, had an alcove with a por- celain wash bowl, mirror, soap of a quality that would not injure the skins so many loved to see, if not to touch, fresh brush and comb, tooth brush and powder, and toilet water that Evans found, on examination, was genuine prewar Kölnwasser. The "cot" was a fine three-quarter bed with sound springs and a mattress soft on one side and hard on the other, to suit individual preferences. The walls were papered with a soothing pattern. The floor was of rub- ber tile, not dingy black but Madras brown.

Homer was about to speak, and touch Reynolds lightly on the shoulder, when he was deterred for a moment by the reluctance he had felt from his earliest years when obliged to wake anyone, favored or unlucky, from the refuge of sleep. As Emile had said, the appearance of smoke was a warning of fire. And when the lieu- tenant in virtual command of a homicide squad, in the third most populous city of the great U.S.A., set a dragnet, it was not for minnows which might contribute to the enjoyment of an afternoon hour beside a purling stream or shaded pond. There may have been a murder, and soon there might be others. Homer Evans had lived too abundantly to be deceived by the rich appointments of surroundings, or the fame or fortune of those who had found modern life too much for them. The late Scott Fitzgerald had said. "To the spoils, belong the victor." And how true! The poor, if they do not find life congenial and are unable to enjoy themselves, do not have to search for explanations and excuses. Those others, blessed with money, and a place in the sun, are also human, and subject to "the ills all flesh is heir to."

"June, bird-song and the scent of jacaranda," murmured Evans. "Eternal allies of the absolute. I must get to the business at hand."

Bob was not hard to awaken, after a few hours of deep sleep. He sat up, blinked, and glanced around him.

"Old chap," Bob said, not at all patronizingly, to Evans, "what is it they call the kind of amnesia that makes a guy forget, not who he is, but where and why?"

"*Lapsus memoriae*," Evans prompted.

"Much obliged. I seem to have it. Any cure?" Bob asked.

At that instant the cop who had been at Dave Chasen's opened the door a few inches and handed in the bottle of Calvados, the cork of which had been loosened. Homer, smiled, removed the cork, and offered the bottle to Reynolds.

Bob accepted, took a good long drag, gasped and felt the glow of the hardy Norman apple juice, distilled and perfected by time's alchemy.

"Now that's great," Reynolds said, as he handed the bottle back to Homer. "I can't remember things any better, but what's the difference?"

"You were thrown out of the Hippocrates Building on Beverly Drive by an emulator, up to a certain point, of the late Florence Nightingale."

Bob frowned and rubbed his forehead. "Sorry, old man. You'll have to toss 'em a little lower. They're all going over my head."

"Some nurse bounced you out of the office of Dr. Hershel Harms."

Bob took this much harder. "Holy cats! Does Shirley know?"

"That's one of the things we'll have to find out," Homer said.

"Ask Ruth Mesker," suggested Bob, as if that were the simplest solution. "Jeese! I hope Ruth isn't sore. I must have got a little tight when I should have been rallying 'round."

Homer shrugged, indulgently, as if that could happen to anyone. "I can't get in touch with Miss Mesker just now. She's hiding from the police."

"The devil," Bob said, petulantly, then the significance of Evans' remark dawned on him. "Ruth? The police? But she's my agent. We all depend on her."

"We'll extricate her, shortly," Homer said. "First, tell me a little of what this is all about."

"We'll have to call Finke Maguire," said Bob. "The private eye Ruth got for me. My stand-in."

"He's being sought in every church in San Francisco," Homer said.

Bob rubbed his head again. "Whatever I had to drink must be having a delayed effect. Things don't seem to make sense."

"If we don't find Finke, he'll find us, in due time," Homer assured Bob. Bob looked relieved. He might have had loads of temperament, as becomes an actor and particularly a baritone whose range goes up into the tenor, but he was not of the jittery kind.

"When you last saw Miss Mesker, and Finke . . ." Homer hesitated and looked inquiringly at Bob for guidance.

"That was at E.P.U. By the way, what day is it?"

"Early Wednesday. Just after midnight."

Bob shrugged as if that were as good a time and day as any for it to be. "If you don't mind . . ." Bob glanced about; at the washstand, paper walls, only slightly rumpled three-quarter bed and the Madras rubber tile. "Exactly where are we?"

"We're now in Beverly Hills in the . . . er . . . municipal building."

"Some can! I seem to have seen it before," said Bob. "Now what is it you wanted to ask. . . . Mr. . . . ?"

"Evans. Homer Evans. I was associated in Paris with Mr. Maguire."

"I read about it. Some bank murder, a Leftist mixup. I didn't know the Reds had any banks. But in Paris, anything goes."

Homer let that pass. The case had been known as "Murder on the Left Bank" and Bob, who never went into matters deeply, was harmlessly confused. The two men shook hands, Bob subdued and grave, but not excessively, Homer completely at ease.

"When you last talked with Finke, Mr. Reynolds, was there anything special he wanted you to do?"

"It was Ruth who wanted me to find Shirley, right away, so we could be reconciled, privately and publicly. Ruth thought we ought to make a statement. We'd had a lovers' quarrel . . . She pulled a gun on me in the projection room . . . So Ruth insisted that we get together and let the newspapermen photograph us . . . You know how they do in case of reconciliations . . . Shots from the waist up, in each other's arms. She looking up, me looking down. Two close-up heads, near together. The public goes for that."

"Miss Mesker must have had a more urgent reason than ordinary publicity," said Homer. "Both you and Miss Hall get plenty of that."

"Shirley's having one hell of a time . . . She's jealous," Bob said. "I try to be patient with her . . ."

"Is that why she's under treatment? By Dr. Harms?"

"Can you *beat* it? That fat head thinks he's going to make Shirley see her love and sex life in a *rational* way. Rational fiddle-sticks!"

"Exactly. But there's no harm trying, is there?"

Bob looked uncomfortable. As always, he disliked taking the defensive. "It's only . . . You're a man of the world . . . The thing isn't as simple as it seems. That nurse . . ."

"The nurse who gave you the vagabond's rush?" Evans asked.

"Did you know? About the big *Fräulein?*" Bob asked, eyes wide. He reached for the Calvados again.

"Deduction," Homer explained. "The simplest deduction. A nurse, especially a German nurse, undergoes a rigorous course of training. Those who specialize in the handling of sufferers from psychic or neurotic disorders—including jealousy—have additional training, and only those with extraordinary control of their tempers and strength have the remotest chance of being registered for that work. The *Fräulein*, so I hear from Emile, is of the heroic stature of the Rhine maidens and the Valkyrie. She did not merely ease you out of the doctor's office, but all the way to the sidewalk where, in the words of Captain Strongfort, you 'fell flat on your face.' Now on the screen, Mr. Reynolds, I have seen your perform some creditable feats of strength and endurance without the need of a 'stunt man.' You are no weakling, and surely were not helplessly drunk. Is it possible that this nurse, of legendary proportions, may have taken a fancy to you of correspondingly ample proportions, in the course of your visits to Dr. Harms' office to accompany, escort or inquire about your famous fiancée, Shirley Hall? Even if that strong passion were undeclared . . ."

Bob took a double shot of the Calvados and interrupted.

"Hells bells. It was declared, all right. The truth is, I got extra pie-eyed one evening, and Shirley'd been unusually unreasonable and suspicious . . . So I ran into Lukie . . . and . . . damn it, I shouldn't have to dot the 'i'."

"I take it you dotted it so thoroughly that it has remained well dotted to this day."

"I suppose so. I wish I remembered it better. Oh, you know. We all get into these pickles."

"How true," admitted Evans, smiling again. "But yours has elements which are not at all banal. Shirley Hall, I assume, must think highly of Dr. Harms to have undergone his treatment so long. If the German Brunhilde were stirred to her full depth, as it were, and wished to aggravate Shirley's very real ailment, the *Fräulein* would have unusual opportunities to see that certain hints or facts, inflammatory to Miss Hall's condition, reached Shirley's mind."

"I've got to hand it to you," Bob said to Evans. "In just a few minutes, you've got closer to my problem than all those others have in months."

"Meaning Ruth Mesker, your fiancée, herself, her doctor, and the *Fräulein*, who, for love of you, has tossed caution and tradition to the winds?"

"What put you wise?" asked Bob, uneasily, in spite of the relief that confession, even backhandedly, affords to the harassed.

"No nurse who did not love you would forget herself and exercise such violence. It was a kind of frenzy—unprofessional and surely out of character. Had the *Fräulein* been addicted to torturing patients or assaulting those who were solicitous about them, she would not have gone scot-free as long as this . . . Or is she very young?"

"She's thirty-five," Bob said, a little too promptly.

"A *Berlinerin?*" asked Evans. "I haven't seen her yet, you know."

"From Tallinn, Esthonia."

Homer whistled, softly. "This case offers challenges from every angle. From Tallinn, indeed. Before the Reds annexed it, that capital was the criminals' paradise. Is Miss Kahler Esthonian on her father's or her mother's side? You know, in selecting fighting bulls, it's the brave cows, the mothers, who determine the strain. But Kahler sounds German."

"You can say that again," agreed Bob.

"She's big, like the Slavs, and persistent, from her German side."

Reynolds reached for the Calvados and groaned.

"If Shirley gets wind of this . . ."

"Don't despair," Evans said. "It may be that Fräulein Kahler's irresistible urge for you will guide us into other channels pertinent to this case."

A light tap on the door was followed by the voice of one of the policemen. "If you don't mind, gentlemen. We're a bit crowded these moonlight nights."

"Don't mention it," Evans agreed courteously. And to Bob: "Lead on. To Shirley's apartment."

"We'd better telephone first," Bob said, reluctant but willing. He glanced around, as if he expected to find a phone.

"I'll speak to the Captain about the service. Meanwhile, we can use the public booth in his reception office," Evans said. They rose, Bob straightened his clothes, which were not much awry, considering, and they set out on their way.

9

Quite Dead

"THE REASON THAT THE PRESENT always appears confused and illogical," Homer said, as, with Bob Reynolds, he rode in a taxi toward Shirley and the Forty-Niners Towers, "is that past events may be reviewed in their entirety, like an ideal motion picture."

"A newsreel?" asked Bob, whose head had cleared somewhat but at its best was not equal to Homer's philosophical asides.

"News material, in perspective, thoughtfully presented and interpreted," Homer said. "Now in what you have told me about this situation, in which you all are involved, and I am trying to be useful, what we call 'the timing' leaves much to be desired."

"Nothing louses up a picture as much as bad timing," Bob agreed.

"A motion picture, in its ideal state, may give us the truest reflection of life. None of us can understand life too well."

"I don't know as much as you do about anything," Bob said. "But if art and perspective get into a movie, you can kiss 'box office' good-bye. I suppose the same goes in life. It's all right having a lot of highbrow ideas, as long as you don't start putting them into practice."

"A very distinguished Christian is quoted as having said: 'By their works ye shall know them'," Homer observed.

"For instance, the Manellos?" asked Bob.

Homer looked pleased. "After all, they're human—to a certain extent. Now, speaking of the brothers Manello; you met Ric Manello six weeks, more or less, *before* the death of Barney Rice.

Ric was establishing an agency and had shown strong influence at E.P.U."

"You make Ric sound legitimate," Bob said.

"In solving a murder case, everyone must be left in the clear until proven guilty of the murder in question. Other unrelated felonies don't count. A suspect may have driven his old mother into the snow to beg and starve, or robbed a bank and got an acquittal before a jury of his peers. Still, one does not accept him as the murderer of a specific victim or victims on the basis of his reputation, character or his previous record."

"Aside from his previous record," Bob said. "Ric tried to force me into signing up with him. He knew Shirley and I were engaged, and worked as a team, and that Ruth Mesker was our agent and had put us in the chips. He wanted me to ditch them."

"He offered you a chance to better yourself—from his point of view," suggested Homer.

"From no matter whose point of view, a guy doesn't better himself by turning into a horse's ass when he's always played it on the level," Bob said.

Homer looked at Bob admiringly, much reassured. "That epigram, in slightly modified form, perhaps, should be carved on the walls of our schoolrooms," he said. "But let me resume. Just the facts—in their order. Ric Manello asked you to sign up with his agency."

"He didn't mention Shirley," Bob insisted, doggedly.

"He didn't say 'without Shirley', did he?"

"He didn't ask Shirley to sign." Bob would not budge an inch from that ground. "He didn't threaten Shirley, either, after Barney had died. Nobody did. Why should she be slighted?"

"It stands to reason, that if the Manellos wanted to get rid of Shirley, they must have had some actress they wished to use in her place."

"There was no one in sight, then, when they first propositioned me," Bob said.

"And later, after Barney Rice had died, and you had turned Ric down again, Señorita Noguera from Mexico appears as if by magic, and fulfills all the requirements. Where was she all that time? She's as lovely, as a brunette, as Shirley is among blondes. She can act like an angel, or she-devil."

"I've only been in this business five years, but the old-timers can remember the days before sound pictures could be made. As far as I know, there's never been a time when a swell role had to be cast, and no actress appeared to fill it, magic or no magic," Bob said.

Then came the leading question.

"You didn't suspect, of course, when you agreed to act with Miss Noguera, that she was being groomed for Shirley's part?" Evans asked so sympathetically that Bob could not possibly take offense.

"Why can't Shirley see that?" Bob demanded. "I didn't know a thing about the material for the test till the script was handed me last Friday afternoon."

"And the test was rehearsed on Friday, shot on Saturday, and shown on Monday."

"I didn't even know it was going to be rushed through Technicolor on Sunday. You could have knocked me over with a feather when the color flashed on the screen."

"You were aware that the cameraman was . . . Didn't Emile say, 'Hagup Bogigian, three times winner of the Oscar for photography'?"

Bob leaned over toward the defensive again. "I only got wise to that Saturday, when the shooting began. And, to tell you the truth, I figured that Miss Noguera had got to Hagup in person—the way she had softened me up. What the *hell*? How can a man say 'no' to a girl like that, with looks and—you know—everything it takes. A guy who wouldn't go out of his way to do Miss Noguera a favor must be made of cream of wheat. How did it happen, let me ask you, that Laslo Sitchev decided to direct the test himself? He hasn't gone that far for a beginner since he discovered Demona Bourbon singing the Hallelujah Chorus on Easter morning at the Hollywood Bowl. Of course, the bloody Hunyak wasn't talent scouting at dawn. He was drifting home from an orgy in Pasadena, and had lost his road. That's the kind of luck Sitchev has. I shouldn't beef, I suppose. He's made six smash hits in a row, with me—and Shirley."

"Let me get this straight," Homer said. "It's important. You attribute, then, Señorita Noguera's meteoric beginning to her own

initiative and personality rather than the heavy-handed tactics of
the Manellos?"

"One doesn't rule out the other. Eulalia plays the field. It gives
me a pain the way she lowers herself, giving the business to Tony
Manello, when it doesn't mean a thing. I've told her off for that, to
her face," said Bob, his eyes narrow with whatever stags feel when
contending for a stray doe.

Homer's face was alight with satisfaction, and, unnoticed by
Bob, he signaled covertly for the taxi man to take it easy.

"Miss Noguera must be especially grateful to you. After all,
agents like the Manellos, a writer like Jack Oehler, a prize cameraman like Hagup Bogigian, a director and discoverer of stars like
Laslo Sitchev, plus the combined resources of E.P.U. and top pri-
ority with Technicolor couldn't have put her across without a leading man."

"Eulalia appreciates that. She's got a lot of sense."

"Does she grasp, also, that Shirley is not as well . . . balanced,
shall we say?"

Bob's face clouded. "She didn't tumble to that until too late.
When first she heard that Shirley was upset—that was Saturday—
she called Shirley up to tell her how wonderful it was to work with
me, and how lucky Shirley was to be engaged to a man who could
let himself go, on the set, and make a love scene convincing, and
then be sweet and impersonal off scene."

"I assume that Shirley was not comforted," Evans said, sympathetically.

"She smashed four pictures of me, in hand-carved frames of
upas wood, that had set me back fifty bucks apiece."

Homer was instantly alert. "Did you say 'upas wood'?"

"That's what the Shroeder woman called it, the one who runs
the shop, Art for Art's Sake," Bob said.

"I know Mrs. Shroeder and her shop. In fact she got for me not
many years ago a few authentic paintings by Raden Saleh done
in his youth, before the paternal Dutch sent him from Batavia to
Europe to learn about 'art for art's sake' and debauched his genius

completely. Those youthful masterpieces, by the way, Saleh him-self had framed in Upas wood, the only ones I ever have seen. . . . I trust that Miss Hall, if she broke such precious and unusual frames, has salvaged the pieces."

"Not Shirley," Bob said, and sighed. "Sky's the limit, when she gets the idea that I'm unfaithful. And, damn it, don't jump at wrong conclusions. I'm not in love with Eulalia Noguera. Or anybody except Shirley. I sat for hours with Eulalia in the moonlight last night, as platonic as hell, after Harmon had raised such a stink about her acting in Tahitian costume. I didn't even kiss the girl, except maybe on the forehead or the ear, forgetful like."

"How does Fräulein Kahler behave when she gets an earful about you from Shirley? After all, Shirley must confide in Dr. Harms, if she's haunted with suspicions that you're playing around, and a nurse would overhear."

Bob had the grace to blush. "I'm usually careful not to see Lukie too soon after Shirley's been to the doctor's office. I slipped up on that last night . . . and, well, that's how you and I happened to get together—in the hoosegow. Lukie, worse luck, hadn't known until then that I'd been helping Miss Noguera. Can you imagine what might happen if Lukie lost her head and sounded off, so Shirley would find out her own nurse was nuts about me?"

The cab pulled up in front of the Forty-Niners Towers. Homer and Bob got out, and the latter was greeted in a tactful comradely way by the doorkeeper, Lazarus Hinckley.

"You're just in time," Hinckley said. "Miss Hall just went up to her apartment."

Bob looked relieved, but he had to be sure. "Did she seem—well?"

The doorman, who had been at the Towers since the day they were opened for occupation, nodded understandingly. "Fair to middlin'," he said. "She put in a call as soon as she got to her phone. A bit excited, you might say."

"To the Omar Gardens?"

Hinckley nodded. "It wasn't for you—directly."

"Indirectly?" asked Bob.

"She asked for another party."

"Ah?" Bob asked, fearfully.

"A Miss Noguera. And when Miss Hall learned that Miss Noguera was not there, she asked the operator the usual questions. Had this Miss Noguera gone out with you? Had you and she been seen together since this afternoon? Had you called anybody? Had anyone called to try to get you? Where you were last night, who with, and what time you got home? Miss Hall seemed to think, if you'll excuse me, Mr. Reynolds, that you spent the night with this Mexican, but she didn't get any satisfaction from the operators at the Gardens. They're pretty good down there at dodging questions."

Bob took from his pocket a twenty-dollar bill and slipped it to Hinckley.

"Don't let me down," he begged.

"Not on your tintype," Hinckley said. "I was an engaged man, myself, before I got nailed. Shall I announce you, and Mr. . . . ?"

"Evans. Homer Evans," Reynolds said.

Homer shook hands with Hinckley, and Bob said, to the latter, "Let me have a word with Shirley—to get the lay of the land."

The doorman went over to the switchboard, inserted a plug, took up the receiver and clamped it on his head. He pushed a button. Waited. There was no response.

"Now that's funny," said Hinckley. "She's up there alone."

"That damned Cockney maid. Where's she?"

"She went out to the drug store on an errand—the front way, as always. Being a Limey she thinks she's too good to use the rear exit, with the rest of the help." Hinckley gave a glance toward the doorway. "Well. Here the maid comes now."

Sensing instantly, by Bob's attitude as well as that of Melissa as she approached, that they loathed each other, Homer interposed.

"We were trying to contact Miss Hall. I've just flown down from San Francisco on purpose to meet her," Evans said. "No doubt she's tired, after such a trying day and evening."

Melissa looked daggers at Reynolds, then back to Homer, but, in his case, without hostility. "After spending hours with that stupid doctor, and for days being worried sick by a party I could mention, who's not worth her salt . . ."

"She's been with Dr. Harms?" Evans asked. "Evidently you don't have much confidence in psychiatric treatment. I know Miss Hall has not been well, and I promise not to stay too long. Unless I'm mistaken, she finds more relief in your company than doctors can give her."

"There's nothing I wouldn't do for my lamb," Melissa said. "But the company you keep!"

The maid glared at Reynolds again.

"You'll be out of a job the day Miss Hall and I are married," Bob assured her. "And if you want to go sooner, I'll make you a present of a ticket back to Yorkshire, where you belong."

"I'm particular who pays my transportation. No self-respecting young woman like Miss Hall can be hoodwinked by a trifler like you, for long. You'll get your walking ticket before I do."

Homer saw a glitter in the English maid's eye and a set to her chin that made it all too plain that, in order to dispose of Bob, she would not stop at murder in any style.

"Let's go on up," Bob said to Homer. "We can't stand here with this crowbait all night." And to Hinckley: "Let her walk, if she doesn't like the service elevator."

It occurred to Homer that their respective "servant problems" had provided another strong bond of sympathy between Reynolds and the beautiful Gardenia. He wondered if they had discussed, by June moonlight, Shirley's Yorkshire maid and Harmon's Dutchman.

Having ascended to the penthouse level of the Forty-Niners Towers, Bob admitted, with another becoming blush, that they would have to wait for Melissa to let them into Apartment 17-A. For his touch of the buzzer had brought no response from within.

"Shirley often doesn't answer the phone or the doorbell. She has so little privacy," Bob said, apologetically. "I suppose," he added, hesitantly, "that you think it odd that I don't carry a key to her place. I'm a bit nervous about keys. Suppose some night I should get a skinful, the way I did when I woke up with . . . You understand how it is. I'm not trying to say I don't want to marry Shirley. But, believe me, I'd rather hold off until Doc Harms gives her the high sign."

"You mean Dr. Harms has hinted that Miss Hall had better wait till she acquires that 'rational view' you spoke about?"

"You get the drift," Bob agreed.

"Dr. Harms understands, of course, how things are with you and Fräulein Kahler?"

Bob almost hopped out of his shoes to protest. "My God, I hope not. The doc's nuts about Lukie. Any dope could see that, without a degree from Vienna. If she asked Doc for the moon, he'd try to fork it over. And he's the gent, mind you, who gives patients rational views of love and sex, while all the time his tongue's hanging out for a dame he travels with, from country to country, and pays by the week. He's about as rational as Charley's Aunt."

The tenants' elevator, having descended, returned with Melissa. The door rolled open, and the Yorkshire maid stepped out, her red-rimmed eyes fixed on Reynolds malignantly, as if to say: "So she wouldn't let you in? Serves you right!"

With an air of indispensability, Melissa inserted her key in the lock, but before she turned it, it must have occurred to her that she should give her mistress some kind of warning, perhaps that she was not returning alone, but had unexpected guests with her. At any rate, the maid pressed the door button and both Homer and Reynolds heard the buzzer sound faintly inside. Two shorts and a long. Again there was no response.

The maid flipped over the key without delay, as if she were in a mild panic, and pushed the door open without further ceremony.

"My precious baby!" she called. "Where are you? You're as quiet as a mouse."

Shirley's lack of response was even quieter than a mouse. It was non-existent. The maid rushed into the bedroom, leaving Bob and Homer agape. Evans recovered in a split second and started for the kitchen. The cold-water tap was dripping, almost in a stream. His instinct to turn it off brought his hand within an inch of the faucet and his stronger impulse as a criminologist held it back, in time. He heard Bob's voice in the living room, berating the frantic maid.

"Well. She isn't here, you dope. You knew damn well that Ruth and I and the newspapermen and the studio have been trying to find her all evening. Then, as soon as she showed up, you streaked out of here and let her get away again. This time I'll make an issue of it. Either you go, or I do. And you can be sure it won't be I."

Melissa, Homer noted, despite her hatred toward Bob and her nature that made her ordinarily as touchy as a hedgehog, failed to reply, or even to seem to notice.

"Come here, please, Mr. Evans," Melissa begged, and Homer crossed the living room and followed her into the bedroom. The maid opened the drawers, one by one, and the doors of the closets. She indicated, in order, the various cosmetics and intimate utensils in ornamental boxes and cases. The small wrapped phial she had brought from the neighborhood drug store she had dropped in her haste to the floor where it lay on its side on the rug.

"What's missing? Not much, I should say," asked Homer.

"Just the clothes my darling had on, her green handbag and gloves. The same dress and shoes she took with her to the studio when she left this noon. That isn't like her. My lamb couldn't have done that of her own accord. The clothes she put on to go to the studio and had to wear to the doctor's wouldn't be right for evening—even this hour in the middle of the night. And she hasn't taken the medicine she sent me out for. She told me the doctor wanted her to have it, right away. Three drops in a half glass of water."

Evans picked up the little drug-store package from the floor, unwrapped it carefully, glanced at the label, took out the glass stopper, sniffed the contents, and nodded.

"The usual," he said. "The combination sedative that gives the illusion of well-being, combined with a stimulant that induces gaiety and activity. Not for sleep. In fact, a mild insurance against it. Mmmm. Signed by Dr. Harms, probably. We must not take too much for granted."

Bob was annoyed, almost petulant again. It was evident that he did not take a serious view of Shirley's absence, although it displeased him, and was, from his point of view, most inconvenient.

"Don't take this too much to heart, Mr. Evans," Bob said. "It's nothing unusual, these days, for Shirley to go off half-cocked, show up when you least expect her and duck out of sight without notice."

"You heartless idiot!" Melissa, now tearful, shrieked at Reynolds. "She may have been murdered for all you care. It's your conceited self you think of. You want her to sit at home, twirling her thumbs, while you make an exhibition of yourself with some greasy foreigner, who wants to do in my lamb. And step into her place."

Without comment, Homer gently took Melissa's hand and led her toward the kitchen. He pointed to the fast dripping faucet.

"There is modern plumbing in Yorkshire, or does one still use hand pumps?" he asked, mildly sarcastic, to take her mind from Bob.

As Homer had expected, Melissa bristled and turned on him, but restrainedly and with respect. "Not likely I'd leave a tap like that, if that's what you're getting at. My poor lamb, distracted as she is, must have got herself some water, here in the kitchen."

"Not in her private bathroom?" Evans asked, blandly.

"Oh, please," Melissa entreated him. "You're a gentleman with intelligence. You can see that none of this makes sense. Someone has kidnapped my darling."

"With astonishingly few signs of violence. I can't seem to find any myself," said Homer.

"Whoever it was wheedled her. She's that sweet and trusting— except in the case of this fiend." The maid thumbed toward Reynolds, who still was refusing to get into a dither.

"Any idea as to who might have lured her away? And by what route? We spoke with Mr. Hinckley, who tends the front door."

"You can't trust that one. He's a two-faced nark."

"Nevertheless and notwithstanding," Homer said, "I think he would have mentioned the fact to Mr. Reynolds and me, had Shirley gone out by the front exit within three or four minutes of the moment we arrived. Mr. Hinckley, as a matter of fact, phoned up here to announce us, and was somewhat surprised at receiving no reply. Miss Hall, I understand, has the habit of ignoring the phone, when she wishes to be uncommunicative."

"She hasn't the 'abit of sending me on the double quick to the drug store, and then disappearing—at night—in sports clothes for the afternoon."

"There's a back door, I assume," Evans suggested.

"Miss Hall never used it. Not once, to my knowledge. And no more have I, with the scum that passes in and out that way."

Then Evans made a request neither of the others had expected, but one which brought him much further into the good graces of the Yorkshire maid.

"Would you mind, Melissa, in this instance, accompanying me to the rear exit? Mr. Reynolds can hold the fort here, in case the telephone or the doorbell rings."

"Why, gladly, sir. I've confidence in you, if you'll forgive my saying so, and there's nothing 'ere he wants, since he's stole my poor mistress' heart away, and thinks everything she's got is his."

"Go on, blabbermouth," Reynolds said, in such a way that Homer, who would have been amused had the situation been less grave, expected Bob to stick out his tongue and make a face. To an outsider, that pair—Bob Reynolds and Melissa—were as good as a vaudeville team. And actually, Homer showed no signs at that moment of having the deep fears for Shirley's safety that he secretly entertained.

Homer and Melissa descended to the basement in the service elevator. The back exit was one floor below the grade level on Sunset Boulevard, because of the down slope to Los Angeles and what is known as "The Miracle Mile" on Wilshire Boulevard.

On duty at the back doorway was a competent and frank-appearing ex-service man named Vulcan Moscone, a former top sergeant in the Commandos. He was working that week a split shift to accommodate a pal, and had been on since eight that evening and expected to be relieved at four. Ordinarily he was on from midnight to eight A.M.

"You know Melissa, of course," Evans remarked as soon as he had introduced himself to the guard. He had noticed Moscone was carrying an automatic, in a shoulder holster, although Hinckley at the front door showed no signs of having been armed. Very likely, in Moscone's case, it was force of habit, Homer thought.

"Pleased to meet you," Moscone said, politely. He had never seen Melissa, quite evidently, and she knew him neither by his name or his face.

"Have you been here all the time since, say, one o'clock to-night?" Homer asked. It was then about half past.

Moscone's honest face fell. "Not all the time, sir," he answered. "The folks up in 16-A phoned me to ask if I could get them a bottle at Escobar's liquor store that closes around two. I'm permitted to do errands like that for the tenants, if they don't take too long, and I lock the door from the outside, so no strangers could get in. So many of the tenants have jewelry and furs, and large amounts of cash for their gin-rummy games."

"Of course. Everything else is done on credit," Homer said and smiled.

"That's the size of it, sir."

Melissa's face froze. She did not hold with gambling.

"How long were you absent tonight—just now?" Evans asked.

"Not ten minutes, sir. I must have got back at least ten minutes ago, and delivered the liquor."

"What was the liquor?"

"French cognac, sir. Cour-voi-sier."

"A very fair brandy, but scarcely cognac," said Evans.

"I drank plenty of it in France."

Evans smiled. "Me, too, although I prefer Armagnac, or the Spanish Gonzalez Byass."

Melissa snorted again. "My poor mistress has been kidnapped while you were traipsing after French brandy," the maid stated.

"Kidnapped, you said, ma'am?" asked Moscone, incredulously.

"Or murdered," insisted Melissa.

Moscone looked at Homer, man to man, hoping to get the straight of it.

"Do the tenants have keys to your back door?" Homer asked.

"They're entitled to them, so they can pass in and out in case the watchman's been called away for a while. But not many of them bother to get keys, and fewer of them use 'em. Miss Shroeder and Mr. De Witt, on the 16th, now and then. They make so many deliveries, paintings, frames and knicknacks of one kind or another, and this door's handy to the garage. The nurse who rooms with 'em comes in or leaves this way, when she's in uniform."

"Fine figure of a woman, Miss Kahler," said Homer, with a grin at Moscone that set off Melissa again.

"I'll say," agreed Moscone, and made a gesture, raising his hands palm downward above the level of his head. "That dame's fanny wasn't built too close to the sidewalk . . ." (to the maid) "Excuse me, ma'am."

"While you two men discuss French liquor and woman . . ."

"German women. *Echte Rabenmüttern*," corrected Homer.

"Bah! My mistress didn't have a key to this door, and if she had, she'd never have used it. Mr. Evans, we're wasting our time."

"I'd like to take a look around the back premises, if you don't mind," Homer suggested.

"And if you don't mind, I'd like to call the police."

"Forbearance! Patience!" Homer said. "But if you wish to call anyone, I think you might try Miss Mesker, Miss Hall's agent."

"I've talked with Miss Mesker fifty times this night, if I've talked with her once, but she's had to call me. Miss Mesker's not been at home, and she isn't there now, or she'd have let me know."

"Say, mister. What is this?" Moscone asked, mystified. He looked puzzled at Homer and frowned. "This canary's—excuse me, ma'am—not serious that some tenant's been croaked!"

"Each one dies at his or her appointed time, and sometimes sooner," Homer said, but reassuringly.

Moscone opened the door, which was unlatched, and Evans stepped out, Moscone following gingerly, Melissa impatiently, lips pursed between grunts of protest.

They did not have long to travel. Ten paces from the exit, Homer caught his breath, seeing something at his left, on the ground. He halted abruptly, motioned the others back, stepped five or six strides in the direction of the object his keen eyes had seen dimly, stooped, retrieved what seemed to be a handbag, straightened and faced his companions.

"Melissa. You may call the police."

"It's her?" the maid wailed.

Homer had had in the course of his brilliant career to be the bearer of bad news in so many instances that he knew the brusque and simple announcement was the best where devoted bereaved ones were concerned, in no matter what station in life.

"Quite dead," he said, kindly, but his two brief words seemed to sharpen the colors of the moonlight and scene.

Seeing how cruelly Melissa was stricken, and how helpless she would be for a while, Homer turned to Moscone, who was standing at attention.

"You'd better put through that call for the police," Homer told him.

"Which police, sir?" the guard asked, in the military manner he had unconsciously assumed in the emergency.

"Captain Strongfort, at the Beverly Hills headquarters, that's the nearest, and then the County authorities—we're in County territory, I believe, here on the Strip—as a matter of form."

10

Nocturne in Spades

To GET OFF THE BEAT where Lieutenant Marcus' dragnet might be extended, Finke had only to slip out the service exit of the Derby and start afoot across Wilshire and along Rodeo toward Olympic Boulevard. Once out of the glow of the boulevard lights he found himself in an ordinary bourgeois area inhabited by Californians who work for wages. Usually, it was next to impossible to find a taxi in that neighborhood, but Finke had luck that evening. He hailed an empty passenger cab whose driver had just quit the 20th Century-Fox lot stand and was on his way home, downtown. The Omar Gardens, whither Finke was bound, was only a couple of miles off the taxi driver's route, and in greater Los Angeles, where one frequently has to drive six miles to buy a box of matches, such a small detour was nothing

Finke hopped out, at the entrance of the Gardens, paid the cabman and not until he stepped into the patio did the prevailing mood of the quiet moonlit evening envelop him and retard his nervous pace. He seemed to be alone and still had the impression that amorphous shapes were forming and reforming beyond the range of the dim reflections and purple shadows on the walls. When he looked closer, the benches, seats and settees were unoccupied. As soon as he turned away, he thought he heard mysterious whispering. The fronds of shrubs stirred as night birds ruffled their feathers and tucked their heads under alternate wings. Magnolia, acacia and phlox sustained the thinner fragrance of the tall flowering bamboo beyond the garage and first cluster of cottages. As Finke passed the pool where the patched goldfish moved in drowsy pattern, and rising to the surface, gobbled tiny gem-like bubbles, he saw that Enrico, the Mexican night mechanic, had forsaken the enclosed stench of gasoline and rubber and was sitting in the dappled shadow of a banana tree.

"To say *'buenas noches'* on a night like this is too much, or too little, Señor," Enrico said.

Finke, his stubborn Irish self-consciousness aroused by such a surfeit of loveliness and language, almost growled, "Is Harmon back?"

The Mexican understood Finke's way of reacting. Not yet, *amigo*," he said. "Won't you join me in contemplation?"

"To hell with contemplation!" said Finke. "What about your countrywoman?"

"Ah," said Enrico and smiled. "Such nocturnal splendor as this is not for pie-faced Anglo-Saxon blondes, who are at their best in the grandstands at fixed sporting events. This *décor* is for brunettes. It touches the soft contours of their faces and forms, and concentrates in their darkly glowing eyes the depth of all shadows, so they seem to recede as they approach. . . ."

"Can the build-up. Is she here or isn't she?" demanded Finke.

Enrico made a gracious gesture toward the Gardenia's bungalow. "She passed that way," he said.

"Alone?"

Enrico sighed and nodded. "If Señor Harmon were as wise as he is rich, he wouldn't leave her to her own devices. Last night it was Mr. Reynolds. Now you, Señor Finke."

"Never mind me. Where's the Dutchman?"

"As much as Señor Van Vleeck loves his trees and flowers, he has the habit of going early to bed, as soon as Mr. Harmon has finished dinner or set out for the evening, and he rises just before sun-up, according to the rhythmic ordinance of the seasons."

"A daytime Nature Boy. O.K. I'll take a walk around the Gardens," Finke said. "Would you mind giving me the high sign when Harmon blows in? Maybe he'll scrape his other fender."

"You wish to talk with him tonight?" asked Enrico, in surprise. It was not idle curiosity on his part. He wanted to be sure not to make a *faux pas* and snarl up the already tangled situation.

"Sure. Tell him I'm here. He tried to find me at my office," said Finke.

He followed tentatively the pathway toward the Gardenia's house and, as he neared the jasmine bushes in which the night butterflies were feeding, he stopped to watch them. He knew nothing about moths, except that there was a criminal variety that gnawed holes in woolen clothes. Of the kinds who seemed to prefer jasmine to cloth, some had a wingspread of more than six inches, with one great eye on each wing, like that on the feather of a peacock's tail. Others were tiny, with a deep coral shade. None of them ate greedily. They did not prey on one another. Individually, they made no noise. Collectively they evoked a rustle just on the border of the hearing range.

The bungalow was dark, except for the faint glow of the night-lamp inside. Eulalia's bedroom windows were slightly parted. Finke concluded regretfully that she must be asleep. He had had such a strong presentiment that he should see her, that he gave it up reluctantly. The loam bed, freshly raked, still smelled of manure, and Finke tiptoed across to look in through the shutters. This time no pair of dark eyes encountered his, from within, then disappeared. Little Tani, who in spite of her schoolgirl's frock was several years beyond the marrying age of her people, was nowhere in evidence.

With an increasing uneasiness, Finke turned toward the Dutchman's greenhouses. He passed the tall staunch bamboo which, high aloft, was in flower. Prompted by an instinct to keep himself inconspicuous, he stepped into the shadow of some lotar palms and glanced beyond the feathery clumps of Calcutta grass. In the tranquil moonlight of the clearing lay the beds of pitcher plants, alternately screened and unscreened. Finke felt gooseflesh rise when he saw, not the Dutchman, but Latacassi. The old crone was not kneeling this time. She was standing, like an antique statue that had deformed itself progressively to correspond with its deteriorating model, beneath a tree—not a full-grown tree, but an immature one, that must be still growing and had reached a height not exceeding twelve feet. Finke ground his teeth with perplexity that amounted to annoyance. He was no Nature Boy, but his powers of observation should work outdoors as well as indoors. He could have sworn that the tree in question had not been standing where it was, or anywhere in sight, when that morning he had seen the garden in sunlight, or earlier that evening, when the moon was rising. Had that tree been occupying the space where now it unquestionably stood, the tall well-dressed man who proved later to have the object lesson Voice would have not halted on that spot to spy on Latacassi. And why did the old witch take every opportunity, when the Dutchman was away, to haunt his garden and grove?

Finke tore the stillness of the night with a resounding Bronx cheer and, before the end of it escaped his lips, where Latacassi had stood there was blank space, presumably with air in it. He faced about stealthily, counting as far as seven, before he detected the almost inaudible fluttering of moths and the click of the Gardenia's door latch. He waited, beneath the lotars, until he was sure that his rude device for scaring off the aged Javanese woman had aroused no one else. Then he walked over, softly, to examine the mysterious tree. He touched the slim trunk, experimentally, and quickly withdrew his hand. His palm had been moistened by a cool sticky substance, definitely unpleasant to the touch and exuding a faint sickening odor that suggested mold or bedbugs. Carefully Finke wiped his hand dry with a handkerchief. He took from his pocket his small flashlight and turned the small beam on the tree trunk, which was not three inches in diameter. A drop of sap was oozing from a round hole in the bark. It looked as if the tree might purposely have been tapped. Distastefully, Finke spread his spare handkerchief on the damp ground, keeping the one intact that had been moistened with the ill-smelling sap. It did not take long to verify his conviction that the tree had been transplanted between the time he had knocked out the Dutchman and the present moment.

"So what?" Finke asked himself, determined not to be diverted from the essentials of his case into the labyrinth of naturalism.

"The Dutchman moves trees around, just to show God what He could do if He only had Harmon's money."

Finke straightened up, impatiently. He would go to Harmon's cottage, wake up the damned Dutchman, and find out why he had been phoning all day, without leaving his name or number. But before he could take a step, there was a click of the Gardenia's door latch and that subdued fluttering of the moths in the jasmine recurred. He faced about, careful not to touch the tree that smelled of bedbugs and corruption. Old Latacassi was afoot again, when she should have been astride a broomstick. Finke watched her glide along the pathway at right angles to the one that had brought him to the pitcher-plant beds and outlandish grasses and palms. He did not want to let her slip out of his sight, so he followed on the parallel path. What he saw was as understandable as his discovery of the tainted tree was mysterious. Tani, not in schoolgirl's pinafore but wrapped in some kind of robe or house gown she must have "borrowed" from the Gardenia, was seated on the doorstep of Bob Reynolds' bungalow, which obviously was dark and unoccupied.

Latacassi, in the manner of an Occidental grandma, was scolding the girl softly in the strange dialect which was the only form of speech, except for about thirty words of pidgin English, that the old woman knew. Tani, not in the manner of a submissive Oriental child, brought up on parent worship, but more like a fresh spoiled young pupil from an American junior high school, was trying to convince Latacassi that a girl of twelve can be trusted late at night, with a perfect gentleman like Mr. Reynolds, who, moreover, was not there. Nevertheless, Latacassi led Tani back to the Gardenia's cottage, the moths fluttered, and just before the doorlatch clicked, Finke could not resist letting out another resounding raspberry. The result was a quick "wipe dissolve," in movie parlance. The old Javanese and her grandchild disappeared inside, but the moths paid no attention and the tree frogs sang without interruption.

When all was still again, and before Finke could get going, a soft voice at his elbow said: "*Buenas noches, Señor.*"

He jumped as if he had been prodded with an ice pick.

"Why, Senor Finke!" the Gardenia said, mischievously. "I thought you were one of those strong silent men, without nerves. You were so calm and cool this afternoon, when you saved Mr. Reynolds."

The Gardenia, slender and lovely in the moonlight, was in a misty kind of gown, insubstantial as her perfume. Her words were real, and so was her silvery peal of laughter. The rest was fantasy.

"You knocked me for a loop," Finke said, crossly.

"This afternoon?"

He looked her over ruefully. "Why don't you go back to bed?" He made a gesture toward the moon, the trees, the chorus of night sounds, and breathed deeply to include the fragrance. "Isn't this setting enough for a guy to contend with, without you to foul him up?"

"I haven't been in bed. Not yet," she said, quite gravely. "Have you seen Mr. Reynolds?" Her tone was a shade too anxious.

"Not for a couple of hours, but he's quite safe. If that's what's eating you."

"Nothing's eating me." She breathed deeply and stretched her arms, throwing back her lovely head.

"It wouldn't prey on your mind, if you were the cause of Bob's getting shot?"

"He won't get shot," she said, back to reality.

"Who told you so? That stuffed orange shirt from Chicago?"

"There's only one Manello who counts. Señor Ricardo," she said.

"That doesn't stop you from giving Señor Antonio the business," Finke said, with more feeling than he had intended.

The Gardenia laughed again.

"Bob is jealous of Tony," she said, but pleased. "Now you, Mr. Finke. Even Mr. Sitchev doesn't like it when I give Tony what you call 'the business'."

"Is it Mr. Sitchev who told you that Reynolds won't be shot?"

"Why do you ask?"

"Mr. Reynolds is my responsibility. I'm supposed, among other things, to keep him alive."

"I don't want to steal him, or Shirley's prestige. I merely want to act, in a picture or two, until I'm satisfied that I've done my best. Then, to please my husband, I'll retire. Or maybe, if Mr. Harmon can't stand an actress for a wife, I'll wait until then to be married."

"Is that Sitchev's idea?"

"Mr. Sitchev needs me. Before my test, he knew that Miss Hall was overtired and needed a long rest. He was at his wits' end, because there was no one to take her place."

"You've got it all figured out. There's only one hitch."

"Shirley?"

"You know damn well that as long as you are with Bob, on or off the screen, Miss Hall won't get well. She'll lose what's left of her reason."

The Gardenia hesitated.

"I think not," she said. "I talked with Señorita Hall tonight. She was relatively calm."

"I can hear her purring," Finke said. "Look, baby. I like you. You've got everything. Please don't take me for a sap. . . . Let's get this straight. You talked with Miss Hall about her taking a rest?"

The Gardenia nodded. "At the Tropics."

"What time?"

"After she'd left the doctor's office. She was hungry and tired, and stopped at the Tropics for something to eat. And also in the hope that Mr. Reynolds might be there."

"Is that why you were there, too?"

The Gardenia, her hand toying with a branch of acacia, looked Finke clearly in the eyes. "I was lonesome. Mr. Harmon had been so unreasonable."

"O.K. Who tipped you off that Reynolds might be there?"

"Mr. Manello, if you must know."

"Which one, Tony, or the boss?"

She shrugged and withdrew ever so slightly. "That doesn't matter," she said. "Am I undergoing the third degree by the clever detective? Or are we friends?"

"That remains to be seen," Finke said. "Maybe you'll tell me who told Shirley that Bob might be at the Tropics?"

"I don't know how Shirley happened to be there, and it was an accident that she sat at my table. The head waiter was going to give her another booth. She caught sight of me and came right over."

"And you pulled the line about a nice long rest and taking care of Bob while she was in the loony bin? Don't give me that," Finke said.

"I told her that I respected Mr. Harmon and was going to marry him."

"Whether or not he let you star in *Tabu?*"

"I did what I could to put her mind at ease."

"You filled her full of baloney. Was she drugged, or something?"

"I wouldn't know," the Gardenia said. "I've never had a sedative myself. Or any of those pills to give me energy. I'm like a cat, I guess. I can go to sleep whenever there's nothing else to do and wake up feeling fine."

"You can take care of yourself, all right."

"Who else? But I didn't deceive Miss Hall. I've no intention of giving up Mr. Harmon's name and position, or the millions. I know the value of such things, and how few girls get them. That I told Miss Hall quite honestly."

"She didn't argue?"

"No."

"She was all in. That's the size of it. Too sick to fight back."

"I offered to see her home, but she didn't want that. She thought Mr. Reynolds might be there, most likely, or get in touch with her. She was almost like a woman walking in her sleep. But Dr. Harms and his nurse were at another table. They saw her go and must have thought it was all right. For her to be alone, I mean."

The Gardenia looked appealingly at Finke, her dark eyes moist, exactly as they were in the closeup he had seen that afternoon.

"I'm sorry for Shirley," she said.

He looked at her noncommittally. "I suppose you are, at that," he said.

Suddenly she seemed to shed ten of her twenty-odd years, just as he had seen her do as Mumu. She touched his hand, let her fingers rest there and said, "I wish you'd help me, Senor Finke. There are only you and Emile who ever speak honestly with me. I've been listening to men who want to be my agents, to those who want me to sign contracts, to Mr. Harmon who wants me to be nothing at all but what he calls a 'dutiful' wife."

"You want to know the score?" Finke asked.

"Sí, Señor," she said.

"You mentioned Emile. He's the one to tell you how the Manellos and the Sitchevs play for keeps. I could tell you some of it, but I've got my angle, as you have, and all the others concerned."

"What is your angle, Mr. Finke?"

"I'm supposed to protect my client."

"Mr. Reynolds, you mean?"

"He's only a property. I mean Miss Mesker—and, most likely, before the evening is out, your beloved Mr. Harmon."

"Don't be unkind," she said, and turned away. "I . . ."

"Go on. Say it. You *love* Mr. Harmon."

She turned on Finke defiantly. "I love myself," she said.

They were silenced by the sound of footsteps coming their way, not stealthily, but firm, as if whoever was approaching wanted to attract their attention tactfully. It was Enrico. Under no matter what stress, he never forgot his manners. He bowed first to the *señorita*, then to Finke, begged their pardon for the interruption, then told Finke, in the Gardenia's hearing, that Mr. Harmon would soon be at home.

That puzzled Finke, who forsook Mexican politeness in the interest of directness. "I didn't see his headlights or hear him drive in. Did he phone? Maybe to ask you to fix his fender?"

Emile spoke softly, and impersonally. "He hasn't phoned or driven in. He's parked the limousine on Concord Drive, near Crescent, and started toward the vacant back lot and the little back gate."

Instantly Finke was alert. "The hell you say." He made a gesture to the Gardenia. "Excuse me!" he said. No man with millions, presumably unarmed, was going to walk alone in that deserted area, for no matter what purpose, while Finke was carrying around in his head an undelivered death threat intended for him.

The Gardenia, who as suddenly had sensed that she could include the obsequious Enrico in the category of men she could confide in, looked at the mechanic for guidance.

"Am I being spied on as crudely as that?"

"I think not, Señorita," he said. "If you'll pardon the suggestion, why don't you go to your room and wait? Mr. Finke will talk with you later, and answer your questions, I've no doubt."

The Gardenia touched his hand, which he turned palm downward because of the roughness of the calluses, and in her filmy robe moved effortlessly away. The moths stirred, the door latch clicked.

"A token," Enrico said to himself.

Mills Harmon entered the back gate, not stealthily, but as if he were trying to preserve his dignity and assuage his frantic jealousy with separate halves of a split personality. He saw, in plain sight, strolling back and forth in the moonlight, Finke Maguire.

"Good evening, sir," Finke said. "I'm sorry I was out when you called at my office."

"You've been waiting here for me?" the oil man asked, not quite able to adjust himself so quickly.

"I had a talk with Enrico, to pass the time. Van Vleeck had gone to bed. In fact, Enrico's about the only one who's neither asleep nor absent."

Harmon's face darkened almost resentfully at the mention of so many, sleeping.

"I've been looking for you at what I was informed are your usual haunts."

"You may have made the acquaintance of Lieutenant Marcus, then," Finke said. "Lieutenant Marcus, of the L.A. Homicide Squad. He's been looking for me, too."

The oil tycoon was not much interested in anything that might interfere with his pressing affairs.

"I trust you're not involved in homicide investigations. What I wished to consult you about will take your full time and attention," Harmon said.

"It may not have occurred to you that I might have other business on hand?"

"Frankly, it had not," said Harmon. He realized that he was getting off to a bad start, and checked himself. "Bear with me, Mr. Maguire," he said, in the tone he reserved for delicate situations. "I've had too much on my mind."

Finke was breathing more freely by the second. Nothing was clearer than that the multimillionaire, if he had been informed that Finke had intercepted one of his telephone calls, did not attach too much importance to the fact. He wanted to be sure of a few more basic premises before he risked showing his hand. "Your man called me several times from five o'clock on. He's a bit eccentric, as you know, and wouldn't leave his name or number . . ."

"Van Vleeck? He phoned you? What on earth for?" asked Harmon.

Finke shrugged. "Probably nothing important. Someone's been tampering with his plants, perhaps. Or plagiarizing the articles he published in foreign magazines."

"In that case, he would ask my advice," Harmon said. "Please, Mr. Maguire. What I wish to talk with you about is more imperative."

"A matter of life and death, I believe you told Miss Cougar, my assistant."

They had been walking back and forth in the bottom of the garden, stepping up the pace as the talk proceeded and they seemed to drift farther apart.

"Maybe you're tired. We can go to the patio and sit down," Finke suggested.

Mills Harmon stiffened. Finke had touched on a sensitive spot. "I am not in my dotage," the millionaire said, icily. "I rise at seven every morning and practice tap dancing, sir."

"All right. Let's dance," said Finke. "Or would you like to hear what I've got to say? Then you can tell me what you have to say."

"I had supposed we'd proceed in the reverse order, Mr. Maguire. I'm not retaining you to listen to your problems, but to obtain your services in solving mine."

"Our problems are interrelated, Mr. Harmon. A good man has been murdered, not a rich man, but an ordinary guy, who was drafted by his country."

"If that is true, it's an outrage, and concerns me as a citizen, no doubt."

"It concerns you as an individual, Mr. Harmon, because the same mob that killed him is out to get you."

Harmon had had time to size up Finke, to control his own emotions and show the sense and judgment which had put him where he was in practical affairs. "Explain," he said, and listened attentively, while the tree frogs piped and in the tallest bamboo two mocking birds vied with each other. The harassed oil man interrupted Finke's statement only once.

"God damn those foolish birds," he said.

"I haven't told your fiancée that she heads the murderer's list."

"I should hope not," Harmon said. He was calmer, more efficient, more impressive now.

"After all," Finke continued. "Barney Rice is dead. These people stop at nothing."

"You can't mean that anyone would kill Miss Noguera to force me to consent to let her act on the screen?" said Harmon. "I've not led a sheltered life. I'm aware that even wars have been fought over oil."

"The movies are big business, too."

"I can't believe . . ." Harmon gave up trying to define just what it was he couldn't believe, so Finke helped him out.

"You can't believe that any Dago racketeers think they can bluff you out and get away with it," Finke said.

Harmon drew himself up. "And what's wrong with that?"

Finke had no comment, but he liked Harmon better.

"Furthermore," said Harmon. "They could not coerce Miss Noguera. She's able to act like a" (his face showed real pain) "a Mumu, when she sees fit."

"Would she risk having you bumped off, just for that?"

"Do you think I'd ask her not to? Because of a threat?"

"Why, no," Finke said. "What I'm thinking is that, whatever it is you want, or don't want, I can't take you on as a client."

And why not?"

"I have a client. Miss Mesker."

Harmon started to swell, puff and growl.

"You've got Miss Mesker all wrong," Finke told him. "If Miss Noguera signs up with Sitchev, and Shirley Hall is eased out, Miss Mesker, my client, is ruined."

"I don't think that actor, Reynolds, would do a dirty trick like that," Harmon said. "Unless . . ."

"Unless he falls in love with Miss Noguera?" suggested Finke.

Harmon started shaking, as if he had the ague. He was suffering, all right. "Unless *she* falls for *him*," he said.

"You think those wise guys are counting on that? Because you're an old man and she's young?"

Mills Harmon had plenty of stamina, but not quite enough. He might have gone into a fit had not Enrico reappeared, his face so grave that both Finke's and Harmon's emotions were short-circuited for the time. The mechanic had in his hand a copy of the Los Angeles *Examiner*, an extra, fresh off the press, on the front page of which was a deep two-column cut of Shirley Hall beneath an eight-column banner headline which read:

JEALOUS ACTRESS SLAIN
AFTER LOVE SHOOTING FAILS
Screen Test of Meteoric Mexican Starlet
Who Spurns Septuagenarian's Millions
Brings Bloodshed in Its Wake

Finke handed the paper over to Harmon, gave him time to pull himself together, and said, "You didn't get around to telling me what you were going to retain me for, but if you still want to, you're on," Finke said. "There's no conflict of interests now."

11

Top Cop on the Totem

A BLACK AND WHITE POLICE CAR, harlequin symbol of the anti-under-world, streaked along Sunset Boulevard, as in response to Homer Evans' summons, transmitted by the doorman, Hinckley, Captain Strongfort of the Beverly Hills police crossed out of his luxurious residential territory into the "Strip." The Strip, a chunk of Los Angeles County, featured offices where only big deals were consummated, clubs where celebrities might enjoy relative privacy because guests were admitted only by appointment; apartment hotels for married bachelors and non-housekeeping concubines, and the only skyscraper in the vicinity, the Forty-Niners Towers. With Captain Strongfort was the County medical examiner, Dr. Hank Bibesco. Until the genial doctor had gone into politics, he had used the name "Henry." For purposes of getting himself elected, a moniker like "Hank" brought him more County votes than a more formal designation.

Dr. Bibesco was a graduate of the Golden Rule Academy of Medicine of nearby Oklahoma, where the courses, thirty years back, consisted mostly of homework in which Hank had been assisted, about ninety-five percent, by his wife, a former schoolmarm. Once he had got his degree, Hank had done passably well for himself and his patients. He knew that the odds against anybody's dying of illness in California were negligible, if sunstroke were avoided, so he prescribed aspirin, in various guises, for everything that calomel did not cure. All surgical cases he passed over to the Balm of Gilead Hospital in L.A. unless the patient would be more con-tent among his co-religionists at the Sacred Heart. The closer any given patient, or his loved ones, stuck to the Party ticket, the less the strain on the family budget under the heading of "Medical Care." Hank was, in fact, the most valuable member of the County's political team, so that both the sheriff, and the county attorney deferred to him. As a matter of fact, in the last election, when the attention of the citizens had been focused on the Truman-Dewey contest, Los Angeles county had had no candidate for coroner and Hank Bibesco had been deputized to act as such, in addition to his duties as medical examiner, and thus be entitled to draw double pay.

It was extraordinary how quickly two such shrewd judges of human nature sized each other up and became firm allies as when Homer Evans and Dr. Hank Bibesco met, in the lobby of the Forty-Niners Towers, to which the shadow and hush of tragic death had spread from the lugubrious back yard. There, where the body of Shirley Hall, beloved and admired by millions while animate, lay cool but not cold, as yet, a truly sad vigil was kept. Bob Reynolds stood silently, murmuring inaudible protests to himself. He was more bewildered, cold sober on account of the shock, than ever he had been in his cups. At such moments, the mind of a man as direct and simple as Bob's gropes for psychic closets in which to hide in the dark. He wished with all his might that he were drunk again.

It is almost too painful to write of the misery endured by Mel-issa, the maid. Such a woman, with integrity, loyalty and force of character too great for a humble station, needs an idol on which to lavish her worthy attributes which otherwise are useless to her-self, ill-favored and unpliable as she is. Gone now was her ban-tam-like fury at the sight of Bob Reynolds, and washed out of him was the scorn and enmity he had felt for Melissa. They might have joined hands as they stood, four feet apart, looking down at Shirley's body, which was face to the earth. The green handbag which Evans had carefully replaced where it had lain, beyond the outstretched left arm and pale hand, was still expressive, as the hand of a dancer. Its gesture said farewell. Exit. Curtain. The cur-tain that, once lowered, does not rise again.

As the others were bowed down by weight of subjective woe or were aghast, like Moscone and Hinckley, with a half-guilty feeling of duty done, but not done well enough, Homer became objectivity itself. And the relief he felt when he saw, with Captain Strongfort whom he had already discounted as an amiable C-minus on the Binet scale, Hank Bibesco, most certainly an A-plus, though uninstructed, made Homer feel that luck was with him. Like the sound American philosopher, Lefty Gomez, Homer experienced many occasions on which he would "rather be lucky than right." "*Mieux la chance que l'adresse*" is the way the French have translated the proverb.

Evans was the only one present who realized quite what was at stake, especially for Finke Maguire, so he acted with dispatch but no haste.

"Gentlemen," Homer said, in the lobby, before they had descended to the scene of the demise, if not the crime, "this is a case in which the time of death can be fixed without technical elaboration."

"Now that's a break," said Hank Bibesco, and Captain Strongfort frowned and nodded.

"On the other hand . . ." Homer began.

"Uh, uh," grunted Hank, in anticipation of the catch.

"On the other hand," Homer continued, "the cause of death, unless I am mistaken, will be so difficult to establish that it is not likely that any doctor, however expert, will care to contradict whatever Dr. Bibesco decides is—shall we say—expedient to assume for the present. I'm sure you'll agree that here in Greater Los Angeles, where there is such an unavoidable conflict of police authority, we must make it easy for ourselves."

"You mean that you'll co-operate?" Hank Bibesco asked. "I don't travel much, Mr. Evans, but I've heard about your famous cases, way back in the County seat."

"I'll do what I can, in the interest of Mr. Finke Maguire. Finke holds, by the way, a County license. In fact, this whole investigation should be, primarily, a County affair."

"You can say that again," said Dr. Bibesco. Then he turned tact-fully to Captain Strongfort. "Ole, here, will play ball with us, and we'll see that he gets honorable mention."

"If I don't get blackballed by the L.A. bunch," the Captain said.

What the County medical examiner said about the L.A. city bunch might endanger the passage of this narrative, in printed form, through the mails. And he mentioned specifically Lieuten-ant Marcus of the Homicide Squad.

"May I make a suggestion?" Homer asked, of Hank Bibesco.

"If you don't make a flock of 'em, we're sunk, Professor," the medical examiner said modestly.

Homer smiled. "We'll get along fine," he said. "Now I'm won-dering if it would be possible, since you, Doctor, are here on the ground, for you to get yourself deputized by the sheriff to act in his behalf, with his full authority behind you, in case Lieutenant Marcus should wish to take over. I've never met Lieutenant Marcus, but any officer who will interrupt the performance of the Berlioz Requiem to find a couple of completely innocent suspects, should not be encouraged, in my opinion."

"Not so's you'd notice it," Hank Bibesco said. He turned to Hinckley and thumbed toward the phone. "Get me Sheriff Mull," he said, and a few moments later, when the sleepy voice of the Sheriff came over the wire, Bibesco spoke and they conversed as follows:

"Ike?"

"Hank. What is it?"

"I want you to deputize me. See? Make it official. You'd better get yourself laid up with arthritis. Take a fortnight off . . ." The doctor glanced at Homer. "Long enough?" he whispered. "A week'll be plenty," Homer assured Hank, also *sotto voce*. Hank continued on the phone. "Oke, Ike. From this minute on, till further notice, you're on sick leave, with full pay and medical allowance, and *I'm* Acting Sheriff."

"Mutually agreed," grunted Ike, and Hank hung up. "Now we might as well view the remains," he said.

"One more detail. The newspapermen. I'd rather they'd get the story from me, and E.P.U. publicity, than from Lieutenant Marcus, or even such an outstanding genius as Chief Pinky Johnstone, who polices the lot."

So Homer got on the phone and caught Charley Morgan, of the *Examiner*, just before press time, for the city edition, gave Morgan the facts and the leads to sources of information, then sighed with relief.

"Now Lieutenant Marcus will be able to get a full account from his breakfast-table paper," Evans said, smiling.

Hank Bibesco grinned and slapped his thigh. "Yes-sir-ee, Professor! Now maybe we can get a look at the body."

Regretfully Hinckley resumed his post at the reception desk, while Homer led the officers downstairs. On their way, Evans said, "Miss Hall's heart stopped beating . . ."

"Ah. Good old coronary thrombosis, for the cause. Is that what you're leading up to, Mr. Evans?"

"When you make a statement, Doctor, say that in the interest of justice, no further details can be disclosed until an autopsy has been performed by the foremost experts in this country, at the Beverly Hills Municipal Hospital, under the direction of Dr. Hamilton."

"Dr. Hamilton is tops, but he's on the staff of the Balm of Gilead Hospital," agreed Hank.

"Exactly. But that fine hospital is in the city of L.A. and we don't want any question to arise as to who has custody of the body. Dr. Hamilton and his colleagues, in this instance, will gladly come to Beverly Hills. This is an extraordinary case, from the medical standpoint. It will establish a world-recognized precedent."

"Now what is your private opinion, so I won't pull any boners?" Hank asked.

"There are no signs of struggle, no marks of violence. The victim was agitated, but not frightened, and under the influence of one of the drugs developed by the Nazi doctors to keep troops in action beyond their normal powers of endurance. Little it mattered to Herr Hitler that after the battle had been won, nine-tenths of the victors died. Miracles of supermanhood were achieved, in the German Army, and later, by the Japanese, by administration of a combination sedative, which kept the mind serene, and stimulant which kept the flesh in motion."

"I fought the war in Texas, damn it," said Hank. "There everybody was half-dopey, anyway. Hop or no hop."

The oddly assorted trio stepped through the back doorway into the silvery night, and their casual manner slipped from them as they approached the dead girl, in her appalling loveliness, and the two chief mourners of the anonymous millions who had adored Shirley Hall.

"Some bastard'll be sorry for this while he's waiting for the sniff of gas in the chamber," growled Hank Bibesco, and for once he was not thinking about votes.

A sob from Bob Reynolds was the only audible comment and Melissa from Yorkshire stepped toward him and rested her head on his chest.

"Any idea who did it?" asked Captain Strongfort, of all and sundry. Only Evans replied.

"Someone who was in this building," Homer said. He shrugged ruefully, and Dr. Bibesco caught on, with his usual aptitude.

"Maybe one hundred and fifty suspects, counting tenants and help?" he drawled.

"Plus a number we may designate by 'X', who may have passed in and out of this doorway while Moscone was fetching from the neighborhood liquor store a bottle of Courvoisier."

"Now what the heck is Coor-vwo-zee-ay?"

"The brandy of Napoleon. Not cognac," Homer said.

"I like drugstore whiskey, myself," Hank said. "I ought to. I made quite a pile, in prohibition days, prescribing it."

Melissa, by that time, had recovered sufficiently from shock to assert herself in her dead mistress's behalf.

"You blighters," she hissed. "Are you going to stand there gabbing all night while my poor lamb is left lying in the cold?"

"It's better—for her sake—if we expect to catch her murderer, to leave her there a while," Homer said. He nodded to Captain

Strongfort, who stepped to the house telephone inside the door-way. He got Dr. Hamilton on the line. Homer exchanged a few words with the famous surgeon, toxicologist and diagnostician who had failed in the case of Barney Rice. The phone was hardly settled back on its cradle before the sound of sirens, from the direction of the front doorway, did violence to the night, now darker because of the waning moon and elongated shadows.

The din subsided and was followed by the sound of windows opening and alarmed occupants of the Towers talking back and forth to ascertain, first, if there was a fire, and, secondly, to ask what, then, was the matter.

Homer looked at Hank Bibesco and sighed. "Unless I'm mis-taken, we're about to be honored by a call from Lieutenant Marcus. Remember, Doctor, that you're Sheriff, and top man on this totem pole of police authority."

"I won't forget. He won't get away with a thing," the doctor said, and thumbed toward Shirley's lifeless figure.

"Be sure he doesn't try to make any arrests. My colleague, the detective actively in charge of this investigation, Mr. Finke Maguire, may be here any moment and the L.A. law may wish to cramp his style—in short, to incarcerate him."

"Nobody gets incarcerated unless you say the word, or my name's not Hank Bibesco," declared the medical examiner, coro-ner and acting sheriff of Los Angeles County.

The elevator descended and a plainclothes man, neatly dressed if a bit on the natty side for a Homicide officer, stepped out, fol-lowed by a smaller and more dapper man whom Homer recognized at once as the well-known producer and discoverer of screen stars, Laslo Sitchev.

"Good evening, Mr. Sitchev," Homer said, extending his hand to the little Hungarian. Then turning to the other, he offered his hand in turn, saying, "Lieutenant Marcus, I presume."

"Where's this Finke Maguire?" asked Marcus, without bother-ing to shake hands. "I want him, and I want him quick."

"He's not here," Evans said.

"And furthermore," broke in Hank Bibesco. "If he were, and you wanted to take him along, it would be no go. I'm Acting Sheriff, and this is County territory, in case you don't know. If anybody's pinched, it might be you, for creating a public nuisance with your bloody sirens and waking honest people from their beds."

"Honest people? On the Strip? Don't make me laugh. My lip's cracked," Marcus said, and added, "Where's the body?"

"It's just where it fell, and there it stays till the medical examiner—that's me, Lieutenant—gives directions for it to be moved."

"So that's the way it is," said the Lieutenant. He might have been mad as a hornet, but he kept himself in admirable control. He didn't even raise his voice. He glanced at Sitchev, shrugged his shoulders, smiled, and said, "Let's go, Mr. Fixit."

Homer interposed suavely. "We've no objections if you wish to look at the body, Lieutenant."

Marcus turned to Captain Strongfort, who was having one of the worst moments of his uneventful career. The Captain had always believed that the less eventful a police career was, the better for all concerned. And now he was caught in the middle of a situation that had all possibilities of disaster. "Who is this bird?" Marcus asked the Captain, indicating Evans.

"You don't know?" asked Sitchev, who was playing up to Homer, in his diplomatic way. Whoever won out in this pickle, the Hungarian did not want to find himself on the opposing side or sides.

"*Should* I know him?" inquired Lieutenant Marcus, more mildly.

"He's Homer Evans, famous criminologist."

"Representing Mr. Finke Maguire," Evans said, in a self-deprecatory way.

"Go ahead. Represent," said Marcus. "I've got lots to do." And again he said to Sitchev, "Shall we amble along?"

"If I were you, Mr. Sitchev, I'd stick around here," Evans said. "There are things I crave to know."

"With your permission," Sitchev said, as much to Marcus as to Evans.

Marcus made an almost merry gesture. "Fine. Stay with the famous criminologist, Shorty. Ta ta!" Then, to Evans: "And ta ta to you, too, sir."

Before he ascended in the elevator, the Lieutenant brushed aside the weeping Melissa cavalierly, stepped out into the yard, looked down at Shirley's body, stared separately at the green handbag, shrugged, glanced contemptuously at Hank Bibesco, who had followed him to make sure that he disarranged no evidence, and departed.

Hank looked uneasily at Evans, who seemed pleased.

"He was too willing to beat it," Hank said. "He's got something up his sleeve." Hank turned on Sitchev. "Any ideas about his intentions, I mean?"

Sitchev shrugged in a manner that would have made Emile or Enrico seem crude. "*I* should know about a cop's intentions!" he said. "I couldn't even swear to my own. Why am I *here?* Because Shirley was my discovery. To direct a girl with talent like hers is to love her. She was to be the star of my next picture. She came to me, like I was her father, for advice. God can strike me dead beside her, if I wouldn't have died in her place."

Melissa's face had been darkening and tightening.

"You little faker!" she said in a terrible undertone. "You'd drag her from a sickbed to cut down a dollar on your budget. You'd work her day and half the night till she was limp. You'd make her go through the same foolish sequence a dozen times, so you could put your arms around her."

Sitchev shrugged, as if appealing to the others to be indulgent toward the desolate old woman. "Nobody knows what we producers go through," he said. "I was happier as a boy in the green pastures of Hungary, mit goats."

"You were born in Lompoc, California," screamed Melissa. "Goats, my eye. You were nothing but a bellhop in the Paramount Hotel."

"Is this a democracy?" asked Sitchev, shrugging again. "Shame on you, that we should bicker in the presence of the grim ripper. . . . *Who* killed her, Mr. Evans, by the way?"

"We shall come to that in due time," Homer said.

He left Captain Strongfort and Melissa with the crew of photo-graphers, fingerprint specialists and technicians who had been assembled at Beverly Hills headquarters and tardily arrived. Once the routine work was done, the body would be removed to the Beverly Hills Hospital. The Acting Sheriff went with Evans and the little Hungarian producer to the seventeenth floor where, in Shirley's "living room," they went over, name by name, the list of occupants of the suites and rooms of the Forty-Niners Towers. Bob Reynolds, still dazed, had trailed along. Hinckley was stationed in the lobby to keep out intruders and to hold himself available to answer questions. Moscone, as soon as he was relieved by the other guard, joined Homer aloft.

If one of the possible suspects, among the residents, held Evans' attention more than another, he gave no sign until he found the name of Mrs. Alma Shroeder, of Apartment 16-A.

"Ah! Mrs. Shroeder, who lives directly below. I'd like to have a chat with her. I've had some dealings before in her shop, Art for Art's Sake, on Beverly Drive." Homer turned casually to Moscone. "It wasn't Mrs. Shroeder who ordered the Courvoisier, by any chance?" he asked.

"No, sir. It was the man who works in her store, has a room in her apartment, and who, folks say, was at one time her husband, although he doesn't act like anybody's husband to me."

"You mean Mr. De Witt, who designs and dyes batiks?" asked Homer.

Moscone nodded as if he would not put that beyond the man in question.

"So Mr. De Witt is an amateur of Napoleon brandy, to the ex-tent that he calls for it at one o'clock or later in the morning," Evans said.

"He never ordered Coor-vwa-zee-aye before. Mr. De Witt drinks rum. Bacardi—the Cuban, not the Puerto Rican. And bottled beer named Heiniken's, made in the East Indies."

"I begin to see light," said Evans, with a smile of satisfaction.

"I'm glad somebody does," the Acting Sheriff said, uneasily.

Evans nodded understandingly. "Moscone! Why don't you go back to Escobar's for a bottle of straight Kentucky bourbon—I.W. Harper or Old Ripey will do—and ask him if, in the interest of the public safety, he could lend me his current account book, the volume in which the purchases in the name of Schroeder and/or De Witt are listed."

"There won't be any under De Witt. That monkey never paid for a bottle of White Rock or even Coca-Cola," Moscone said.

"You see? Progress!" said Evans to the sheriff, pleased, almost triumphant, as if that explained a lot.

"Please?" asked Laslo Sitchev, who was deeper in the fog than any of the others.

Evans rose. "Mr. Sitchev," he said, sympathetically, "if you follow this investigation, you'll be astonished, most likely, by certain dissimilarities you may observe between the sound methods of making motion pictures, and the way we proceed in modern detective work. Both are indispensable media, still in their infancy. In your industry, you perfect your script, assemble your cast, approve sets and costumes, and photograph your sequences, not in order, but by no means haphazardly, to achieve a result which exists only in your own creative imagination, until the rushes of each day are sorted, cut and pieced together, with appropriate dissolves and fadeouts. We detectives reverse the process. Our illusory film is finished and complete when we begin. Incident by incident, character by character, scene by scene, we take it apart and restore clever artifice to its elements of stark reality."

Homer indicated that Hank Bibesco was to join him. He still had the list of tenants in his hand. As soon as they were alone, on the sixteenth floor, Evans touched with his forefinger another name listed under Apartment 16-A. The Acting Sheriff blinked and looked again to be sure.

"To these dimming old eyes it looks like Lukie Kahler," Hank said.

"A woman's name," mused Homer. "By profession a nurse," he added. "By coincidence, possibly, the nurse employed by Dr.

Hershel Harms, who, in turn, is the psychiatrist under whose treatment the late Shirley Hall was being 'cured' of jealousy."

"Some cure! She tried to take a pot shot at her man this afternoon. One of her last acts," Hank said.

It had been the advance proofs of the Los Angeles newspapers, delivered according to routine at the police department in advance of publication, which had sent Lieutenant Marcus to the E.P.U. lot and thence to the Forty-Niners Towers. The first city edition, delivered to Enrico, who hastened to show it to Finke, cut short abruptly the consultation in progress between Finke and Mills Harmon. Finke urged the multimillionaire, now his client, to confirm the fact in writing, which was hastily accomplished. In parting Finke implored the oil tycoon not to arouse Señorita Noguera until she put in an appearance in the morning, if she waited that long, and in any case to break the news to her gently. He asked Harmon also, under the circumstances, not to upbraid or even question the Dutchman about his attempts to contact Finke.

"I'll be back the moment I can. Meanwhile, if Lieutenant Marcus comes nosing around, tell him I'm still at that wake in San Francisco."

So saying, Finke was on his way, in the Harmon limousine with the dented right fender. There was no time to waste in waiting for a taxi.

12

If a Body Meet a Body

THE BIG BLACK LIMOUSINE came to an abrupt stop in front of the Forty-Niners Towers, taking its place in a motley line of cars that were parked there in collective violation of the No-Parking-at-Any-Time sign. First was the Beverly Hills police runabout, then the county medical examiner's vehicle with its doctor's license number. Behind it was a photographers' car and two press cars which also were loaded with jutting paraphernalia.

Finke barged into the lobby, all ready to take a swing at Lieutenant Marcus, if the latter looked at him cross-eyed. Instead he found no signs of excitement or disorder. Hinckley, at the desk, bowed and smiled.

"We've been expecting you, Mr. Maguire. Go right upstairs."

"Who's been expecting me?" demanded Finke.

"Mr. Evans."

Finke recoiled as if he had been doused with cold apple sauce. "You said 'Evans'?"

"Homer Evans. He's acting in your behalf," Hinckley said, unable to understand why Finke was so astonished and seemingly ready to burst.

As quickly as he had lost his temper, Finke got hold of himself, more resigned than deflated. "I might have known," he said. "I suppose he landed in a giro right here on the front sidewalk, in time to see it happen. Or did the murderer have to wait a while?"

"Mr. Evans was not present when the murder was committed," Hinckley said.

"He's slipping, the son-of-a-bitch," muttered Finke.

"Oh, no, sir," Hinckley assured him. "He was here within a few minutes of the time of death . . . to represent you, sir."

"Do you think I should disturb him? Now he's getting on so well? You didn't tell me if he'd solved the crime," Finke said.

"Not yet, sir. But according to the Sheriff, he's seen some light."

That was too much for Finke. He knew that when Evans saw light, generally a comet landed squarely in somebody's lap.

"Could a body see a body?" Finke asked.

"If you don't mind my suggestion . . . Mr. Evans hoped you'd join him directly, upstairs. He's not in the late Miss Hall's apartment."

"He wouldn't be. That would be too simple," said Finke. "Can you direct me to him or shall I try the apartments, in order?"

"Mr. Evans is in 16-A. If you care to take the elevator, Mr. Maguire."

"No, thanks, I always walk," said Finke, but he did not suit his action to the words. He got in, jammed down the button and ascended. He swore to himself all the way to the eighth, and from there up to the sixteenth felt an immense flow of relief. Again Homer had saved him from his own limitations. But where, Finke asked himself, was that fat-head, Lieutenant Marcus, who had twice as many reasons for running him in as Finke could offer in the negative? He recalled that years ago, under California law, a roughneck had been acquitted because the statutes said nowhere, specifically, that a white man could not kill a Chinaman. Most likely there was no law, either, against furnishing apes with automatic pistols. The offense Finke had committed, which in his own mind he could not justify, namely, having filched Mills Harmon's telephone call and failed to tell the old man he was under a threat of death, as was also his beautiful fiancée, no longer was valid. Finke had made a clean breast of it to Harmon, and had in his pocket the millionaire's written endorsement of their professional relationship. He could not wait, once he had seen and thanked Evans, to find Lieutenant Marcus and have a showdown. It seemed to him as if he had been a fugitive for ages, when actually only fifteen hours

had passed since he had climbed the E.P.U. fence. The first murder victim was still in that shabby Santa Monica graveyard,
unavenged, and the second—come to think of it—where the hell
was she? The *Examiner* had said something about the Towers back-
yard, and nothing of the upper floors of the skyscraper hotel.

The luxurious hallway of the sixteenth floor was quiet and deserted. Finke found the door marked 16-A, and touched the button. Faint gongs inside sounded Do Mi Do. The door opened without fuss or fury, and before him, in a becoming negligee, with her
head wrapped in a Javanese turban, was the woman he had seen
with the nance and Big Lukie at the Derby.

"I'm Mrs. Shroeder, Mr. Maguire. Won't you come in?" she
asked, hospitably and not at all worried, so it appeared.

She led the way into the living room, which because of its
exotic appointments brought back to Finke that weird sensation
of walking again in his Oriental dream. And still in dream sensation he saw Homer Evans, sartorially elegant and spiritually serene, rise and offer his hand. Finke caught on that, although there
were explanations forthcoming, Homer thought it better that they
should wait.

"I see Alma . . . Mrs. Shroeder, has introduced herself," Homer
said, as if it were three o'clock in the afternoon, not three in the
morning, and tea, not blood—or poison—had been dispensed. Well,
by God, Finke said to himself. If these cookies can play a scene
this low, so can I. So he tried not to bat an eyelash when Homer
introduced him to Dr. Henry Bibesco, sheriff, coroner and medical examiner of Los Angeles County; and Mr. Boris De Witt, foremost American exponent of the ancient art of batik, and connoisseur of orfevrerie, laquerage and both wet- and dry-point engravings.

De Witt, tall and somewhat limber, in his Persian lounging robe,
rose in a desultory way, trying to bear up, though not amused.

"Your erudite pal lays it on rather thickly, what?" he remarked
listlessly to Finke, although he was awake enough to smile rather
appreciatively into Finke's Irish blue eyes.

Finke had a close call with apoplexy, first, because he had heard
that Voice twice before, and, secondly, because as this fantastic

realization swept over his brain with an atomic flash, another counter-flash counteracted his impulse. Evans' voice from way back seemed to be repeating, urgently: "Steady, my friend. *Never volunteer information!*"

Afterward Finke let himself believe that he was getting on, that Homer's prize instruction had not been wasted. He swallowed hard, realizing with the utmost dismay that his hesitant manner was being interpreted by De Witt in a fatuous way, and merely acknowledged the introduction. But simultaneously he was aware that had he given Homer Evans written notice two weeks in advance, Homer would not be less certain that Finke had something about De Witt to disclose in private and that, meanwhile, the tall well-house-gowned slender young esthete was not to escape surveillance.

Homer, of course, continued his disarming monologue most effectively, to cover Finke's consternation. Evans turned to Mrs. Shroeder, smiled and said, "Mr. Maguire is recently from France, and would relish a long cool glass of Courvoisier and soda. I'm sure you must have that dependable brandy on hand."

Instead of waiting for an answer, Homer, as if to save the hostess too much exertion in their behalf, strolled over to the teakwood liquor cabinet, and, opening the precious hand-carved door, glanced inside. There, in its original wrapping, untouched and undisturbed, was a fifth of the brandy of Napoleon, aged twenty years.

"Mind if I open it?" Homer asked. Finke was about to offer to pull the cork, when the slight lift of Homer's expressive right eyebrow again prompted him to subside.

"Now this Coor-vwa-zee-aye I got to try myself," said Dr. Hank Bibesco, as Evans stepped into the kitchenette with the bottle in his hand.

Mrs. Shroeder, evidently puzzled by the prolongation of the call at such an unearthly hour, was careful not to fail in courtesy. De Witt, on the other hand, was definitely fed up, if not sleepy. Finke decided that the connoisseur of all those things Homer had mentioned was either an utter idiot or the best actor in Southern California. What was Evans driving at? Finke could see that the County

Sheriff was also itching for action, and had been getting only talk, and talk so far over his head that he was not even reaching for it. The situation was not clarified when Homer returned to the living room, with two tall highballs in hand, gave Finke one and the Sheriff the other. For Finke, sipping promptly to assuage his thirst, tried not to give the show away by a change of expression. His drink contained not a drop of Courvoisier. Unless he had gone daft, it consisted of St. Charles brandy, from Central California, and White Rock from . . . who cared?

The Sheriff, mesmerized by his own anticipations, carried on enthusiastically, smacking his lips and clucking praises.

As soon as the drinks were finished, Homer put an end to the interview with his usual relentless ease. Finke knew, while the Sheriff did not, that Homer had accomplished exactly what he wanted. Lukie Kahler had not been in her room, because Homer absent-mindedly opened the wrong door, on the way out, and the nurse's spacious double bedroom was unoccupied.

As soon as they were safely beyond earshot in the corridor, Homer said, "It would be indelicate for us to inquire after Fräulein Kahler at Dr. Harms's hotel. Don't you think so, Hank? We can chat with both of them, together or separately, tomorrow."

"I happen to know that this Lukie Kahler doesn't go for Dr. Harms," Finke said.

Evans smiled. "Precisely," he agreed. "That makes it the more significant that, on occasion, they pass a night together, sometimes here, sometimes there."

"They ate dinner together, at the Tropics, when Shirley was there with Señorita Noguera," Finke said.

Instantly Homer was all attention. "Fräulein Kahler saw Shirley leave the Tropics or wherever she was to come home here to the Towers?" he asked.

"Surest thing you know," said Finke, and although he knew he was being bolstered in his morale, he could not help feeling better when Evans gestured toward him in a congratulatory way.

"You see, Hank," Homer said to the bewildered Sheriff, who still was trying to find something unusual in the after-taste of

Courvoisier. "While we've been idling at the scene of the demise, Maguire has revealed what may prove the key to the situation. I've been troubled because of the hiatus between the hour Shirley left Dr. Harms at his office and the time of her arrival at the front entrance of the Towers, as noted by the reliable Hinckley. Now, thanks to Finke, we are aware that the doctor had a precise idea as to when his patient would get home, and send Melissa to the drug store for her medicine."

Homer paused, for Hank to catch up, then said, "And, as medical examiner, Hank, don't forget to point out to Dr. Hamilton that while he will find ample traces in the body of pheno-indizene-dexadrol, the small phial of the same sedative-stimulant which the good Melissa obtained at the Cedars Pharmacy, while her mistress was dying, is unopened. That is another most important point."

"You'd better tell Doc Hamilton yourself. He's a smart man. He'll know that I wouldn't recognize pheno-indo what-you-may-call-it from Murphy's five-dollar corned beef and cabbage in the stomach of no corpse. And how you did it, without looking into anything but her handbag, beats me."

"You'll get used to Mr. Evans and his methods, but don't think he's kidding. Not ever," Finke said to the Sheriff, as if they were brothers both over and under the skin. "I'll bet anybody whatever odds they name that the departed will be so full of pheno-whoozit that the chow mein she had at the Tropics will be practically dissolved. Still, you might tell Dr. Hamilton that she did have chow mein, with soya sauce, and a frozen Daiquiri."

"Indeed! That would accelerate rigor mortis . . . the Daiquiri, I mean," Homer said. "I was a bit puzzled by that, too."

"Any time Hank and I can set you right, let us know," Finke said. "Now what's the play?"

"Let's leave the technicians to their technical work, and Laslo Sitchev and Bob Reynolds to comfort each other, and Melissa," Homer said. "If I did not misunderstand Emile, Harmon's Dutchman is a botanist. . . ."

"You can say that again. He grows things from the East Indies that would make your hair stand on end."

"From the East Indies? He grows things here, from there?"

"Meat-eating plants, bamboo that blossoms, trees that stink like bedbugs . . ." Finke began.

Homer interrupted him, looking as grave as ever Finke had seen him.

"Not upas trees!"

"I don't know what you call 'em, but he transplanted one tree tonight, long after dark—by moonlight."

"We must hurry. There's not a moment to lose. It's amazing how much you've uncovered. Is it possible that I shall, at last, see an upas tree?"

"Unless it's transplanted again, already," said Finke and they all three got into the elevator, albeit that it was somewhat small for three, and descended as fast as the machine would go, which, for none of them, seemed fast enough. In the lobby, Homer paused to urge Hinckley to have both exits guarded, and to ask Captain Strongfort to assign his best man to tail Boris De Witt, and on no account to lose him until further notice.

That started Finke boiling again, internally. It was not enough for the cerebral criminologist to beat them all to the corpse. He had, also, to hand Finke the Voice, on a platter. But the limousine's engine started so smoothly, and imparted such a sense of well-being to Finke, that he relaxed again, and grinned. What the hell was the use of palling around with a cerebral whiz, if he didn't come through?

They had hardly cleared the frontage of the Forty-Niners Towers before Homer pulled from somewhere, as a prestidigitator produces a rabbit from a silk hat, a wrapped unopened bottle of Courvoisier and, handing it to Hank Bibesco, said lightly, "You might keep this, Sheriff, as Exhibit 'A'. We'll drink it, after the trial, if there's no Armagnac."

What with daylight saving and "omnipollent nature's corrupted benefaction" who can say that, touched with Aurora's rosy fingers, the Omar Gardens in Beverly Hills were less enchanting than they had appeared in hours of full moonlight. As Harmon's dented limousine approached the patio gate, with Finke at the wheel, Evans in the front seat beside him, and the awe-struck Acting Sheriff of Los Angeles County resting on cushions to which the hindfaces of Midases and Croesuses of our criminally flamboyant and pacifically bankrupt twentieth century were wont to hide themselves from public view, birds who had been somnolent were emitting paeans to nothing in particular and insects who had been quiescent were foraging.

Moths gave way to butterflies, owls to jays and larks, June bugs to humming birds, mosquitoes to the busy bees. The native plants were symbolizing provincial satisfaction while the exotic imports were offering lush extravagance in lieu of proprietary privilege. Windows, dim to Lady Lune, flamed with the sheen of sun. Walls, blended in dimness, were pieder than pipers in pre-dawn. Contrast of chance democracy. Communism of spectral cacophony. Of the majority of tenants who were sleeping, little need be said. The members of the coterie, whose mutual bond is the thread of this story, will be reviewed in order.

The mechanic and philosopher, Enrico, was back at his post in the garage, taking a nap while seated on a running board. Mills Harmon was seated in a straight hard chair he had moved to a living-room window, through which he could see the wrought-iron gates of the patio. He had fought a hard fight with himself, and, having been accustomed through the years to discussing his important decisions after he had made them with subordinates, he was waiting with impatience that was almost painful to talk with Finke again. So when the millionaire saw the black car turn neatly into the area and come to a halt, he rose, walked briskly (considering his age) to the patio and addressed Finke as the latter was stepping from the driver's seat. That his private detective was accompanied by two other men did not escape Harmon's observant eye, but so compelling was his urge to talk with someone he felt sure would agree with him that the oil man found it convenient to ignore Evans and the Sheriff until after he had got his message off his chest.

Homer and the Sheriff made themselves tactfully unobtrusive.

"I've made up my mind," Harmon said to Finke.

You have?" said Finke to Harmon. "That's fine."

"I've reached a decision, and it's final," Harmon said.

"Good," said Finke.

"I'm not the man to fail to acknowledge a mistake."

"Well, all right, then." Finke was determined to act as straight man until he got the drift of what the talk was about.

"Mr. Maguire, I was wrong," Harmon said.

Finke's rejoinder was on the sympathetic side. "Who doesn't pull a Snodgrass now and then?"

"Snodgrass," the millionaire said, somewhat pedantically, "merely dropped a ball which he had, to all intents and purposes, in his hand. My conduct has been more like that of Fred Merkel, who, neglecting to touch second, was not eligible to proceed to third and home. In other words, Eulalia shall act for the screen."

Homer felt that Finke's wealthy new client would loosen up and be more explicit if he and the Sheriff withdrew, so he led Hank Bibesco toward the garage, where Enrico opened his eyes just in time to greet them.

"Could I trouble you to direct me to the greenhouses?" Homer asked.

"That way, Mr. Evans," Enrico said, indicating the area where the bamboo grove, the greenhouses and the flower beds were expressing what Grieg had summed up as "Morning Mood."

"And may I say how glad I am that you are honoring us with your presence?"

"What little I may contribute," Homer said, in plain sincerity, "will be less than I shall receive. I've never seen the *phyllostachys pubescens* actually in bloom. A plant of sturdier practical value and more fickle caprice does not exist on our planet, Don Enrico."

Enrico was touched and bowed. He had never even heard of *phyllostachys pubescens*, but he was sure it must be significant.

"This is the Acting Sheriff of your county," Homer said, introducing Hank Bibesco.

"I've been expecting Lieutenant Marcus, of the Homicide Squad," Enrico said. "To meet you instead, Señor, is a most welcome surprise."

"You don't have to take any guff from Marcus here. He's off his territory on the Strip," the Sheriff said.

"I shall refer him to you, Señor, without my compliments," said Enrico.

"Got anything against him? Almost everybody has."

"His manners . . . over the phone," Enrico said.

"He called, then?"

"He phoned," said Enrico. "He asked for Señor Maguire, who, I informed him, was absent; and Señorita Noguera, who, I said, could not be disturbed at such an hour."

As Homer, with the Sheriff trailing behind him, went on to the gardens, the dialogue between Finke and Mills Harmon progressed.

"I had to find a formula," Harmon said.

"You did?" asked Finke.

"There's always a middle ground."

"When a guy gets out on a limb," agreed Finke.

The millionaire looked at him sharply, because of the mixed metaphor, but he was not to be diverted from pursuit of his objective, with dignity.

"Eulalia has talent. I was taken by surprise in the projection room, and failed to adjust myself in time," Harmon continued.

"I shed a few tears, myself," admitted Finke. "But that's supposed to be good for you."

"I hadn't caught on how much acting meant to her."

"She knocked me for a row of brick privies, and I don't care who knows it."

"The hunger for self-expression . . ." continued Harmon. "That shouldn't be suppressed, damn it, Finke."

"By no means, within bounds," Finke said.

Harmon paced the floor, his hands clasped behind him.

"It isn't every man of his age who can do that," Finke thought. There was something boyish, quite refreshing, in the oil magnate's underlying humanity. He was boyish—old-boyish—and took himself seriously. But who did not take seriously a man in good health who had maybe a billion dollars and was under no indictments?

The hard part was coming, and Finke waited. Harmon at last got under way.

"Seeing her face, so eager, in one of those closeups, do you know what I thought?"

"You yelled like a stuck pig," Finke said. He had been a yes-man as long as he could stand it.

"Don't interrupt, please," said Harmon, gruffly. "At the time I'll admit I was fit to be tied. Who wouldn't be, with the woman he loves stripped naked, to all intents and purposes? . . . But later . . . just now . . . tonight . . . while you were off seeing an unfortunate actress' dead body . . . I got face to face with myself."

"Look, Mr. Harmon. An ex-soldier's dead, and now a fine young actress, a blonde. We've got to get down to cases, sir."

"I stand rebuked," Harmon said. "Let me be brief."

"Yes, sir."

"No false pretensions."

"Get with it."

"I recalled that when I was Eulalia's age, and just being gradu-ated . . . with some difficulty, Maguire. . . . from Harvard . . . my father . . . a stern man . . ."

"But a just one."

"Exactly. My father tried to place me in a broker's office, where he had arranged for my rapid advancement . . . from the bottom, up . . . you understand."

"Why not?" Finke said. "Go on."

"My father . . . God rest his judgment . . . had faith in securities . . . stocks, bonds, negotiable paper."

"I've heard of 'em," said Finke.

"My father scorned commodities. He spoke of oil, Maguire, as if he had sat in it and soiled his trousers."

"The formula, sir," prompted Finke.

"I'm coming to that," said Harmon. "I went into oil."

He broke off the dialogue to pace the floor again, twice left, then right, this time his hands at his side, with his extended fin-gers touching the bottom of his well-cut jacket. His hours of stress did not affect detrimentally his correct attire.

"Please follow me, point by point," he began.

Finke assumed his most receptive position, one ear cocked slightly toward the millionaire.

"The Manellos," Harmon began, now in his firmest tone which had dominated so many boards of directors. "The Manellos have had the effrontery to try to intimidate me."

"Don't forget Barney Rice," Finke said, drily. "They tried, as you say, to buffalo Bob Reynolds, too."

"We must get that boy's murderer, Maguire. Spare no expense. But I can show no signs of weakness. If, by relenting, and giving my permission for Eulalia to follow a screen career, from which those crooks would profit, it should appear that I've been coerced, my reputation . . . my credit . . . my prestige would . . ." Harmon groped for words and started pacing again.

"Go belly up," agreed Finke, supplying the conclusion.

"That brings us to the formula," said Harmon, calmer now.

Finke grinned. "Eulalia acts. We freeze out the Manellos," he said.

"We sign with a rival agent . . . Any reputable person. Eulalia's choice."

"She ought to be a woman—the agent," Finke suggested. "The relationship between an actress and her agent is so intimate . . . Think it over, Mr. Harmon. Miss Mesker—the smartest agent in town—made the same mistake you did. She underrated your fiancée's talent until she'd seen that test. That Hunyak director had spread all over the studio that Miss Noguera stunk . . . I should say, stank."

"He shall eat those words," growled Harmon, swelling like a pouter again. Then he calmed himself, red from the strain, and admitted, "I get your point, Maguire. Eulalia shall choose, and better Miss Mesker than some fatuous young chump who holds nothing sacred. . . . But there's another danger . . . another intimate relationship, and that has to be with a male."

"You mean she'll play opposite Bob Reynolds? What could be better? Bob is Miss Mesker's client, too. Ruth can keep him in line."

"Would she agree to have that stipulated in the contract?" Harmon asked. "I've always found it safer to have everything reduced to writing," said Harmon.

"Some reduction!" mumbled Finke, but aloud, he said, "You want my advice?"

"Speak your mind, Maguire."

"Why the hell don't you marry the girl? Put that in writing, too. You've made the big concession of letting her act. She'll agree to spot you the Dutchman. You won't have to can him. He can hang around and press pants and pot plants, but put in a proviso that he keep out of her boudoir when she's not there."

"Do you think her marriage vows would deter Reynolds?"

"Don't trust Reynolds, or me, or yourself. Trust her. A Mexican girl of her quality, once she's made a promise, fulfills it to the letter. Ask any guy who has one."

"I'll marry her today," Harmon said. "She shall sign my name to her first movie contract. 'Twill be the most precious wedding present of all I give her, in a way."

And Mills Harmon relaxed his dignity to tear off a few nifty steps in soft-shoe style as he reached for his check book, and humming a tune entitled "I'm Just a Lucky So-And-So" said, "For expenses, Maguire. Don't spare them."

It was in this frame of mind that Finke caught up with Evans, in the shade of the young upas tree, amid the pitcher plants. He found Homer as ebullient and self satisfied, in his manner, as Harmon had been.

"Finke," Homer said. "This is a toxicologist's paradise. All the inscrutability, all refinements of cruelty of Java, most favored and decadent of islands, flourishes here before our eyes."

"Not mine," groaned Hank Bibesco. "Cock-eyed-looking posies with dead flies and live tree-toads in 'em. Bah!"

"Ah, *nepenthes gracilis*," Homer touched fondly a little golden-lined goblet suspended from a wickedly coiled tendril. "The florid pitcher plants of our continent, called side-saddle flowers, or the *sarrenciae drumondi*, as you observe, have veined leaves which drown their victims in plain water. This little arch fiend of a notoriously fiendish family, the nepenthes, distills little pots of poison, with lids that open to lure winged creatures, and wax rims to un-steady their faltering feet. Then the cover closes."

Finke, however, was not as much intrigued as Evans with the pitchers of the dangling kind. He pointed to the bed of what Evans had called *sarrenciae*, with translucent leaves of yellow green, subtly veined, and aloft on stems which honked gracefully to in-vert the cup-like flowers of soft wine-brown, brick dust, and rus-set purple with pale lilac on the underside.

"These are the ones that give me the heebie-jeebies. I see them, and all those snaky colors in my dreams. Also I saw them in the Technicolor sets for *Tabu*, and in Dr. Harms's reception room. And again tonight in Mrs. Shroeder's apartment."

"Of course. There's a connection," Homer said.

"Don't tell me we got to fool around with these stink trees and bug-eating begonias," the Sheriff protested. "If that's the kind of case we're mixed up in, I'm going to get myself undeputized, but fast."

"There'll be work for all of us," Evans said. "More, I'm afraid, than we bargained for. I am fed up, and the world is with me, with the tendency lately to link purely personal murder intrigues with international complications. Man longs, again, to be an individual—one who can slit a throat or sprinkle a pinch of arsenic without involving satraps and principalities, democracies and dictator-ships, or pitting one whole race against another."

"Amen," said Hank Bibesco. "Up in the County seat, in war time, if a deputy pinched a drunk, for his own good, one or both of them turned out to be subversive. What's become of our old-fashioned felonies and misdemeanors, good enough for the founding fathers and grandfathers?"

"I've been messing around in counter-spy work quite some time. It's the botanical stuff Evans raves about that gives me cold feet," Finke said. "Let's plow up this damned disgusting garden, give the bamboo poles to kids for fishing rods, and keep this case in the animal kingdom, where crime belongs."

Homer gestured toward the screened and unscreened beds of pitcher plants. "Our astute Dutchman seems to be proving, what a few great men, including Darwin, have at least suspected: namely, that some plants kill insects—a form of animal, to be sure—just for sport. You'll note that the specimens of *nepenthes, sarrenciae,* the Venus fly traps, *darlingtoniae,* butterworts and sundews, all represented here, are as lusty and beauteous when deprived by screens of their prey as when so situated that they may devour whatsoever they can lure, and digest the carcasses."

"What the hell bugs and flowers have to do with a dead blonde's love affairs is too deep for me. Now this bottle of Coor-cafacha is tangible. I can pat it, heft it, and, after the trial, take a swig from it. I don't know how many California judges you've had dealings with, Professor, but I've run up against quite a few, and juries of twelve picked slobs, or citizens drafted at random. Just you lug in one branch of a tree that makes the courtroom smell of bedbugs, and tell 'em that polygamists way over in Borneo or somewhere tap the things to knock off their women, when they get sick of 'em . . . Just trot before the bench with a few pots of meat-eating Venus flaptrap and claptrap, and we wave our free defendant 'So Long' on our way to the nearest nuthouse."

"I've had experience, too, with judges and juries," Evans agreed. "I promise that whatever Finke presents, in the interest of his clients, will be as clear as day."

"I still say: 'plow this garden under, and pave it' beginning today," Finke said.

"You'll appreciate the beauty and the menace of it as soon as I can have a few words with our Dutchman, who has served science and his government so well," Homer said.

"Did he, or didn't he bump off Barney Rice and Shirley Hall? Can you answer us that?" the Sheriff demanded.

"I wish we were faced with no problem more difficult than that. I'll let you judge for yourselves, while I'm questioning him, in your presence. We must remember, in this exotic case as in ordinary ones, a murderer must be in a certain place at a given time."

"You'll pardon me, Professor," the Sheriff said. "I don't want to horn in where Einstein and Beebe would fear to tread, but what you just said gives me a horrible thought. If Dutch botanists are like Jap gardeners or white farmers, they get with their produce before this hour of the morning. It's been daylight quite a while."

The effect on Evans was electrical.

"Gentlemen," he said, with the utmost chagrin. "I've been a consummate ass. Mynheer Van Vleeck . . ."

Finke was already on his way to Harmon's cottage.

"I'll bring him, dead or alive," he said, without thinking of what he was saying.

Evans winced. "I implore you, Finke. If he's not alive, don't touch any object—not even the doorknob."

The Sheriff's jaw dropped. He saw, and a shudder shook his lean frame, that Homer was in earnest. Hank hustled after Finke. Evans, sighing humbly, sat on a cushion of moss, beneath the feathery Calcutta cane.

"It was wisely said that pride goeth before a fall. While I was acquiring the tangible Exhibit A, I may have let pass into eternal silence my most likely interpreter of Exhibits X and Y. Alas!"

13

No Signs of Violence

MILLS HARMON, still exuberantly tap dancing in his living room, for which purpose he had rolled back the rug, desisted as he saw Finke Maguire and Hank Bibesco approaching. On the front walk, they parted, and while Finke unceremoniously burst into the front entrance, Hank was heard by Harmon to crash the back door. The tycoon instinctively puffed and bristled, then his better judgment caused him to withhold his unspoken protest. Something pressing was afoot, and no mistake.

As Finke hurried past his bewildered host he beckoned Harmon to follow, and so the millionaire, remembering that he had been a halfback on the 'varsity eleven at Harvard ('02), picked up a set of brass fire tongs and brought up the rear. Before a closed door beyond the bungalow kitchen, one that could only belong to a servant's bedroom, Finke skidded to a halt, as the Acting Sheriff, barging into the scene from the other direction, did likewise.

"Touch nothing! Not even the knob!" admonished Finke, and the oil magnate and county doctor nodded assent as Finke called out, "Van Vleeck! Van Vleeck!"

As they all, by that time, had feared and anticipated, the reply was silence. In human adventure, as in music, the whole tones, crochets and quavers, are punctuated with equally effective rest notes.

Finke looked at the Sheriff, who frowned and shuddered. The sheriff looked back at Finke. They both shrugged and looked at Harmon.

"What is it?" asked the multimillionaire, breathing hard. "Not dead?"

Already Finke had taken out his second spare handkerchief. With it he protected his hand which reached for the doorknob. It turned without resistance. He pushed, and the door opened. On the three-quarter bed of extra length so that the head and feet of the Dutchman both had ample space, the obstinate and erudite Hollander was lying, face down, and fully dressed. The arms and legs were spread in a position so similar to that which those of the late Shirley Hall had assumed, before rigor mortis set in, that the Sheriff was struck at once by the fact. Finke, who had not yet viewed Shirley's remains, was appalled for another and very personal reason. Those gawky arms, had, not many hours ago, seized him from behind and those enormous hands, now rigid, had groped for his throat. Finke had lost his temper and hit the old Dutchman harder than had been needful to knock him out. In apology, Finke reverted to his boyhood and made the motion of crossing himself, which for some years he had not done.

"This is insufferable!" Harmon roared. "Maguire! I want the murderer of my faithful old friend, who also served me, brought to justice, and at once. Do you hear?"

The oil magnate's emotions now were as mixed as they were powerful. His wedding day! Death in his house! Mills Harmon was no more egocentric than most men of large affairs. He had an orderly mind and had kept his bachelor life and his business well ordered. Now his inner arrangements seemed to be wide open to criminal interference from all angles. The result was turmoil.

In contrast, the grim emergency had brought to their sharpest peak the faculties of Finke and the Acting Sheriff, both men of action and as sure-footed between crimes as Harmon was in a field of oil wells or on a slippery directors' room floor.

"We'd better call Doc Hamilton again. He'd better do both post mortems at once. These deaths are linked, as sure as hell, if you ask *me!*"

Finke nodded. "They're linked, all right," he agreed. He turned toward Harmon, who was still staring bug-eyed at the grotesque corpse of Sprouls Van Vleeck, which was stiffer than a bundle of beanpoles.

The Sheriff mumbled, quoting Evans, "No signs of violence. No struggle."

"You may find a few bumps or scars on his puss, when you turn him over," said Finke. "He tried to throttle me, last evening, and I had to slap him down."

"Don't tell that to Marcus. It looks like you had a motive, yourself," cautioned Hank.

Seeing that Harmon was reaching the limit of his remarkable endurance, Finke led the host to the living room and, with the aid of the handkerchief, reclosed the death room door and latched it, but left it unlocked as he had found it.

"We must think things over," said Finke.

"Shouldn't we call Professor Evans?" Hank asked.

Finke scowled. "I suppose so," he admitted. "Go ahead."

Hank started out to fetch Homer. Finke and Harmon sat down, and Harmon absent-mindedly pushed a button.

"We'd better have a drink," he said, and then he realized what he had done. Van Vleeck would hear no more bells. His huge hands that had the delicacy to sort the dust from pollens as well as the accuracy to measure whiskey, ice and water, would not function again. No more was said of refreshments, just then.

"Eulalia's going to feel this deeply," said. Harmon, whose own eyes were wet. "I hope it won't dampen the occasion. Christ, Maguire. Must we postpone the ceremony? We'll have to do it quietly, at any rate. A Mexican girl of Eulalia's quality makes a big thing of a death. While we were down there, in Mexico City, she blew a swimming race just because somebody told her, just before the start, that the old woman who'd nursed her as a baby had been crushed by a truck. I dread breaking this news to her. It wasn't as if she'd been on good terms with Van Vleeck. She hated his guts. . . . You follow me, Maguire?"

"She'll find a formula," Finke said. "Now you listen to me, and try to follow, point by point. Bob Reynolds has a servant—or, if you like it better, an employee—who's also his friend. The party dies, from nobody knows what, and Bob gets the Object Lesson message over the phone."

"If those Manellos . . ." burst out Harmon.

"Keep your shirt on, Mr. Harmon," Finke admonished him. "No mugs are guilty of a given murder because of anything they've got away with, previously. If they wangled acquittals, up to date, they stand. See what I mean? Those Manellos play close to their vests. We've got nothing on 'em yet. So we don't jump at conclusions. *But* they wanted something from Reynolds, so Reynolds' closest pal gets killed and Bob is threatened. It may be just a coincidence that the same mob wants something from you, so your valet is bumped off. The murderers, in your case, give you your Object Lesson routine before, and not after, the death of the victim. What difference does that make? It looks like the same operators, with the same technique."

"If it takes my last cent . . ." began Harmon.

"Just a minute," said Finke. "I thought at first that Miss Noguera was in danger. Then I saw the flaw in that little pipe-dream. How could the Manellos use Miss Noguera after she was dead? And what would they need from you then? They've got money salted away. Besides, if they take over E.P.U., and spring a sensational new star like Eulalia, your pals, the bankers, will be all too glad to finance the picture."

While Finke had been talking, Homer Evans and the Sheriff had entered, unobtrusively. Homer interposed, so gently that his voice did not startle anyone.

"Just supposing," Homer suggested, "that the Manellos in this instance are innocent of murder. Supposing a murderer we shall call 'X' had a motive for killing *both* Miss Hall and Miss Noguera, and was diabolical enough to dispose of Shirley in a way that would throw the guilt on Miss Noguera, and send the latter to the lethal chamber, in infamous disgrace?"

"I cannot imagine why anyone would want to hurt Eulalia. She's as generous and open-hearted as a child, and has done no one any harm," Harmon said.

"The late Mynheer Van Vleeck?" suggested Evans. "As I understand it, our late gifted botanist didn't rate Miss Noguera very highly."

"With Van Vleeck, distrust of women was a fixed idea," Harmon said. "And not that of a man who might be suspected of senility. Van Vleeck's mind was clear as crystal, except on that one point: that women, especially young women, were not to be trusted. That twisted view he had held through many bitter years."

"He never talked with you about a disillusioning experience, to account for his prejudice?" asked Homer.

"I've never known a more reticent man. He thought it indecent to speak of one's personal affairs, once they were experienced. In trying to protect me from Eulalia . . . . from a misguided urge to serve me well, whatever the consequences to him . . . he was determined . . . quite fanatically . . . to safeguard my future."

"And his own?"

Harmon replied sincerely, and with the tolerance he had extended the Dutchman while the latter was alive. "He saw the future as a resumption of the past, as it had been before I met Eulalia, when he had his work . . . his scientific research, I mean . . . and I was . . . what he called 'free and unencumbered'."

"There are many who would hold that Van Vleeck had a most unusual and enviable berth, with a congenial employer, duties that were not onerous, and leisure time and funds to carry on his rare vocation."

"You can say it was rare once again," said Finke. "Stink trees, plants that trap bugs just for the fun of it, bamboo that blooms only when it pleases, century plants that shoot up ten- or twelve-foot stalks in one night. You might ask the bug-doctor, Harms, if a man who spends his life with the craziest things that grow, and nurses them like babies, couldn't lose a lot of his buttons, even if he had a full set to start with. It's possible that our Dutchman was just plain nuts."

"It's possible, too, that a man sitting pretty like he was, who gets the idea, all of a sudden, that he's about to lose his job; might bump himself off. Aren't most of those weeds and bug-traps full of poison?" the Sheriff asked.

"Let's not make conjectures until we've sifted our facts," Evans said. "And furthermore, men as stubborn as the late Van Vleeck do not end their own lives in the middle of a conflict. As recently as last evening, Mynheer Van Vleeck tried repeatedly to contact Finke. What for?"

"I'd like to know what for. It was unauthorized by me," Harmon said.

"Did he ask you when he could telephone, and to whom?" Finke asked.

"He never used a telephone except in cases of the most extreme necessity. Not three times in the last ten years, I should say. That was another of his—eccentricities," Harmon said.

Evans spoke with great deliberation. "We must all approach this problem dispassionately—without false pride or concealment of pertinent trifles. You, yourself, Mr. Harmon, went to Finke's office last evening to consult him. Do you mind if he tells us for what purpose?"

Harmon flushed a deep red, and averted his eyes.

"Exactly," Evans said.

The Sheriff this time looked chagrined. "I guess I don't hear very good, any more. What was the purpose?"

"Mr. Harmon never told me. Late last night, when we were in the middle of our first conference, and hadn't got as far as his stating what he wanted, Enrico broke it up with the news that Miss Hall had been killed," Finke explained. "This morning we got side-tracked on virtue and marriage."

Again Harmon looked painfully embarrassed. Homer took the floor again, to spare the oil man unnecessary humiliation.

"Let me put the case," Homer said. "For Mr. Harmon *and* the late Van Vleeck. They were associates and friends, with mutual respect and anxiety for each other. One believed implicitly in Miss Noguera—and the integrity of womanhood. The other, a scientist and admittedly an eccentric, if not a zealot, was equally positive that his protector's fiancée was exploiting him; that, in fact, she was deceiving him with other and younger men."

"What the hell," Hank Bibesco said. "I've spent most of my life in Los Angeles County, but human nature's about the same, one place or another. On a proposition like you just stated, Professor,

I'd take four to five, any day in the week, without knowing the parties' names."

"A Mexican girl of Miss Noguera's quality . . ." began Finke.

"The Mexican population of Los Angeles County," said Hank, "runs up as high as thirty percent. Within the County, I'd take the short end of that bet, and made the odds five to four."

Harmon, who had stood all he could, went off the deep end. "If you think I'm going to stand here and listen to a vulgar discussion of the character of my future wife . . ."

"Mr. Harmon," Evans broke in, "again, let's be realistic. Not twelve hours ago you went to Finke's office to ask him to investigate the character of your future wife—or, rather, the conduct. That, incidentally, most surely was what Van Vleeck was going to retain Finke for. Only you wanted confirmation of your faith in Miss Noguera, to set his mind at rest, as much as yours; and Van Vleeck wanted proof of his suspicions, for your protection more than his."

"The less we know about our loved ones, the sounder we snooze," said Hank Bibesco.

"Gentlemen, you misunderstand me. If I hadn't been sure Miss Noguera was beyond reproach, I would have shot any man who spied on her, not paid him."

"Van Vleeck spied on her, and you paid him, although not specifically for that, I assume," Homer ventured.

"That is *why* I've slept nights," Harmon said. "Can't you understand what it means to a man of my years, if you like, to have that assurance? Van Vleeck was a painstaking scientist. Also, a woman hater of the most pronounced type. If *he*, watching constantly, could produce not an iota of proof against Miss Noguera . . ."

"Has she promised, in so many words, to be faithful?" Finke asked.

Harmon colored, gobbled and glared again.

"Gentlemen, you take me for a fool. Would any man on earth trust a girl who had to *promise* to be faithful? An innocent girl never mentions being virtuous, at all. She doesn't know what sex means."

"The less parents know of their children, the sounder both the kids and elders snooze," said Hank.

A clock struck five.

Mills Harmon, who with all his millions and problems had retained some sense of humor, relaxed, breathed deeply of the summer morning air and smiled wryly.

"This strikes me, gentlemen, as an odd conversation to be holding on one's wedding morning. Van Vleeck has passed on, and with him his obsession."

"Also, unluckily for me, his unparalleled knowledge of the *nepenthes, phyllostachys, sarrenciae, darlingtoniae*, the fly traps sacred to Venus, butterworts and sundews," sighed Evans.

"Those he can have," muttered Finke.

"Amen," said the Sheriff.

A tap on the door was followed by the entry of Enrico, whose face was imperturbable only in moments of inner agitation.

"Enrico. Congratulate me! I'm the happiest man in the world," Harmon said. "At last I've found my formula."

Enrico's mobile face could never be classified as a "dead pan" but the flash of polite felicitation that dimly lighted it was accompanied by a worried look as he spread before Homer a fresh extra which had been put out by the *Examiner*. Finke, Harmon and the Sheriff gathered around and stood on tiptoes to read over Homer's shoulders:

CHICAGO EX-GANGSTERS HELD
IN E.P.U. LOVE MESS
Ric Manello and Brothers Implicated
in Murder of Blonde Screen Star
OIL MAN'S MEXICAN BRUNETTE
ALSO SLATED FOR GRILLING
County Authorities Smuggle Corpse
to Beverly Hills for Secret Post
Mortem in Defiance of Los Angeles
City Homicide Police
BEREAVED BOB REYNOLDS
DROWNS HIS GRIEF
IN ALCOHOL

Harmon read as far as the line which stated that Eulalia was "slated for grilling" and began, once more, to holler and growl.

"Enrico. Please ask Latacassi to awaken Miss Noguera. I must speak with her on a matter of the utmost importance," Harmon said.

The garage man bowed and looked at Evans.

"Any one will think twice before 'grilling' Mrs. Mills Harmon without pretext."

Finke interposed. "After all, sir. Miss Noguera was one of the last to see Miss Hall alive. It's police routine to question those who had the opportunity and a motive for killing a victim."

"What opportunity, may I ask?"

"The *señorita* sat with Miss Hall in the Tropics, while Shirley ate chop suey . . ."

"Surely not chop suey. Chow mein . . ." corrected Homer.

"That Chinese grub's all the same to me," said Finke. "Anyway, Miss Hall ate some of it. Both she and Miss Noguera were drinking. Miss Hall wasn't stabbed, shot, clubbed or scared to death. If it turns out she was poisoned, Miss Noguera had a wonderful opportunity."

"And the motive? Eulalia had proved herself an actress. She'd been offered a contract. Except for my approval . . . which I suspect she knew she would get, in the end, I've never denied her anything . . . if we overlook Van Vleeck," Harmon said. He breathed deeply, threw back his shoulders, and resumed his ecstatic mood again. "My wedding morning! Death in the house. My bride *slated* for grilling. Gentlemen. I trust you, individually and severally, to deal with these obstacles and annoyances. Do you think that, under the circumstances, I could call on her at seven? Mexican girls of her quality make quite a thing of marriage—the outward forms, I mean. In Mexico, marriages are performed by judges, and the certificate is a judicial act."

The excited oil man turned to Hank Bibesco. "You know a judge, no doubt, who'd waive the technical barriers—publication of intentions, blood tests, all that sort of thing."

Hank was not a man to make extravagant promises. "I might speak to Judge Weintraub, of the Superior Court in L.A. It just happens that when he was up for appointment, another slick lawyer, and a better politician—Aloysius O'Flaherty—seemed to be getting the inside track. It was me who swung the pendulum—that fat head governor we had—Judge Weintraub's way. The Judge isn't a man to forget past favors."

Homer Evans was again deep in thought. He heard what was being said, but only as an obbligato, as it were, to the main trend of his cerebration. Unlike the others, he was facing the window commanding the pathway from the patio and he saw, approaching, Lieutenant Marcus, of the L.A. Homicide Squad, and with him a bulky state police sergeant in uniform. Homer signaled to Enrico, and whispered, "You'd better see that Miss Noguera is awakened, and let her know that it's urgent that she get dressed, in one-tenth, let us say, of the usual time it takes any girl of her quality to accomplish her morning toilette. And, go out from here the back way, in a manner not too conspicuous."

The Mexican garage man nodded and was off.

Finke was continuing, not so much to dampen Harmon's ardor, as to induce him to take a glance, at least, at the score.

"These two murders are linked," Finke said. "The police routine is to find and question all the persons who had both opportunity and motive for killing both the victims. To put it plainly, Miss Noguera fits into both pictures, as Cinderella's feet fitted both golden slippers. Shirley Hall stood between her and Bob Reynolds, as leading man, and everybody around these gardens knows that Van Vleeck had been trying to prove she was two-timing you. Don't forget, Mr. Harmon, that if you've got—roughly—a billion dollars, under California law the day a woman marries you, she's worth $500,000,000. With that much at stake, two murders, at $250,000,000 apiece, would be worth almost anybody's while."

"Eulalia's an artist. And Mexican, to boot. She has no sense of money at all."

"Harpo Marx is a wonderful artist, and says himself that he's got a strong sense of double-entry bookkeeping," said Finke.

"If Eulalia's under suspicion, in what to her is a foreign country, the more reason I should marry her and shield her. We must do it this morning. Right away."

The tap on the door which Evans had been expecting some minutes, softly sounded, then the gong began sounding "Do mi do."

Homer opened the door.

"Ah, Lieutenant Marcus, again. With one of our State Cossacks. I saw you approaching, but thought you might like to eavesdrop a while before entering. Do come in!"

"Meet Sergeant Spode, whose jurisdiction isn't cramped by city and county boundary lines," Marcus said, in his blandest smirking manner. "He has a writ for . . ." The Lieutenant hesitated and the State cop, read out, laboriously:

"Eulalia Julia Maria Noguera y Mendes Cajigal Zeraceria."

"She must be some pippin to rate a moniker like that, but I understand she is," Marcus said.

Homer and the sheriff glanced at the document Sergeant Spode extended. It was, in fact, a summons, signed, sealed and attested, requiring the presence of Eulalia . . . etc . . . Noguera . . . etc . . . forthwith in the Superior Court of the State of California as a material witness in the case of California versus Ricardo, Antonio and Pietro Manello et al, etcetera, etcetera . . ."

When they got as far as the signature of Jacob Weintraub, Homer looked at Hank, raising his right eyebrow, and Hank's face broke into a grin, as he nodded, and said, "Now isn't that just fine?"

Harmon stepped up to the officers, and informed them, in his most impressive manner, "Miss Noguera and I are to be married this morning."

"You make me very happy," Lieutenant Marcus said. "But would you mind holding the ceremony at Lincoln Heights jail? You see, sir, the Superior Court, where under the laws of the sovereign State of California Miss Noguera must present herself forthwith, is in the city of Los Angeles. There I can take over."

"No judge will send Miss Noguera to jail when I'm at hand to vouch for her, and furnish unlimited bail," Harmon said.

"That I'll grant, but as soon as the judge releases her, I'll take charge of her myself, and hold her as a witness. But I won't be too tough on you, Mr. Harmon. As I offered, I'll let you marry her through the bars."

"May I make a suggestion?" Evans interposed, in his most tact-ful manner.

"Why, certainly, Mr. Amateur Criminologist. I'm only sorry that this case isn't difficult enough for you to solve. It's open and shut."

"The murder in connection with which you're about to hold Miss Noguera?" Homer persisted, smoothly.

"That's the one," Marcus said, gaily.

"Are you referring to the murder of Miss Shirley Hall?" asked Evans.

"Perhaps you've stumbled on another?"

"As a matter of fact, I have, or rather, Mr. Maguire has."

"The fink you represent?"

"Exactly."

"Don't make me laugh," Marcus said.

"Will you step this way?" invited Homer, starting toward the servant's bedroom.

Marcus looked at Sergeant Spode, who was utterly indifferent.

"Why not?" said Marcus, and the members of the group filed through the living room and kitchen, in the order named, to wit: Homer Evans, Lieutenant Marcus, Sergeant Spode, Finke Maguire, Hank Bibesco and Mills Harmon. The latter was not depressed or alarmed. He hummed as he brought up the rear of the small pro-cession, "I'm Just a Lucky So-And-So," and cut a softshoe caper.

Pausing in front of the closed door of the servant's bedroom, Homer said to Lieutenant Marcus, "This case—or series of cases—on which we all are engaged, one way or another, is much more open than shut. I hope that after I've shown you what I have to show you, you'll see the wisdom of co-operation."

"When the L.A. force needs help, we'll ask for it," the Lieuten-ant said. "While you and your boys have been fooling around with fancy post mortems, I've got some of the murderers. As soon as you produce Miss Noguera, I'll have another, maybe."

"Mrs. Mills Harmon," sighed the oil man. "Murderess, indeed! If Eulalia had been obliged to commit murder, she would not have accepted any role except the principal one."

"The leading lady, in a lot of pictures I've seen, gets stooges to do her dirty work," said the Lieutenant.

"Let's not digress," Evans said. "So far, Lieutenant Marcus, you've made one blunder after another."

"I have? Now isn't that just ducky?" Marcus cracked.

"You've arrested the Manellos, not for any of the crimes of which they might possibly be guilty, but for one they didn't commit. You've given them, by jailing them without proof, a perfect alibi for a second murder which is so obviously related to the first that you won't be able to hold them ten minutes, once the second crime is publicized. I don't mind your making an exhibition of yourself, because that might be good for you. As a citizen I hate to see the public confidence in its paid protectors shaken."

"Where is this corpse No. 2?" Marcus asked, still unruffled.

Homer took out his handkerchief, wrapped it gently around the doorknob, and opened the bedroom door.

"Well, I'm damned," said Sergeant Spode. "He wasn't bluffing, after all."

"Bear in mind, Lieutenant Easy Marcus. We're still in County territory. You can have a look-see but you mustn't touch the exhibits," Acting Sheriff Bibesco said.

"You'll notice," Evans said to the dazed Homicide Lieutenant, "certain points of similarity between this cowardly crime and the killing of Shirley Hall. The position of the bodies are identical. No signs of violence or struggle. No marks or bruises, except in this victim's case, a few scars or bumps may be found on his face when Dr. Hamilton turns him over."

"How do you know about those, if you haven't tampered with the evidence?" demanded Marcus.

"The deceased had a fist fight a few hours before he died with a colleague of mine," Homer said.

Marcus nodded and thumbed at Finke. "The same who slugged a guard at E.P.U., stole a gun, slipped it to Shirley Hall, and then was on hand to disarm her after she'd tried to shoot Bob Reynolds. The same Joc who got rid of said gun the second time by handing it to a blue-bottomed ape."

"No apes have blue posteriors," Evans said. "You must be referring to a drill or a mandrill."

"You can't give loaded guns to monks, no matter what kind," Lieutenant Marcus said. "No more than you can to women under treatment for mental illness and who your innocents, the Manellos, are trying to get rid of."

"Now, really," Evans said. "You can't think that Mr. Maguire's in league with the Manellos, and tried to help them get rid of Shirley Hall by inciting her to shoot Bob Reynolds."

"I happen to know that one of the Manellos slugged Mr. Maguire night before last on the Derby parking lot, with a sack of BB shot," Marcus said.

"Fine teamwork among fellow conspirators," was Homer's comment.

"It's an old Sicilian way of keeping *fellow conspirators* in line," Marcus said.

"The Manellos have never been in Sicily," Homer said. "They're from Naples, where crime has for centuries been raised to the level of high art. Ricardo Manello is a very clever man, as clear-headed and balanced as any in the land."

At last Lieutenant Marcus relaxed and looked pleased, without putting on his provocative act. "Professor," he said, "suppose I let you in on something for a change. Ricardo Manello has been having himself psychoanalyzed for the last three months by the same bug-doctor who was treating Shirley Hall."

"That only stresses the advisability of our working in harmony and exchanging information," Evans said. "I'm frank to admit that what you have just said is news to me and that I'm amazed."

A clock struck seven. "Gentlemen. If you'll excuse me," Mills Harmon said, beaming, and started for the door.

"Go with him and serve your paper. Give him ten minutes to propose, if he can get down without spraining a knee."

"Sir," said Mills Harmon, "I can touch my hands to the floor palms flat without bending my knees. Can you, you young upstart?"

And suiting the action to the word, the septuagenarian multimillionaire touched his palms to the floor, humming "I'm just a Lucky So-and-So."

With that, Harmon straightened, readjusted the lapels of his jacket, pulled down his vest, and preceded Sergeant Spode toward the Gardenia's cottage. The Sheriff, leaving Marcus with the dead Dutchman, Finke and Evans, tagged along.

"Have you seen enough here, Lieutenant?" Homer asked.

Marcus smiled his aggravating smile. "I'll arrest the live ones. You dig up the dead ones," he said. "You don't have any more corpses, in reserve, I take it."

"As a matter of fact, a man who'd been murdered died a week ago in your territory, to wit, the Balm of Gilead Hospital. He was an ex-veteran, disabled . . . In some way, it's the most outrageous crime of our related murders. You seem to have overlooked him, utterly," Homer said.

"I'll admit that much, if there is such a corpse, and I'll charge you formally for obstructing justice, if you've kept this ex-veteran on ice a week, without notifying the proper authorities. That bunch of high-priced doctors at the Balm of Gilead are getting too big for their britches. Perhaps I can take them down a peg, too."

"I'm afraid you won't make any charges stick, against me or the excellent staff of the hospital," Evans said. "The cause of death of the victim—whose name was Barney Rice, and who acted as Bob Reynolds' stand-in—was not revealed to me until this morning, just after dawn."

"So I'll accuse the guy who waited that long to reveal it. Who is he?"

Evans gestured toward the body of Sprouls Van Vleeck, prone and stiff on the bed.

"Can you talk plain English, for a change?" Marcus asked.

"English has to be lots plainer to some than others," Finke said. "But here's some, plain enough even for you. Before these *related* cases are filed away, I'm going to take a poke at you."

"Why not here and now?" Marcus suggested. "I'm outside my jurisdiction, so there's no legal comeback."

There would have been action had not Homer interfered.

"Gentlemen," he said, "there's work to do. Would you mind coming with me to the gardens the late Van Vleeck maintained with such devotion? In the sad absence of Holland's foremost botanist, the late Mynheer Van Vleeck, I'll try to elucidate."

"That means 'throw light upon', shamus," Finke said to Marcus.

"Does the Professor throw left-handed, by any chance?"

"He's ambidextrous," Finke said. "Look that one up, after you get busted and fired."

"Gentlemen," again remonstrated Homer, "there's no time to be lost."

"After all, Professor," Marcus said. "There are three corpses, so you say. Am I to understand you expect to have more?"

The effect on Evans was not at all what anyone, not even he, himself, expected.

"Great heavens, Finke," he said. "I'm not at my best in this preposterous affair. Take the limousine, quick, to the Towers and collect Bob Reynolds. We must keep him near us till the real culprit's behind bars."

Finke, seeing Homer was headed for the pitcher plants, upas tree and pools of live bladderwort again, was not loath to fulfill his assignment. Evans led Lieutenant Marcus, however, past the meat-eating *sarrenciae* and the dangling poison cups of the *nepenthes* to the growth of sturdiest bamboo. There it stood, the most useful of plants, straighter than cedar, rising in sections to the height of sixty feet or more and luxuriant with light amber-colored flowers which glowed in the slanting morning sunlight.

"The learned scholar, whose remains you have just seen, was the only man who ever succeeded in transplanting the *phyllostachys bambusoides* from its native soil in the Indies to North America and caring for it so skillfully, and with such patient ingenuity, that it would burst into bloom," Homer said.

"You slay me, Professor," said Marcus. "But, as a practical matter, when flowers grow that high, how's a guy going to pick 'em? And, if he did, what would they have to do with the death of a disabled ex-veteran?"

For answer, Homer pointed toward the center of the grove, where thick stumps a few inches high, most of them already obscured by new sprouts, indicated that several, perhaps a dozen stalks of the giant bamboo had been carefully cut with a jig saw, and removed.

"One hell of a job for a few yellow flowers no bigger than mustard you can pick along the trolley tracks," said Marcus.

"Precisely," Evans said, and the baffled Lieutenant saw he was in dead earnest. "The difference is, that mustard, or *brassica hirta*, yields a harmless pollen beloved of bees, and a condiment or pungent without which certain foods like boiled beef would scarcely be worth while. On the other hand, the pollen of those dainty bamboo flowers, from the *phyllostachys bambusoides*, consists of microscopic needles, too fine to be detected by the naked eye, and harder than powdered steel. Actually, almost as sharp as diamond dust."

Homer looked at Marcus expectantly. The latter was, as he expressed it, "nowhere."

Evans sighed. "Since Dr. Hamilton and his consultants were baffled by these deadly instruments of death and torture, I can be patient with you."

"You mean . . . that dead Dutchman used this stuff on a disabled veteran? Now, by God, Professor! In that case, who wouldn't co-operate?"

"Not so fast," Homer said. "I appreciate your attitude, and the feelings which prompt it. But Mynheer Van Vleeck did not murder Barney Rice or Shirley Hall. Those unfortunate victims, and Van Vleeck, himself, were killed by one and the same hand."

"You know who did it, of course. You cerebral bozos always do until we working cops produce the guy who confesses," Marcus said.

"I know who did it, with a fair degree of certainty. What we lack is proof."

"Oh, that," said Marcus, smirking again. "We just need evidence?"

"We have enough evidence to convict a regiment of criminals. I said 'proof' that can be grasped by a jury. A nice distinction, but, in this instance, a significant one."

"Do you know what we lowbrows and roughnecks of the regular police do in such cases? We pinch the guilty party and give him such a going over that he just begs us for the lethal gas. Or we keep him covered, and wherever he is, phone him or brace him, and ask pointed questions, about once every twenty minutes, night and day. He either goes nuts, or confesses, or both. And if he doesn't ask for the gas chamber, the crowded conditions in our public institutions soon make him wish he had. So let's corral this party."

14

Cross-Examination

WHILE HOMER WAS EXPLAINING to Lieutenant Marcus certain properties of *phyllostachys bambusoides*, or common bamboo, about one hundred yards away in the Gardenia's bungalow a spirited sequence was unfolding itself. She had last been seen, as the reader will remember, in silvery moonlight, clad in a diaphanous robe, in the waning hours of the night whose natural beauty had been so sharply offset by the ugliness of its eventualities.

"Where's Mr. Finke?" she had asked, when awakened by a soft voice outside her bedroom window. She had been lying on the coverlet, her lustrous head of black hair loosened, and had fallen asleep that way, in the cat-like fashion she had described to Finke when he had brought up the subject of sedatives and stimulants. Indeed, the lovely *señorita*, who already had been hailed in press dispatches as "the brunette Jean Harlowe the world has long been waiting for," had no need of pills to put her to sleep, or ampules, capsules, lozenges, tablets, powders or injections to make her more thoroughly alive once her long-lashed eyelids had lifted. She sat up, without haste, and if the gesture suggested languor, it was spiced with vibrant anticipation. "Oh, it's Don Enrico," she said, and beckoned him to come in through the French windows, to spare her the exertion and exposure involved in her getting out of bed and going to the front door to open it.

Enrico hesitated, and murmured "*Con su permiso*" although the permission had already been granted. Then he moved aside the curtains and hopped hesitantly over the sill.

"You come from Mr. Finke?" she asked, and laughed merrily. "A nice funny man."

"Before we talk, I must show you this," Enrico said, and held out the first extra the headlines of which she read:

JEALOUS ACTRESS SLAIN AFTER
LOVE SHOOTING FAILS
Screen Test of Meteoric Mexican Starlet

"Starlet! Indeed. I'm five feet four," she said, with a becoming little frown, looking down over her figure which seemed, even in daylight, to be revealed rather than obscured by her robe.

"*Mi madre!*" exclaimed Enrico, so receptive to beauty that the experience was on the borderline of pain. "I beg of you, Señorita! If there were time to spare, I'd save myself and call later."

The Gardenia started to laugh, then caught the significance of the banner line and registered consternation. "Please, Enrico! Not Miss Hall! It can't be she who's slain."

He bowed his head and nodded. Tears filled her eyes and blurred the words as she continued reading. She broke off, protestingly. "But I haven't spurned Señor Harmon's millions, not forever. And what means this horrid word 'septuagenarian'? It sounds like infection of some kind. And bloodshed! Was poor Shirley knifed or shot?"

"Mr. Finke thinks she was poisoned. You were one of the last to see—and drink with her, were you not?" Enrico asked. "I was sent to warn you that you must get dressed very quickly. You are to be arrested and married this morning."

As he spoke he handed her the second extra which announced:

CHICAGO EX-GANGSTERS HELD IN E.P.U. LOVE MESS
OIL MAN'S MEXICAN BRUNETTE ALSO
SLATED FOR GRILLING

"They suspect you, Señorita—the police, not Mr. Finke—because you had a chance to poison Miss Hall's drink, just before she died, and later were on these premises when Señor Van Vleeck was murdered," Enrico said. "The police are here, city, county and state, Señorita."

Her eyes blazed. "Am I to be arrested first, and then married, without my consent, or vice versa?"

"Señor Harmon desires that your first film contract shall bear his name. He's admitted his mistake in denying you a career."

"To whom does he make these admissions? To the city, the county, the state? Why not to me?"

"You were asleep, Señorita. He thought and paced the floor all night, and, as he describes it, found a formula. You've no cause to be angry with Señor Harmon. He's behaving as a gentleman should. He defies the police, and wishes to marry you through the bars, to show his faith in your innocence. And under such unusual stress, he's considerate enough not to wake you before 7 A.M."

The Gardenia's face, at first tempestuous, was wreathed in smiles. "We're to be married through the bars? *Through the bars!* Enrico! Think of that. My box office is assured. Meteoric Mexican Starlet Jailed for Double Killing Weds Spurned Septuagenarian and Millions Through Bars. Are you sure my public won't misunderstand and think we all are drinking? Ah! Why doesn't the public speak Spanish, our smooth expressive mellifluent Spanish, in which a drinking bar is a *café*, prison bars are grilles or obstacles, a starlet at the bar of justice is an *accusada*, and 'bar none' means *todo el mundo*. A bar of music is a *mesur*, and being barred from a theatre, like a Negro or one of us in Texas, is an interdiction."

"You've overlooked bonbon or candy bar," Enrico said. "I agree that English is illogical, and American is absurd, as a medium of communication, especially without gestures, in print."

He saw the moths abandon themselves to what amounted to panic, and added, regretfully, "Our precious time has been expended in talk, Señorita. Here come the groom, the Cossack and the Sheriff. The latter, by the way, is on the side of Señor Finke. It's only the plump one in uniform who does not wish you well. Shall I try to hold them off a while longer?"

Again the Gardenia glanced down at her figure, as presented by the filmy robe. "Should I receive them this way? Those who admire me will be grateful, and the plump one will be self-conscious." Then she frowned and touched her forehead. "Don Enrico. I'm heartless. It's only that you've sprung on me so much, in so short a space of time. I can't realize yet that the poor lonely Dutchman has died, and, except for my generous future husband, friendless and bitter, as he had lived. I forgive all his insults to me. I wish to tell you, and no one else, that really, before I found out from you about his death, I had relented, and was ready to agree that Señor Harmon should retain him—with the proviso that I should act for the screen as long as it pleased me, and that Van Vleeck should be forbidden to enter my quarters or to spy on me."

"But that is Mr. *Harmon's* formula," Enrico objected.

"Let him continue to believe so," said the Gardenia. The gong rang in a minor cadence "Mi sol re."

"Ask them to wait in the living room, just a moment," she said. "I should appear in black."

Although the "moment" they were asked to wait lengthened into a good half hour, Sergeant Spode, the plump state officer, showed no signs of impatience. He promptly chose the best easy chair and fell sound asleep. The Sheriff picked up an album absently and found, to his delight, that it contained prints of numerous "stills" from the scenes included in the screen test.

Mills Harmon, on the other hand, found nothing to divert him. Having been accustomed for years and years to have subordinates handy who might be summoned for immediate consultation, day or night, he could not wait to tell his fiancée of his change of heart and the resultant plans. That she might not agree or might punish him for his outburst at E.P.U. by keeping him on tenterhooks had not occurred to him until he had been left a while to cool his heels, with others, in her living room.

"You gave her my message, Enrico?" Harmon asked the mechanic, quite diffidently for him.

"She was deeply shocked," Enrico said.

"Shocked? By my proposal of immediate marriage?"

"By the news of the death of your Hollander, sir," said Enrico. "She thought it best to dress in black."

"In black? To be married!"

"You, as groom, will be in black, will you not?" asked Enrico.

"God! I suppose so."

Harmon rose and began pacing the floor, three steps left, three paces right, his hands clasped behind his back. He had entered like a lion, and already was feeling like something with mint sauce.

"Your honest impression, Enrico? Will she forgive and forget?" the oil man asked.

"A Mexican girl of her breeding forgives like an angel, but she almost never forgets."

"You can say that again," broke in Hank Bibesco, who was relishing a particularly candid shot of Mumu as she stooped, profile to camera, to pick a *percebes* from a Tahitian lagoon, in order to offer it to Timomo. "That goes, too, for the well-bred Portuguese, Armenians and Greeks. When it comes to forgetting, a woman makes an elephant look like Edward Everett Horton."

At that point, he heard Eulalia's voice calling, "Mills, dear. Please come in and hook me up the back."

The Cossack, who had been, to all intents and purposes sleeping, opened one eye and cocked his head. Hank Bibesco looked at him and grinned.

"You ain't seen her yet," the Sheriff said, with a chuckle as he shut up the album. "You and your fat head city Lieutenant! I'd like to watch you pick your jury. You'll have to challenge all the men."

"We got two strikes on any Mexican, whatever she looks like," the Sergeant said.

It was impossible for those in the living room to hear what was taking place in the boudoir, but eventually Mills Harmon emerged, the joy on his face so eloquent that no verdict had to be announced. Behind him was the Gardenia, her oval face solemn, her eyes downcast, as if grief and remorse were more poignant in June morning sunlight than ever shades had found them on the far banks of the

Styx. She approached to within a pace of Sergeant Spode, raised her luminous dark eyes, her slender hands crossed on her breast and whispered in a husky voice, "You wanted me, Sergeant?"

Spode, who had awkwardly stumbled to his feet, cap in hand, dropped his cap without knowing it and gasped, "Jeepers Crow."

Finke drove pell mell into the patio. In the front seat of the limousine, beside him, was Kay, who had spent a sleepless night but was quite ready for a few more, if only she could do something constructive, and not be parked in odd corners to give inquirers false directions. In the rear seat was Ruth Mesker, between Laslo Sitchev, with whom she avoided contact, pointedly, and Bob Reynolds, who was dozing on her shoulder.

As they were helping Bob to his bungalow, Lieutenant Marcus and Homer Evans saw them moving in in irresolute, unorganized cortege. Finke was supporting Bob and lending him moral support with some well-chosen profanity. Kay was on Bob's other side, so much interested in Finke's curses on passers-out who had no regard for timing that she almost dropped Bob's left elbow and upset the trio's unstable equilibrium.

Bringing up the rear, coldly isolated in their antagonism, which was all one-sided, however, were Ruth Mesker and Laslo Sitchev. Ruth was vibrant with sorrow, and would have been stunned by it had not her indignation proved too strong to permit her to indulge in an outburst of grief. Sitchev was on the defensive. If he had been coaching Iago how to needle Othello, he could not have expressed interested innocence more eloquently.

"Who's the dame behind the other dame?" Marcus asked.

"I haven't met the lady, but I assume she is Ruth Mesker," said Homer.

Marcus nodded and thumbed a notebook. "The one who talked Mr. Harmon into going to the studio to see the Hall-Reynolds shooting that didn't come off? The agent?"

"The agent your agents were looking for in San Francisco. It was that ill-considered attempt on your part that convinced me you'd need help, so I flew down."

"What's so ill-considered about looking for a woman where her sweet silver-haired old mother says she's at?" Marcus demanded. "That old dame had me fooled, all right. She was so smooth you'd have believed her, yourself," said the Lieutenant.

"Mmmmm," agreed Evans, rather distrait. For he had seen, as the escorting group with Reynolds had paused raggedly at the doorway of Bob's bungalow to fish his pockets for the key, a streak or shadow movement which seemed to emanate from one of the vine-embowered French windows on the wooded side and whisk into thin air within a yard or two.

Marcus repeated his question, in modified form. Of what did his alleged big boner consist?

"The Berlioz Requiem Mass," Homer began. And he outlined the career of the great French composer and the mighty funeral music, the breadth of its significance, the infrequency and meagerness of its performances.

"I'm a detective, not Oscar Levant. Get to the point, and if it's about music, to hell with it."

"Tickets and standing room for the American *première* of this colossal composition were booked up, to the last chair and inch of standing space, two months ago. So you were shagging a couple of suspects who on the spur of the moment had lit out for parts beyond your jurisdiction in a cathedral which had been sold out sixty days previously." Homer shook his head, reproachfully. "Such a detective needs guidance."

"Don't forget, Professor Crapola, that I've got all the heavies— the Manello boys for Murder No. 1, and now your Black Gardenia for killing the Dutchman. Who else but her, I ask you, could have a motive for that one? She had to bump him off, or lose the $500,000,000."

"You promised Mr. Harmon before witnesses that he could marry her through the bars at Lincoln Heights. Is your word not worth a farthing?"

"I'm not sure what a farthing is, but Old Money Bags may not want to marry this tamale after he's heard the earful he's going to hear from my witnesses this morning. . . . I'll tell you what I'll do with you. We've got quite a few suspects and what-have-you on these premises now. Let's round them up, and find out where they were last night, between the time the show broke up at E.P.U. and the present. I'll ask a few questions, in my dumb routine way, and you can give lectures on bugs, blooms and this mug you call Berlioz. Is it a go?"

Quite formally Evans held out his hand, which Marcus looked at for a second, shrugged "what the hell" and shook it.

Enrico's garage would have been an ideal place for the assembly, except for the odor of gasoline and the presence of only one chair. Harmon's bungalow, the most spacious, still contained the corpse of Sprouls Van Vleeck, and the technicians, this time to be led by the famous Dr. Hamilton of the Balm of Gilead Hospital, were expected any moment. The Gardenia's cottage was pervaded with the fragrance of Caron's "Bellodgia," which is to alluring brunettes what Guerlain's "L'Heure Bleue" (believe it or not, pronounced "llur blur") does for blondes. So the get-together was staged in Bob Reynolds' living room. Bob, himself, was to be interviewed last, so they left him in the bedroom to get a few winks of sleep which, it was hoped, would put him in better shape for questioning.

The questioners, who sat facing the others, were, from left to right:

> Sergeant Spode of the State Cossacks
> Homer Evans, amateur
> Finke Maguire, licensed private detective
> Hank Bibesco, Acting Sheriff of Los Angeles County

By common consent, Homer Evans was chosen as Chairman and M.C.

Counting Bob Reynolds, singing actor, blissfully sleeping in the next room the questionees outnumbered the questioners, seven to four. They were, besides Bob:

Kay Cougar, private secretary to a private eye

Ruth Mesker, agent

Eulalia Noguera, the brunette Jean Harlow the world
had long been waiting for.

Enrico Rodriguez y Puig, garage mechanic and erst-
while motion-picture extra.

Laslo Sitchev, motion-picture producer, director and
discoverer of Demona Bourbon, Doodie
Howland, Fatima Buckleinekoff, the late Shirley
Hall and others.

Mills Harmon, socialite financier and oil man.

In opening the meeting, Homer explained that its purpose was merely to establish a timetable determining the whereabouts of everybody concerned between the hours of six o'clock P.M. on Monday and this morning, Wednesday, up to the present moment.

"Please don't be nervous, and suspicious of one another," Homer said. "It is an unusual circumstance in such assemblies as this, but the murderer of Barney Rice, Shirley Hall and Sprouls Van Vleeck may not be present."

Those out in front relaxed and glanced at one another with relief and congratulatory friendliness. But this mood was short-lived when Lieutenant Marcus broke in.

"No you *don't*, Professor! *I* say, *one* of the murderers of Shirley Hall and the Dutchman, Van Vleeck, is sitting right here before me, and has the nerve to dress in black. As far as this Barney Rice goes, if there ever was such a guy, all the doctors in Los Angeles haven't decided what he died from yet. So we won't go into that."

Homer smiled reassuringly at the Gardenia, who, with all eyes upon her, was comporting herself with quiet dignity so dramatic that even Sitchev, who was squirming and viewing her from all angles, found no suggestions to offer and just stopped himself in time from yelling "Camera."

"We have our little differences of opinion, of course," Evans said. "In fact, some of us are right, some are wrong, and others are somewhere in between."

Quite resolutely the Gardenia smiled.

"Miss Cougar," Homer continued. "This is an impromptu meeting, to clarify the situation. Would you mind, since you are the only one among us who has shorthand, making a record of the questions and answers?"

Kay agreed, recorded from memory what had already been said, and then was given first place on the list. She wrote down with consummate ease the questions, and her own answers, which were brief.

"In your own words, Miss Cougar, can you tell us where you were, and why, if you can, beginning at six P.M. yesterday?"

"I was waiting in Mr. Maguire's office, in the Griffith Building, 777 Sunset Boulevard, from long before 6 P.M. yesterday afternoon until about 8 P.M. At that hour I drove to the Tropics, on Rodeo Drive, to confer with Mr. Maguire, my employer," Kay began.

"Just a minute! Just a minute!" Lieutenant Marcus said, cockily. "The E.P.U. records show that at 8 P.M. yesterday, Mr. Maguire was somewhere on the lot in Cheviot Hills."

"Let that pass, shamus," Finke said. "The same records show that I'm still on the E.P.U. lot."

The Lieutenant was as amiable, on the surface, as he could be.

"Of course, none of you birds are under oath," he said. "But it's an odd thing. When parties make statements under oath, in court, and they don't check with statements they made without swearing to tell the truth and nothing but, jurymen get suspicious. That's not so good for you ladies and gents, but for me, it's just fine."

"Continue, if you please, Miss Cougar," Evans said.

"What Mr. Maguire conferred about is confidential. We drank a bottle of rum. Then he started for the Omar Khayyam Gardens, to talk with Miss Noguera."

Harmon rose like a Jack-in-the-Box. "He did! Eulalia! You didn't tell me that. Neither did he."

"Or Van Vleeck?" the Gardenia countered with spirit.

Marcus looked gleeful, but Homer interposed.

"Patience, my friend. Peace! Philosophy!"

The Gardenia recovered and said gently, "Your blood pressure, dear."

Kay went on. "After Mr. Maguire left me, and the rum was gone, I went back to the office. Within a few minutes, Mr. Harmon called."

It was the Gardenia who erupted that time. "You did! Mills! Was it to ask Señor Finke to start spying on me, like your detestable Van Vleeck, God rest his soul at the utmost possible distance in space?"

Harmon looked like a schoolboy caught using a trot but he smiled with effort and said, "Remember our formula, dear. No suspicions. No more recriminations. This very day we shall be wedded."

"And you lose 500,000,000 smackers," the Lieutenant reminded the oil tycoon. "That wouldn't be so bad, if she didn't win 500,000,000 smackers. I've seen half that amount make a dame very independent."

Kay again tried to get on with her story. "At ten o'clock, P.M., I closed the office and went home. There I read till three o'clock this morning, when I drove back to the Tropics, picked up Ruth Mesker, and took her back with me to my apartment. We talked till 5 A.M. or so, when the newsboy brought the city edition of the *Examiner*. We took one look at the top headlines and I drove as fast as my Austin would go, and took Miss Mesker to the Forty-Niners Towers. There I stayed with Miss Mesker; Melissa, the late Miss Hall's Yorkshire maid; Mr. Reynolds, who was drinking ginger beer with vodka; and Mr. Laslo Sitchev. At just before 8 this morning, Mr. Maguire arrived at the Towers, and drove Miss Mesker, Mr. Reynolds, and Mr. Sitchev here. And here we are, Mr. Chairman."

"Very neat. Very jolly," said Lieutenant Marcus. "I only want to ask (a) why you didn't shut up shop yesterday at 7 P.M. as usual; (b) why, after having stuck around until 10 P.M., you closed the door so fast and beat it to your hideout, where your telephone's under a phony name, and your address unlisted in any directory? And (c) after reading until second cockcrow, did you suddenly decide to 'pick up' Miss Mesker at the Tropics and whisk her to your hideout, too? (d) Why, when you and Miss Mesker were hid out, safely, did you both happen to wait up for the *Examiner*, at 5 A.M., mind you, and then make a contrived and innocent-appearing entrance to the place where Shirley Hall was murdered and was lying dead?"

Kay, having an orderly mind, answered the questions in order, and succinctly:

"I kept the office open after seven because Mr. Maguire had not phoned or called to give me the all-clear signal. I closed at ten, and went home, where I have arranged to have relative privacy, because you, Lieutenant Marcus, had phoned and said you 'wanted' Mr. Maguire, and when I informed you he was in San Francisco, you threatened to come in person, arrest me on trumped-up pretexts and rifle our office files."

Finke grinned at Marcus. "That's teamwork, punk, in case you never heard of it."

Instead of getting huffy, Marcus took the ingratiating tack. "If this false alarm you work for gets fresh, and you want to quit, there's always a job in my department," the Lieutenant said.

"I regret deeply," answered Kay, her head held high, "that Mr. Maguire's intentions have thus far proved strictly honorable."

Hank Bibesco chuckled. "Now there's a witness for you, Lieutenant. With her, and this lady in black on the stand, you've got the chance of a snowball in hell."

"And snowballs to you, hilly billy," retorted Marcus, then sharply, to Kay: "Why did you tell me Mister Maguire was in San Francisco, listening to some funeral march by Cecil de Mille? When you'd just conferred with him and helped him polish off a bottle of rum in Beverly Hills?"

"I knew Mr. Maguire had important work to do, and I was anxious to prevent you from bothering him. In my position, Lieutenant, I pick up quite a bit of law, and I knew about the limits of local jurisdictions," replied Kay.

"But this is magnificent dialogue, if only I could understand it," Laslo Sitchev cried. He hopped from his place and whispered a request to Kay about making an extra carbon for him. She nodded assent, good-humoredly, and continued her answers to the Lieutenant's questions.

"I read, till second cockcrow . . ."

Evans interrupted, apologetically. "For the record, Miss Cougar, cocks do not crow at regular or predictable intervals. In populated districts, where the flashing of headlights at night frequently stirs in roosters fleeting suggestions of the coming day, they crow as a purely automatic reflex, then go fast asleep again."

Lieutenant Marcus shrugged and sighed. "Folks," he said. "The Professor's off again. This time it's cocks. Wait till he spouts about bug-eating forget-me-nots and French slow music. Our chairman's a card. He can yodel the right fin off a Nile seahorse. Too bad he can't spot a murderer who's near enough to bite him."

The Sheriff chuckled. "I'd give her the first two bites, by cracky, myself."

Sergeant Spode giggled and said to Harmon, "Not bad, eh, Gramp?"

Homer let them have their little recess, then dismissed Kay from the stand, as it were. "Thank you, Miss Cougar. You've been very helpful," he said.

"Not to me," Lieutenant Marcus said. "She and that agent, Ruth Mesker, knew that Finke Maguire had slipped a hot gat to Shirley Hall just after lunch yesterday afternoon. To shoot Bob Reynolds? No. Because Maguire was on hand to stop her after she'd tried to do that. Let's trot out that Mesker dame."

"I'll tell you what I can," Ruth said. "As authorized agent of Mr. Reynolds and the late Miss Hall, I can't disclose their confidential affairs."

"In a murder case you jolly well can, and you'd better, if you know what's good for you."

Before Ruth could get started, Laslo Sitchev slapped the black-clad Gardenia on the knee. "Don't forget to remind me to tell our writer to put a swell trial scene in *Tabu* before you go into the fadeout, to be strangled with the buru vine." The producer-director turned to Evans. "By the way, Professor. You know everything," Sitchev said. "Just what is a buru vine?"

"A figment," Homer said.

Sitchev's expression showed that he knew less about figments than buru vines.

"Too bad we can't conduct this inquiry in Spanish," Enrico whispered, sympathetically, to the Hungarian.

"I know less of Spanish than English. But to hell with words. What we don't make clear can't hurt us."

Ruth took the floor. "I left E.P.U. last evening, after the showing of the rushes of Miss Noguera's screen test. About 6 P.M., or a little after."

"You left your private eye behind?" asked Marcus.

"He was to meet me on the parking lot," Ruth said.

"And did he?" Marcus persisted.

"No. I waited a half hour, decided he'd been delayed, and started looking for Miss Hall."

"Why Miss Hall?" asked Marcus.

"To square things between her and Mr. Reynolds."

"Who, as usual, was getting another skinful," Marcus said.

"They were my most important clients. I had to keep them together, alive, happy and in harmony. That's what an agent is paid money for," said Ruth.

They all heard a lusty yawning sound and, turning, saw Reynolds standing in the door of his bedroom, stretching and trying to orient himself in the scene that revealed itself slowly before him.

"Did someone mention a drink?" Reynolds asked.

Marcus spoke up, but to Kay. "Get *this* for the record. Broken-hearted affianced of slain actress wisecracks as he wakes."

Bob looked from one to another, until his eyes rested on Evans. "Thank God you're here," he said. "I loved Shirley, the way a man can in the show business, and all my friends know it. So will the sons-of-bitches who killed her, when I get my hands on them."

Marcus, now, was fairly glistening. "On them? More than one? Any ideas as to who they might be?"

"I have," said Bob. "The same dirty rats who killed my friend, Barney Rice."

"Not the Dutchman, too?" Marcus was leading him on, and Finke, all ready to stop him, caught a side glance from Homer which prompted him, with misgivings, to subside.

"What Dutchman? You mean Van Vleeck? Mr. Harmon's valet?"

"He grew plants on the side," Marcus reminded him.

"Is he dead, too? What for?"

"You say that as if you knew why Shirley was dead."

"Of course," said Bob. "Who doesn't, for God's sake?"

"Just for the record," urged Lieutenant Marcus, who was so gleeful that he was most incautious. He would soon learn, for keeps, that when things seemed to be going against Homer Evans so smoothly, the buyer had better beware.

"The Manellos killed her, to break our partnership, with the notion that they could scare me into signing with them. Ask Mr. Sitchev, the double-crossing little skunk . . ."

"Now, Bobbie," Sitchev said, cajolingly.

"Look!" said Reynolds to Marcus. "Why go further, when those thugs are already in jail? What did they do? Not much. They muscled in at E.P.U. and scared the top executives. They looked around the lot for birds of a feather to help foul the nest, and found this Hungarian weasel."

"Now, Bobbie! Peace. Philosophy," Sitchev said.

"Shut your trap," said Bob. "I've been hushed long enough. Ric Manello tried to get me to trim Shirley and Ruth Mesker, and sign him as my agent. I told him where to go. He tried it again, a few weeks later, after Shirley was taken sick."

"What was wrong with Shirley?"

Bob was embarrassed. "You know how it is, Lieutenant. When a girl gets crazy about a fellow. She was jealous. She got out of control. I was her whole existence, so when she'd catch me with another woman, she'd see red and start breaking things "

"Did she ever try to kill you before?"

"Not with a gun," Bob assured the Lieutenant.

"How, then, exactly?" asked Marcus.

"Oh, just ice picks and picture frames." Bob touched his forehead gingerly. "Once she took a swipe at me with a book end. I had to have six stitches that time."

"Just lovers' spats, you might say," said Marcus sympathetically. "Too bad *you* didn't kill her. You might plead self-defense.

You didn't by any chance, steal every picture you and she worked in, as Mr. Sitchev says?"

"There's nothing that louse wouldn't say. If he thought it would get him anything, he'd swear on a stack of Bibles that I was the bum, and Shirley was carrying me along because she took pity on me."

"But what would it get Mr. Sitchev, to sell her short, and give you the build-up?" Marcus asked.

"Look at him," Reynolds said, indicating Sitchev, contemptuously. "He's scared spitless of the Manellos, even now when you've got them locked up. Just figure out what's happened, since those racketeers blew into town. Sitchev was working on a story idea for me and Shirley, *Sin on an Island*. I was to sing and act, Shirley to dance. Cripes. We've made the same picture three times already, on three other islands."

"Hot dog," escaped from Sergeant Spode. "Sin on four islands."

Bob continued, hotly, "So the Manellos muscle in and start taking over E.P.U. What happens to our script? The beach at Waikiki become Tahiti, wherever in hell that is. The star mustn't do American dances, or the hula. That's old hat. And what must the star do? The one thing Shirley can't do? Swim."

Sitchev could not resist taking over, suavely. "And why should poor Shirley swim, if she doesn't like the water? I'm the one who suffers. I have to find a swimmer, somewhere, so Shirley can take a nice long rest, like the doctor's ordered. And Bobbie can keep on working, so the public won't forget him. The result?"

The little Hungarian director turned to the Gardenia in black and extended his arms. "A godsend right from God. To save the situation."

Marcus fixed Laslo Sitchev with a sardonic eye.

"Was it you who brought the *señorita* here from Mexico?"

Sitchev was willing enough to take the credit, but caution born of experience restrained him. "I didn't pay her fare," he insisted. "There's a comeback, if you discover a girl across the state line and she turns out to be a flop and a tramp."

Mills Harmon rose up, roaring. "You are speaking of the woman I love," he began.

Evans checked him smiling, and the Gardenia patted his hand.

"Ah. This wedding morning conversation. It gets better and better," he said. "Don't be disturbed, Mr. Harmon. We'll have a chance for rebuttal."

"Your blood pressure. The formula, you old bear," the Gardenia said.

"You weren't discovered by this insignificant little shrimp! Say that for the record, sweetheart," Harmon urged.

"It was another lily found her, way across the Rio Grande," Marcus said. "Mr. Tony Manello!"

Harmon's eyes began to bulge and his Adam's apple started gobbling again. "You mean to admit that you had this mania for screen acting *before* I brought you here."

The Gardenia's eyes flashed dangerously. "I'll refund you the fare, if that's what's on your mind."

"The formula. Philosophy," Evans cautioned them.

Marcus asserted himself. "Señorita. Take the stand. Stand up, I mean. Now who was it put the bee in your bonnet about a Hollywood career? Was it Sitchev? Was it one or all three of the wops? Or was it—just by chance—that you'd fallen for Bob Reynolds and couldn't think of any other way to get into his strong manly arms?"

"This is outrageous," Harmon shouted. But the Gardenia arose in such a manner that a hush fell over the room.

"I'll admit that I developed a strong admiration for Mr. Reynolds, as an artist," she said.

"What pictures did you see?" asked Reynolds, all agog.

"*Aloha Means Good-bye*," the Gardenia replied.

Harmon was fit to be tied. "So you brought me way up here . . . not so you could see something of the world before we settled down. You had to meet Bob Reynolds. You had to act with him. You wangled this whole thing yourself."

"*And* why not?" the Gardenia said. "And what does it matter if I met Tony Manello and found that he was useful to me? You've said a lot, Señor, about being master of your fate. Should I be mistress of mine?"

"Your fates are not irreconcilable," Evans said, and his voice had a calming effect. "Mr. Harmon. Women have ways of getting what they want, and if they're not quite like us, as the French say 'Vive la différence!'"

"Hot dog," said Sergeant Spode, and rocked back and forth in his chair.

Lieutenant Marcus stepped nearer to Harmon, and called the oil man's attention, with a gesture, to Bob Reynolds. "Ask Mr. Reynolds who induced him to act in a screen test that drove poor Shirley Hall crazy."

"I did! And Miss Hall was very ill, and in need of a rest!" the Gardenia said.

"Ask Mr. Reynolds where he spent night before last. The night he was supposed to get the death threat, by nickel phone."

"That's nobody's business," Reynolds said.

Again the Gardenia rose and the effect was so dramatic that Sitchev bit his tongue to stop himself from yelling "Camera!" The Gardenia's contralto voice was low and husky now, like Mumu's in the bamboo love-nest scene.

"Mr. Harmon and I have nothing to hide from each other," she said. "I spent hours, night before last, with Mr. Reynolds. He doesn't need to spare me by avoiding direct questions."

"Eulalia!" exclaimed Harmon, swelling, gurgling, sweating and almost paralyzed from shock. "You spent the night . . . with Reynolds?"

Enrico could not restrain himself. "They were in the patio. When a Mexican lady of her quality gives her word, it is her bond," the garage man said, proudly.

Marcus grinned. "Mr. Harmon's in the oil racket. He knows there are bonds and bonds," he said, and slapped his own knee.

Swiftly, taking two paces forward, the Gardenia confronted the Lieutenant.

"Do you dare question my conduct?" she asked, burning.

"Peace. Formulas. Philosophy," Marcus said, in imitation of Homer's manner. "Let me ask your countryman . . . Did he watch you all the time you were in the patio? Did Mr. Reynolds—or you, for that matter, know you had a chaperone? Or was Enrico asleep for hours at a stretch, while you and your crush were frisking in the moonlight?"

"Do you care to ask me that question, Señor?" she asked of the frantic billionaire. "Or do we trust each other, according to our recent arrangement, which you yourself proposed?"

Marcus interrupted hopefully before Harmon could answer.

"I can withdraw my permission for the wedding to take place in my jail," he suggested. "Why be in such a rush? Why not wait till this case is closed, and you know all the score?"

"Speak up. It's now or never," the Gardenia said.

"I can't live without you. It's now," the oil man said.

"I've got one more little surprise for you," Marcus cautioned. "Ask *Mister* Maguire where he was, last night—before you got home?"

"Señor Feenke was with me—in the moonlight. Alone," the Gardenia said.

The Sheriff spoke up, to bolster Harmon's morale.

"Cheer up, old-timer," Hank said. "You can't be jealous and suspicious of the wide wide world."

With a game effort at a smile, the tycoon said, ruefully, "You can, worse luck. You can. It *is* a disease. My heart goes out to poor Miss Hall."

The Gardenia, eyes moist, reached over and patted his hand. "There're such things as confidence and faith, Mills, dear," she said. "I come to you as you would want me, and others may believe it or not. You will have no possible doubt."

"Hot diggety dog!" said Sergeant Spode, and rolled from side to side in his chair, clasping his knees as he swayed. "Hot diggety jeepers. Jeepers Crow."

The Lieutenant subsided and Homer could not repress a smile. That last reassurance from the Gardenia had been the clincher. There was little doubt about the marriage now. Finke looked at Homer, bewildered. He couldn't figure out why it was that Evans was so eager for this June and December romance to culminate that day. Or any day.

Evans, in sooth, seemed well pleased, but Marcus wasn't exactly crushed. The Lieutenant seemed to feel that he, too, was sitting on the world. The sun was rising higher, and Homer, with the long day's work in mind, did his best to expedite developments.

"Let's simplify matters as much as possible," Homer said. "Before we disperse, may I ask Mr. Sitchev if he was cognizant of the mysterious circumstances surrounding the death of Barney Rice, Bob's stand-in?"

"A man with my responsibilities should know the troubles of a stand-in," he said, shrugging and lifting his elbows, palms upward and spread outward.

"Ask him if he knew that the evening after Barney's funeral, that was Monday, I was called to the pay phone in Enrico's garage," Reynolds insisted.

"For what?" asked Sitchev, repeating his gesture.

"Shall I give the exact words?" asked Reynolds of Finke.

"Why not?" Finke said.

Reynolds quoted, so deeply resentful that his own blood-pressure was higher than Harmon's had been. "'You're having an object lesson. What happens to someone close to you can happen to you. Don't be obstinate. Think well about the matter. What happens to someone close to you can happen to you.'"

Marcus didn't bat an eyelash. "And who was closer to you than Shirley Hall? Who'd bother picking on a stand-in, at seventy-five a week? And give you a warning after he's dead and buried? And who besides a stiff gets a good long rest these days?"

The Lieutenant turned to Homer, with a smirk of triumph. "I still say, I'll give you Barney Rice. I'll ask my boys to dry clean the Manellos, on this object-lesson stuff." He faced Bob, still pleased with himself. "I suppose you'd recognize the Voice if you heard it."

"*I* would," said Finke.

Marcus didn't seem astonished.

"How come, shamus?" he asked Finke. "Did one of your other clients get this 'object-lesson' threat, in practically those same words?"

"He would have got it," Finke said, nonchalantly. "Only I figured it was my duty to stand between him and the bird who was blackmailing him. So who got the hemlock, or whatever's going round? Not Señorita Noguera, who's closest to Mr. Harmon and the $500,000,000 dollars, but the nutty old Dutchman who pressed pants and sewed plants. You're all wet, shamus, trying to pin this on Miss Noguera. You was born all wet, and never got dry behind the ears."

"All right, shamus," retorted Marcus. "Try *this* on your pornograph. Who stands to gain by the death of Shirley? The Manellos and the *señorita*. The Spick steps into Shirley's step-ins, the Guinneys drag down their ten percent. Who wins if Van Vleeck gets croaked before he gives the bride away? Señorita Eulalia Provolone y Chile Con Carne, and the Wops get no cut. I've got the *señorita* here, in spades. And hey chums from Naples and Chicago, I've corralled at Lincoln Heights. We're just where we were when we all came in."

"I daresay you are," said Evans. "As for me. I seem to have learned a thing or two. I'll tell you what, Lieutenant. Let me have a little chat in private with Miss Noguera. So many of the gentlemen have. Then you toddle along with her, Mr. Harmon, our capable Sheriff and your obliging Cossack. Finke and I'll gather up a few threads, with the help of Miss Mesker and Miss Cougar. Bob Reynolds can use a bit more sleep, with Enrico on guard."

"You haven't mentioned me, Professor," Sitchev said, uneasy at being neglected.

"If you've nothing else to do, Mr. Sitchev, pray go on with your script. You'll have your talented Mumu, and Timomo, however hard hit by his bereavements, will realize that 'The show must go on.' Although, with most shows of today, I've never understood exactly why."

As they all made ready to go, in one direction or another, the Gardenia, more beautiful than ever, approached Homer.

"You wanted me?" she asked, looking into his eyes.

"Hot diggety," he said, and led her toward the *nepenthes, sarrenciae, darlingtoniae, phyllostachys bambusoides, melocanae,* upas tree, Venus fly traps, bladderworts, butterworts and sundews, over and among which multitudinous insects, both pestiferous and benignant, horrendous and decorative, were swarming in ambrosial and pollenistic orgies, beneath the California sun, and sub-tropical shade.

The others waited in the patio, and when, after a few moments, the couple, so graceful and distinguished, respectively, returned, side by side, the Gardenia was heard to murmur:

"Don Homer. You're a very sympathetic man, and an erudite one. I'm thrilled that you can repose a trust in me."

"Let me be the first to address you as Doña Eulalia," he gallantly said. "Let me felicitate you in French fashion. *Les moindre des difficultés!*"

Homer turned to the others, and said, as a sort of afterthought. "We'll meet again tomorrow, wherever it proves most convenient. I'll be nearer to your murderer then."

With that he bent gallantly and brushed the Gardenia's fragrant hand with his lips.

"And crapola to you, too, sir," the Lieutenant said, in parting.

15
The Labyrinth

"I'M BOUND FOR YOUR STUDIO. Would you like to come along?" Evans asked Sitchev, who after the Los Angeles-bound contingent had departed still was hanging around. The Hungarian accepted with almost pitiful alacrity. Enrico brought Harmon's "second car," a brand-new Chrysler, around and placed it at Homer's disposal. Finke, in response to Evans' nod, got in, but to the right of the driver's seat. He thought well of himself as a driver, but had ridden with Homer before, and knew he was not in his class. This had rankled Finke at first, because he had formerly considered that driving cars was for men of action, and not for the cerebral type. Ruth squeezed into the front seat between them, leaving Sitchev, somewhat hurt, to have the rear all to himself.

Kay was dispatched to the Balm of Gilead Hospital, for data Evans had specified, thence to the Pioneers' Insurance Company, on an errand for Finke.

So Homer, Ruth, Finke and Laslo Sitchev rode toward Cheviot Hills. When they brought up in front of the E.P.U. administration building Finke hesitated.

"I'm not supposed to go in the front way," he said.

Sitchev took him by the arm, as if he were a long-lost brother. "For a friend of mine, here, the best is not good enough," he said. And, to the surprise of all of them, when Sitchev made his appearance before the reception desk the handsome types in uniform, selected for their sensitivity to E.P.U.'s variable winds of fortune, almost bumped their foreheads on the flawless mahogany. It was

Mr. Sitchev this, and Mr. Sitchev that. And of course . . . his guests. A pass was thrust into Finke's hand, made out in flowing script, as if by magic, with his names spelled right. And how was Miss Mesker? *And* Mr. Evans. Long time no see. Of course. And since when did Mr. Homer Evans need a pass? A gesture toward both doors, as if presenting Homer ceremonially with a golden key.

Ruth, eyes narrowed, looked hard at Sitchev. "Well, worm! What gives?"

"I'll explain," the Hungarian promised. "This morning, I'm aces wild."

"You mean ace high?" Finke asked. Then he remembered his Chevvy. "In that case, excuse me. I'll join you in a jiffy, in your office, if that's where you're headed for."

Homer smiled indulgently as Finke made his quick exit, by the same door that he had come in, and beckoned for his companions to follow him back into the reception room to watch.

The first-class parking lot for E.P.U. executives, where Finke had mistakenly left his car the day before, was just across from the porte-cochère (or Port Kosher). Through the sun-conditioned plate-glass windows (at $100 the square foot) they all saw Finke go straight to his Chevvy. The attendant, who had not seen him with Mr. Sitchev, tried to intercept Finke with a peremptory gesture.

Something happened. So much quicker is the hand than the eye that our group saw only that where two of them had been standing, one remained erect, and he was Finke. The other lay flat. Together they looked like the clock hands at a quarter to twelve, although it was barely nine A.M. Finke got into his Chevvy, drove it a few yards and parked it at the curb squarely in front of the Port Kosher and the marble stairs. Then he rejoined the Sitchev party and, without comment, followed them back inside the main building.

They ascended one floor and walked along the marble corridor to Sitchev's suite of offices, where Natalia gave Laslo a greeting that she could not have topped if the Tsar had come to life. Again Ruth Mesker looked hard at the Hungarian and he shuddered, gulped and repromised to explain. Natalia Borodin, woman and maiden, had developed a remarkable deadpan, but when she saw among the group entering her lord and master's office the detective, Finke Maguire, she moved a face muscle or two.

"No interruptions, please," Sitchev said.

"Not even—" Natalia gestured upstairs "—the Chairman of the Board?"

"Not even John Jacob Astor," said Sitchev. And he closed his private office door behind him.

"Now," said Ruth. "To business. We haven't got all day, and don't stall. What does this mean? This reception at the door, and from Natalia? Your about-face with the Manellos. You sang to Lieutenant Marcus, and got them into jail. How come?"

Sitchev was persuasiveness and glibness dually personified. "Don't you see, Ruthie, darling? You're smart yourself. I'll make you a producer. You should work here with me—for blank checks you fill in yourself."

"Can the barn salve. You sold out the Manellos, and sent them to jail, after kissing their backsides all these months, getting my top client ready for Alcoholics Anonymous and my second top client killed. If you don't give us the straight of this, I'll see that you get the same, only slower and painful. See?"

Finke, who still had old-fashioned ideas about women—some women—was appalled. Such fury was shocking, and Ruth was in earnest. Not even Homer tried to soften the way she was laying it on.

The harder Ruth got, the more bland grew Laslo Sitchev.

"You've said it. The whole point. The Manellos are in jail. E.P.U. can breathe again. No more hold-ups. No more fancy prices for properties that stink, and hams who can't act. Sure, I had to play ball with the Manellos. I like, above all, to stay alive. I let them have rope, and they stretched it too far."

"And what if they aren't guilty, as Mr. Evans says, and they get out again?" Ruth asked.

"They've got to be guilty," Sitchev pleaded, appalled by the horrid new thought.

Homer asked Ruth to take them to the E.P.U. school. There, near the center of the lot, on the boulevard side, a model building had been put up in the silent days and had been remodeled with the advent of sound and, more lately, of color. The children, boys and girls, whose tears, evening prayers, lisps, precocious cracks and trick haircuts, curls and braids were known to millions, in the odd way screen writers and directors believe children are effective on the screen, reacted to the studio class instruction as normal kids do. In short, they were bored. Their good luck, which had given them such an edge on their non-professional acquaintances, did not exempt them from the law. They had to put in a specified number of hours, studying cut-and-dried stuff they knew Clark Gable or Betty Hutton had got along so well without, and it soured them on the world while they were enduring what their contracts called "education."

"The Gardenia's old servant has a daughter, has she not?" Evans asked. When Ruth said she had, with misgivings in her voice, and Finke's face broke into a grin, Homer asked Ruth if she would step inside the schoolroom and tell the teacher that Mr. Sitchev wanted Tani to have a few words with his friend, Mr. Evans.

Both Finke and Homer noticed that Sitchev's standing, so brusquely elevated during the night, was "aces wild" in the school as elsewhere, both with the dear kiddies whose uppermost thoughts were to find new ways of attracting attention to themselves, and the teachers who were being paid to keep their charges "normal."

Tani, as she was notified that "a gentleman" had asked to see her, was the envy of all her classmates, most of whom were taller than she was, and about one-sixteenth as bright. Tani, herself, was not thrilled. At the age of thirteen, according to records, and much older in experience and understanding, Tani had already suffered the most deadly handicap and misfortune that can overtake an actress. She had been typed. Her name was never called when kids were needed for a Bowery sequence or a field hockey game in merry England. Because her grandmother had lived in Java, her mother had married an American redskin, and she, in order to converse with all her parents and relatives had had to pick up Javanese, Malay, a Dyak dialect, and the Blackfoot language, Tani was tagged and labeled for pictures set in the Orient, the tropical islands or the wild habitats of American Indians. She had been stripped in February, to paddle in coral coves, and stuffed into papoose baskets in July to accompany her old man, Chief Elkdown, on the war path, in spite of the fact that he had been turned down for flat feet and corns in World War I. Tani's mother and father had both been out on location, in Wyoming, several weeks and therefore have no part in this story. At such times, Tani was left with old Latacassi, not because the kid could not take care of herself, but because Latacassi had never learned more than thirty words of English, and they were intelligible only to sailors. Tani, herself, could remember interpreting long before she said anything on her own. This early training, which had only been part of her odd family life, had sharpened her linguistic turn of mind, so, at the studio, she had learned French, Spanish and Italian with the greatest of ease, and Portuguese and Nazi German on the lot, while E.P.U. had been shooting a spy picture in Lisbon because the same story had gone over big when located in Nicaragua.

Homer Evans had a way with children. He addressed Tani in French and slipped into Malay. Her eyes brightened, in spite of the fact that she was languid and doleful. The man with the Charlie Chan whiskers was playing an amusing game with her, she thought.

"Miss Mesker and Mr. Maguire want to be alone. Shall you and I take a walk?" Homer asked.

Tani brightened a little more, as she gave Finke the eye, approvingly. "I knew they'd be having an affair," she said. "Hells bells. Will I ever grow up?"

They took a few steps along the walk while Finke and Ruth headed for the commissary to have coffee and—from Finke's angle—in the hope that he would run into Pinky Johnstone. Finke wanted to see how Pinky would treat him, now that he was Laslo Sitchev's pal.

Homer did not try any roundabout tactics with Tani. He ignored the absurd schoolgirl frock and put his case directly.

"You're a detective," she said. "How do you stand with Mr. Finke?"

"We're working together," said Homer. "To find the murderer of Shirley Hall."

"Shirley Hall was crazy," Tani said. "Any girl ought to know that you can't keep a man like Bob Reynolds in a glass case. Men like Bob have to have their freedom. They'll come back to the woman they love, whenever they get tired of playing around. Shirley ran him ragged."

"Girls can't be killed just for that," said Homer.

"If they are, a man like Bob'll find someone else," Tani said.

"You think he has, already?" asked Homer.

"I'm afraid so," Tani said. "Only this one isn't jealous. She's too conceited. She can't imagine that if a man can have her, he'll go chasing someone else."

"Does Mr. Reynolds want her or does she want him? Which one wants the other the most?" Homer asked.

"I don't know, and neither do they. He's never made a pass at her, yet. You wait! Some fine day he's going to get drunk and then anything might happen."

"Ah, well," Homer said. "Time will tell."

They walked farther, toward the zoo. "I wish I could talk with Latacassi," Homer said.

Tani grew cagey at once. "What for?" she asked.

"Did you know Mr. Van Vleeck very well?"

"No one knows that old screwball," said Tani.

"Someone killed him, too. Last night or early this morning," said Homer. "Latacassi didn't know?"

"She'd have told me, if she knew. And she wouldn't have stayed a minute in the Gardens. She thinks—all the women do in Java—that when somebody dies who hates them, they have to hide away and go through a lot of magic junk, or the soul of the dead one will get inside 'em and get 'em into trouble," said Tani.

"So Latacassi did spend the night in Miss Noguera's cottage."

"She was roaming around the garden, most of the time. She does that, when the moon is high. That's what women do in Java, and Grandmother can't change her ways. She'd seen Van Vleeck in

Java, years ago and thought he was a demon or something when he showed up in L.A. Of course, he didn't follow her. It just happened."

"Did Mr. Van Vleeck know your grandmother had seen him in Java?" Homer asked.

"Of course not," Tani said. "To him, one old woman looked just like another, and he hated 'em all. He hated children, too."

"He didn't get along with Miss Noguera," said Homer.

"I'll say he didn't. That's an understatement."

They had paused in front of a monkey cage. Inside was a drill with a bright blue behind. At their approach, the four-foot monkey began to chatter and scold, turning somersaults, banging himself against the bars. Tani laughed and got perilously near the cage to tantalize the furious monkey.

"That's the monk who got the gun, and shot it off last evening," Tani said.

"What gun?"

"The one Shirley tried to shoot Bob with. Mr. Finke took it away from her, as it said in the paper. I saw him do it."

"You didn't see him give it to the monkey."

"Well, somebody did. I wish I'd seen that, too. I see so little excitement. A murder happens right in the Gardens where I am, and I don't know a thing about it."

"Won't you take me to Latacassi? I won't frighten her, or hurt her. She can help me, and Miss Noguera, and Mr. Reynolds, if she will, and you'll be interpreter."

"Will I get into court?" asked Tani. "I'm a pushover for courtroom scenes, and I've never been in one."

"Mr. Sitchev's going to have a courtroom scene in *Tabu*. I'll see you're in that and have a few good lines."

Tani was overjoyed. "Lines? You will? Gee, Mr. Evans. If you knew how I want to be a success. I can act right now as well as Miss Noguera—or almost as well. She's got what it takes all right. But so have I. I want to show some of these kids who make fun of me because they think I'm a nigger."

For the only time, Evans spoke to her sharply. "None of that," he said. "We're all in the same boat."

"I didn't mean any harm. Some of my best friends are colored. I've heard that somewhere. It must be a line from a script."

"Can you remember all the scripts of the pictures you've played in?"

"Sure. Try me."

"Ever heard this before? If you can tell me what picture it's from, I'll get you a part in an American picture that's set in New York or even Boston. I'll see that you're cast as a Mayflower girl. Or one of the Little Women," Homer promised.

"You can do that?"

"Mr. Sitchev and I are just like that," Homer said, and snapped his fingers.

"Give me the line you want to spot," Tani said, eagerly. And added, in the manner of Robeson in *The Emperor Jones*: "Brains! Do yo' stuff."

"You've seen a lot of pictures," Homer remarked.

"I've never missed one, if I could help it," Tani said. "Now give me that line."

With a remarkable imitation of the voice of Boris De Witt, Homer quoted: *"You're having an object lesson. What can happen to someone close . . ."*

Tani, a child again, hopped up and down with glee.

"I've got it," she said. "You'll keep your word? You'll get me in an American picture, as a white girl? You will?"

"You haven't told me, yet," said Evans.

"The Sheltering Palms," she said. "I worked in it, myself. With Melvyn Douglas and Joan Crawford, and . . . who were the others? Oh, yes. Peter Lorre and Anna May Wong. I was Anna's kid sister. A Jap. I had a line. 'So solly.' Jeepers Crow. The things I've had to do to stay in this business."

"Where was the action in *The Sheltering Palms?*" Homer asked.

"Let me think. Was it Hong Kong or Hawaii? No. Some desert island, where they could bring in Ubangi dancers. They were so black they had to be made up, all over, in light brown, and turn out to be descendants of some Egyptian sheiks and houris so Joan Crawford, who was a native, could marry Melvyn Douglas, who was a white, a wonderful white doctor who operated on Anna for some kind of paralysis no surgeon had ever cured. So Anna gave up Melvyn, and let Joan take him away, on a liner."

"They forgot the kitchen sink," Homer said. "Thanks, Tani. I'll come through. I'll keep my promise. Now will you take me to Latacassi? Just tell her I'm her friend, and your friend, and let me talk with her. Can I use Malay?"

"She'll understand you, but how the Sam Hill will you understand her? Her dialect, I mean. It's as different as Leslie Howard's kind of English is from Wendy Hiller's in the first few reels of *Pygmalion*. Can you get me in an English picture, too, where I can have lines like 'Not bloody likely'?"

Tani's imitation of Wendy Hiller was fabulous.

She was leading Homer away from the frantic drill and toward the Tarzan lot, the jungle kept intact through all the seasons for the pictures in which women love apes who turn out to be eligible according to the Hays love code.

"This is where Latacassi hides, when she wants to get away from it all," Tani said. "You'd better wait here."

Tani stepped toward a bamboo thicket (*sasa tesselata*) and vanished before Homer could identify the species. He waited, and perhaps after two minutes, two figures materialized. One was Latacassi. The other was Tani. Tani, to make sure her grandmother did not escape, was holding her firmly by the hand. Homer greeted the trembling old woman in Malay.

"Go on. Answer. He's smart. He'll understand you," Tani said.

"Tani," Evans said, kindly. "Find Miss Mesker and Mr. Finke, take them to Projection Room A and wait for me there. We're all going to see *The Sheltering Palms*, but don't give anything away. I want our lines to surprise the others."

"I'm hep, Mr. Evans. The play within the play routine," Tani said. "We used it in *Pearls for Mine*."

"And Tani," added Homer. "You've got a good memory."

"Terrific."

"You might ask Mr. Maguire, on the Q.T., mind you, to ring Lieutenant Marcus and invite him to bring his suspects along, if he's so minded. It might prove worth while, don't you know?"

Tani was enraptured. Her emotional range was truly from girl-hood to where brook and river meet and on downstream from there.

"Then you and they will see me act," she said.

"I can hardly wait," Homer said, and the girl looked up at him quickly. She felt sure he really meant it, and, as a matter of fact, he did.

"One thing more, Tani," he added. "Tell Mr. Maguire, from me, not to fret if he has quite a wait before I show up. And whoever drops in to the projection room, in the meantime, make sure that they stick around. If some of them react this way or that toward some others of them, he might keep his eye peeled, his ear cocked and his reflexes limber."

"Eye peeled, ear cocked, reflexes" (Tani struck her leg above the knee with the side of her hand and kicked daintily) limber," she repeated, to be sure of the message. "G-e-o-r-g-e!"

As Tani tripped away, Homer turned to Latacassi. They talked earnestly, for half an hour, in the course of which the old woman gained confidence and unburdened herself. At the end of the strange conference, which, if nothing more, proved Kipling was all wet about East and West and never the twain shall meet, Homer phoned Alma Shroeder and Boris De Witt, and Latacassi went back to the Gardens, to take care of the neglected East Indian plants, and no harsh hostile voice called out "*Raus!*" to frighten her away. She watered what needed watering, dusted pollen from this and that, patched and adjusted a few screens but her especial atten-tion was not given to the *sarrenciae*, the *darlingtoniae* which bore the name of California, the sundews that were passing dying bugs from tentacle to tentacle, the trap leaf butterworts, the Venus fly trap, or the medicinal *melocanae*. The *phyllostachys bambusoides* and *phyllostachys pubescens*, hardy as they were, required no daily

care. Not so the *nepenthes gracilis* and *nepenthes bicalcarata*, with
their lids both luminous and mucilaginous, their accumulated chiti-
nous exoskeletons, live tree frogs, and their haunting hues of blue
and lemon green, saffron yellow, wine, lilac and the blush of the
shell pink rose.

Bob Reynolds, waking from sleep, took a look from the window of his bungalow and shuddered, and so did Enrico, who so
seldom seemed vulnerable.

They jumped and bit their tongues as the telephone rang.
"We're both to go to the studio," Enrico said.

"Yeah? Oh, *no!*" said Reynolds, aghast. "I can't face E.P.U. just
now."

"Mr. Evans wants us . . . In Projection Room A," Enrico said,
and started laying out appropriate clothes, which Reynolds, numb
with misery, obediently put on.

16
A Census of Suspects

As Evans walked leisurely past the E.P.U. barber shop toward the automobile entrance reserved only for top top-level executives, technicians and stars, he was happy to see Kay's diminutive Austin drive onto the parking lot, a few yards away. Homer halted to watch what would follow, an amused smile on his face.

As Kay unwrapped her long legs from the absurd little car's mechanism and stepped out, all knees, shins, nylons and a flash of flesh and garters, the attendant who was nursing a sore jaw and a bump on the back of his head darted over like a Black Widow's husband.

"What do you think *you're* doing, Highpockets?" the man asked huffily.

Kay, caught unawares, flushed and murmured something about Mr. Sitchev, since it was from the Hungarian's office that she expected to get trace of Finke and Ruth.

At the sound of the word "Sitchev" the parking-lot attendant almost did a backward somersault. "Before God, lady," he said. "I didn't know it was you. Beg pardon. Let me put your car away. Out of the sun." The dazed man looked up to make sure the sun was shining, although he was suddenly drenched with sweat.

Homer's laugh from the sidelines brought a rueful smile to Kay's intelligent face and keen eyes.

"That's the secret word this morning. Sitchev the Deliverer. The lot is yours," he said.

He took Kay by the arm and led her to the Port Kosher. No cop had yelled at him to put himself on record when he had stepped off the sacred premises beyond the auto gate and when he escorted Kay into the marble room where the chosen receptionists, all rosy-cheeked aspiring young men who could be affable or icy by instinct, started bowing and scraping and making a pass for Kay, not at her. All women looked alike to them.

For privacy, Homer led Kay down the short flight of plush stairs to the red leather alcove off the main reception room from which the corridor, equipped with red and green lights, gave entrance to the projection rooms.

"First, the news you have for Finke," Homer said, as they seated themselves and lighted monogrammed E.P.U. cigarettes which were at hand in gold-plated holders on which a humped bison's rear view was engraved.

Kay spoke briefly and clearly, without reference to her notes.

"In this region, between Malibu and Playa del Rey, and east to west from the San Fernando Valley to the Pacific, about 200,000 automobiles (exclusive of trucks, station wagons and special ve-hicles for delivery, etcetera) are circulating—of which approxi-mately, according to insurance statistics, 10,000 would be Plymouths. Of these 300 would be red, and of the red ones 24 would have tall drivers. Luckily I didn't have to sound a general alarm and involve a police investigation. I consulted with the Plymouth agents and got a list of the persons to whom new Plymouth se-dans, maroon in color, had been sold. The thirteenth name on the list was Art for Art's Sake, Inc., of which the proprietor is Alma Shroeder De Witt . . ."

"Ah," Homer said, smiling, "they *are* married, then."

"What is called, I fear, a marriage of convenience," said Kay. "I've known both of them, slightly, for years. De Witt decorated our office, and the objects of art were chosen by Alma. They see eye to eye in matters esthetic, and seldom get that close in *amour propre*, let's say."

"A nice distortion of the French," Homer said. "But we mustn't speak of love now there's so much work to do."

"Alma goes by her maiden name, and Boris works for the corporation on salary, commission and a drawing account."

"Limited by the bank balance and Alma's moods, I take it," Evans said. Kay nodded.

"The number of the maroon sedan in question?" Homer asked.

"DT 3-4938," said Kay.

Homer selected and lighted another cigarette for Kay.

"Please withhold your report from Finke just a little while. I've an idea—just the faintest premonition—that he may find the car he seeks parked behind his Chevvy, before the porte- cochère," Homer said. "We're seeing an old picture called *The Sheltering Palms*, with Melvyn Douglas, Joan Crawford, Peter Lorre and Anna May Wong. And also Tani Elkdown."

"Tani Elkdown? Have I ever seen her?"

"Not yet. But note her work, particularly, please."

"Mine not to reason why," sighed Kay. "If she's one of those girl prodigies, I'll have the vapors."

Homer lighted an E.P.U. for himself.

"Now, Miss Cougar. The thumbnail biographies, if you please. First the light one, bright one, who cashes in on the stuff that dreams are made of."

Kay began, again without having to scan her notes.

"Born in Stuttgart, 1902, therefore 48 years of age. Got his degree, *summa cum laude*, 1931. Post-graduate work at Eitel Friedrich, Berlin, 1933, at which time he was forced to join the Nazi Party."

"All out, or with reservations?"

"He hated it, so it seems, and, from distaste of excesses in Berlin, took a post in Batavia, Java, East Indies, in the Dutch hospital there. In Java he remained from 1934 to 1937."

"As psychiatrist or general diagnostician?"

Kay touched her right temple with her right forefinger and rotated the latter. "Psychiatrist," she said.

"Proceed."

"In 1937, after a brief stay in Berlin, he was transferred to Amsterdam, Holland, where he got increasingly nervous, according to his own story, and escaped just before Hitler's invasion, which devastated the city and overwhelmed the Dutch in 1940. He was accepted by the New York authorities and admitted, as a refugee. He followed his profession with distinction at Bellevue Hospital from 1940 to 1945, when he came to Beverly Hills."

"And found the streets—or, at least, the couches paved with gold," Evans said, concluding Kay's sketch of the career, to date, of Hershel Harms, M.D.

"And now, Lukie Kohler," began Kay. "Born, Tallinn, Esthonia, 1915. German father, Esthonian mother. Fled to Berlin long before the Soviets took over. Trained as nurse at Eitel Friedrich Hospital, qualified and registered, 1933, age 18. Obliged to join Nazis. Did so, just before Dr. Harms became a party member. Went to Batavia in 1934, two months before Harms did. On Harms's 'invitation' got work in Amsterdam in 1937. In summer of 1939, went to New York, where she took out first papers, before World War II broke out. There was a serious shortage of competent nurses, even then, and it got more acute as the months went on. Miss Kohler made an excellent record, before and after Dr. Harms joined her, in 1940. She came with Dr. Harms to Beverly Hills, in 1945, and has been his assistant and receptionist ever since. Meanwhile, attended U.C.L.A. and got degree of M.D. to be of greater service to Dr. Harms as his practice developed."

"Finke should know this at once. Let me summarize, more for my benefit than yours, Miss Cougar. And correct me if I err. Dr. Harms is 48, Miss Kohler is 35. Their respective journeys along the path of life brought them together first at the Eitel Friedrich Hospital in Berlin, in 1933, and both had to Heil Hitler and join his crusade for the New Order, which became old before its time. Lukie embarked first for Batavia, in the East Indies. Hershel caught up with her two months, later, in 1934. Hershel was first 'transferred' to Amsterdam, and invited her to join him. As European affairs went from bad to worse, he sent her on to New York, for her safety, no doubt, and made his own escape a step ahead of Hitler's invasion of Holland. She did well at the Bellevue, and so, when he was welcomed to America, did he. They worked 'with distinction' until 1945; then it was westward ho. He has made what to a European professional man is a fortune. She's now also an M.D. Right?"

"Right," said Kay.

Homer rose gallantly. "You'll find Miss Mesker, Finke and Tani Elkdown in Projection Room A," he said, indicating the proper corridor. "Join them if you like. I'll be along later. And, meanwhile, whoever drops in, persuade him or her to stand by. If some of them react this way or that toward others of them, you might keep an eye peeled, an ear inclined and your deadpan on straight."

"Jehosaphat Crow," she said, softly and hurried off, smiling.

Evans took the elevator to the second floor and walked leisurely to Sitchev's office, humming softly, under his breath, the sublime tenor solo from the Sanctus of the Berlioz Mass. On entering the outer room, where Natalia sat, he went straight to her desk, and said, with all his charm:

"*Gospodya* Borodin! I wish to consult with *Gospodin* Sitchev, little dove. Have the obligeance to walk to the zoo. The air will do you good, little wild duck of the North. Please to count the drills and mandrills when you arrive at the cages, and if one of them seems to be missing, stay there."

"*Da!*" she gulped, and hurried to obey. By that time Sitchev was in the doorway of the inner office, extending his arms to make Homer twice welcome. What they talked about will become self-evident later. It is only necessary to note here that the moment Evans had finished and retired a few yards to an easy chair on which the red leather had been replaced by white, Laslo brought his guest a phone marked "Private," unconnected with the studio switchboard. Evans dialed a number. "Hello! Mike?" he asked.

"*Mister Ev*ans!" exclaimed the famous restaurateur.

"Would you mind calling Maître Douthé to the phone? Tell him who's calling."

"If I shouldn't tell him, he'd crown me with a skillet," Mike said.

Romanoff evidently transmitted the request, for after a few seconds the usually irritable voice of the famous *chef de cuisine* came to Homer over the wire, but overjoyed.

"Monsieur Evans!"

"André," Homer responded. "A certain Doctor Hershel Harms, ex-anti-Nazi from over the Rhine, has an office on your street. Ergo: He has money and, possibly, taste. He lunches *chez* Romanoff?"

"Weekdays excepting Sundays," the chef said promptly. "He is a slight little man, very amiable, with a discriminating taste but no more than the average appetite, which flags during the cheese course as the hour for his nap approaches. Therefore he omits dessert and liqueur. He arrives punctually—ah, these punctual Boches—at noon."

"As early as that?" Evans asked.

"His magnificent nurse, Mademoiselle Kahler, prefers to lunch at one. They can't abandon the office together. So the doctor goes back and dozes in his chair until two, when she, also punctual— the she-Boche is more deadlier punctual than the male—returns. But La Kahler's appetite is beyond belief. Yesterday . . . No! Day before yesterday, she ate a *gigot entier*. A whole leg of lamb."

"Not yesterday?" asked Homer.

"Yesterday, *nom de nom*, since you mention it, she ate almost nothing. And tore her *serviette* in two . . . Her napkin, not her brief case, of which she carries none."

"Thanks, André. I hope, if the pressure of affairs relaxes, to taste your unparalleled cooking no later than tonight. Let me see. Today's Wednesday. Would you be having sweetbreads Masson?"

"My friend, you'd eat with pleasure of Monsieur Romanoff himself, if I prepared him with a truffled sauce like that," Douthé said.

Evans hung up the receiver, after the appropriate exchange of civilities and amenities, then handed the instrument to Sitchev, who sat at his desk again. He dialed a number from memory.

That fact did not escape Homer Evans. Soon a woman's voice, forceful but modulated, was heard to answer, "Here, the office of Doktor Hershel Harms! And who is calling?"

Sitchev told her.

"Al*so*," the voice said. Another voice followed, almost too quickly.

"Mister Sitchev, this is truly a pleasure, although the occasion is sad. Our loss is poor *Miss Hall's gain*. She suffered much—as only can an artist."

"I'd almost rather to have died myself. And in the bargain get murdered. But no matter what happens, can a director in this business take time to grieve and moan? The first thing this morning, I'm called upstairs. 'What about Mr. Reynolds?' He's temperamental like you can't conceive. He's prostrated. Can the picture go on? You understand, Doctor, that the very least one of my budgets runs, for a feature in color like Mr. Reynolds plays in, is two, three million dollars. Our Chairman and Board of Directors have hearts, but also they have fingers to count on. In this case they're unanimous. They say 'Scrap the script. Let Bob take a voyage on the ocean, at $6,000 a week, minus tax, till he recoups and gets sober, and then we can risk three, four million on one of his pictures again. For myself, what could be sweeter? I get, maybe, a rest. Not on the ocean, God forbid, which just to mention makes me sick as a dog. But up in Palm Springs where it's quiet and you can find a few fellers to talk with who don't know English. . . ."

"You mean, Mr. Reynolds wants psychiatric treatment?" Dr. Harms asked in real alarm.

"No. We just want your opinion."

"We?" asked Dr. Harms cautiously.

"Me, then. You can't refuse me," Sitchev said. "I talked the Chairman over, till he's willing to take a chance and go ahead with my picture, if you guarantee Bob won't go nuts till after it's in the can. I want you should come, for any figure you've got the nerve to ask, and see, at noon today, a picture. Bob Reynolds'll sit with friends, up front, and you—Miss Kahler, too, if you like—sit behind where you can keep your eye on him. Then after lunch you should meet the Board and give them the signal that Bob's all clear."

Homer, standing closer, and Sitchev, ear glued to the phone, heard a muffled exchange in German.

"I'll be at your studio at noon," the doctor's voice said. "But I shall have to give the Board an honest opinion."

"As honest as you like, so long as you say Bob can still act sane. *Auf wiedersehen!*"

The Hungarian turned to Homer. "I know a man like you can't be bought with money. But if the Manellos get gassed, even if in this case, as you claim, it might be unjust . . ."

Evans shook his head, good-naturedly. "Crooks must be taught to respect the law," he said.

The harassed director, torn between fears and hopes, took up the phone. He dialed—again from memory—and when a woman's voice responded, "Art for Art's Sake, Alma Shroeder speaking," his rejoinder was, "Put Boris on the other phone if he's not already there. . . . This is Lash. How are you, Alma, darling? You know what I've offered, how many times. The minute you should get tired of Art for Art, come mit me and try art for box office. I'll O.K. your designs on blank paper, before you draw them, yet. You'll get blank checks you fill in yourself. Bring Boris too. Who cares?"

"Oh, I say," said De Witt. "Is that nice, after I've been technical adviser on six of your silly pictures, and no critic's found anything wrong except the story, the dialogue, the casting and the revolting emphasis on sex?"

"This time, we're doing something different! Original! Gripping! *Deep!* I wish I was as sure of living to accept the Oscar as I am that I'll get it, posthumous, in case I don't."

"Either way suits me, dear," De Witt said, and seemed to be indulging in a yawn.

"You must be flush, to be indifferent, like this," Sitchev said.

"We'll drive over, Laslo. And thanks," Alma said.

"Damn and blaast!" Homer heard Boris whisper, with a very short "a" in "damn" and an extra long one in "blast".

In Projection Room A the barometer which, while only Tani, Finke, Ruth and Kay were present had indicated "Fair and Warmer," had fluctuated with the entrance of Bob Reynolds and Enrico. Bob was wearing heavy dark glasses, the lenses and rims turned obliquely from the nose bridge up and outward, so that he looked as if he were in a rakish mask. Enrico stood beside him, also in dark-rimmed glasses, but owlish and circular.

"I can't see what this is all for?" Reynolds said. "Evans last night seemed like a reasonable chap. He won't even let me have an eye-opener till this show is over."

"He didn't tell you what this is all about?" Finke demanded. He could have used a snifter himself.

"Not bloody likely," Tani said. "Didn't you see *The Maltese Falcon*, or *The Lady in the Lake?* The master mind keeps everybody guessing through eight reels to build up suspense."

"As far as I'm concerned, the suspense is tight enough right now."

Bob and Enrico came in and took seats, five rows from the front and in the center. The house lights were on and the screen pale and blank. The projectionists had not yet brought over the cans containing *The Sheltering Palms*, so the projection booth was empty. The same messenger who had taken Finke the afternoon before to the de-luxe telephone booth looked in the door, saluted politely and retired.

"I don't get it," said Bob. "There's too much God-damn politeness around the studio this morning. Or is it all hush-hush because my feelings must be spared? Why can't people act natural? Wherever I go, they pussyfoot and look away, and remind me that Shirley's dead. Why can't we come right out, and talk about it? Sure, I treated her rotten. I was an s.o.b. She was swell. When she went for a man, and she never went for any man but me, she went all out. And what did she get? I know all that. And I know the worst trimmers and two-faced louses in this business are the ones who sigh the loudest and put on the most sickening act."

"Hell," Finke said. "Don't blow your top. Each man kills the thing he loves . . . Well, I didn't mean exactly that."

"That reminds me," Kay said, and she pulled from her handbag a small pearl-handled automatic, a very early model, and handed it to Finke. "You might need it, boss," she added.

"Thanks!" Finke said, and slipped the gun into a jacket pocket. "You think of everything." And Kay felt happy inside.

Bob clenched his hands and pounded the arm of the seat.

"Has everybody gone nuts around here? My nerves can't stand this too long."

Kay took a pint from her handbag. "Just one," she said, and the others, who saw Bob's reaction to the act of mercy, realized that she had done well in exceeding her instructions.

"How does it feel to get a skinful?" Tani asked.

Nobody answered, but Ruth and even Enrico looked at the pint with eager eyes, and decided to abstain.

The left-hand door opened, and into the lighted auditorium, which was at once so roomy and so intimate, led by Pinky Johnstone, who seemed to be trying to offer his pale smile and his bottom simultaneously, stalked Lieutenant Marcus. But he only stalked one pace, and then became ironically gallant. For, still in black—lovely, fragrant and dignified—the Gardenia floated rather than stepped into the room. Behind her was Mills Harmon. The oil tycoon somehow cleared Marcus from the space the Lieutenant was about to occupy and took her arm. Behind them, as they filed down the aisle, as solemn as the rest, walked Ric Manello. Next in line was Tony (appearing more grotesque than can be imagined, in his loud clothes) and then Pete, who was tough and nonchalant. To bring up the rear, Sergeant Spode waddled down the aisle.

Finke, a sardonic grin on his face, rose to greet them, one and all, but addressed himself to the Lieutenant.

"*So*, shamus. You changed your mind and decided on an outing, after all."

"Commissioner's orders, shamus," Marcus said.

"What's wrong? Did you make such a mess of your *habeas corpus* dodge that the D.A. threatens to horn in. Take my advice, shamus. Let the D.A. have this case."

Disdaining to answer directly, Marcus sat down, in the row ahead of Finke and his companions. "Where's the Professor?" he asked. "I don't hear his voice."

"He said for you to wait. He's busy this morning," said Finke.

Harmon, glowering, was still standing in the aisle, with the Gardenia beside him. Finke turned to her and smiled admiringly.

"Mrs. Harmon, I presume," he said.

"Not yet," snapped Marcus. "I wasn't born yesterday. Has it occurred to you that a husband can't testify against his wife, and vice versa? That billion dollars'll have to stay in one chunk till after the trial. Let 'em get hitched in the death house."

Neither Ric Manello nor his brothers had said a word. They had taken three seats, a little off by themselves, tossed their hats on three more, and were idly watching the projectionists, who had lighted up their booth and were sorting cans of film.

The door opened again, and Pinky Johnstone, who had sat quietly in the rear, as if hoping nobody would notice him and start involving him, sprang to his feet.

"Come right in, Mr. Evans," Pinky said, looking around Evans and the others for Laslo Sitchev. He still remained effusive, on the chance that Sitchev, whom he could not locate, was in the offing. In rubber heels the Hungarian director, as Pinky well knew, could make a tomcat sound as if he were stamping.

The look of relief on Harmon's face, to say nothing of Finke's, Tani's, Ruth's and Enrico's, was touching to behold. The Gardenia, veiled and immobile, somehow conveyed more poignant welcome than those who inhaled, exhaled, gestured, slumped, stiffened or exclaimed. And for once, Ric Manello's thoughtful, even wistful face, revealed his thought. "Well. Here's a man a man can talk with," it seemed to say. "Now we'll get on with it."

With Evans, in order of entrance, were Dr. Meyerson Ruloff Hamilton, eminent surgeon and diagnostician, from the staff of the Balm of Gilead Hospital; Hank Bibesco, in his capacity of medical examiner of Los Angeles County; and Captain Strongfort of the Beverly Hills police. Pinky Johnstone sidled over beside Strongfort, and was not chased away. Yesterday the Manellos were sitting on the world. Today Sitchev was the darling of the Chairman of the Board. Who might be King of the May tomorrow? Pinky had stuck it out through many changes of administration and policy. He hoped he might make it, once again, if, like Latacassi, he kept in hiding from the evil spirits.

Marcus beat the others to the sixty-four-dollar question.

"Well, Doctor! What killed Shirley Hall? We know who, and where, but we got to know how 'twas done," the Lieutenant said.

Everyone except the Manellos and the languid De Witt sat up straight.

Dr. Hamilton looked uneasily at Homer, who stepped into the aisle, where all could see and hear him without effort.

"Miss Hall was drugged and then poisoned," Evans said. "The drug was administered to allay her suspicions and make her susceptible to suggestions. It is called pheno-indizene-tridexadrol. Am I right, Doctor?"

Dr. Hamilton nodded confirmation. "Or possibly, didexadrol."

"The poison that killed her is compounded by nature and made usable by human artifice. We can't disclose details concerning it, right now, or say how or where it was obtained," continued Homer.

Marcus leered resignedly. "Now there's the professor running true to form. He knows all about this pheno-chafadrol, that's probably mostly aspirin and can be bought without prescription in any drug store. But the stuff that killed her, where it grows, or where these mugs and the future Mrs. Harmon found it and used it—those facts are just too pertinent for words. Let's skip routine items like that. Those things are confidential."

"You'd favor warning the murderer, I suppose, so he or she could cover up, and go free?" Evans asked. "You're too impulsive, Lieutenant. But I'll not hold out on you. The late Barney Rice died in your jurisdiction, and the post mortem was conducted there. Dr. Hamilton, only this morning, was able to announce, not for publication, that Rice died from swallowing the fertilizing element of local *phyllostachys*, presumably from the groves of the Omar Gardens."

"You mean to say that the Dutchman killed Miss Hall, then bumped himself off? Come off it. Come off it!" Marcus exclaimed.

"There you go. A jumping bean is poised compared with you, Lieutenant."

"And beans to you, sir," Marcus said. "If that's all you got to offer, me and my charges will toddle along, either with or without bracelets, as they choose."

While Marcus was threatening to break up the meeting before it got fairly under way, Pinky Johnstone and a figure in a rear corner whom no one, thus far, had noticed, but who turned out to be Natalia Borodin, sprang to their feet and started making the obsequious kind of motions, erect, that subjects of the King of Siam make while prone. Laslo Sitchev had materialized in the doorway and started down the aisle, followed by Dr. Hershel Harms and the statuesque blonde, Lukie Kahler. Behind them, in turn, came Boris De Witt, and the self-effacing Alma Shroeder.

Introductions were effected all around, by Homer, who thrilled Tani by presenting her first to Sitchev as a coming star about to be discovered, and who might eclipse Demona Bourbon, Doodie Howland, and Betty Buckeleinikoff (née Bresnahan).

Since all the men had stood up to meet Lukie and Alma, and the Gardenia had risen, also, and for the first time turned back her veil, there was some reshuffling of the seating arrangements when the projectionists signaled Sitchev that they were ready with the film. Homer, himself, went back to the steps of the booth to whisper a suggestion to the chief projectionist.

Covertly he was watching the others in front and noted that Ric Manello was doing his best to sit next to Dr. Hamilton; Sitchev and Tony Manello were stumbling all over Harmon to get a place on the left of the *señorita*; and Bob Reynolds was appalled at finding himself between Lukie Kahler and Dr. Hershel Harms.

Boris De Witt was making quite a play for a seat behind Finke. Eventually he landed it and at once he leaned forward to chat. Kay, seeing Pete Manello sitting by himself, so tough, boyish and neglected, planked herself down at Pete's right.

Alma, Ruth and the Sheriff were together, and Tani was between Sitchev and Sergeant Spode. The Hungarian was dimly aware he had seen Tani before (she had been in the background of ten of his pictures) and was noticing that, in spite of the clothes she wore, she might have everything Evans had said. Her voice was spontaneous and flexible to the point where already it sounded quite like the Gardenia's and unconsciously Tani had adopted the *señorita's* delicate air. Why not let the kid understudy Mumu, and maybe, do a few stunts with sharks and a waterfall, for instance, that would be too hazardous to permit a star to do, with the risk that a million dollars' worth of takes might have to be scrapped if she got hurt? Sitchev was thinking of a possible bargain. If Evans would trade him the Manellos, dead or deported, for Tani, he would build up the kid and put her name in lights.

When Sitchev had entered, he had not seemed to notice the Manellos, and they had not bothered either to look at him or away from him. The intellectual tussles for advantage in cinematographic circles are like the classic rough and tumbles on the screen. The actors deal each other blows that would stagger the stone ghost in Don Juan, throw around furniture that three furniture movers from the Southern California football team couldn't lift. First one combatant is flat, belabored and bleeding, then the other is stunned by a chair which is smashed to bits by the impact. When the sequence is over, neither hero nor heavy has to pause for breath or even to straighten his tie. It is an accepted routine, and they have done it. The next sequence, apparently, has no connection, and still the picture makes the kind of sense that is cinematographic, and slowly is taking the place of banal reality in the public mind. Children may cry with disappointment when they take a swing at a little playmate, and he does not fall off a balcony into a nest of rattlesnakes, but simply slaps them back. Still, they do not lose their faith that Tyrone Power can knock Lionel Stander over six rows of seats in a Malamute saloon, if Osa Massen seems to require it.

The Manellos had never played for marbles, and they knew Sitchev was as slippery as an eel in a pail of pudding sauce. So what? They'd been on spots before and nevertheless had sent cartloads of flowers later to the funeral of the guys who'd outsmarted them. Sitchev was longing with all his heart to smile at them, as a first step toward letting bygones be bygones, but he didn't dare, not yet. Meanwhile, he and they were supposed to act like certain characters in an old-fashioned play who had entered from separate sides and remained some time on the stage, oblivious to the presence of the others, until the cue prompted them suddenly to get their eyesight back and let out a cry of effusive recognition.

The ringside seat for the sharpest by-play had gone to Finke. He was bowled over by the forces of resentment, jealousy and hatred which played around and through him like bolts of radio-activity. Finke was not the object of these frightening passions. Bob Reynolds was the target, like a radio tower without a trans-mitter, and all its receiving apparatus tuned to concert pitch.

"Holy cats," Finke muttered, as he turned from the Junoesque Hun in white to the pulsing Latin beauty in black. "Are these murders over yet?" Of one thing he was sure. Bob Reynolds was squarely in the middle. Finke wondered how many of the others were aware of that.

The house went dark. The Humped Bison, rear view, switched his tail, and the credits were flashed on the screen:

THE SHELTERING PALMS
with
Joan Crawford
Melvyn Douglas

Anna May Wong
Peter Lorre
Sessue Hayawaka
Lionel Stander
etc.

Produced And Directed
by
Laslo Sitchev

and so on, until near the end of the credit list:

Technical Adviser
Boris De Witt

The story was of the simplest. Melvyn Douglas, a beachcomber who had been a mesmerist with ambitions to make his way through medical school, and whose failure to do so had driven him to sea, had been shipwrecked on the island of Foo N'Lan. A few weeks earlier in the season Peter Lorre had landed from a junk in a leather-sailed "ghost boat," which was never supposed to be used by mortals, but had been built according to native superstition in order to furnish tempting free transportation to any demons who wished to quit Foo N'Lan for some other island. Peter had brought with him, unconscious from the deadly coconut fever, Joan Crawford, and both Peter and Joan had narrowly escaped being strangled with ocelot thongs because of the foreign spells which Peter, who was Chinese, used on Joan who, being white, was held by the rank-and-file natives to be the ghostly carrier of the terrible fever of the polluted palms.

The high priest, Sessue Hayawaka, and his high executioner, Lionel Stander, were arousing native opinion to the pitch necessary to tie Joan and Peter to large stones and feed them to man-eating giant clams. The clams, once they had digested their victims, would have to be caught by native divers and ceremoniously fried on a pyre of *phyllostachys pubescens*, the toughest of bamboo leaves.

Just in time, Melvyn Douglas swam in with an old phonograph the natives had never seen. The mysterious threat to the fanatic old chief and Lionel Stander struck terror to the Foo N'Lanians when it was intoned in English:

> "YOU'RE HAVING AN OBJECT LESSON. WHAT HAPPENS TO SOMEONE CLOSE TO YOU, CAN HAPPEN TO YOU . . ."

Homer Evans, sitting in the rear, gave an almost imperceptible signal. The film was torn, there was a bewildering flash, then whiteness. As suddenly, the house lights went up, catching one and all completely unprepared. What none of them except Homer realized was that they had been photographed.

There was a soft thud, then another. Two members of the group had fainted. They were Natalia Borodin and Alma Schroeder.

The action, on the positive side, came from Bob Reynolds. Bob, blinking, caught sight of the supercilious face of Boris De Witt, who was looking especially bored, even for him. There was the man, within reach, who had threatened him with death in behalf of the Manellos, Bob was sure. Before he realized what he was doing he had swung from way down near his knees, as he rose, and caught De Witt with such a haymaker that the batik specialist fell backward over the seat which had been occupied by Finke. Finke caught De Witt and tossed him back to Bob. Bob grabbed Basil by the padded shoulders and started shaking him, as if there were no other way he could vent his blind rage.

There might have been another fatality if Nurse Kahler, who in the course of her practice had been faced with many similar emergencies, had not put her powerful arms around Bob *and* Basil and addressed herself to Bob.

"*Liebling!* Bobbie! Don't. If you kill him, they'll kill you."

Bob continued to struggle, even more frantically.

"Bobbie! It's I. Forgive me for yesterday. I got crazy. I didn't know what I was doing."

Reynolds' head cleared enough so he could see the gleeful expressions on the faces of Lieutenant Marcus and Finke. Lukie began to croon to calm him.

"Aw, nix, Lukie. Nix!" Bob begged, trying to push the tender Amazon away. De Witt, ignored, slid down to his knees. Lukie held Bob in her ample and tender embrace.

There was a flash of black, as if cloud and lightning had reversed effects, as in a negative. The Gardenia had torn herself from Harmon, who was trying to shield her, and had taken a swift dive. Her slender hands gripped the German giantess by the hair and her perfect knees in the sheerest of nylons jack-knifed up to Lukie's muscled midriff. Bob, between them, caught the force of the onslaught and was catapulted against Lukie with such momentum that his forehead flattened her nose and made her lose her grip.

Tony Manello was yelling and rooting. "Four gets you five on the little one in black," he said, and Hank Bibesco hauled out a ten. Ric looked on with impassive disapproval. He, like Finke, had old-fashioned views about the conduct of women, unless they were out-and-out molls.

Mills Harmon was roaring and hopping, trying to step over or across De Witt, who, sitting in the aisle, was fixing his hair and straightening his tie.

"Don't tread on me, you a-a-absurd old man," he said, pouting.

Finke had looked to Homer for his cue, the moment he could collect his wits. Evans was purely the observer. It fell to the sculptor, Rodin, to make the symbol by which civilized men should personify "The Thinker." Had Rodin been still alive and present in Projection Room A he would have caught Homer's pose and sculptured "The Observer." So Finke observed, too. He observed the powerful hands of Lukie Kahler, whose head had cleared, reaching, nails ready, for the lovely face of Eulalia Noguera. The huge nurse was accustomed to exertion and violence and was trained to rise above confusion. The action was deliberate and would have disfigured the Gardenia, perhaps unfitted her for the screen, had not Finke intervened. Somehow, Finke stripped the *señorita* from Lukie, as if she had been a live black sheet draped over a white statue about to be unveiled. The *señorita* fell back, with strands of blonde hair in both hands, landing on Boris De Witt.

"Oh, brother," the batik expert exclaimed in disgust, and pettishly readjusted the Gardenia's clothes to cover her matchless legs, which seemed, somehow, to annoy him.

For a moment it looked as if Finke had bitten off considerably more than he could chew. Lieutenant Marcus rocked and chuckled with delight, then was sobered instantly. For Marcus had seen what luckily Finke had sensed also. The big German nurse's right thumb and forefinger formed themselves into a "V" not three inches apart. She feinted with her left and her right, fingers still in "V" formation, darted straight toward Finke's eyes.

At such instants, trained fighters, like wild animals, act on atavistic impulse. Finke ducked his head down, so his face was protected by the starch and soapy uniform on Lukie's resilient bosom, and brought it up with all the force the real danger and narrow escape from being permanently blinded had added to his own, never inconsiderable. The back of his head hit Lukie's chin, which was not set for it. Her head bobbed back, and then, Homer, the observer, saw Dr. Harms transformed. The little Berlin doctor, who specialized in the realm of nerves and mind, reached into Finke's pocket, took out the automatic and, holding it against Finke's stomach, pulled the trigger. Too late, Homer yelled a warning, and came down the aisle at top speed. There was a sharp report. Another and another. Alma Shroeder, who had revived, all by herself, promptly fainted again, and Natalia smothered Sitchev in a protective embrace.

Finke, who had not been in a position to see the doctor attack him, or feel the gun slip from his pocket, thought he had been shot and already was in a kind of limbo. Lukie had drawn back, also counting Finke for dead, and dazed by the prospects. Dr. Harms had dropped the smoking automatic back into his pocket and was begging, not Finke's, but Lukie's pardon, as if from years of habit that had become second nature to him.

Then, in the course of a few seconds, during which Finke was bewildered because his whole past life did not seem to be unreeling backwards before his mind's eye, he realized definitely that he was still alive. For he had caught a glimpse of Kay's face, on which was a contented, though enigmatic, smile. His hand went to his midriff, where the cloth of his shirt was scorched and warm. Coincidently, his eyes, still on Kay, telegraphed to his brain that his secretary was sitting quite detached and alone, where formerly Pete Manello had been beside her.

Finke made a gesture to Homer that all was hunky-dory, and turned to Marcus.

"Nice work, shamus," he said, with a derisive grin.

Marcus was, for once, sincerely apologetic. "Now have a heart, shamus," he pleaded. "Would you have figured such a thing could happen, if the shoe was on the other foot? This funny little squarehead doctor, who couldn't hurt a fly even if he would. Frisking you for a gun, and shooting it!"

"I didn't mean that," Finke said.

Marcus hardened again, in self-defense. "Then what in hell did you mean?"

"Have you counted your suspects lately?" Finke asked, his blue eyes alight.

One of the quickest things that had happened in a very quick oleo was the turn of Marcus's head toward the Manello brothers. Ric was sitting as before. Tony and the Sheriff were deciding that their bet, in all fairness, would have to be called off. Pete was nowhere.

When slowly the awful truth dawned on Sitchev that the hardest of the Manello brothers was on the loose, and doubtless with one sweetly solemn thought in mind, he began to bawl like a calf, and ran to Homer to implore protection.

"I'm a dead man already. I knew something like this would happen. You wouldn't listen, Mr. Evans. Now where can I go? Palm Springs? Tahiti, yet? A boy like Pete'll get his man, and his man, Mr. Evans, is me. You got to help me, Mr. Evans," Sitchev wailed. Natalia again embraced him like a mother who had given birth to a gnome about forty-five years old, and loved it for its faults.

Ric Manello looked on impassively, and the sight of him caused Sitchev to cry out again. "I'm already embalmed. I smell flowers."

Tony grinned and said, "Yeah?"

There was a pause. Sitchev, had he dared, would have run away and hid, but there was nowhere to go, least of all in the studio which Pete knew as Latacassi and Johnny Weismuller knew the Tarzan lot.

"I might have known, shamus," Marcus said, sarcastically to Finke. "Any dame who works for you would pull a fast one."

Kay looked pleased, in her modest unassuming way.

"Think nothing of it," said Finke. "The others'll be free soon enough."

"The *señorita* won't," Marcus retorted. "I never thought you'd be much help, but you and your professor have just given me what I want. Something swell for a jury. Just why, when the nurse began fussing over Reynolds did the *señorita* start pulling her hair? The *señorita's* nuts about Bob. What do you say, Dr. Harms? You're an expert on jealousy."

Harmon was swelling and purpling again.

"I knew it," he said to Eulalia. "He's infatuated you. This Mumu and Timomo business! He's turned your head. Can you deny . . ."

Eulalia straightened herself sadly and looked Harmon in the eyes. "I didn't want him for myself," she said. "You must believe me, Señor."

Marcus almost crackled with joy. "Still making a play for that half billion dollars," he said.

The Gardenia turned on Marcus and said with quiet self-possession, "If you'd seen what I've seen, in the slums of Mexico City, you wouldn't keep up your foolish American pretense that a woman, in love or out, mustn't think about riches. What other security is there?"

Anyone could have heard a pin drop in that recently so noisy auditorium. She turned back to Harmon.

"You understand, Señor. You know what plenty means. Have I ever led you to believe that I didn't look forward to unlimited wealth right in my hands?"

"You attacked Miss Kahler when you saw Reynolds in her arms," the oil man said. "I suffer, too, regardless of bank accounts and assets. You've made me realize how lonely I've been. It's life itself, not money, that has to be shared."

The Gardenia kissed Harmon on one cheek. He bowed his head and patted her shoulder. "Then why, my darling, did you forget yourself?" he asked.

"I didn't want that great blonde beast to have him," she said. "I hate her without knowing why."

"I've felt the same way—to a milder degree—in business transactions. I've risked impoverishing myself to prevent a man I detested from getting a good thing I myself didn't need."

The Acting Sheriff laughed merrily and slapped his thigh. "Still want that one on the stand, before a jury of her peers, if any can be found?" Hank asked Marcus.

Disgusted, Lukie strode up the aisle and Dr. Harms would have followed her out had not Sitchev grabbed him.

"Not yet, Doctor," Sitchev pleaded. "You got to O.K. Bobbie's nerves to the Chairman of the Board." The little Hungarian took a check from an inside pocket and waved it like a pennon.

Dr. Harms, after tearing his wistful glance from the door through which Lukie was disappearing, looked at Bob Reynolds and swallowed hard. It was Tani, this time, who was drying Bob's brow with her handkerchief and murmuring comfort and endearments.

"Might it not be better to observe Mr. Reynolds a few days longer?" the psychiatrist suggested.

"Better not give time for the Board to hear you took three shots at Finke. That wouldn't do much good to your reputation if it got bruited about."

The psychiatrist got the point. He sighed and looked at Bob again and Tani's ministrations. "The classic examples," he murmured to himself. "Cellini, Henry the Eighth, Don Juan, Valentino. They feast while others starve, and who can blame them?"

Homer Evans, as he had seen Big Lukie make her exit, glanced at his watch and nodded.

"The subconscious acts, under no matter what stress and strain. It's exactly her lunch time, one o'clock," he said. "I must ask my friend Douthé about her appetite today. Will it be two legs of lamb or none?"

Homer called the others to order. "Has anyone else an appointment just now?" he asked.

Only Boris De Witt responded, and the Gardenia. De Witt had a customer due at the shop, one with money and no taste, who might not wait. So Homer excused him.

"Great God, Evans. He's the Voice. You're letting him give you the slip," Bob objected.

"Not in a new maroon Plymouth, or any other way," Homer said, with his disarming but deadly suavity. "You understand that, all of you," he added. "We all must hold ourselves available till this is over."

The Gardenia asked with her eyes for Homer to step aside from the others.

"You're not disappointed?" she asked.

"I shall always be grateful," he said, "and so will the lady with the scales, whose toga, not heart, is of stone."

Of the company, Homer asked if they would kindly follow him and they responded, two and two:

Tani with Bob Reynolds, who held her by the hand.
Dr. Harms with Laslo Sitchev, who, for other rea-
    sons, held him by the hand.
Enrico and Kay
Ruth Mesker and Alma Shroeder
Finke and Marcus
Harmon and Dr. Hamilton
The Gardenia and Ric Manello
Natalia and Pinky Johnstone
The Sheriff and Sergeant Spode
Tony Manello and Capt. Strongfort.

The procession, which, incidentally was the cynosure of all the eyes along the route they traversed, filed out of the projection room, through the corridor and reception room to the plush stairway, up to the ground floor, along the marble corridor to the exit within the bounds of the lot, across to Stage One, and a block down the studio street to the Music Department. There in a filing room larger than the weapons warehouse not far away was a collection, supposedly complete, of the Voice recordings for off-screen effects. They were arranged according to year, picture titles alphabetically, and in the order of appearance in the film.

Sitchev, at Homer's request, found the recordings for *The Sheltering Palms*. There were not many, only three involving a voice. The middle one, the envelope of which was there but with the disc missing, had been spoken by Boris De Witt, and was labeled "Object Lesson".

"Not here," Homer said, his eyebrows raised.

"Not there?" asked Sitchev, uneasily.

"As I suspected," Homer said. "Before I myself tried to find it earlier today."

He turned to Marcus. "I thought we might start even," Homer said to the Lieutenant. "Whoever finds this record will take a long step toward solving this case—if he is careful not to jump at false conclusions. Now Hank and I propose a deal. You let my protégés and helpers enter and leave your city territory unmolested, unless you have something on them. Hank will not question your right to arrest any culprit in the County, again provided you have a valid reason for detaining him. In a pickle like this, we must trim, if not clip, the red tape. Do you agree?"

"I still keep the Manellos, the two that are left, and Señorita Noguera?" Marcus said.

The *señorita* looked at Evans with a question in her eyes.

"That wedding through the bars," said Homer. "It shall take place? Miss Noguera and Mr. Harmon can make a deposition before they are one. You can use their statements, made before the ceremony, no matter how thoroughly they are married just afterward."

At that point, Dr. Harms absent-mindedly put his hand in his pocket and found the still warm automatic. He let out a little scream, which still was enough to make all hands jump and contract like startled crabs.

"What shall I do with this?" he asked.

Finke, grinning at Pinky Johnstone, pointed toward the zoo. "Give it to one of the monkeys, Doc," he said. "That's an old E Pluribus custom."

"Is that the one you took from Shirley?" Pinky Johnstone asked.

"Now what do you think?" Finke said. "Would I give Miss Hall a rod to shoot my client's top client? I know you told Marcus a story like that, but I didn't think you'd be dumb enough to believe it yourself."

The E.P.U. Chief was nervous and hesitant. "It didn't really seem to make sense," he said.

Finke took a step nearer. "So you did call in this shamus *before* Miss Hall was killed? And started him scouring San Francisco for me and my client, Miss Mesker? You weren't playing ball, by any chance, with the Manellos?"

"I try to be nice to everybody," said Pinky.

Finke stepped up so near he could have flicked Pinky's nose.

"You told shamus" (thumbing at Marcus) "or so he told the Chief of Police in Frisco, that Miss Mesker and I were wanted as witnesses in a murder case. *What* murder case? Miss Hall was still alive. So was Van Vleeck, the Dutchman."

"None of this stuff makes sense," Pinky said evasively.

"You do," said Finke. "You're a lousy gold brick and a stool pigeon."

That was too much for Pinky. "I don't have to answer your questions or report to you," he said. "Your nose isn't so clean. You slugged a guard and stole a gun. And if you didn't slip it to Shirley, who did? And what gun did she use?"

"So you don't have to answer my questions," repeated Finke. "Whose questions do you have to answer? Ric Manello's? Sitchev's? Maybe the Sheriff's? Come over here, Hank. Ask this Alabama clam who told him Barney Rice had been murdered! And what he did about it. Ask him when he told Marcus, and what Marcus did about it!"

Finke was going full steam ahead, and Homer watched, approvingly.

"You come on over here, too," Finke said to Sitchev. "Go fetch that guard who says somebody slugged him, and let's see if he identifies me. It could have been one of *your* pals who gave Miss Hall that gun. You wanted to get rid of her."

"I'll go, Mr. Finke," Sitchev said, hastily. "I'll bring the guard."

The Sheriff let Finke ask Pinky questions, and backed him up with County authority. It was routine at E.P.U. for Pinky to look into any death of an employee, important or insignificant. Pinky had called the hospital . . .

To everyone's astonishment, Dr. Harms stepped forward in confusion. "Let me explain," the psychiatrist said. "When Mr. Johnstone applied to the hospital for information he was referred to me, since no one at the Balm of Gilead was in a position to state the cause of the ex-soldier's death. But since it was I who sent the late Mr. Rice to the Balm of Gilead, Mr. Johnstone's inquiry, as a matter of form, came to me."

"Most interesting," Evans said. "Pray continue."

"It isn't a suspicious circumstance," said the psychiatrist anxiously. "Miss Hall was my patient."

"So I understand," agreed Homer.

"Mr. Reynolds was her fiancé."

"Granted."

"Miss Hall had confidence in me."

"I daresay."

"So she advised Mr. Reynolds, when he got worried about Mr. Rice's pains, to send him to me. She thought, naturally, that if I couldn't treat him, I'd recommend a reputable doctor who could. That I did."

Dr. Harms bowed to Dr. Hamilton, and the latter, as meticulously professional as he was competent, said, "You're too kind, Doctor. One can hardly say that I distinguished myself on the case."

"You've made up your mind what killed Mr. Rice?" Dr. Harms asked.

"With the help of Mr. Evans," Dr. Hamilton said.

"Only they can't announce it to the regular police," interposed Marcus, skeptically.

Dr. Hamilton spoke again with professional courtesy to the little psychiatrist, who had beads of sweat on his forehead and was fumbling his cuffs with his hands.

"I'm sure we'll all be discreet. You'll understand why. It was the sharp sabulous fertilizing element of *phyllostachys bambusoides*. But even had I known what the irritant was, in the beginning, nothing whatever could have been done to save the patient," Dr. Hamilton said.

"You mean," Finke asked in horror, "that if one party feeds another party a dose of this stuff, which can't be seen with the naked eye, then the party who swallows it dies—weeks later? And this sabulous cafacha grows wild, and costs nothing? We may as well write off half the population, if this gets out."

"How about Shirley Hall?" Marcus put in. "She didn't take six or eight weeks dying, or six minutes, if you ask me."

Dr. Hamilton looked around him, lowered his voice, and, after a nod from Homer, said, "Miss Hall, according to the autopsy, died of poisoning, after the administration of a large dose of sedative to make her incautious and pliable."

"And the poison?" asked Dr. Harms.

"A concentrated infusion of the acid from *nepenthes gracilis* in a glass of cool water, which rendered it practically tasteless, especially to one who had been drinking frozen Daiquiris and was dosed with a pheno-indizine-dexadrol compound."

Dr. Harms sighed and looked relieved. "I regret, Doctor, that the practice of my specialty has caused me to forget what little I ever knew about the toxic vegetable acids. One becomes as ignorant as a cannibal outside his own restricted field. Alas."

Homer Evans was never as disarming. "You were at the Batavia hospital, Dr. Harms, in 1936?"

"Now, have a heart, Professor. Let's not go back fourteen years, after all," Marcus said.

"I wouldn't be born," Tani said. "Isn't that a rotten break?"

Dr. Harms ignored the by-play. He was on his guard, again, or so it seemed to Finke—and also Ruth and Kay. "One couldn't practice mental healing in Berlin, where madness was the order of the day," the little doctor said.

"You were working in behalf of the Dutch Government, were you not?" Homer asked.

"You'll be astonished how many Hollanders, staid and stolid as they seem in their own country, shed their inhibitions or gather new and dangerous ones in the East Indies," Dr. Harms said. "The psychiatric ward was always filled, and there was a long waiting list."

"I've heard," Evans said, "that some of the Dutchmen were well served—oh, very well, indeed—by native Javanese women, in the interval between the men's arrival and the time, some weeks or even a year or two later, when the Dutch wives joined their husbands."

Dr. Harms shrugged and smiled. "Inevitable," he said. "Sometimes I had to treat the man, more often the wife."

"And never the native women?" asked Homer.

"Native girls preferred to be stabilized in Javanese fashion, and I must admit the native cures were quite effective."

"You mean the female casualties *d'amour*, let us say, were married to complacent Javanese males, and started raising children? Or slaving over hot wax and tubs of batik dyes?"

"I was so busy," the doctor said, "that I had little time to study native customs."

"Or native plants?" suggested Homer.

"I've always been an indoor man," Dr. Harms said, ruefully, looking down at his small stature, as indicated by the creased legs of his pants.

"You never met, out there, by any chance, a learned Dutch botanist, one Sprouls Van Vleeck?" persisted Homer.

"I don't seem to recall the name," the psychiatrist said.

Homer asked what seemed to be a quick question of Tani, in Malay, then another, more deliberate, of Dr. Harms, before he dismissed the latter.

"You don't remember a housemaid called Norma, because her native moniker was far too difficult for everyday use?" Homer asked.

It seemed to Finke that there was a flicker of dismay, or a slight significant hesitation before Dr. Harms replied. Anyway he paused, seeming to search his mind, which might have been a play for time.

"Look, Professor. I couldn't even say for sure who was vice-president then," Marcus objected.

Dr. Harms recovered his modest aplomb. "You might ask Miss Kahler. She managed the servants," the doctor said, and blushed to the roots of his hair.

"She would," muttered Finke and blinked his eyes thankfully, to make sure they still worked. Turning to Marcus, Finke said, "Take the witnesses."

"Thanks for nothing, shamus," Marcus said, and scratched his head.

17

Where Fancy Is Bred

FINKE WATCHED MARCUS WALK OUT of the Music Department and suddenly felt one of the unaccountable spasms of uneasiness that came to him now and then when he realized that he was noticing something that should be indicative and was muffing the significance.

"I don't like the way he beats it out of here. He's got a hunch," Finke said to Kay and Ruth. They agreed that the Lieutenant looked purposeful, and found it a little strange that he should leave the rounding up and escorting back to Lincoln Heights such a slippery pair as the remaining Manellos and a girl as unpredictable as the Gardenia to Sergeant Spode.

Homer, who had been receiving the heartfelt thanks of Mills Harmon for having fixed the wedding day, observed the uneasiness of his trio of associates. "Think nothing of it," he said, and the others relaxed.

"If this keeps up, I'm going to get an inferiority complex," Finke said. "I'm not supposed to be smart, but I used to be tough. And what happens? I've been crowned by a punk, frisked by a monk, judoed by a dame and shot in the pantry by a practicing psychiatrist, and all I got to show for it are a couple of K.O.'s—a poor working stiff who wasn't set for it, and a Dutchman in the dark."

"Never mind, boss," Kay said.

Laslo Sitchev, who had gone for the guard, returned with him. "I want you should look around and tell me if you see the man who hit you and pinched the gun," said Sitchev. "But if you should make a mistake . . ."

249

The implication was that, in case the guard picked an innocent friend of Sitchev's, he would join the ranks of the unemployed and be blackballed in the bargain. So the guard shook his head.

"No, Mr. Sitchev. I'm sure, Mr. Sitchev, he's not in this room."

Pinky ground his teeth and his eyes narrowed, but he had to take it. So he tried to smile and asked Finke privately if he would mind telling him how he had got off the lot.

"Not at all," Finke said. "I climbed the fence, like any human fly."

"And the Chevvy you left behind?"

"I didn't need it, anyway," said Finke. "Am I still entitled to a pass?"

"Of course, of course," Pinky answered, and added in an undertone. "As long as Sitchev lasts."

As if he had overheard, which he had not, Sitchev moaned. "I'm embalmed. I'm stretched. I don't exist." He turned to Alma Shroeder. "You tell that Boris of yours that the next time he puts a flea in my ear and it turns out to be a spider . . ."

"Most interesting," Evans said. "Did Boris suggest that you frame the Manellos?"

Sitchev was abject. "Now, Professor. Be reasonable! Who would you have picked, in all Southern California, to be guilty of a crime that would net them at the very least one hundred thousand grand, in cash? Would you have said they'd overlooked a bet like that?"

"You did. Or *did* you?" asked Ruth, her eyes ablaze.

"What could I do? They'd have larded me like a rabbit if I'd tried to take a cut," Sitchev said. Again he tugged prayerfully at Homer's sleeve. "Just let 'em get ten-twenty years."

Ignoring the Hungarian, Homer approached Kay.

"Your gift for statistics, Miss Cougar, is exceptional. Would you exercise it again in our behalf?"

Kay nodded.

"Get a note from Mr. Sitchev, commending you to his banker. I'm curious to know about the bank accounts of our suspects. Doubtless you know those I mean," Evans said.

"If you do, you're way ahead of me," Finke muttered.

"I'll include everyone, police and all," Kay said.

"Now look a here," blurted Pinky Johnstone.

"Omit Chief Johnstone. He plays the races," Homer said.

Alma Shroeder sat down, limply, and began to cry again. "There's nothing the matter," she protested.

Homer, looking at her with the deepest compassion, touched her forehead. "Why not lunch with us at Romanoff's? Afterward I'd like to toddle over to your shop."

The proprietress of Art for Art's Sake seemed inconsolable and could hardly follow what Homer said. Again he touched her forehead. "There's an old New England saying: 'Good riddance to bad rubbish'," he said.

For company at lunch Homer selected Dr. Hamilton, Ruth and Alma, Hank Bibesco and Finke.

Dr. Harms had appointments at his office, Natalia had to stay at her desk to tell all inquirers that Mr. Sitchev had gone to Palm Springs. Pinky Johnstone did not dare leave the lot until he was sure Sitchev's standing was going to last, at least through the day. Captain Strongfort, who lately had worked nights, needed sleep in the daytime. Bob Reynolds, too nervous to be of use, and Tani, who had no intention of being shunted back to school, went to see *The Man Who Sought the Truth* in French, with Raimu.

The lunch at Romanoff's passed very pleasantly and with the cheese, the famous chef, Andre Douthé, forsook his kitchen to pass the time of day with his friend, Evans, and get direct word about how things were in Paris. Homer had ordered for everyone: *saucisse de Toulouse* and black olives, a *matelote* of eels with red wine sauce and Spanish Val de Peñas; chicken breast Rossini; salad Pharamond; *brie* and coffee with Armagnac.

After paying his respects to the chef and introducing each of his guests, each one of whom, incidentally, Douthé would remember and favor during the rest of his career, Homer asked casually, "Which was it, today, André? Two gigots or one?"

"Unfortunately, none. I'd prepared goose with parsnips, since the party in question can eat half of the bird, and I can count on the other half . . ."

"*One* person. Half a *goose?*" asked Alma Shroeder, and her eyes seemed to widen with horror before she burst out crying again.

Bravely she tried to smile through her tears. "I'm the death's head at the feast," she said apologetically.

Douthé bowed. "Had I known you were in sorrow, madame, I should have not served you sauce Rossini. He was an enormous irrepressible Italian, with their national relish for flour. No one whose heart is breaking should indulge in white flour. An aid toward a stoical attitude, your native American Indian cornmeal is *de rigeur*. It produces the wholesome attitude and emotional balance of your sturdy savages, who, by the way, knew much more about *amour* than our Jesuits who came to convert them."

When Douthé had retired to the battery of ranges he fondly called "his piano," the natural restlessness of the companions began to manifest itself again, until soothed by the Armagnac. That settled their moods, even Alma's. School could keep or not, into each life some rain must fall, so what? The art of Douthé and the discrimination of Homer Evans had produced its effect.

Over the precious distillation of the grape known to the Gauls, Homer turned to Dr. Hamilton, and the others, glasses in hand and bottle on table, were content to listen.

"In the early nineteen thirties," Evans began, "the Dutch—that is to say—the most perspicacious among them, began to foresee, with the rise of Hitler, that they might be invaded. Therefore, the advisers to the Queen urged Her Majesty to use all ways and means, without consulting the German-born regent, of securing the Dutch hold on the East Indian colonies, where there was a spontaneous nationalist movement among the natives which was being perverted by Nazi propagandists to direct it against the Dutch. The Führer wanted to weaken both the patriotic natives and the Dutch by pitting them, one against the other, with a view to easier Nazi conquest of them both."

"It's all right, Mr. Evans. Take your time. Start with the Stone Age if you want to, so long as the Armagnac lasts," said Hank.

Homer smiled. "We must sketch in the background," he said. "We may skip the political and military phases and focus our attention on the medical implications. Ever since the Dutch had taken possession of Java and the nearby islands, the home Government

had made it a practice to send men to the East Indies, to get accli-
mated and prepare the way. The wives were shipped to join the
colonizers, some time later, after it had become apparent that the
Dutchman in question was fitted by physique and temperament to
stay. The Dutchmen got along famously with the native girls, and
formed attachments which were inevitable, and mutually benefi-
cial. But no matter how deeply the temporary attachments proved,
the Government, with the routine obstinacy governments have,
kept sending blonde, blue-eyed and relatively innocent young
women, as wives or brides-to-be, in order to avert the formation
of an intermediate race which might well prove dominant in the
region. The population of Java alone is 48,000,000, that is,
8,000,000 larger than that of France or Holland.

"Statistics soon seemed to show that blonde, blue-eyed Dutch
women had little chance of survival in the Javanese climate, until
it was observed that most of them died in mysterious ways not suggestive of maladjustment. The Javanese had always been extraor-
dinarily adept as poisoners. Polygamy was practiced by the sultans and the rich, and the swarms of wives and concubines, by
Hindu tradition, were supposed to die when their lord and master
did, either by stabbing or on the funeral pyre. Those girls who were
shy of blood and blade or who dreaded the agonies of fire found
ways of poisoning themselves, in which they were abetted by
old women, and seldom by the eunuchs who guarded them. The
eunuchs were impaled alive on sharpened bamboo poles (and all
their male relatives with them) in case their charges got hold of
contraband poisons and rendered themselves unfit for the traditional public ceremonies of knifing or roasting."

It was at that moment that Mike Romanoff, who always had a
wistful desire to get in on rare discourse that took place in his restaurant, stepped over and handed Homer a telephone instrument.

"Enrico? Ah. Indeed! I thought so. From Moscone?"

Finke remembered that Moscone was the sentinel of the rear
door of the Forty-Niners Towers.

Homer was still responding tersely. "Good! The excellent Pablo,
too? Now what should we all do without Boris?"

The wine and Armagnac had died in Alma, leaving her without the force to cry out. Homer, disregarding her distress, hung up. "Remember where we were, Doctor?" he asked of Hamilton.

"The roast and the blade," the famous specialist said. "Why is it, through history, men like to see ripe women slaughtered and cut from the vine? Wild beasts and the lady Christians. Adolescent Hindu girls and wild pigs. The scalpel parting the skin of American maidens for unnecessary appendectomies. The Siamese practice of lopping off girls' hands. The rites of Suttee. The Fascist ordeal of the purge and the stoppage. Ah, me! And we thought all that was behind us, or some of it, at least."

"The least attractive trait we humans have is the cruelty we learn from Nature. Our pet cat with the mouse. Our faithful dog who shakes the cat to death. The grasses on the lawn, which conduct total wars whose relentlessness never seems to diminish. And our *nepenthes gracilis*. And all the other pitcher plants the late Van Vleeck nurtured and studied so faithfully. They kill, not as much to vary their diets as for sport. The sport of luring, outwitting, trapping, handling and killing."

"Amazing, if disgusting," exclaimed the doctor. "Now who would have suspected? What I can't fathom is how a man like Van Vleeck would go so far, and show such originality in research, and still not publish his findings, except those few articles you pointed out to me."

"I suspect—we'll verify this later—that Van Vleeck was waiting for his controls to survive another season before sending in his final revised manuscript for publication," Homer said.

"Bottoms up!" said the sheriff to Ruth and Finke.

"I'll get to the end, for now," Homer said. "The Dutch wives and sweethearts were being poisoned by old women who knew all the tricks of the trade. There was a standard fee, much less in actual cash than the price of a 'permanent' in Beverly Hills."

Finke tore himself away from the glowing relaxation the brandy was providing and so did Hank.

"Did the Dutchman have a wife who got croaked on account of a Javanese Jane? Is that what soured him on women?" the sheriff asked.

"He had a wife, unless I'm mistaken, who survived the Javanese girl he loved to distraction."

"You mean some outsider got an old witch to poison the native cutie?" asked Finke, and Ruth shuddered. Alma had reached the limit of her suffering, and suddenly was calm and very attentive.

"All witches are not old, or ugly, or even male or female. At the time the poisoner in question was as neutral as one of Dr. Hamilton's marble slabs."

"How many of the suspects in this case have been in Java?" Ruth asked.

"Quite a number," Homer said. "But don't assume that others can be eliminated as suspects. Anyone who can read and walk around might have killed all three victims. Now let's see. Those who've been on Java. Mills Harmon, Dr. Harms, Fräulein Kahler, Latacassi. *I* have."

With an effort Alma got to her feet. "I have. I've been there," she said.

Homer smiled disarmingly. "Of course. In connection with your trade. Few dealers have your grasp of East Indian art."

As if regretfully, Homer rose, too, as a sign that the lunch was over.

Alma's eyes got wide with horror, but she got hold of herself. She could not let the subject drop, it seemed, without knowing the worst. Quietly she said, "Why don't you say it right out? Boris was there. But he was only a boy of eighteen. A student."

"He was eighteen, you say?" Evans asked. "Well," he sighed. "Some mature early. Look at Tani, for instance. She's as old as time, and her grandmother's a child. Think of Marie Bashkirtsev, who wrote of love when she was six, and quite as well as D. H. Lawrence. Mozart composed one of his profound symphonies at the age of eight, or was it nine?"

Two girls from the check room arrived with hats and summer wraps, and Evans led the way toward Art for Art's Sake, not fifty yards away.

"Unless I'm mistaken," mused Evans. "Our precocious Boris decorated Dr. Harms's reception rooms."

"My office, too. Including Picasso's three-faced dame with a mackerel for a kelly and a Caligari chair," said Finke.

Evans continued. "Boris also sold a few odds and ends to Mr. Harmon, for himself and the Gardenia, and furnished the upas wood frames for Bob Reynolds, who gave them to Shirley Hall. And Boris lives, or doesn't he, at the Forty-Niners Towers?"

"That's our address—and we're still married, don't forget," Alma Shroeder said with a show of defiance.

After noticing that the maroon Plymouth was nowhere to be seen, Homer entered the art shop and found Kay waiting patiently, notebook in hand.

"You must have had some lunch," she said. "The banks are closed. Even the help has left, except for Mangini, himself, and the watchmen."

"Get what we wanted?" asked Homer.

"You'll have to be the judge of that," Kay said. She opened her notebook, as they stepped aside from the others. Her long forefinger indicated a name and a notation.

"Now isn't that intriguing?" Homer asked, and smiled.

The name was Boris De Witt.

The entry was American Express checks, ten 1000s, five 500s, fifty 100s, one hundred 50s, two hundred-fifty 10s.

"Mmmmm," mused Homer, as pleased as Punch. "I make it just twenty-five grand."

"A nice round sum, the bastard," said Kay.

Meanwhile Alma Shroeder had been looking around the shop. There was a sizable display room, with modern furniture, lighting fixtures and shades, statuary, trays, etc., in front, and three back rooms. The smallest of these was used by Alma as an office; another was devoted to Boris' finished batiks and others from Java or Bali. The third back room, with a roomy modern safe as large as a meat dealer's ice box, contained prints, drawings, engravings, paintings and reproductions, also frames. First Alma had gone straight to the frame rack, and, after examining its contents, had recoiled. Her lips quivering and her hands clenched, she had almost torn open a large folder of wood cuts.

"I take it the rich customer you'd been expecting didn't show up," Evans suggested at her elbow.

She wheeled like a vixen, eyes blazing up at him.

"Does that concern you?" she demanded.

Now this is for the book, Finke said to himself. He had seen Homer get on famously with so many zany women, especially of the type who knew about art, that he had caught on that Homer was deliberately provoking this inoffensive little dame.

While Finke was thinking, Homer softened toward Alma and took the opposite tack. "The customer was here and couldn't get in, perhaps. I wonder where Boris might have gone. In your new Plymouth. He looked most displeased when I said we'd all have to stay on call, as it were, till our case is over. May I?" As he concluded with the question, Evans had already started dialing.

"E.P.U.?" Homer asked. "Thanks. Mr. Sitchev, please. Never mind Palm Springs, Natalia. This is Evans." Homer's voice sharpened. "I don't care how or where he is. Connect me, please! . . . Ah. Laslo? . . . Homer. Who in your vast studio do you call when you want transportation? Fine. Ask her, will you, if she has within the last fortnight booked two tickets for New York on the *City of Los Angeles* or the *Superchief* for a Mr. De Witt and friend. Get also the name of the friend."

Alma had sat down, eyes dry, knees trembling. Finke had an impulse he could not control, and did not. He stalked over to her side, placed his hand on her hot forehead and said, so Homer couldn't help hearing, "Chin up, sister. I'm putting my chips on you, the whole pile."

And as Finke and the others looked anxiously at Homer, they were relieved to see him relax and smile. "Exactly," he said. "Whatever Mrs. Shroeder may have done, or not done, has been under extreme provocation. Of course, this is murder, which nothing approaches as far as extremity's concerned."

The voice of Sitchev issued from the receiver again.

"That any cheap technical adviser could prove so ungrateful! I picked him up from the gutter. Now I need him, he slips the cup from my lip."

"Where to? Gotham?"

"No. New York," Sitchev said.

"Alone?"

"Better he had been. He's taking that sissie who dresses just alike with him."

"The name?"

The Hungarian seemed disgusted. "Sinjun Rochelle—who turns out to be Cyril Heukolom on his pass, yet."

Finke, still patting Alma, took notice.

"The drip who speaks Malay and rides with Boris in the maroon Plymouth sedan," he said, to Homer, who had replaced the phone.

"So that's why Boris wasn't anxious to take a paying job with Laslo in *Sin on an Island*," Homer said. "He'd already made other plans."

Homer took up the phone again. This time he said, in a jovial mood, "Lieutenant Mox Klop? As I live! I want you should go to the union railroad depot by Los Angeles. . . . Yes. It's the Professor. I've just been talking with your No. 1 source of misinformation, Mr. Sitchev, and his habits of speech are contagious. Please drop whatever you're doing, sashay over to the depot. The U.P. Streamliner leaves for Chicago and New York in twenty-five minutes. Take off one Boris De Witt. He'll have abandoned a maroon Plymouth sedan in the public parking lot. It's not his. You'll find with De Witt, in Compartment D, Car 63, called *Minetta*, a certain Cyril Heukelom. No. I'm not kidding. He goes by that name, and also the name St. John Rochelle, but let that pass. By no means detain Cyril. On the contrary, encourage him to continue his journey as if nothing had happened. I'm not in favor, as a rule, of giving citizens what you Los Angeles police call 'floaters,' but circumstances alter cases. You might suggest that if he is ever seen in these parts again, you'll pick him up under Paragraph 3, section 7, Chapter 213, of the Revised Laws of California, 1932, as amended by . . . You understand."

"Look! Why fool around with young men's fancies? The case is sewed up," said Marcus.

Alma was crying softly. This time it was Homer who laid his hand on her fragrant hair and batik headdress.

"He isn't worth all that," he said. "But, if it comes to a showdown, who is?"

There is a moment in each California afternoon, and markedly in June, when, while the sun is still high, a subtle change is noticeable in the air, as if the heat had reached its peak and progressively the hours of sunset, twilight and dark would be cooler. So that in desert freshness, the moths, owls, bats and tree frogs would come forth.

At that hour, on the same Wednesday of which I have been writing, a solemn but eager group sat in the patio of the Omar Gardens and a delegation, including Homer Evans, Dr. Myerson Ruloff Hamilton, Don Enrico Torres y Montero, Finke Maguire, Latacassi and Tani were standing in the shade of the bamboo grove, near the transplanted upas tree, the pitcher plants, screened and unscreened, the greenhouses, moon lilies and the other Oriental rarities of the late Dutchman's collection.

As he had done quite a few times before on that day, an action that was by no means habitual with him, Evans glanced at his wrist watch.

"Now is the hour," he said. "The brunette Jean Harlow the world has been seeking so long should be in the process of acquiring five hundred millions of Yankee dollars, and a husband we all respect and admire, with one of Manhattan's most illustrious old names. I should have liked to have been best man, or at least the No. 2 witness, had not Mox Klop and Sergeant Spode craved the honors.

Tani clapped her hands. "Goody, goody," she said. "She won't be able to keep up her play for Bob, as brazen as if she were single. Does she lose the money if Mr. Harmon has cause for divorce?"

"For shame," Enrico said, quite formally. "A Mexican girl of her quality who gives her word, and gets millions of dollars, will honor her promise to the letter."

"Four gets you five," Finke said, and Enrico produced a ten.

Homer cleared his throat and addressed himself to Dr. Hamilton. "To make a long story short," he said. "The manuscript in Dutch we just examined in the bedroom of the late Mynheer Sprouls Van Vleeck, M.S. Bot. Doc., Ph. D. . . ."

"Pants presser and fertilizer spreader on the side," muttered Finke with a look of distaste at the *sarrenciae*.

"The manuscript," continued Homer, "presents the results of a lifetime of study. No longer need Occidental toxicologists grope in Stygian darkness where the poisonous plants and fruits of Java, Bali, Sumatra and other East Indian or Polynesian islands are concerned. To the growing library of beneficent science, a department has been added. All honor to Van Vleeck, who in order to accomplish this fine purpose, did not hesitate to work as a servant and valet, live in virtual exile, and bear in silence his great sorrow."

"The Javanese cookie?" asked Finke.

"Perhaps its better," Homer said, "that he never knew she was a daughter of Latacassi, a sister of the absent Mrs. Elkdown, and an aunt of Tani, who bears her a haunting resemblance."

"Unfortunate man," Dr. Hamilton said. "A great scholar who dies before his work is quite done."

"His work, I shall finish myself," Homer said, simply, and Enrico impulsively wrung his hand. Homer continued, embarrassed but warmed by the Latin demonstration. "You noticed, Doctor, that the next to the last completed chapter was missing?"

The doctor looked regretful. "I don't read Dutch," he said. "German, Latin, French, Italian. But no Dutch or Slavic, or Scandinavian. I'm practically an ignoramus. There's so little time," he said and sighed.

"Who pinched the missing chapter, or is that a top secret?" asked Finke.

"We'll get to that tomorrow, at the final ensemble," said Homer. "But I can reassure you in advance. The missing text will be recovered. Who knows? Meanwhile our friend, Mox Klop, is chasing phonograph records and a chapter of a book which will have a pitifully small circulation, and from which the author, even were he alive, would derive less recompense than little Tani, here, does from acting in a picture like *Scruples Away*."

"That was fun. I'd have done it for nothing," Tani said.

"Exactly," said Homer. "Van Vleeck was that way, too, about things he enjoyed. And that chapter to which I've just referred, when we locate it, may convict his murderer, who was also Shirley Hall's and Barney Rice's."

"You still maintain they're three in one?" asked Finke.

"As sure as the Mills Harmons are now one in two," said Homer, and was about to join the ladies and the sheriff in the patio.

Dr. Hamilton detained him deferentially. "A few questions, if you don't mind, Evans. The upas tree, for instance."

"I'll translate from memory what Van Vleeck has written on that subject," he said. "An adventurous English physician and traveler claims to have witnessed in 1752 the 'execution' of nineteen concubines of a sultan in old Weltereden, now known as 'The Hague of the Far East.' This 'execution,' was a veritable execution but by other means, more or less secret. In brief, the unshakable conviction that persists today to the effect that the juice of the upas tree is deadly poisonous has no foundation. The old belief that bad odors spread disease or death is partly responsible, and so is the careless English doctor, Abel Simmons, and the London *Times* who credited his slipshod findings. Native executioners in all the islands pretended to use upas juice to deceive the relatives of the women executed, who down to the third or fourth generation were likely to attempt revenge with poison themselves. No doubt those eighteenth-century executioners, and others who date back a thousand years or more, sampled the juice of upas, as I have, and found it unpleasant but quite harmless. For purposes of poisoning, either official or criminal, the upas juice was reinforced by concentrated liquid from the pitchers of *nepenthes gracilis*."

Homer stopped quoting and made a gesture toward the beauteous, frightening and luxuriously colored pitcher plants.

"All the others, aside from the *nepenthes*, are content to drown their prey with rainwater," Evans explained. "Our *nepenthes* poison the insects."

Tani nodded. Dr. Hamilton and Finke started in horror.

"You know about all these damn weeds that kill and poison?" Finke demanded.

"I know whatever granny knows," Tani said and touched the old witch's hand affectionately. "We talk all night, sometimes."

"Maybe it wouldn't be such a lousy idea for you to take up Sitchev, and beat it back to wherever in hell you'd like it best," said Finke.

Tani smiled provocatively. "You're a nice funny man, Señor Finke," she said, in such perfect imitation of the absent Gardenia that everyone was astonished.

"You don't miss much, at that," Finke admitted. "How much else have you overheard—from Bob, and me, and God knows who else?"

"Maybe everything," Tani said, as mysterious and noncommittal as Evans could be.

"If you'll answer me one question, you'll still get that speaking part, in *Tabu* or *Sin on an Island*," Evans promised.

"May God strike you dead?" Tani asked, in Sitchev's tone.

Homer placed his hand on his heart.

"All right, shoot," said Tani.

He asked his question in Malay and Latacassi started jabbering.

"Man the pumps," Finke muttered, and gave up even trying to make out the drift of what she was saying.

"Thanks," Homer said, and to Finke, "We're in luck."

Dr. Hamilton groaned. "My God! He has Malay, too. Most likely Hindu and Chinese. I'm a dunce. I should resign."

"Just how are we in luck?" Finke demanded.

"When Bob Reynolds was with the *señorita* after his visit to Ruth there were eavesdroppers—besides Tani and Latacassi."

"Who was spying? The Dutchman?" asked Finke.

"As a matter of fact, the learned Van Vleeck was watching from a distance, beyond the range of hushed voices. But there was another. And that one was watched by still another, who guarantees, in many easy lessons . . ."

"To give a patient rational views of sex and love, for instance?" demanded Finke, suddenly enlightened. "He and his helper must gather their data at night."

18

Exhibits B and C

"WE CAN'T BE TOO SURE of the times of death," Homer said, as Dr. Hamilton was about to take his leave and return to the busy hospital.

"For Miss Hall, it's between 1:05 A.M. and 1:20, at the earliest and latest, Wednesday morning," the renowned doctor said. "Moscone can vouch for that, and the findings of the post mortem confirm those limits."

"It's fine we got *something* in plain words and figures," said Finke.

"In the case of Mynheer Van Vleeck, death must have occurred about the same time, surely between 1:00 A.M. and 1:30," the doctor said.

"Ah, yes. Quite," said Evans, and shook hands with Dr. Hamilton before the latter started away. "Of course, Doctor, we'll see you tomorrow for the final get together," Homer said. "Always a melancholy occasion. Friends and enemies must part. That sort of thing."

"Elevenish?" the doctor asked, and Homer, already deep in thought, absently nodded.

"Say! *Wait* a minute. Just a *min*ute," called Finke. "You said the Dutchman died between one and one thirty? This morning?"

Homer nodded and waved the doctor the all-clear signal.

"Elevenish," he said. "Projection Room A."

Finke braced Homer before he could slide into another of his inaccessible moods.

"Look. Between one and one thirty this morning, I personally was in these Gardens, afoot, awake and on the job, and so were

Enrico, Latacassi, that kid, Tani, who knows more than Mozart, not to mention the Gardenia. Even discounting the others, and me, Enrico was on watch," said Finke.

"Not constantly," Evans said. "Enrico had a couple of minor repair jobs. Besides, just after you arrived, and *before* he brought you the *Examiner* extra that upset you so, he had to drive a few miles along Sunset to tow in a client."

"All right. Try this one. Who was loose in the Gardens who could have wandered in to knock off Van Vleeck? Who could get into Harmon's bungalow and find his way around?"

"There's only one who might have done all those things," admitted Homer. "That may be why Mox Klop, bless his heart, has been so cocky today. He got a report of Dr. Hamilton's findings, according to our pledge. So he's made his timetable and put a double lock on the Gardenia's cell."

When Finke was worried, he did not try to hide it, unless it was a special occasion when a poker face helped. And Finke was not one of those detectives who always win at poker. Whenever he broke even, he felt lucky. "We've got to do something," he said.

Homer agreed reluctantly. He led Finke to Harmon's cottage, deserted except for the Sheriff's representative, who was dozing on the most comfortable divan.

"As you were," murmured Homer, and as the county man complied, he led Finke to Van Vleek's bedroom. On the bed table, some leaves of the manuscript and printer's proofs were spread, weighted down with a block of polished sapan-wood. Evans took up a galley of proof and handed it to Finke. The text was in Dutch.

"See anything there—just a narrow chink of light?"

"Not bloody likely," Finke said.

"Look closely," advised Homer. "The top lines are in English, of a sort."

Finke started at the head, and found the following abracadabra:

Gal.179 Siebold (5-12-50) late ME, t. F: *f* non-NON
plus pareil equal etc.

Mathieusen.

By the time Finke had got far enough at sea with the galley heading, Homer had found the place for which he was looking in the telephone directory.

"Siebold stands for Siebold Press, let's assume." Homer explained. "As I live. Here's a coincidence. In Beverly Hills. The office and some of the layout are in the Hippocrates Building. We ought to go there, anyway, to pay a call on Dr. Harms. He must be in a state, poor fellow."

"Nerves," said Finke. "He pulled the trigger three times, at point-blank range," Finke said, feeling gingerly his belly. "By all means, let's cheer him."

So they set out in Harmon's No. 2 car, the Chrysler, and parked in front of the Hippocrates Building.

Potts greeted Finke warmly, for himself as well as in memory of the $5.00 tip.

"All copasetic?" Finke asked, thumbing toward Harms's office. "Big Lukie behaving?"

"Oh, yes, sir. No trouble today. And Mr. Reynolds? I trust he's feeling no bad effects," Potts said.

"He doesn't have hangovers. There isn't time between bats," Finke said, and introduced Homer to Potts. To the latter's surprise, they did not walk down the corridor toward Dr. Harms's office, but entered the cage and asked about the Siebold Press.

"Fourth floor, back," Potts said.

After the elevator door was closed, Homer said to Finke, "You read the report of the autopsy—the one on Van Vleeck?"

"Sure. Most of it was like that Dutch galley, as far as I'm concerned," said Finke.

"The contents of the stomach? Do you remember that part?"

"He'd been drinking Holland gin."

"Fockink?"

"That's what they call it. Those Dutchmen would."

"I've got a thing or two to discuss with Mr. Siebold. Should you chance to find a bottle of Fockink, would you sequester it, unobtrusively, using your best silk handkerchief? We'll label it 'Exhibit B'," Evans said.

ELLIOT PAUL

"You mean the Dutchman was here?"

Homer shrugged. "His printing was done through Mr. Siebold. They both hailed from Amsterdam."

"I'll be damned," said Finke.

Their next visit, with Exhibit B in their possession, was to the excellent liquor store presided by Pedro Escobar. When Evans mentioned as references Lazarus Hinckley and Vulcan Moscone, Pedro put them at their ease with all his Latin charm. He was an exile from Monarchist Spain, fifteen years before the ill-fated republic.

"Have you sold much Fockink lately?" Finke began.

"Not much. But I had one customer for that gin yesterday morning," Pedro replied, glad to be of service.

"Man or woman?" Finke asked.

Don Pedro couldn't say.

"How come?" Finke asked.

The customer was waiting in a taxi and sent in the driver of a Yellow Cab. Naturally Don Pedro did not notice particularly the driver or the number plate. He was too busy opening the case of Fockink, for which he had had no call for some weeks or months. When Finke showed him the bottle, which had been opened and was about one-third gone, Don Pedro showed mild surprise when asked not to touch it. However, he examined it while Finke held it in his handkerchief. Exhibit B, as far as Don Pedro could tell, was the same bottle he had sold the day before to the unknown in the unknown taxi. The taximan had paid for the fifth of Fockink, $11.63, including tax. He had handed Pedro a new twenty-dollar bill, and had received his change. Don Pedro, in reply to Finke's question, said that he had tasted Fockink once or twice and that, for him, it had a strange perfume of juniper and algoroba. "One might become fond of it after one was used to it," Pedro said.

Homer was now in the best of spirits, so Finke bore up as best he could. He was determined that if he must be a dunce, he would not in any event be a killjoy. So when Homer bought another bottle, asked Pedro to open it without precautions as to fingerprints, and they all sampled the genuine Holland tipple, faintly redolent of the bread fruit and the bright berry boars love so well, Finke smacked his lips. He had been prepared to say "Not bad" out of courtesy. Then the fine glow and aftertaste struck his palate as he exhaled. Enthusiastically he let out an ejaculation of approval he had learned from Tani, which sounded like "Waah."

"Exhibit C," Homer said.

The bottle was then wrapped, but in a manner which left the label somewhat exposed. Don Pedro was cautioned not to mention their visit to anyone, come whoever might, and by no means to comment on the sudden heavy demand for Fockink. Then Homer and Finke did a few small personal errands to pass the time until the *apéritif* hour. When they approached Dr. Harms's office, Homer again suggested that the little psychiatrist would be contrite and badly upset because of his impulsive behavior toward Finke in the projection room.

"Let him down easy. If not out of plain humanity, please have in mind that we shall probably need him tomorrow, in the pink of condition," Homer said.

So Finke, not one to hold a grudge, nodded and smiled when Evans gave Dr. Harms and Fräulein Kahler an earful about knowing how it was in show business, at sword's points one minute, embracing the next. How show people were tuned to concert pitch, which was contagious. How every lively incident becomes charged in movie land with drama, as nearby clouds accumulate electricity, until positive meets negative and in a flash the lightning leaps, followed by the crack and rumble of displaced air which, when still, is silent and soothingly static.

With a shrug Finke looked at big Lukie, then at haggard little Harms.

"You'll get used to Evans' line," he assured them.

Homer rose. "*Auf wiedersehen*, my friends," he said. "I'll see you, Doctor, about eleven tomorrow, in Projection Room A."

Dr. Harms sighed without protest. "I shall have to break numerous appointments," he said. "But, if you wish, I'll be there."

Perplexed, Finke refrained from comment until after he and Homer were in the corridor. "You didn't invite Kahler," Finke reminded Evans. "Was that intentional?"

"She'll come, as she did the last time. On Bob's account," Homer said.

When darkness occurred that Wednesday evening, not falling, exactly, and expressly not having been pushed, certain of the companions were seated at the Tropics, and others were not. As the gamelan played, Homer mused aloud.

"Apropos *Tabu* or *Sin on an Island*. If in as popular a film as *The Sheltering Palms* Ubangi dancers from South Africa may exercise their art, in a *décor* that purports to represent one of the lesser known Caroline islands, why not a super-gamelan in Tahiti?"

"No one, least of all that Judas, Sitchev, would bat an eyelash," Ruth Mesker said.

Her mother nudged her reproachfully and glanced toward a side booth.

"I know he's listening, the earwig. That's why I said it," Ruth said.

"I'm not crazy," the voice of Sitchev said, shamelessly. "While Pete Manello is loose, and his brothers still living, I stick close to the Professor, wherever he goes. And if it's gamelans he wants in any picture of mine, he can have 'em in Wichita, Kansas, at the D.A.R. hall, playing 'God Bless America'. All I ask is that Pete be caught and all three of them get twenty-thirty years."

"This strikes me as an odd conversation for a man's wedding night," Mills Harmon complained, but manfully.

Homer touched the lonely tycoon on the shoulder of his tailored cutaway. "Just this one night she's safer under lock and key," he said.

Kay was doodling and made haste to cover it up.

Finke, whose mind was groping, suddenly thought of Exhibit C and, excusing himself, went to the parking lot to look for it in the Chrysler.

"It's gone. The Fockink. We must have left it somewhere," Finke said, on returning. There were two and possibly three bottles of that gin in circulation, then. One he had found in Siebold's place, another had been bought by the anonymous morning customer in a taxi from Pedro, and Exhibit C was the third, or second.

"Think nothing of gin," murmured Homer, whose fingers still moved with the gamelan's beat.

"Hey, waiter. Some more rums Collins," yelled Bob Reynolds, but not brusquely. "In matters of plurals and pronunciation I string along with Claude Rains."

So they sat, soothed by the sound of the kapok, sambesi and tymbos which blended with the tinkle of glass and ice, the susur-rus of the wings of moths, owls and bats in the light of the silvery moon.

Bob Reynolds reached for his rum Collins. He raised his glass to Mills Harmon. "Five hundred million days. Five hundred mil-lion dollars," he said.

19
The Morning

AT ELEVEN O'CLOCK THURSDAY MORNING, June 8th, all hands were present in Projection Room A. The investigators were seated on the low stage, back to the blank screen and facing the empty projection booth. From left to right they were:

> Finke, Hank Bibesco, Lieutenant Marcus, Homer
> Evans and Captain Strongfort.

Those who were being held as suspects or material witnesses were in the front row, with Pinky Johnstone on one side of them, between them and the doors. Sergeant Spode held the corresponding position on the right-hand side. Studio guards in uniform were posted outside each exit. The "prisoners," as it were, numbered four—to wit:

> Tony Manello, the Black Gardenia, Ric Manello, and
> Boris De Witt

The witnesses and spectators were grouped as follows:

> Ruth Mesker, Alma Shroeder, Kay Cougar.

Around Bob Reynolds, to give him support and comfort, were Mrs. Mesker, Melissa the maid, Tani and old Latacassi, Emile from the Derby, Kertojoyo of the Tropics, Mike Romanoff and André

Douthé, Frank Whitbeck, keeper of the E.P.U. zoo, and Mano, the E.P.U. barber, and the Derby waitress, Diana. All these were fond of Bob and he of them, but their soothing presence was somewhat counteracted by that of Lukie Kahler, who sat directly behind him, with Dr. Hershel Harms on one side and Dr. Myerson Ruloff Hamilton on the other.

Mills Harmon sat in Row 4, center, in solitary dignity, wearing the only starched standup collar, a black frock coat of moderate length just barely to the back of his knees, a black Ascot tie, gray striped trousers of a conservative pattern, black socks, black shoes, and black gloves on the seat at his left. From time to time he glanced at the empty seat at his right and sighed.

The Gardenia, in Row One, was in black and wore a black mantilla. From where he was sitting, the groom could see only the arch of her proud neck, the dark profusion of her hair and her slender shoulders, which seemed slighter because of the mournful lack of color. Since, to get a glimpse of his accused wife, the oil magnate was obliged to lean this way or that, to see around Fräulein Lukie Kahler, he suppressed the urge unless it became unbearable, in order not to appear nervous.

Detached from the others and three or four rows back, so there was plenty of empty space between, sat Laslo Sitchev and Natalia. In the last row were Hendrik Siebold, of the Siebold Press; the E.P.U. guard Finke had slugged; Pedro Escobar of the liquor store that served the Forty-Niners Towers; Lazarus Hinckley, who kept the front door of that de-luxe establishment; Vulcan Moscone, guardian of the back door; and Gregory, of the Brown Derby, who had tagged along to find out where Emile and Diana were going. Also there was Phil Cedars, of the Cedars Pharmacy, and the driver of the taxi who had taken Finke on his long, long ride while the Chevvy had been, to all intents and purposes, impounded.

In the E.P.U. parking lot, exclusively for executives and guests, only, stood Harmon's great limousine, the No. 2 Chrysler, the maroon Plymouth sedan that De Witt had tried to abandon at the depot, Kay's Austin and Finke's Chevrolet.

"Ladies and gentlemen," Homer began. "We're here to investigate three deaths: Barney Rice's, which occurred on Thursday, June first, a week ago today, at the Balm of Gilead Hospital, Los Angeles, after an illness of about two months; the death of Shirley Hall, internationally beloved as a musical-comedy dancer, who usually was paired with Mr. Robert Reynolds on the screen, and was engaged to marry him. Miss Hall died in the back yard of the Forty-Niners Towers, in Los Angeles County, but not in the city.

"The third fatality, which also overtook the victim in County territory, was the death of Mynheer Sprouls Van Vleeck, M.S., Bot. Doc., Ph.D., one of the world's leading botanists, contributor to technical and scientific literature in the horticultural, vegetable and entomophagous fields, and body servant of Mr. Mills Harmon. The latter is with us today."

At that the Gardenia turned her head slowly, raised her great eyes until they looked, across the intervening aisles, into those of her husband, and wiped a tear away, with a black lace handkerchief. For the moment, the scene was hers. Homer stood patiently until the accused faced front again.

"Less of it," Lieutenant Marcus said airily. "He's dead, the old Kraut. You killed him, Señorita."

The lovely Mexican straightened before the hushed gasp could rise and subside in the well-proportioned room, which had been built with no thought of expense but much attention to acoustics. The acoustics had never served better than when the Gardenia, with a glance at Marcus said, not too loudly, not too low, two words, "*Pobre loco!*" (Poor fool.)

That got under the Lieutenant's skin, and no mistake. Homer glanced at Finke and smiled. "A sound beginning," Homer's eyes seemed to say. Finke could not respond with his customary resilience. For in the sealskin case in which Marcus had brought some of the state's "exhibits," Finke had glimpsed a certain article, or object like a phonograph disc.

Anyone as sensitive as Homer could feel the tension rising in the room, and when it got to the pitch he required, he resumed.

"Lieutenant Marcus," he said, "is at the head of the homicide detachment of our fair Pueblo de la Reine de Los Angeles—the city of the Queen of the Angels. He has detained, in connection with the three murders I have enumerated, four persons, only one of whom has escaped. In spite of the absence of Pete Manello, you see four persons on the bench of the defendants. I, myself, requested that Mr. Boris De Witt be included."

Marcus interrupted:

"Never mind the high-sounding talk. The Gardenia killed Shirley Hall and old Van Vleeck. The Manellos were in on it, and I can prove it," he said.

"Pray do," Homer urged. "This isn't a formal trial, so we all can use greater latitude than is prescribed by rules of evidence in court."

"Two murders are enough," Marcus began quite brightly. "So, for my part, I'll skip Barney Rice. He's been dead so long . . ."

"A whole week," said Homer.

"He was so long dying . . ."

"Not much of an advantage," Homer said.

"He wasn't in the public eye, then," Marcus said, still trying to appear unruffled.

"Just one of those who'd offered his life for the lot of us," Homer said.

"Look, Professor. If you're trying to get my goat, you're fiddling away your time," Marcus said. "It's like this. This mug with the orange shirt and pink tie" (indicating Tony Manello) "whose brother had some racket in Chicago, went to Mexico City. Do I make myself clear?"

"Every word," said Laslo Sitchev.

"While Tony Manello was in Mexico, his brother Ric quit Chicago—which probably was too hot for him—and came out here to Hollywood. Right?"

"Every word."

"Ric had been tipped off how the Chairman of the Board at E.P.U. could be made to part with dough. So Ric and Pete began to take over the studio? Correct?"

Sitchev was so earnest he almost turned himself inside out. "Before the Manellos moved in, the studio from A to Z was peaceful. Making money, too. All happy. Then, of all the things a crook can do, Ric has to go into the movie business. I ask you why? Why not smuggle diamonds, or Chinese, sell artichokes, snow, hop, maybe reefers. Who cares? Let him kidnap babies. Duck old women in chairs. Burn misers in the feet, like we did in Robin's Vood. No, for Ric it has to be movies. And since it has to be movies, it can't be Monogram, Republic, Eagle-Lion, or even Fox or Warner, or maybe Universal-International, or J. Arthur Rank, which it might be good enough for him. It has to be E.P.U. And of all the producers in E.P.U. he couldn't squeeze blood out of a mallet-head like Repp or Passkey who's old enough to be Moses anyway, what a lucky bum he is . . . It must got to be Sitchev."

The little Hungarian was getting warmed up. "Twenty-five, thirty-five years they should get. Each one of 'em apiece. In solitary for all I care. Otherwise, I'm cooked before I lay me down to sleep, let alone I don't awake. Do me a favor, Lieutenant. Take care of them. Good. I'll make a picture of your life story, a musical, instead of K. Egbert Hoover's, yet. You'll be the bigger shot, the way I'll fix it up."

Tony Manello spoke up, and Ric made no move to stop him.

"What's your beef, Sitchev? Isn't this a free country? So we muscle into the movies. Ric and Pete stay here, to make the arrangements. I mosey around and about to pick up talent. And what do I nail, right off the bat?" Expansively Tony made a proud gesture toward his first and only acquisition. "Eulalia Noguera," he said, answering his own question. "And what do you say, when you arrive by next plane and see her in a swim tank? All wet? Colossal! Divine! She's better than Demona Bourbon, Betty Buckeleinikoff, Felia Fray and Doodie Upsopke put together."

Homer interrupted at this point, but tactfully.

"At this rate, Lieutenant, Dr. Harms and Dr. Hamilton will miss all their appointments for today, and possibly tomorrow. Shall we step up the tempo a little? What do you say?"

"I've got plenty of time," said Marcus. "You gifted amateurs erupt genius for a while, then lay off, with a jug, encyclopedia and Judy. With us regular policemen, it's a long steady grind, and little reward except duty well done and a two weeks' vacation with double pay if we don't take it." The Lieutenant signaled to Ric. "All right, big brother. *You* talk!"

Ric rose, faced the assembly and bowed to the ladies, in turn. His bow to the Gardenia, who was sitting beside the place from which he had risen, was a separate quite deferent act—a European tribute. It seemed to say, *Chère mademoiselle* . . . or pardon, *Chère madame*, we have shared a trying experience. You've borne up well. All my felicitations.

Touched, Ric's co-defendant responded. Again there was merely a bow, almost imperceptible, but it conveyed at least the following, and more: Sir, from others I've heard nothing but evil of you. To me you've been the soul of courtesy and consideration. I long ago learned, *chèr monsieur*, to trust no one but myself. We understand each other.

The exchange above interpreted took less than three seconds. What Ric said to Marcus was finished in fifteen.

"When you put one card face up on the table, I'll cover it. Not before. You've got nothing on me, and never will have. In case there's any talking to be done, for me, I'd like to ask Mr. Evans to do it, if he'll take me as a client," Ric said, and sat down.

"With pleasure," Homer said, pleased. "I consider it an honor, under the circumstances."

Ruth looked aghast and Marcus' lip curled as he laughed a loud guffaw. Sitchev was trying to pray.

"Some honor, Professor," the Lieutenant said. "This new client of yours could hide behind a corkscrew."

"You wouldn't understand the honor," said Homer. "The law bequeathed us by our Founding Fathers has some rare poetic strains. Every man is innocent until proven guilty. Once acquitted by a jury of his peers, he cannot be placed in double jeopardy. Whatever his color, creed, race, nationality or previous record, if he is under no indictment when he steps into a courtroom, he is judged by the evidence. The charges against him must be specific, and must be stated clearly. I accept Mr. Manello and his two brothers, not because elsewhere they may not have transgressed. They did not murder, or connive in the murder of the late Barney Rice, Shirley Hall or Sprouls Van Vleeck. Ricardo Manello has an exceptionally high I.Q."

"I never claimed he was dumb. He's too smart to be at large," Marcus said.

"You, Lieutenant, have implied that he was and is a fool, that a man of Ric's intelligence would risk murdering a poor war veteran, just on the chance that Bob Reynolds might be frightened by the 'Example' into ditching his principal girl, cheating his loyal agent, and signing a shady deal involving such a reassuringly upright specimen as Laslo Sitchev," Homer countered.

Marcus turned on Ric. "Did you want Bob Reynolds as a client or not?"

No reply.

"Did you want Shirley Hall frozen out, to make room for this Gardenia your brother Tony dug up?"

Ric did not even look up at the Lieutenant, let alone move his lips. He did not stir or change expression when Homer spoke up for him.

"I'll answer all three questions in Mr. Ric Manello's behalf. He did wish to sign Bob Reynolds. As who wouldn't? He'd been convinced that Miss Hall was so ill that she'd collapse before she could finish another picture, and therefore my client wished to move ahead of his competitors and pair up Mr. Reynolds with Miss Noguera. All that is well within the scope of ethics accepted in the agency business."

"I hope to kiss a pig," said Tony.

Homer turned to Dr. Harms. "I've been informed by Lieutenant Marcus, who occasionally is helpful, that Mr. Ric Manello has been under treatment by you for some months," he said.

"Again I must beg leave not to violate a patient's confidence," the psychiatrist said.

"Do you wish to explain?" Homer asked Ric.

Ric shrugged and said, "You're doing fine."

"Very well," continued Homer. "If I'm wrong, correct me. Before leaving Chicago and sending Tony to Mexico, Ric Manello reached an intelligent decision. He concluded that the time for the type of gangster work which characterized the prohibition era had passed its zenith and that smart men could get along better, just now, in promotion ventures either within the law or to which no laws yet applied. He found himself slipping, occasionally, into the old direct ways, and felt bored and uneasy when he was keeping absolutely straight. Fearing to become weak or fanatic, he figured out that if he spent a few hours a week with Dr. Harms, and talked freely about the dear dead days, his adjustment to a lawful environment would prove easier."

"My visits to Dr. Harms did me a lot of good," Ric said. "I told him, among other things, that I didn't have to threaten any executives at E.P.U. They jumped at conclusions. So I sold them odds and ends. Sitchev naturally assumed I had the outfit where the hair is short, and did his best to get on the good side of me. He thought he had to."

Bob Reynolds was on his feet, eyes blazing.

"Not so fast!" he said to Ric. "Who told you, and the Chairman of the Board, and spread it all over Hollywood, that Shirley was losing her mind? That she was finished?"

Bob swung his arms free and wheeled on Dr. Harms. "Did you, you little shrimp?"

The distressed psychiatrist ducked and stammered, but before he could say "yes" or "no," Tony Manello horned in.

"Doc didn't tell me. Or Ric," Tony said, with a lighthearted leer at the Gardenia.

Marcus pounced on that quickly. "You see, folks. The lady in black. Why not? Who'd gain more than she would, if Shirley was rushed to the snakepit?" The Lieutenant stepped over to the edge of the stage, leaned perilously so that his face was within a couple of feet of the Gardenia's. "Come clean, Señorita. Was it you who told Ric that Shirley was nuts?"

The Gardenia rose, evoked a hush which enabled her to drop her voice to a low throaty pitch, looked at the Lieutenant more contemptuously than ever, and said: "*Sí, Señor.*"

"You admit it?" barked the Lieutenant, knocked off his perch by the unexpected reply.

"*Sí, Señor.*"

"And who told you, Señorita Noguera?" Homer asked, kindly. Then he shifted his tactics. "No. Don't answer that question," Homer begged. "It might have been . . ." He looked from one to another. "Who could it have been? It might have been almost any-one in this auditorium. Whoever did it can be exposed by Miss Noguera whenever I say the word. Meanwhile, the guilty party is putting himself in danger every second he remains silent." Homer held up his wrist and looked at the wrist watch as if counting.

Laslo Sitchev flew out of his seat like a Jack-in-the-Box. "I told the *señorita*, but somebody told me."

The situation was a set-up for Homer. All he had to do was hold up his wrist watch again, glance from one nervous witness to an-other and smile his most disarming smile.

But this time it did not work. No one spoke up. So Homer pointed at the shrinking Hungarian. "You gave him a chance. Who was it?"

Sitchev did not say a word, but he made a helpless gesture of appeal toward Boris De Witt.

Homer faced De Witt, who looked at him superciliously, and showed plainly that he was not going to say a word, one way or the other. Alma Shroeder rose prayerfully. "Please, Boris. Answer, dear."

"You answer for him, if you wish," Evans suggested. "O.K., Lieu-tenant?"

Marcus shrugged. "A swell daisy chain," was his comment.

Alma said, trembling. "Boris told Mr. Sitchev, but someone told Boris, and Mr. Sitchev's done Boris a lot of favors, thrown good jobs his way, designing sets, costumes, acting as technical adviser . . ."

"Making phonograph records . . ." continued Marcus. "For off-scene effects. Voices. Narration. Boris knows what it costs to make a picture, and what happens if a star gets sick, and expenses go on and on without the cameras turning. If Boris was loyal to Mr. Sitchev . . ."

"Sit down, Alma," Boris said, wearily, looking at her and Laslo Sitchev with equal distaste. "Dear Lasli'd steal the fleece off the Lamb of God, if he could pinch a pair of shears. And if Shirley Hall was going utsnay, who cared? Better actresses than she have spent lilac time in the old asylum, with their ears to the ground to listen for worms. And who can remember their names, or, thank God, their silly faces, a fortnight later?"

"Mr. Evans. Please understand Boris," Alma pleaded. "He does things for everybody, but if anyone implies that his motives are high, it embarrasses him. He pretends to be indifferent."

"If you only knew, darlings, how indifferent I really am!" said De Witt. "Noguera told Manello. Sitchev told Noguera. I told Sitchev. And a little bird told me. What of it? Shirley Hall was obviously nuts, or she wouldn't have been mooning over a ham like Bob Reynolds who'll chase a skirt if it's only hanging on the line."

Dr. Hamilton rose, more indifferent to De Witt's vapors than De Witt seemed to be to life itself. "There's only one man here, it strikes me, who's qualified to tell us about Miss Hall's condition. I refer to Dr. Harms," Dr. Hamilton said.

Homer invited Dr. Harms to describe Shirley's condition.

"Miss Hall was ill, but her state was not hopeless. Naturally of an intense possessive nature, her jealousy had been inflamed . . ."

Marcus broke in. "By seeing Reynolds and the *señorita* making love to each other? You see, it all fits. Wherever you slice it, it's the *señorita* again."

"Was it Señorita Noguera who first aroused Miss Hall's jealousy with regard to Mr. Reynolds?" Homer asked the little doctor.

Dr. Harms hesitated. "Must I reveal a dead girl's innermost secrets?" he asked.

"To help catch her murderer," Evans said. "Either here, or under oath, in court."

Dr. Harms sighed, and his eyes strayed toward the back of the room. "The first woman Miss Hall mentioned . . . This is monstrous, gentlemen. Whatever happens to me as a consequence, I'm forced to decline . . ."

In the very last row, up rose dainty Diana, the waitress from the Derby, Southern accent and all.

"I want to help," Diana said. "Perhaps it was po' little me. I was just being nice to Mr. Reynolds, and I must have paid him too much attention. Because Miss Hall complained, and wouldn't stand for my waiting on Mr. Reynolds any mo'."

"Was Diana the first?" Homer asked Dr. Harms. "She's been very kind to volunteer . . ."

Dr. Harms looked more harassed than ever. "I believe that Miss Hall did refer to Miss Diana, but the first . . . Let me see . . ."

Alma Shroeder rose. "Perhaps it was I. One evening, when both Boris and Bob had been drinking heavily, they got into an altercation about me. Bob struck Boris and nearly injured him for life."

Finke grinned and asked a question, for a change.

"You mean Bob made a pass at you, and sloughed De Witt for resenting it?"

Alma dropped her eyes. "It had that effect on Shirley. She was frantic. But the fact was that Bob attacked Boris because he made an uncomplimentary reference to me."

"Sir Galahad, eh?" put in Marcus. He turned to Doctor Harms. "So Mrs. De Witt, alias Shroeder, was the babe who got Shirley's angora?"

"Not exactly. The very first . . ." Harms began.

"It might have been me . . . or I," Tani said, looking pleased with herself. "Miss Hall thought Bob liked *my* looks, and got Granny fired from her job in his house to remove me as temptation."

Harms looked harassed. "She did mention you, Miss Elkdown. But the first . . ."

There was a stir as Laslo Sitchev said, "Go ahead," and practically pushed Natalia to her feet.

"Miss Borodin!" said Homer, looking astonished but not exactly pained. "*You* were fond of Mr. Reynolds?"

"I was not," Natalia said, positively. "Not very . . . I'm afraid I'm a one-man woman. But Mr. Sitchev was terribly anxious to make one more tropical feature with Mr. Reynolds. Mr. Reynolds had a fear that he was being typed, if you get what I mean."

"Of course. He had to be persuaded," Homer said, understandingly. "You act, in certain cases, when Mr. Sitchev suggests it, as a kind of decoy. Am I wrong?"

An expression momentarily suggestive of rapture swept over the Russian secretary's face. "Ah, Mr. Reynolds, compared with some I've had to persuade, was heaven."

"She'll do anything for me, the little pigeon," Sitchev said proudly.

"There's nothing like loyalty," Homer said. "Did Natalia also arrange for Object Lesson discs to be played on occasion? And then plant them where their discovery would divert the guilt from you? For instance, in this case, in Ric Manello's drawer at home, where he keeps his contracts?"

Ric let his almost sleepy eyes wander over Sitchev's way, and Tony grinned, broadly.

"Brother! It'll seem good to be free," Tony said.

Melissa, eyes distended, shook her fists at the stage, and then the audience. "You beasts! You all killed my lamb, piece by piece. Every night my darling'd come home crying her heart out."

Homer admitted that Shirley had had quite a list to worry about. "Doctor Harms. We have Natalia, Alma, Diana, Tani, and according to Marcus, Eulalia Noguera. Were there more?"

"Yes!" cried Lukie Kahler, rising Junoesquely. "While Miss Hall was consulting with the doctor, and Mr. Reynolds was outside, with me, she got the same wild ideas. She couldn't have me fired from my position. I'd been too long with Dr. Harms. So she forbade Mr. Reynolds from calling at our office, either to escort her, wait for her, or even inquire how she was."

The Gardenia's eyes were smoldering. "You lie!" she said vibrantly to Lukie. "He was with you in your office Tuesday night before Miss Hall was murdered. She told me so, herself."

"In that case," the big nurse said, coldly, "you must have seen her after I did. I saw you leave the Tropics the minute Shirley was gone from there."

"Don't miss any of this," Marcus said. "The *señorita* must have been the last to see Shirley alive."

"You're forgetting that Melissa saw her long enough to be sent out to the drug store," Homer said.

"The *señorita* could have been anywhere then," Marcus said. "Don't you forget that Shirley was hopped up to the gills with that sedative and was wide open to suggestion."

"Why did the *señorita* go to the Tropics, and later, to the Towers? She was chasing Bob Reynolds, trying to find him. She'd been able to turn the heads of all the other men—Tony Manello, Ricardo Manello, Sitchev, that nosy Maguire, the silly old man with too much money, you, too, Mr. Chairman. But she got nowhere with Mr. Reynolds. Bobbie's a man of the world. He knows too much for her. He's too clean," Lukie concluded.

"Fine! Fine!" said Marcus, delighted. "So the *señorita* gets jealous and bumps off Shirley to clear the way to Bob, who's, holding out on her."

"Then what would Miss Noguera need with three mugs like our new clients? Sitchev and Natalia already confessed about scaring Bob, and trying to scare Harmon, with the Object Lesson Voice. And those Voice messages stopped short when someone found out, through Pinky Johnstone, that Harmon's message was delivered to me," Finke said.

"Why bother about details like that? You got two murders right under your noses—Shirley Hall's and the Dutchman's. The *señorita* had the motive for both of them. She can't account for her time while either of the victims was being killed. As far as Barney Rice is concerned, he might have swallowed that bamboo dust by accident. It must have been blowing all over the Gardens."

"In that case," said Dr. Hamilton, "the inflammation would have appeared on the mucous tissues of the nasal passages, the mouth, throat and windpipe. No. Barney must have taken the fatal pollen mixed with food, or drink, and well mixed, so carefully prepared that it passed through the stomach without damaging the tender lining. It was the grinding . . . grinding . . ."

"Don't," begged Alma Shroeder and had to use her smelling salts again.

Marcus looked sharply at old Latacassi. "It still fits," he said. "So it has to be mixed with food. Who did housework in the bungalows, by the day or hour? This old witch is like that" (he snapped this thumb and finger) "with the *señorita*. The old crowbait knew all about bamboo dust from her girlhood in where-the-hell-ever it grows wild. She got the stuff for the *señorita*, and got the job with Reynolds after Barney was sick. Shirley caught on, and raised so much hell that Latacassi had to go, and the *señorita* took her in, full time, to keep her satisfied and quiet."

Tani stood up, indignantly. "That isn't so. I was the reason Granny had to quit Bob's bungalow."

"How old are you, kid?"

"Thirteen. But I'm smarter than you are already," Tani said.

Marcus was not offended, but amused. "How come?" he asked.

"I know who killed all three of the corpses," Tani said. She looked in a friendly way at Ric Manello. "He didn't," the girl said, positively. And, indicating the Gardenia. "She didn't, either."

Homer beckoned for her to hop up on the platform and whisper in his ear.

"That's right, Tani," he said.

"Say. What is this. An act?" asked Marcus, suspiciously. "If it is, I don't like it."

"The person among us who has killed three victims already might get the impulse to try again, knowing that the jig is up. But now our murderer would have to shoot little Tani."

"I've never seen a real shooting," Tani said, alight with anticipation.

Dr. Harms rose nervously. "All this talk about shooting is bad," he said. "The mind of a murderer is sick with worry and fear. It's wide open to suggestion."

"I've been in this room three times, and two of those times somebody's tried some shooting," Finke said. "This joint, with the acoustics and all, seems to cry for it."

"Don't!" implored Dr. Harms.

Boris De Witt yawned. He looked really pale and wan. "If I get shot, I'll sue E.P.U. to the hilt, whoever's taking it over."

"You're too blasé, De Witt," Homer said, "for a man with American Express checks amounting to twenty-five thousand dollars in your pocket."

"I didn't go through his pockets," Marcus said to Evans. "I haven't got a thing on him. He was your idea from the start." He turned to De Witt. "You carry around twenty-five grand?"

De Witt avoided Alma's eyes and also Sitchev's.

"I was going on a journey . . . to New York," Boris said.

"You have reservations for two on the *Ile de France*, which docks at Le Havre, the nearest port to Paris," Homer said.

"Oh, Boris. You wouldn't!" Alma said.

"Did I ask you for any money?" Boris said.

"And what about *Sin on an Island?*" demanded Sitchev. "I need you for the technical advising . . ."

"Did I ask you for the job?" said Boris. "You all make me sick."

There was a blur in the minds of all present, excepting a few who never lost their heads. Finke was across the platform and Homer was holding his breath. After the gun was in Finke's hand, and the safety catch had clicked, everyone realized that De Witt had been knocked across the laps of Ruth Mesker, his weeping wife, and Kay Cougar, and that Pinky Johnstone and Sergeant Spode had hold of him, at the feet and head, respectively.

"Aw, no. Not that one," said Marcus, for the first time deflated. "Don't tell me, Professor, it's that swish."

"I need his evidence. . . . and now he's made this gesture, perhaps I shall clinch it." Homer turned to Finke. "Never again apologize for being a man of action," he said, sincerely relieved and grateful. "You've saved the day."

As soon as Boris De Witt, minus his gun, had been brushed, combed and patched by Alma, who was forgiving him for everything, he was obliged to resume his place beside Ric Manello, who politely made room for him. Ric had been in some very low spots, himself, and always held in awe a man who could make a plausible suicide attempt, whether he meant it or not. Ric was inclined, in this instance, to believe De Witt had really intended to end it all.

"Five gets you four," the Sheriff said, on that point, and when Ric, reverting absent-mindedly to the practice of the Chicago underworld and produced a five-hundred-dollar bill, Hank Bibesco gasped and choked. Ric blushed and begged his pardon, and borrowed from Tony five silver dollars, which Tony kept with him because he liked to clank them on bars.

"If that revolting little jail bait knows who killed everybody, why don't you make her tell us?" De Witt asked Homer, sulkily.

Homer, occupied in an aside with Finke, paid scant attention, so De Witt turned to Marcus.

"You're not so tough, peeper," De Witt said. "Are you running your silly old murder squad or not?"

"I'm sick of you, Clarence," Marcus said. "I should send for your pal on the train, and send you both up for years."

De Witt turned gray. It was then that Homer pounced on him and asked, sternly, "How long have you known St. John Rochelle? Alias Cyril Heukelom?"

"It's not an alias," De Witt said defensively.

"Do extras have stage names, Mr. Sitchev?" Homer asked the Hungarian.

Sitchev shrugged. "Who knows about extras? It's bad enough to remember their faces."

"Does an innocent boy, just because he knows me, have to be dragged into this, through the mire?" De Witt asked.

"Not far," Homer said, kindly. "I simply want to establish where you met him, and when."

"Well, smarty. It wasn't around here, or very lately," Boris answered, more animate now he had a chance to show off. He could make himself look good, if he parried Homer to a standstill. "How far into the past must we delve?"

"You were sweet sixteen plus two. An art student," said Homer, "and very promising."

"You really think so?" asked De Witt. "I've made such a fizzle of things since." He sighed. "Ladies must live," he said, again quite hopelessly.

"I daresay," agreed Evans. "Although I'm open to conviction to the contrary. I see you're in the mood for a long chat, but we're all busy men . . ."

"Let me make him talk," Marcus urged. "He's yours, as I said before, but don't be stingy."

"The problem is not in making this witness talk. It's sifting the wheat from the chaff," Homer replied.

"Or the dust from the bamboo," De Witt suggested boldly.

"Did Cyril teach you about that?" Evans asked.

"As a matter of fact, he did—and many other things "

Alma, gasping, was on her feet, bracing herself by placing one hand on Kay's shoulder and the other on Ruth's.

"Was Cyril there? It can't be, Basil. That was seventeen years ago. You've been . . . That unfortunate affair goes back—*before* we were married?"

"Yes, it has. And I'm glad. That's the only break I got. And *you* had to spoil it," De Witt said bitterly.

Melissa broke out again. "I saw what went on at the Towers. She" (pointing at Alma) "had to support him (Basil) and he took care of that other one."

Homer made a gesture to end the little flurry.

"I only wanted to establish that in Batavia, on the island of Java, in 1933, Mr. De Witt, then eighteen years old, an art student, met Cyril Heukelom, then twenty-two years old. Heukelom was a male nurse."

De Witt, wreathed in a beatific smile at the recollection, murmured. "Yes. Oh, yes."

"Do you remember Heukelom, by any chance, Dr. Harms?" Evans asked.

The doctor started as if he had felt a spider drop down the back of his collar, but the moment he was able to collect his thoughts he replied, quite normally, "Mr. Evans, how could I remember a male nurse from 1933, halfway across the world? All nurses dress in white. The females are much better, even for strength and endurance," the little psychiatrist said.

De Witt was gazing at Dr. Harms in speechless wonder. "You don't remember Cyril? When he was right in your own department? The psychiatric ward?"

"That's where the bunch of us'll end," said Marcus in despair.

"My point is," Evans interrupted tersely, "Cyril learned about bamboo dust and told Boris, seventeen years ago, in Batavia. And then, this year, in 1950, when the boys were reunited, as 'twere, at the Omar Gardens . . ."

"I really tried to give him up," De Witt said to Alma, who had sobbed aloud.

"Don't stop me," Homer said. "We're getting warm. Cyril and Boris, at the Gardens, were reminded of old days by the tall straight bamboos, the feathery Calcutta grasses, the pitcher plants, the lotar palms and the light of the silvery moon. They both recognized Mynheer Van Vleeck because they had seen him waiting and pacing in the rooms, corridors and outside the hospital in Batavia and occasionally being called into consultation."

He turned to Dr. Harms. "You don't remember Van Vleeck?" he asked, casually.

"He must have been outside my department," said Dr. Harms.

"I see," said Homer, passing over the matter lightly.

There was a muffled exchange between Tani and Latacassi. Tani raised her right hand, as if she were in school and Homer was a teacher she was anxious to please. "Granny remembered," the girl said.

"Van Vleeck?"

"Of course. But I meant Mr. De Witt and" (she giggled) "the other one. She says they dressed just alike, to go walking in the moonlight."

"They still dress alike, to sail to Paris," Homer said.

"I know," Tani said, and whispered to Granny, who smiled, her ancient eyes alight, her wrinkles forming a rugose pattern that had an element of time in formation.

"We haven't got all day," Marcus said. "What is this leading to?"

"I'll be succinct," Homer promised. "Does it strike you as strange that when Bob Reynolds at the suggestion of Shirley Hall took the late Barney Rice to Dr. Hershel Harms, and Barney had the symptoms that were the talk of Batavia when Harms, Van Vleeck and, of course, Miss Kahler, had been sent there by the Dutch Government to find out why so many Dutch wives and sweethearts were dying from an ominous and mysterious complaint— does it excite your curiosity in any way to learn why, under such circumstances, Dr. Harms could not diagnose the case? Instead his mind is a complete blank, seemingly, about his effective work in Batavia, for which, incidentally, he keeps in his desk drawer a decoration he received at the hands of Queen Wilhelmina."

"I keep telling you," Dr. Harms said patiently. "The intestinal cases were outside my department."

"Unfortunately for that theory, Doctor," Evans said, "there's a record."

Dr. Harms looked at Lukie, who was looking bewildered.

"There is?" Harms asked.

The big *Fräulein* sighed and shrugged. "Not that I know of," she said.

"The *imaginary* cases were in your department. Weren't you aware of what frightful fear was running around, and of its basis?" Homer asked, kindly, and when Harms failed to respond, apparently taking refuge in bewilderment, almost as if he had forgotten his English, which under stress he sometimes actually did, Homer said to Finke and to Hank, "Open up the suitcase with the proofs and exhibits, would you mind?"

The tension in the room, so long building up, was electric. Painfully electric, as if everyone had hold of a shock machine with both hands and could not let go. The designer, or electrician had made some awful mistake, and they were getting more than they could stand.

There was no anticlimax when Finke took out first an unopened bottle of Courvoisier.

Alma clutched at her head and Kay fumbled in the fainting woman's bag for her smelling salts. "I ordered it," she said.

"Somebody ordered it, and sent Moscone away from the back door of the Towers. Then the bottle was left unopened," Homer said.

The next was a bottle of rum, and two glasses. Kertojoyo came forward.

"Those are the ones. I marked them, as you said, Mr. Evans. That bottle was the one from which were made the frozen Daiquiris, and those are the glasses Miss Noguera and poor Shirley Hall drank from."

Finke fished out a bundle or two of galley proofs and tossed them aside for the moment. Then he produced from the depths of the bag an opened bottle of Fockink. At sight of the Fockink Dr. Harms took a few steps forward, so he could face the audience, held up one palm for silence and said, with sad dignity, "I confess."

Marcus was on his feet, threatening and raging, shaking his finger under the psychiatrist's nose. "You confess to what?" the Lieutenant demanded.

"The murders," the little doctor said. "All of them."

"What murders?" barked Marcus. Homer was standing by, with a real poker face, except that he was blinking his eyes now and then. And little Tani was squirming in her chair to such a point that her Granny had to hold her down with a wrinkled hand over her mouth.

"Come on. What murders?" Marcus snarled, as if to reach for Harms's small-sized collar and shake the answer out of him.

"Barney Rice—with *phyllostachys bambusoides*," the psychiatrist said. "He came to my office. There was nothing to hinder."

"Who else?" Marcus asked, scornfully.

"Shirley Hall, with a distillation of *nepenthes gracilis*, in the rum you see as one of the exhibits. I was also at the Tropics. There'll be traces in the glass," the doctor said.

Homer Evans emitted a heartfelt sigh that brought forth all the merits of the room's inspired acoustics.

"Amazin'. 'Pon my word. Just think, Lieutenant. Those glasses and the excellent Bacardi rum are as pure driven snow. I took the precaution of having them analyzed, just this afternoon."

The doctor became frantic. "The Fockink! You haven't tested that! With that I killed Van Vleeck."

As if beseechingly the little psychiatrist held up his wrists. In exasperation, Marcus clamped a slender pair of cuffs on, somewhat tight, since they had been selected for the Gardenia.

"Great sequence!" exclaimed Sitchev. "Each bottle comes along and tops the last." The Hungarian yelped as from the projectionists' cage came a derisive raspberry and the head of Pete Manello popped out. Pete pulled out a standard sling shot and peppered the cringing Hungarian on the forehead with a pea.

"Sleep tight, peeper!" Pete said.

20

More Deadly Than the Male

THERE WERE SO MANY little items to explain to our companions whose destinies had been interwoven by the intricate nature of the crimes that, since lunch time was approaching, Homer had a whispered consultation, first with André Douthé and Mike Romanoff, then with Lieutenant Marcus and Mills Harmon. The Gardenia was permitted to go to her husband's side; the Brothers Manello were allowed to chat freely together. Dr. Harms was relieved of the handcuffs on the promise that he would stay within reach of Captain Strongfort. Alma Shroeder, who seemed at long last to be rid of her obsession for De Witt, stood close to the haggard psychiatrist's side, like a ministering angel seeking new occupation.

Lukie Kahler, so subdued by the morning's revelations that all her aggressiveness was gone, was surrounded by a sympathetic group, like the lesser figures around the central theme of a monument.

"This is a free and wonderful country," the nurse said. "I must not brood and mourn. I shall take some courses at U.C.L.A., U.S.C., and some other local schools and fulfill my lifelong ambition, impossible in Germany, and get medical degrees to carry on the practice."

The psychiatrist smiled wanly and touched her hand. She smiled down on him and murmured to Bob Reynolds, "He'll plead insanity, of course. For a long time I've suspected" (she made the telling gesture with forefingers at her lofty temples) "and for a short time I've known. What could I do?"

Mills Harmon voiced the invitation and they all repaired to Mike Romanoff's for the fadeout. In that famous restaurant, where the 100,000,000 movie fans have sat so often in their dreams, a horseshoe table was prepared, so that not only our assembly of investigators, suspects, witnesses and friends could be accommodated, but the rest of the spacious main dining room could be made available to well-known motion-picture stars, executives and bankers, and the lucky tourists of that day.

To Mills Harmon was accorded the place of honor, with his lovely bride in black at his right, and Homer Evans at his left. The seating of Bob Reynolds presented some difficulties, and eventually he was placed at the tip of one of the prongs of the horseshoe and along the sides sat Diana, Natalia, Tani and other fair ones too enticing to be enumerated.

It is not necessary to praise the fare and the refreshing *apéritifs*, wines, liqueurs and *digestifs*. Douthé was chef, and Romanoff the restaurateur. When the coffee was served, the guests shifted their chairs, Homer rose, and began.

"We have improved the tradition that the condemned shall eat a hearty breakfast by serving a memorable lunch," he said, with a bow to Douthé, who had joined them.

"This time, since I now have all the evidence, I'll not try your forbearance. The murderer . . ." he glanced pityingly at Harms, "we shall designate as 'M.' I, for one am tired of 'X' or 'Y'. For this is a human equation we solve, and not an algebraic one."

Marcus, about to explode, reached for his glass.

Homer proceeded. "This time, I shall describe in detail, from beginning to end, the series of related crimes. As is an ideal motion picture, the fundamental is the love interest, and the secondary, money. Without these, neither crime nor the ultimate in human baseness or nobility exists.

"'M', like so many of the others around and beyond this table, had a passionate nature set so deeply in frustrations that for years it was never released. Then the spark touched the fuse, the beam completed its circuit and the rest was inevitable. Shall we call it fate?"

Marcus reached beyond the glass to the bottle and grasped it. That, at least, was tangible.

"'M'," continued Homer, "had learned many secrets, had been entrusted with grave responsibilities. So, when temptation flared irresistibly, 'M' was possessed of a rich and unusual equipment, physically, spiritually and morally. That is to say, 'M' had no morals or inhibitions whatsoever. For relentless accomplishment and fulfillment of uncontrollable desire that is ideal. 'M' encountered the affinity 'M' wanted, had to have, would move mountains to get. In other words, one evening Bob Reynolds, goaded by his late fiancée's reproaches, got roundly drunk. Following the reasoning so often inspired by the cunning demon rum, he got himself involved with 'M' and 'M' with him We've all seen that when anyone gets involved with our popular baritone and actor, involved she stays."

The Gardenia's slender hand had clenched so hard that her liqueur glass parted from its stem.

"My dear! Try not to be nervous," her husband said.

"'M' found inconvenient the presence of Barney Rice in Bob's bungalow, and knowing the properties of bamboo in flower, removed him. He was only an obscure ex-soldier.

"In the case of Shirley, Bob's fiancée, 'M' had to follow a safer method of procedure. 'M' had unusual facilities for planting the seeds of jealousy, or even insanity, in Shirley's sensitive mind."

Disgusted, but in a way expansive, Marcus made a gesture of freeing Dr. Harms. "Go where you like. I knew your confession was phony. I said it was a woman all the time."

"All right," Homer said. "The murderer is a woman, a most unusual example of the gentler sex, who, as Kipling told us, can be more 'deadly than the male'."

The men glared at the women, with mixed emotions, in which awe was predominant. Since each of the men had known, himself, that he was innocent, they had felt safe all along, except for the chances of a miscarriage of justice.

Dr. Harms made one final and desperate attempt. "I did it," he said. "I had the chance to kill Barney Rice and I did. I poisoned

Miss Hall's drink at the Tropics, before she went home, to die in her back yard. I was there. I did it. I admit it. Who else, except Van Vleeck could prepare the poison, to disguise its sharpness in the case of Barney Rice, and its taste to Shirley Hall?"

"'M' could, and did. That narrows our field again."

"Van Vleeck had all the details written in a book he was preparing. I saw the proofs, every chapter," Dr. Harms insisted. He was like an earnest evangelist whose glowing faith was also his belief.

Marcus reached for the psychiatrist again. "He may be bughouse at that. Gripes! Won't I be glad when this is over."

"The book is in Dutch, and has not yet been published, let alone translated," Homer said. Looking straight at Siebold, he continued, "That narrows our field to those who read Dutch. Will all such raise their hands?"

Hands went up. First, Homer's; then, in order, Siebold's, Dr. Harms's, De Witt's, Alma's and Fräulein Kahler's. At the end Sitchev spoke from his seat. "I may as well raise mine. I know Dutch as good as English, most likely."

"Who knows Russian, yet?" asked Mrs. Mesker, hopefully. Homer, Sitchev, Natalia, and, belatedly, Mike Romanoff responded.

"We're getting along, but not fast enough," Homer said. "I'll shift my method once again."

"Stout fellow," said De Witt. "I suppose you're bound to strike it right some time. What about Van Vleeck? Anybody might have wanted to kill Shirley, but why pick on a nice clean old man?"

"I was coming to Van Vleeck, and to you," Homer said. "As one of Europe's most brilliant young botanists, Van Vleeck was sent to Java to study the poisonous plants. He met an aunt of Tani's, as beautiful and then as young as today Tani is. Van Vleeck, a lonely character, whose life had been his studies, poured out his love on the Javanese girl. And a blonde white woman, sent to the island ostensibly by Dutch officials, killed her with the pollen of *phyllostachys bambusoides*."

Nearly everyone in the assembly groaned in sympathy. The tension was mounting again.

"I wish to say now that the murderer of Tani's aunt and Lata-cassi's second daughter was none other than our 'M'. For 'M' was after the ancient secrets of Javanese poisons, not for Holland's queen but a paranoid paperhanger whose right name was Schickl-gruber."

"Under the direction of Dr. Harms," Finke said. "I figured that out already."

"It was the standard Nazi practice," Homer said, "to send out agents in pairs. The one who seemed to have authority in the eyes of the world would be subordinate to the other, who seemed to have a secondary role. 'M', still a woman, was the boss. Dr. Harms merely followed instructions, or else."

"I still don't see why 'M' had to bump off Van Vleeck," Hank Bibesco objected.

"I'll explain," said Homer. "What Van Vleeck found about Javanese poisons, in the light of his own tragedy, seemed to him to be too dangerous to report. He pretended he had learned noth-ing, and was dangerously near the abyss of melancholia and self-destruction when Mr. Harmon visited Batavia by chance and be-friended him."

Harmon, who was relishing the champagne, nodded sadly.

"The rest is easy," said Homer. "Van Vleeck, embittered by the treachery of one woman and the loss of another and motivated by the gratitude he felt toward Mr. Harmon, started patiently from scratch, right here in California, where anything will grow. He raised, tended and transplanted the trees, shrubs, plants, bushes, grasses and flowers, recommenced his destroyed manuscript, and chapter by chapter has bequeathed us a most important document. Incidentally, he has demonstrated not only that plants think, which has been suspected, but that they indulge in carnage for sport—real hunting or trapping."

"Nature stinks, just having fun," said Laslo Sitchev.

Ric Manello nodded thoughtfully. "Human nature, too. What about those Object Lesson warnings that were blamed on me?"

Homer replied sympathetically. "Sitchev wanted Bob and the Gardenia as co-stars. He knew you were approaching both of them and because of your record would be suspected of blackmail. Only Dr. Harms knew you had gone straight, as a matter of policy."

"Not fanatically. Just legitimate. Today's the day of promotion. Racketeering's old hat," Ric explained. "But who peddled the secrets in the Dutchman's book to 'M' and how did the peddler get them? That kind of a deal could be on the borderline—inside the law, or out, I mean."

"De Will was asked to consider drawing certain illustrations," Homer explained. "So he, needing money to lavish on his boy friend, rented out Van Vleeck's book, chapter by chapter, for a total of $25,000. The buyer had each chapter photostated, and the understanding was that, once the deal was concluded, De Will and Cyril would go to Paris and stay there, or, at least, not return to Southern California."

Ric sighed almost enviously. "I can imagine what could be collected for that information, the exclusive rights," he said. "Still, nobody legitimate could do a thing like that, except for his own Government.

"I didn't tumble that 'M' was going to murder Van Vleeck," said De Witt.

"'M' had to prevent Van Vleeck from publishing his book," Homer said.

"I hoped the book would never be printed," Dr. Harms said in horror.

"But I had it in type, practically all of it except the stuff about controls, and the summary," said Siebold, with stolid Dutch indignation. "Why wouldn't it be printed?"

Again Homer produced, from under the table, a bottle of Fockink. "You were expected to drink of this," Homer said. "And get a strong dose of the poison from *nepenthes gracilis*."

Siebold turned and fixed one of the assembly with an accusing finger. "Van Vleeck drank. I didn't, because I felt sick."

"You see," Homer explained. "This poison, which killed Shirley Hall and Mynheer Van Vleeck, does not work instantaneously. The ancient sultans and their populace, when a number of concubines were 'executed' simultaneously, liked to see them drop, not in turn, but unpredictably, over a period of a couple of hours, while the gamelan played. You've noticed that Shirley, who was given the poison in her drink in her kitchen at the Forty-Niners Towers, got all the way downstairs before she collapsed. 'M' asked De Witt to send Moscone out for Courvoisier so she could ride from the Tropics, enter the back door of the Towers, to which she had a key, give the stuff to Shirley in a glass of water so cold that her taste buds were dulled, and, since Shirley was already drugged with the latest stimulant-sedative, it was easy to persuade her to accompany 'M' down the service elevator through Moscone's untended back door, and out into the yard.

"Who was it, Mr. Siebold, who knew that you and Van Vleeck were to confer about format and cover late Tuesday evening, and who told you she had just been given a bottle of Fockink you and he might relish? You've no idea how the flavor of juniper and breadfruit cover that of *nepenthes gracilis*."

Before Siebold could answer, Finke, again waving his arms, asked, "Why did this 'M' have to kill Rice so slowly, and then bump off the others so fast?"

"As I said, she failed in Batavia to learn the Javanese secrets. As she got a look at Van Vleeck's book, chapter by chapter, the bamboo pollen was dealt with first, and only in the last few days was the pitcher-plant technique set down."

Siebold was a slow thinker but a sure one. "Then she meant to poison me, and take the manuscript, proofs and all. Who would know? I keep my own records, mostly in my head."

"Right," said Homer. "So our murderer is a fiend in female form, who has been in Batavia, speaks Dutch, is a die-hard Nazi agent, has had Dr. Harms dizzy with unrequited love since they met in Berlin, while she was training—in more ways than one— who followed him to the Indies, back to Holland, preceded him to New York, and followed him to Southern California. Finke! Quick!"

Lukie had shot from the sitting position; Finke had made a lunge for her arm; the Gardenia had fallen.

Surrounded by Marcus, Finke, Hank, Spode, Strongfort and Kay Cougar, all with automatics drawn, Lukie towered. Only Kay's gun

was trained her way. All the others were holding off the companions and spectators who were wild with indignation.

"Do what you like. She won't have my Bobbie!" Lukie cried.
But Dr. Hamilton, who had been bending over the limp Gardenia,
arose with relief.

"There's nothing to prevent it. The wound's only a scalp crease,"
the renowned physician said.

"Sir!" said Mills Harmon, bristling.

Postscript

THE BUSINESS ARRANGEMENTS were concluded amicably between Ruth Mesker and Ric Manello. Ruth kept Bob. The Gardenia went to Ric because Tony had found her. To compensate for the loss of Shirley, Ruth got half of the big piece of the show that E.P.U. conceded to Ric. E.P.U. is more than content because *Sin on an Island* already promises to gross twice as much as any of Sitchev's previous smash hits.

COACHWHIP PUBLICATIONS

COACHWHIPBOOKS.COM

The Mysterious Mickey Finn

Elliot Paul

The Mysterious Mickey Finn
ISBN 1-61646-293-0

COACHWHIP PUBLICATIONS

ALSO AVAILABLE

Hugger Mugger in the Louvre

Elliot Paul

Hugger Mugger in the Louvre
ISBN 1-61646-294-9

COACHWHIP PUBLICATIONS

COACHWHIPBOOKS.COM

Mayhem in B-Flat
Elliot Paul

Mayhem in B-Flat
ISBN 1-61646-295-7

COACHWHIP PUBLICATIONS
ALSO AVAILABLE

Fracas in the Foothills

Elliot Paul

Fracas in the Foothills
ISBN 1-61646-296-5

COACHWHIP PUBLICATIONS

COACHWHIPBOOKS.COM

I'll Hate Myself in the Morning

Murder on the Left Bank

Elliot Paul

Murder on the Left Bank
ISBN 1-61646-312-0

Murder Ends the Song
ISBN 1-61646-298-1

COACHWHIP PUBLICATIONS

COACHWHIPBOOKS.COM

Murder on Tour
ISBN 1-61646-170-5